THE SENILITY OF VLADIMIR P.

THE SENILITY OF VLADIMIR P.

MICHAEL HONIG

PEGASUS BOOKS
NEW YORK LONDON

THE SENILITY OF VLADIMIR P.

Pegasus Books Ltd.
148 West 37th Street, 13th Floor
New York, NY 10018

ISBN: 978-1-68177-156-4

10 9 8 7 8 6 5 4 3 2 1

Printed in the United States of America
Distributed by W. W. Norton & Company, Inc.

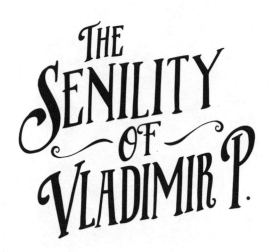

THE SENILITY OF VLADIMIR P.

I

HE DIDN'T KNOW HOW long he had been sitting there. Could have been two hours. Could have been two years.

Suddenly, a connection in his brain sparked to life and set off a chain of ignitions, like a momentary flickering of stars lighting up across a darkening, dying galaxy.

'Why am I here?' he yelled angrily. 'What am I doing?'

'Waiting,' said Sheremetev, plumping up one of the pillows on his bed.

'What for?'

'For the meeting.'

Vladimir's eyes narrowed. 'Have I been briefed?'

'Of course,' replied Sheremetev calmly.

'Good.' Vladimir nodded. His expression changed, losing its anger. Already, he was forgetting what he had been upset about. The connection, wherever it was in his brain, had been snuffed out, perhaps never to spark again, and the self-awareness that had erupted momentarily into his consciousness was gone. He sat quietly and watched Sheremetev work. Vladimir couldn't have said exactly who the other man was, but nonetheless he was at ease with him. Somehow, he knew that it was right for him to be making up the bed, and he had a feeling that it might even have happened before.

Sheremetev was a small man, dressed in a simple white shirt and a pair of dark trousers. He had never worn uniform when looking after Vladimir, but the deftness and economy of his movements as he tidied the bed betrayed a long career as a nurse. It was almost six years since Professor V N Kalin, the renowned neurologist, had asked him to become Vladimir's personal carer. That was shortly after Vladimir announced that he would be stepping down from the presidency. In those days, although the president's condition was evident to those who worked with him closely, he was still well enough to hold his own in tightly scripted public appearances for which he was carefully prepared. His successor, Gennadiy Sverkov, had even continued to have him wheeled out on occasion to try to draw some of the old wizard's magic onto his own increasingly lacklustre administration. Back then, Vladimir still had a valet to dress him and a pair of aides to keep him abreast of events, and Sheremetev's role had been limited, but as Vladimir's memory deteriorated, so Sheremetev's responsibilities multiplied. Within a couple of years, Vladimir's public appearances had become so erratic that even Sverkov's people grew wary of parading him, and rumours of his condition – never confirmed – began to circulate. The appearances ceased. First the two aides were dispensed with, then the valet, and Sheremetev was left alone with him.

The nurse had never concerned himself with politics and had never kept track of who was doing what to whom in the Kremlin. To him, the whole business was a murky soup out of which names rose and sank without apparent rhyme or reason, and what was happening under the surface – and surely things must be happening, as everyone said – wasn't something he tried to understand. He hadn't been aware of the rumour that Vladimir had been forced out as his ageing cronies scrambled to hold on to their positions in the dying days of his power. All he knew was that the president announced that he was retiring – and a few weeks later Professor Kalin summoned him to his office.

'Do you know my mother?' asked Vladimir, as Sheremetev plumped the last of the pillows and set it down on the bed.

'No, Vladimir Vladimirovich. I never had the honour of meeting her.'

'I'll introduce you. She'll be here later. I've sent a car for her.'

Sheremetev turned around. 'It's time for your shower, Vladimir Vladimirovich. You'll have to get dressed in something special today. The new president is coming to see you.'

Vladimir looked at him in confusion. 'The new president? Aren't I the president?'

'Not any more, Vladimir Vladimirovich. Someone else is president now.'

Vladimir's eyes narrowed. In the early years, hearing that might have driven him into a rage. But the rages were less frequent now, and when they did occur, didn't last long. Nothing that Vladimir was told stuck for more than a minute or two in his mind. If he was agitated, it was probably because he was thinking about something that had happened twenty or thirty years ago.

'Is someone coming?' asked Vladimir eventually. 'Is that what you said?'

'Yes. The new president, Constantin Mikhailovich Lebedev.'

Vladimir snorted. 'Lebedev's the minister of finance!'

Sheremetev had no idea if Lebedev had ever been minister of finance, but he certainly wasn't now. 'He's the new president, Vladimir Vladimirovich. He wants to get your blessing. That's good, isn't it? It shows how much he respects you.'

'My blessing?' Vladimir frowned. 'Am I priest?'

'No.'

'Then why does he want my blessing?'

'It's a figure of speech, Vladimir Vladimirovich. In this case, you're as good as a priest.'

Vladimir watched Sheremetev suspiciously. 'Where are we?'

'At the dacha.'

'Which dacha?'

'Novo-Ogaryovo.'

'Novo-Ogaryovo? Why am I meeting Lebedev here? Why not at my office?'

'Today you're meeting him here.'

'I'm going to fire that bastard. Have we got cameras?'

'I think there'll be cameras there.'

'Good. We'll see how he likes that!' Vladimir chuckled. He remembered getting rid of Admiral Alexei Gorky, the commander of the Northern Fleet, in front of the television cameras at Severomorsk. That had gone down a treat.

Suddenly Gorky was right there in front of him. The look on the admiral's face! The old peacock in his big peaked cap saw all the cameras pointing at him and thought Vladimir had come to pin another medal on his overdecorated chest, and now, before he knew it, he was getting the sack. 'Didn't see that one coming, did you, Alexei Maximovich? Who's the boss, huh? Teach you to speak out about not having enough money for the fleet!' Vladimir laughed, banging the armrests with his fists.

Sheremetev had left him to go into Vladimir's dressing room. For the new president's visit, he was determined to make sure that his patient looked like a president as well. He took his time in front of the heavily stocked hanging rails and shelves, considering various options, until finally he settled on a dark blue suit, light blue shirt, a red tie with white dots, and a pair of black leather shoes. From

Vladimir's impressive collection of watches, he chose what he considered to be a simple but elegant timepiece with a thin gold case, white face, gold hands and a leather band.

He brought everything back to the bedroom and laid out the clothes on the bed. 'Come on, Vladimir Vladimirovich. Time for your shower. We have to get you spruced up.'

Vladimir gazed at him doubtfully. 'Why?'

'Constantin Mikhailovich is coming to see you.'

'Lebedev? Is that who you mean? He should go to a priest.'

'Why?' said Sheremetev.

Vladimir frowned. He had a feeling that Lebedev needed a priest, but he had no idea why. 'His mother's dying,' he proposed.

THE CAMERAS HAD BEEN set up in a formal reception room on the ground floor of the dacha, which hadn't been opened for years but had been aired and cleaned that morning for the purpose. Two armchairs had been placed at forty-five degrees to each other on either side of an ornate fireplace, under a pair of studio lights. In the kitchen of the dacha, Viktor Stepanin, the chef, and his brigade had been working since dawn to produce a buffet of canapés and snacks that was now laid out on tables along one side of the room. Near the end of the tables stood a big man in a dark grey suit with an exuberant head of grey hair accompanied by two serious looking presidential aides. Other aides, television technicians and security men milled around behind the cameras.

As Sheremetev led Vladimir in, a hush descended on the room. Every eye turned on the old man in the blue suit who had stopped in the doorway. A few wisps of grey hair clung to his scalp, the face was wrinkled and jowly, and yet with its square chin, broad forehead, close-set and slightly slanting cold blue eyes, it was still immediately recognisable as the face that for thirty years had been the most photographed in Russia.

Vladimir looked at Sheremetev in confusion.

'It's alright, Vladimir Vladimirovich,' he whispered. 'It's just the people who have come for the meeting.'

'Am I going to a meeting?'

'Yes.'

'Have I been briefed?'

'Of course.'

Vladimir looked around again, reassured now, taking in the lights and the cameras. Some last remaining instinct stirred within him of the leader that he had once been and he straightened his back, raised his chin, and a slight supercilious smile curled his lip.

'Who am I meeting?' he whispered.

'Lebedev,' replied Sheremetev.

'Of course. Lebedev!' he muttered, and there was a note of combative relish in his voice as he glimpsed the big man standing with his aides on the other side of the room. 'The time has come!'

Constantin Mikhailovich Lebedev had got his foot on the political ladder as mayor of Moscow, combining an ebullient public persona with a private, craven submissiveness to the Kremlin's commands that made him seem like the perfect placeman. In power, he rapidly became known for his insatiable corruption, more interested in money than power, the kind of politician who posed no threat and whom Vladimir was always happy to advance. But in retrospect, even in the early days there were signs that there was more to Lebedev than met the eyes. What he took in graft with one hand, he gave back – at least in part – with the other, cannily keeping the common Muscovite happy with a string of populist measures that did nothing for the city's future but cheered everyone up with a few extra kopecks in their pocket. Soon the media were calling him Uncle Kostya and he revelled in the moniker. A politician who craved money and wanted to be loved seemed even less of a threat, and Vladimir allowed him a second term as mayor. But Vladimir had to admit that he underestimated him, taken in by Lebedev's talent for playing the gladhanding buffoon. In reality, greater than Uncle Kostya's greed – gargantuan as it was – was his cunning. From the start he had his eyes on prizes more glittering than the mere mayoralty of the capital. By the time Vladimir realised this, Lebedev had Moscow in his pocket and was a force to be reckoned with.

Vladimir set out to destroy him. He brought him into the federal government, only to sack him a year later on charges of incompetence and corruption. Lebedev crawled away wounded, but not mortally, having energetically used his government appointment to distribute the proceeds of a brief but monumental ministerial plundering to a group of influential supporters who had every reason to expect more from him if he could recover power in the future. He had also accumulated an impressive store of secrets that reached to the very top of the Kremlin – the *very* top – and shielded him from further attacks that might have finished him off. So back Vladimir brought him, keeping him close as he searched for another way to dispose of him. For the next decade, the cycle repeated itself – in and out of the government waltzed Uncle Kostya, shamelessly pillaging whatever ministry Vladimir handed him, skimming off even more wealth and spraying it around ever more liberally to entrench himself with another cohort of supporters before being ignominiously sacked, at each sacking playing on his avuncular reputation to portray himself as the innocent victim of Kremlin plotters. Vladimir loathed him

7

with a gut hatred, the type of unbearable disgust that comes from knowing that the only reason this person exists is because of your own mistake in building him up and then not cutting him down when you still had the chance, an existential hatred that comes from looking at someone you despise . . . and finding that when you look past the appearances, what you see is a mirror.

Now he left Sheremetev and strode across the room towards him, as if all of this was happening twenty years ago and he was about to deliver the *coup de grâce* to this bugbear who had swung like an albatross around his neck for so long. 'Constantin Mikhailovich!' he greeted him loudly.

One of Lebedev's aides rushed forward. 'Vladimir Vladimirovich, President Lebedev has come today to pay his respects and to ask you to say a few words for the Russian people on the auspicious occasion of his election. If you could, for example, say—'

'Sit,' said Vladimir to Lebedev, pointing at one of the armchairs that had been prepared.

'But Vladimir Vladimirovich . . .' said the aide.

Vladimir walked to the other chair, and then stood imperiously. Lebedev glanced at his aide. 'I'll handle it,' he murmured.

A pair of makeup specialists hurried forward as the two men sat and proceeded to dab at their faces. Vladimir raised his chin, impatient for them to be finished. After a minute or so he shooed them away. 'That's it! Enough!'

The makeup specialists retreated.

'Constantin Mikhailovich, are you ready?' said the producer behind the camera.

Lebedev nodded.

The lights went on. Suddenly, the scene was bright. Vladimir immediately thumped the armrest of his chair. 'So? What have you come to report, Constantin Mikhailovich? I am not satisfied! The Ministry of Finance is a disgrace. You promised me a year ago that you would clean it up. Now it's worse than ever!'

'Vladimir Vladimirovich—'

'Well, Constantin Mikhailovich? What have you got to say?'

Lebedev turned briefly to his aides and rolled his eyes. Then he looked back at the ex-president. 'You fired me from the Ministry of Finance once already, Vladimir Vladimirovich. It's the exact same speech. Are you going to do it again?'

'Did I appoint you again?'

'No,' said Lebedev.

'Why are you here, then?'

'For this.' Lebedev grabbed Vladimir's hand and turned to the cameras with a smile. 'Look at the cameras and give us a smile, Vladimir Vladimirovich.'

Vladimir pulled his hand away. 'You're a crook, Kostya Lebedev! You were always a crook.'

'Well, if I was a crook, I had Russia's greatest teacher,' replied Lebedev out of the corner of his mouth, the smile still on his face. 'Come on, let's be honest, Vladimir Vladimirovich.'

'Honest? Fine, let's be honest. You're nothing but a thief.'

Lebedev leaned forward, still smiling. 'And you? You knew how to get your share. Where should I start? The Olympics? The World Cup? Or what about Kolyakov's ring road? That was the best! That'll choke Moscow like a noose for the next hundred years. How much did you get on the ring road, Vova? Twenty percent?'

'I should have you thrown in jail. You're worse than anyone.'

'Me? Look, I'm the president now. Put a smile on your fucking face, Vova, and congratulate me.'

'Go and fuck yourself, Kostya.'

'Say: I wish you all the best, Constantin Mikhailovich. In your hands, Mother Russia is safe.' Lebedev waited. 'Well, Vladimir Vladimirovich? Say it.'

Vladimir laughed.

'I wish you all the best, Constantin Mikhailovich. In your hands, Mother Russia is safe.'

'In *your* hands? You'll never be president, Kostya Lebedev. Not even Russia would do that to itself.'

'Okay, I'll never be president. Fine. It's just a game. Let's pretend. Say: I wish you all the best—'

'Can you smell something?'

Lebedev stopped. 'What?'

'Smell!'

Lebedev sniffed. 'I can't smell anything.'

'Sure?'

'Is this a joke?'

'You can't smell it?'

'What?' said Lebedev.

Vladimir gazed at him, then smiled to himself knowingly.

Lebedev took a deep breath. 'Okay,' he growled. 'Look. Say this for me: I wish you all the best, Constantin Mikhailovich. In your hands—'

Vladimir beat his fist on the arm of his chair. 'I am not satisfied, Constantin Mikhailovich! The Ministry of Finance is a disgrace. You promised me a year ago that you would clean it up. Now it's worse than ever!'

Lebedev looked around at the producer. 'Have we got enough pictures? I've had it with this old fool.'

'Just a moment, Constantin Mikhailovich.' The producer huddled with a couple of technicians behind a computer monitor. They looked through the footage at double speed, trying to see if there were enough shots they could extract to make it seem as if the two men in front of the cameras had had an amiable meeting. There were images of Vladimir smiling to himself, laughing at Lebedev. Maybe with the right cutting and splicing ...

The security men stood around scoffing the snacks that the cook had laboured to produce.

Vladimir beckoned to Sheremetev. 'What's my next appointment?' he whispered.

'You have time for a break now, Vladimir Vladimirovich.'

'And then?'

'Lunch.'

'Who with?'

'I'm not sure, Vladimir Vladimirovich.'

'Find out.'

'If we have to, we can stitch something together,' the producer informed Lebedev. 'But it's not great. Maybe try again, Constantin Mikhailovich.'

'Mother of God!' hissed Lebedev. 'Whose idea was this anyway?' He glanced at Vladimir, then shook his head in disgust. Unable, or unwilling, to restrain himself, the new president told Vladimir again what he thought of him. Vladimir responded with gusto. Soon the two men were swearing at each other without restraint, the reeking guts of a decades-old animosity spilling out in front of everyone in the crowded room.

Abruptly, Lebedev stood up.

'Constantin Mikhailovich,' said one of his aides, 'please, perhaps try once more.'

Lebedev gritted his teeth. Then he reached for Vladimir's hand with about as much pleasure in his expression as if he was reaching for an orang-utan. 'I wish you all the best, Constantin Mikhailovich,' he hissed. 'In your hands, Mother Russia is safe.'

'I'm not Constantin Mikhailovich, you idiot. I'm Vladimir Vladimirovich.'

Lebedev forced a smile for the cameras. 'No, you say that to me. *In your hands, Mother Russia is safe.* Say it.'

'You want me say it, Kostya?'

'Yes, Vova, I want you to say it.'

Vladimir gazed at him, a smile forming on his lips. Somewhere in the depths of what was left of his mind, he still knew that power is power, and there is no greater manifestation of it than the ability to thwart the will of another person, no matter how slight the occasion or how trivial the apparent consequence – even if it is only refusing to utter a sentence that would cost nothing to yourself.

Lebedev waited for a moment – then turned and stormed out.

The room drained of people. Security men and aides ran after him, stuffing the last of the snacks into their mouths. In a minute, only the television technicians were left.

'You can take him,' said the producer to Sheremetev over his shoulder, as the television people began packing up. 'We're finished.'

Vladimir looked around in confusion.

'The meeting's over, Vladimir Vladimirovich,' said Sheremetev.

'But I leave first! I'm always the one to leave first.'

'I know. This was unusual. It doesn't mean anything. Let's go upstairs now.'

Sheremetev got Vladimir to his feet. By the time they reached the door, Lebedev's convoy was already gone, sweeping down the drive to the gate.

2

AS FAR AS SHEREMETEV could tell, he had been given the job of caring for Vladimir because of a reputation for probity. This was quite surprising – not because he didn't deserve the reputation, but because previously it had earned him only laughter and contempt.

The Soviet Union was in its final days when Nikolai Ilyich Sheremetev, born to a foreman who worked in a pharmaceuticals factory and a mother who was a bookkeeper with the Moscow metro, was finishing primary school. By the time he completed high school, it was dead and buried with a stake through its heart. Sheremetev dutifully did his army service, spending most of his time digging foundations on construction sites in Omsk. Naively, he imagined that he was working on military buildings – although even he was not so naïve that he didn't wonder why the army had decided that it needed several large apartment-style blocks in a residential district of a city on the edge of Siberia. Eventually a fellow conscript enlightened him, revealing what everyone else apparently already knew, that the platoon was being hired out by the captain as labour to private builders. Sheremetev's expectation that this abuse would soon end with the exposure of the captain's criminality, followed by swift and exemplary punishment by the regimental colonel, was dashed when another conscript revealed that the colonel himself was not only aware of the exploitation, but was being paid a commission by the captain. The conscripts were not exactly choirboys either. Equipment went missing from the construction sites, only to be glimpsed briefly in a corner of the barracks before disappearing again the next day. Others would go off for days with one of the sergeants on missions from which they would return with wallets bulging. For some reason, no one involved Sheremetev in anything, and he became aware of the goings-on only after they were finished. Even if he had known, he would have been too scared to take part, which presumably was obvious to his comrades. Next time they do something they'll get caught, he thought to himself – and then he thought it again each time after they weren't.

The captain, incidentally, was promoted to major shortly before Sheremetev's conscription ended, for heroic action in the service of construction, as the joke in the barracks ran.

Following his army service, Sheremetev trained as a nurse, encouraged by his mother, who said the profession suited his caring nature. Laughably, he then tried to raise a family in Moscow on a nurse's salary. Not that he didn't see what was happening around him. Doctors took money from families to put patients in hospital. Nurses took money to look after them once they were there. Cooks took money to feed them. Launderers took money to wash their sheets and cleaners took money to clean their wards. Nothing happened without a few rubles greasing the way. Somehow, he couldn't do it. Maybe it was simply the fear of being caught again. Maybe it was something else as well. When he looked at two patients on the ward, something always drew him to the poorer one. Saint Nikolai, his coworkers called him, but not admiringly, in the tone one might use for a revered and incorruptible colleague, but tauntingly, at best, pityingly, in the tone one would use for an idiot.

His wife's tone oscillated between one and the other. At times

Karinka told him what a good, humble man he was and how much she loved him for his honesty – at other times she told him he was a fool. They had one son, Vasily, who was now twenty-five and had had to make his own way in the world, Sheremetev having nothing to offer but advice – which Vasily had never listened to, anyway. He was involved in some kind of business that Sheremetev knew little about, and from the little Vasily did tell him, he didn't want to know more. He said his job was to help people, but when Sheremetev asked what kind of help, there was never a straight answer. Without even knowing the details, Sheremetev had the same thought he had had in the army and the hospital. Someone would find out. Something would happen. Vasily laughed. 'It's okay as long as you keep the right people happy,' he would say, as if he were the father and Sheremetev the artless son. 'In Russia, there's no other way. Everyone does it but you, Papa.'

What Karinka would have said had she seen how Vasily had turned out, Sheremetev didn't know. She had died of an inflammatory disease that eventually destroyed her kidneys. At that time Sheremetev was working as a senior nurse on a public ward for dementia patients. A few months after Karinka died, Professor Kalin, the director of the unit, summoned him to his office. This was a surprise to everyone, not only Sheremetev. Professor Kalin normally found time to visit the ward which he supposedly directed roughly twice a year, and unless everyone had magically fallen asleep for five months, it was only four weeks since his previous appearance. Yet there he was, walking down the ward without the slightest sense of impropriety and asking for Sheremetev.

In the office that day, Kalin said he had been told that Sheremetev was a nurse not only of the highest competence but of exceptional integrity, if such a description didn't make him an oxymoron in

Russia. Sheremetev shrugged, not knowing what an oxymoron was, much less if he was one. Kalin said that he had recently diagnosed someone with dementia who had been an extremely important public official. Even today, the diagnosis was a matter of the strictest secrecy. He asked if Sheremetev would be prepared to leave his hospital job and care for this person. Sheremetev hesitated, thinking of the patients on the ward whose families were too poor to produce the rubles required to lubricate the wheels of care. Kalin wondered what could possibly be going through his head. He leaned forward across his desk. 'Nikolai Ilyich,' he said. 'Your nation calls you. You can't say no.' Sheremetev felt obliged to respond to this patriotic exhortation – and thus discovered that the patient was none other than Vladimir Vladimirovich.

Naturally, Sheremetev knew that Vladimir had recently stepped down from the presidency, but like the rest of Russia he had no idea yet of the real reason. He hadn't even heard the rumours. Despite his long experience as a nurse, at first he was somewhat awestruck. It was no small thing to discover that the man who had been president of the federation only a few months earlier was suffering from dementia, and that he was now your patient. Still, he tried to overcome this reaction and treat the ex-president as he would treat any other patient, pragmatically, sensitively and gently. But Vladimir didn't make it easy.

When Sheremetev first came to him, the ex-president retained considerable insight into what was happening to him. He was aware of his ever more frequent memory lapses and what they portended, and would frequently get into rages, which could sometimes go on for hours. Sheremetev did his best to be a calming influence, but still he often suffered volleys of verbal abuse. After all, his very presence was a reminder to the ex-president of his condition. Sheremetev absorbed it all. Agitation and anger, he knew, are common in the early stages of dementia, when people can still understand the future that confronts them, and he had often encountered them in other patients. Why should Vladimir Vladimirovich, just because he had been five times president and twice prime minister of the Russian Federation, not have the right to rail against the cruelty of fate as others did? A man who had been president, thought Sheremetev, must have a superior intellect, and the loss of it must be proportionately painful. Why shouldn't he mourn it?

Yet the rages threatened to become more than verbal, and there was a danger that Vladimir would injure not only others but himself. So Professor Kalin prescribed tranquillisers – tablets at night, and injections, if required, when the tablets weren't enough.

The tranquillisers didn't stop the rages, but they muffled them, turning the outbursts from roof-raising hurricanes into gusts of wind that rattled the shutters and passed on. Only occasionally would some whirling eddy of frustration erupt into a full blown storm. Eventually, over time, the rages petered out. As Vladimir's condition progressed, his awareness of it diminished, and with it the anger that it had engendered. Instead, different preoccupations became manifest, ones that rose up out of the past.

By this point, Vladimir's memory for the people and events of recent years had dissipated. His mind wandered in a world constructed of events that had happened ten, twenty, thirty or more years ago. He spent his time in animated conversations with invisible people who weren't there, most of whom were long dead. Sometimes Vladimir became disturbed by what he was seeing, especially if he awoke at night, when he would be disorientated and bellicose. So Professor Kalin continued the tranquillisers for Vladimir's agitation at his delusions that he had originally prescribed for the ex-president's agitation at reality, checking on the effects each month when he came to the dacha to assess the progression of Vladimir's dementia.

On the morning that Vladimir met the new president, it was clear that he had mentally been far in the past. Even so, Sheremetev disliked the way Lebedev had presumed to tell Vladimir what to say, walking in and expecting to put words in his mouth. He might have been the president, but it was barely a week since he had taken office, and he was talking to someone who had occupied the position five times, even if Vladimir wasn't quite the man he had once been. Sheremetev had been shocked at the language that ensued between them, but he felt a flicker of satisfaction – if not pride – that his patient had given back as good as he got.

Afterwards, they went up the stairs together and back to Vladimir's suite on the second floor. 'I'll get you some other clothes, Vladimir Vladimirovich,' said Sheremetev as he settled him in his chair, and he left him there as he went to the dressing room.

Dima Kolyakov was sitting in an armchair opposite him. Initially Vladimir was surprised to see him, but soon the businessman was explaining a scheme he had hatched to build a new ring road around Moscow. Vladimir listened patiently, not allowing so much as a flicker of an expression to betray what he was thinking. The billionaire was nothing to look at – heavy jowls, bags under his eyes and a pair of moist lips that wriggled lubriciously as he spoke – but there was plenty of lipstick on the pig. He wore a beautifully cut suit, probably from London, where his wife, children and two of his mistresses lived. The neck tie was Hermès. The diamond embedded in his pinkie ring was five carats at least, and brilliant white. The wrist watch, which the billionaire flashed more than someone who wasn't conscious of it would have done, was a Vacheron Tour de l'Ile, worth probably two million dollars. At the sight of it, Vladimir's fingers twitched. He had two of his own that had been given to him over the years, amongst Pateks, Breguets, Piquets, Richard Milles and anything else that the most elite Swiss horologists could devise in their mountain workshops. In the early days, he had taken Rolexes, but after a while anyone who turned up with one would get a quiet word in their ear from Evgeny Monarov, his closest consigliere, even before they were brought in to meet him, and a courier would turn up the next day with something more select.

Vladimir heard the businessman out. At the end he said simply: 'So you think Moscow really needs this new ring road?'

Kolyakov shrugged. 'Vladimir Vladimirovich, would I be suggesting it if I didn't? The traffic problems are immense.'

'But another ring road? Is that the best way to solve them?' Vladimir raised a vodka. 'Your health,' he said, and took a sip. 'How long is it that we've known each other, Dima?'

'Twenty years,' said the billionaire.

'I remember the first time you came and sat in that chair.'

'I do too! Without you, I'd be nothing, Vova.'

Vladimir laughed. 'No one would be anything! Russia would be nothing! Do you know what a shitheap it was when I got hold of it? If you think you do, think again. Tell me, how much did you pay the first time?'

'To see you?'

Vladimir nodded, downing his vodka.

'A million dollars.'

'That was cheap.'

'Very cheap. Ridiculous.'

'Today it's five million, Monarov tells me. Maybe it's more. I don't even know.'

'It should be more. Your time is priceless, Vladimir Vladimirovich.'

'So, was it a good investment?'

'A very good investment,' replied Kolyakov without hesitation. 'At ten times the price it would have been a good investment.'

Vladimir nodded. Not as good an investment as it was for me, he thought. To make people pay to meet him, only so that they would have the chance to offer him even more money – who could imagine such a business? The first time he saw how this kind of thing could be done, when he came back to Russia and found himself in the city government in St Petersburg during the wild days as the Soviet Union collapsed, he could barely believe it. An eye-opener. At the start he was barely a spectator, getting the crumbs of the crumbs, a percentage of the percentages, but as he rose in influence and got the hang of the game, the money came flooding in. Commissions, fees, markups, kickbacks – call it what you want. Set up a company and watch the businessmen queue up to route their business through it and leave you twenty percent as they did. Sometimes thirty or forty percent. Import, export, food, oil . . . Never in his life had he imagined it could be so easy or that he could take so much. But as it turned out, even that was small beer. Once he got to Moscow, everything would have an extra zero on the end, or two, or three.

'I'm not sure about another ring road,' he said. 'Didn't the latest report say another ring road would make things worse?'

'That's just a report, Vladimir Vladimirovich,' said Kolyakov, waving a hand airily. 'A word from you, and it's forgotten.'

'I thought it said extensions to the metro or even a light rail system would be better.'

Kolyakov shook his head gravely. 'That's very expensive.'

'This isn't?'

'Well, more metro . . .' Kolyakov shook his head again. 'We'd need foreign partners. You know what they're like, Vladimir Vladimirovich. They have laws in their countries about what they can and can't do – who they can and can't give to, I mean. They don't really understand how things are done. This is much better for us. Nice and simple. Let's build a road! Five years, twenty billion dollars – we're finished.'

'Well, this doesn't concern the president of the federation,' said Vladimir. 'It's an issue for the mayor of Moscow.'

'Lebedev wants it.'

Vladimir smiled slightly. 'How much are you giving him?'

'Ten percent.'

'So? If he's happy, you'll do it.'

'I also want you to be happy, Vova.'

Vladimir watched the other man. There were two reasons he liked Kolyakov. First, he was only a businessman. All he wanted to do was make money, and when he had made it, to make more. He had zero political interest or aspiration, unlike others who, as they got wealthier, thought their money gave them the right to some kind of say in how the country should be run, and whom Vladimir had had to deal with. And second, he understood the vertical of power, which Vladimir demanded should be respected. Even though this proposal was something that in principle would be decided at the level of the Moscow city administration, Kolyakov knew that in Russia all power started in the Kremlin, with one man, so he made sure to come to Vladimir as well, as he always did.

Kolyakov cleared his throat. 'Twenty percent for you, Vova. Tell me what company to put it through, and I'll do it.'

'That's generous.'

Kolyakov shrugged. 'Who gets rich from making other people poor? Share our fortune with the world, isn't that what the priests say? And the people of Moscow will have a wonderful new road.'

'Which they desperately need.'

The billionaire laughed. 'The process will be official, Vladimir Vladimirovich. Lebedev's people will write a public tender. It will be a very fastidious process, all above board.'

Vladimir raised an eyebrow.

Kolyakov laughed again.

But Vladimir didn't crack a smile. After a moment, the expression on Kolyakov's heavy face became confused, as if he was wondering whether his offer to relieve the state of twenty billion dollars to build a road that would condemn Moscow to years of traffic misery, for twice the price it should have cost, had somehow missed the mark. Vladimir enjoyed the spectacle, seeing the panic he could sow with a mere twitch of his eyebrow.

He let his gaze wander to the watch that was on the billionaire's wrist. You didn't see a Vacheron Tour de l'Ile every day, even on the wrists of the people who came to see him.

Kolyakov realised where he was looking. He glanced up at Vladimir questioningly, then began to unfasten the watch.

Vladimir waved a hand dismissively. 'What are you doing, Dima? I was just admiring it. A Tour de l'Ile, right? I've got two myself.'

The billionaire kept his fingers on the clasp, still unsure if he was serious.

'Dmitry Viktorovich, please! It's your watch, not mine.'

'Everything I have is because of you, Vladimir Vladimirovich.'

Vladimir laughed, not in such a way as to deny the remark, but in acknowledgement of it.

'Build your road,' said Vladimir. 'Talk to Monarov about the arrangements.'

The billionaire smiled and nodded gratefully. Sometimes, thought

Vladimir, the businessman's obsequiousness was sickening, just like a dog. For an instant, he imagined him as a monstrous chimera with the body of a lapdog and a heavy-jowled Kolyakov-face looking up at him, desperately seeking a sign of affection.

Vladimir wondered whether he should have taken the Tour de l'Ile, but in some ways, to show that you could take something but that you deigned not to, was even better. Besides, in the next day or two, Vladimir knew, a packet would arrive for him.

Suddenly Vladimir was aware of a nauseating, fetid odour. He sniffed. 'Do you smell anything?'

Kolyakov sniffed as well.

'It's the Chechen,' said Vladimir. 'The fucking Chechen never leaves me alone.'

'There's a Chechen here?' asked the billionaire.

'Can't you smell him?'

Kolyakov's eyes narrowed. 'I think...I'm not sure...'

'Smell! Come on! Try! That's him. It's the Chechen.'

Vladimir had first seen the Chechen on a visit to Grozny early in the war that he had started, while inspecting an area of the city that had recently been taken back from the rebels. The Chechen's head protruded from a reeking shed or outhouse or shack of some kind behind a house that had been almost totally destroyed. Vladimir couldn't see whether it was still attached to a body. From the look of it, the head must have been there for a few days. The lips were retracted from its grinning yellow teeth, and the tongue emerging from the mouth was swollen and black, like a gigantic slug crawling out of his throat.

'He never says anything,' said Vladimir. 'Just hangs around. You know, I told the whole world once we killed him in a toilet. Just to see what they would say, the western press. Everyone went crazy. One dead Chechen in a shithouse and they're up in arms. If only they knew what else we did!'

Vladimir noticed Kolyakov shifting uncomfortably. He was as ruthless as anyone in business, but when it came to things of flesh and blood, he was squeamish. Vladimir had no real respect for him, but he was a goose who knew how to lay golden eggs, and knew how many he could keep and how many to give away. Kolyakov was said to be worth eight billion dollars. Good luck to him. Vladimir himself had no idea how much he was worth, but it was many times as much.

'Usually he comes at night,' said Vladimir, enjoying the spectacle of the billionaire squirming. 'That's when I see him.'

'What does he do?'

'What do you think he does?'

Kolyakov stared at him. 'I don't know,' he whispered.

'I'd cut his head off, but I think someone already did that. At least he's dead, huh?' Vladimir laughed. 'The only good Chechen . . .'

The billionaire, who had a Chechen grandmother, said nothing.

'Look!' said Vladimir, 'it's Monarov.'

'Sheremetev,' said Sheremetev.

'Monarov, Dima has an arrangement to tell you about. Deal with it in the usual way, huh?'

'It's Sheremetev, Vladimir Vladimirovich,' said Sheremetev again, unsurprised by the fact that Vladimir was addressing him as someone else. For much of the time, Vladimir would engage in conversations with chairs and benches on which, presumably, he believed that people were sitting, and if Sheremetev came in while the conversation was in full swing he often took him for someone out of his past.

Vladimir looked at him in confusion.

'It's alright, Vladimir Vladimirovich. It's almost time for lunch. You'll enjoy it. The chef's made chicken in the Georgian style for you.'

A smile came over Vladimir's face. He rubbed his hands enthusiastically. 'Georgian chicken! Is it ready?'

3

THE CHEF AT THE dacha, Viktor Alexandrovich Stepanin, was a
barrel-chested man with a seemingly permanent stubble. Stepanin
was a creature made by nature and perfected by nurture for the
kitchen – classically trained, as he often reminded people – totally
entranced and enraptured by cooking, ugly, crude, loud and frac-
tious, and yet despite all those qualities – or perhaps because of
them – surprisingly attractive to women. He was having an affair
with one of the maids, and she wasn't the first one who had found
her way to his bed.

Stepanin had developed a habit of chewing the fat with Sheremetev at the end of the day. Normally, Sheremetev gave Vladimir
dinner at around eight and settled him in bed at nine-thirty, after
which he would come downstairs for his own meal. By then, the
rest of the inhabitants of the dacha had usually eaten and Stepanin would make sure there was something set aside for Sheremetev.
The staff dining room with its long green formica table would be
otherwise deserted, and the cook would march in through the
connecting door from the kitchen as Sheremetev ate, apron tied at
his waist, dishcloth over his shoulder, a bottle of vodka in one hand
and a plate of chillied pork scratchings in the other, and pull up
a chair. At that time of the evening, he would have only a set of
snacks still to prepare for the security shift that would be working

overnight. For half an hour he would sit and talk and drink a glass of vodka and chew on the scratchings, occasionally getting up to throw open the door and yell at his assistants and potwashers who were cleaning up inside.

Sheremetev couldn't help but like the big-hearted, voluble cook who wore his heart on his sleeve. Stepanin's great dream, as he had told Sheremetev countless times, was to open his own restaurant in Moscow. Russian Fusion! Minimalist décor! Sheremetev didn't know how cooking here at the dacha was going to help him do that, since the pay, to judge by his own salary, was nothing special. He also didn't know how Stepanin – classically trained, after all – got much satisfaction from cooking for the dacha staff, who probably had never in their lives eaten at the type of establishment he dreamed of opening and were not – Sheremetev included, he would readily admit – the most discerning in the culinary arts. Yet somehow the cook seemed certain that he would one day realise his dream, and in the meantime he strode around his kitchen like a fuming colossus, berating his assistants and inventing startling recipes which, he assured Sheremetev, would feature on the menu of the fantasy restaurant that Sheremetev was equally certain would never come to be.

That night, the cook was eager to know about Vladimir's meeting with Lebedev, and most importantly, what had happened with the delicacies he had sweated so hard to produce.

'Everyone loved the food,' Sheremetev assured him.

Stepanin beamed with pleasure. Then he sat forward, a glint in his eye. 'But Constantin Mikhailovich, Kolya, what about him? What did he say?'

Sheremetev shrugged, as if it was beyond question that the new president had enjoyed the food. The truth was, Sheremetev hadn't seen the president touch a thing. As far as he could tell, the snacks had disappeared down the gullets of his security men and aides. The cameramen too, he noticed, had started grabbing them as they packed up to leave.

'Well?' said Stepanin, eager for details. 'What did he like? What about the *bulochki*? Huh? The ones with cheese. They're not the usual ones – a new invention! Russian Fusion: traditional, but with a twist. I put a bit of quince in, and just a tiny pinch of sumac – a hint, a sniff, that's all. *Lebedevki*, I'm going to call them, in honour of the new president. What do you think? Did he eat them? Did he like them? Come on, Kolya! For God's sake, tell me!'

'I think . . . he liked everything.'

'Everything? He tasted everything? But what did he *say*, Kolya?'

'I can't, Vitya. It's . . . you know, when it's the president, they make you promise you can't repeat anything you hear.'

Stepanin's eyes widened. 'Do they?'

Sheremetev nodded.

Stepanin sat back, his imagination overflowing with images of President Lebedev scoffing his miniature cheese *bulochki* with quince and sumac and praising them in compliments so rarefied, so exorbitant, so . . . presidential that they couldn't be repeated, not even between two people sitting in an otherwise deserted dining room. After a moment he looked up. 'Seeing two presidents in one place! You're lucky, Kolya. That doesn't happen every day.'

'Thank goodness,' murmured Sheremetev.

'Why?'

'They didn't exactly like each other.'

'Really? What did they— no you can't tell me, can you?'

'Let's just say a few choice words were exchanged.'

'You mean words you wouldn't use with your mother?'

Sheremetev nodded.

The cook laughed.

'Vladimir Vladimirovich gave back as good as he got.'

Stepanin roared. 'What fuckery! Two presidents swearing?'

Sheremetev was laughing as well now. 'Like Cossacks!'

Stepanin had tears in his eyes. He wiped at them and took a deep breath, trying to control his laughter. 'Why not?' he said eventually. 'They're just men, after all.'

The cook sat musing on it, shaking his head and grinning. Then he got up and opened the door to the kitchen to yell at one of the potwashers. He came back and poured himself another vodka. 'You want one?' he said to Sheremetev.

Sheremetev shook his head.

'You should drink more, Kolya.' Stepanin threw back his vodka. He put the glass down with a thud, grimacing, and sat quietly for a moment.

'I had another chat with the new housekeeper today,' he said eventually, his tone more restrained, even sombre.

'How was it?'

Stepanin shrugged. He picked up a pork scratching and threw it into his mouth. 'Have you spoken with her?'

Sheremetev nodded.

'What do you think of her?'

'She seems okay.'

'Some of them, you know, they start like that, and then the claws come out.'

Sheremetev, who had had little to do with housekeepers, couldn't say if Stepanin was right or wrong.

Stepanin rolled his empty vodka glass between his fingers, a troubled frown on his brow. Sheremetev wondered what was

'It should be more. Your time is priceless, Vladimir Vladimirovich.'

'So, was it a good investment?'

'A very good investment,' replied Kolyakov without hesitation. 'At ten times the price it would have been a good investment.'

Vladimir nodded. Not as good an investment as it was for me, he thought. To make people pay to meet him, only so that they would have the chance to offer him even more money – who could imagine such a business? The first time he saw how this kind of thing could be done, when he came back to Russia and found himself in the city government in St Petersburg during the wild days as the Soviet Union collapsed, he could barely believe it. An eye-opener. At the start he was barely a spectator, getting the crumbs of the crumbs, a percentage of the percentages, but as he rose in influence and got the hang of the game, the money came flooding in. Commissions, fees, markups, kickbacks – call it what you want. Set up a company and watch the businessmen queue up to route their business through it and leave you twenty percent as they did. Sometimes thirty or forty percent. Import, export, food, oil . . . Never in his life had he imagined it could be so easy or that he could take so much. But as it turned out, even that was small beer. Once he got to Moscow, everything would have an extra zero on the end, or two, or three.

'I'm not sure about another ring road,' he said. 'Didn't the latest report say another ring road would make things worse?'

'That's just a report, Vladimir Vladimirovich,' said Kolyakov, waving a hand airily. 'A word from you, and it's forgotten.'

'I thought it said extensions to the metro or even a light rail system would be better.'

Kolyakov shook his head gravely. 'That's very expensive.'

'This isn't?'

'Well, more metro . . .' Kolyakov shook his head again. 'We'd bedroom nearby, he was the only resident of the upper floor of the dacha, but to look after him the staff quarters housed a small army. Four maids, three male house attendants, and a general handyman who could manage plumbing and electrical problems took care of domestic duties, while a complement of three gardeners and a dozen labourers managed the grounds and greenhouses. A contingent of twenty security guards provided seven-day, twenty-four-hour cover for the estate in rotating shifts. A driver, his wife, and two grown up sons, one of whom also acted as a second driver when needed, lived in the flats over the garage. This horde was fed in the staff dining room, adjacent to the kitchen on the ground floor, by Stepanin and a brigade of half a dozen assistant chefs and potwashers. And ruling over the entire crowded roost, hiring and firing, paying the bills, was the housekeeper.

Until a month previously, the housekeeper had been Mariya Pinskaya, a plump, garrulous woman with a fondness for cheese. Then, without warning, she had walked out. One day she was there, snacking on Stepanin's cheese *bulochki* – not Lebedevki, but traditional ones – and the next morning, she announced that she was leaving with her truckdriver husband for a villa in Cyprus, and her suitcases were already at the gate.

In reality, who the housekeeper was made little difference to Sheremetev. Unlike most of the other staff, he wasn't answerable to her, but to Professor Kalin, Vladimir's neurologist. But the departure of the longserving housekeeper was naturally unsettling, the suddenness of it doubly so. When he first began to look after Vladimir, Sheremetev had kept his own two-room apartment in Moscow, imagining that he would use it on his days off, but a few years later he sublet it. To all intents and purposes, the dacha was his home now, and he expected that he would be here until Vladimir died. He had grown accustomed to the life in the dacha and to the people who inhabited it with him, Pinskaya included.

But change happens, Sheremetev knew. In one form or another, it was inevitable. Three weeks after Pinskaya ran off, a new house-keeper had arrived to take her place, a short, gimlet-eyed woman with dyed brown hair who introduced herself to the staff as Galina Ivan-ovna Barkovskaya. It was obvious immediately that Barkovskaya was no Pinskaya. She was more sparing with her words, more watchful, and ate little cheese, whether wrapped up in *bulochki* or neat. Still, Sheremetev saw no reason for there to be any problems. Things in the dacha had run smoothly before Pinskaya left, and once the new housekeeper had settled in, he imagined, they would continue to do so. The dacha was like a small village. Everyone seemed to have their niche and to get on with everyone else.

THE NEXT EVENING, STEPANIN seemed preoccupied once more. He sat moodily in the staff dining room, gnawing on his pork scratch-ings and watching Sheremetev eating a plate of chicken fricassee.

'What do you think?' asked Stepanin, nodding at the dish.

'It's good,' said Sheremetev.

For a moment, Stepanin forgot whatever it was that was trou-bling him. 'I got some beautiful mushrooms,' he said, putting his fingers to his lips with a smacking sound. 'So fresh, you could still smell the dung on them! Dill, green peppercorns...' he smacked again.

Sheremetev nodded as he ate.

'Barkovskaya said she liked fricassee. I had some lovely plump chickens.'

'So you made it for her? That's nice.'

Stepanin shrugged. 'We had a chat again today, Barkovskaya and me.'

Sheremetev didn't think anything of it. The chef seemed to be having a lot of chats with the new housekeeper, but he imagined that it was natural for a housekeeper and cook to have things to speak about, particularly when one was new to the job.

From the kitchen, where the assistants and potwashers were still working, came the sound of pots crashing. Stepanin took a slug of his vodka and refilled his glass. 'What do you think of her, Kolya?'

'Barkovskaya?' Sheremetev shrugged. 'She seems okay.'

Stepanin leaned forward. 'No, what do you *really* think?'

Sheremetev had no idea what the cook was getting at. 'I don't know. She seems efficient.'

'Efficient...' Stepanin sat back and blew out a long breath. 'Well, that's true. That's one word for her. More efficient than Pinskaya.' Stepanin sighed again. 'What fuckery!'

'What?' asked Sheremetev.

'It's a fuckery that Pinskaya should go and this Barkovskaya turn up to take her place. A grand piece of fuckery with a cock on top!'

'What's so bad about it?'

The cook gazed at Sheremetev, as if trying to decide if he should say anything more. Suddenly there was a noise from Sheremetev's pocket. When he wasn't with Vladimir he carried a baby monitor with him, like the one parents use to listen for cries from their sleeping infants.

'Is he awake?' asked the cook.

Sheremetev took out the monitor and put it to his ear. There was a low staticky rustle which always came out of it, but nothing more distinct.

'Maybe you're going to have one of those nights.'

'I hope not. The doctors are coming to see him tomorrow.'

'Is there a problem?'

'No. Just the monthly checkup.' On a good night, the sedatives' that Sheremetev gave to Vladimir before the ex-president went to bed helped him sleep until seven – but not every night was a good one. Sheremetev listened to the monitor again. There was nothing now but the background rustle that always came out of the speaker. He put it down and took another mouthful of the fricassee.

The cook toyed with his vodka glass. Whatever was worrying him, for once he had apparently decided not to say anything else. He picked up his glass and downed the rest of the spirit, then got up. 'Better see what those fuckers I have to work with have been up to,' he said, heading to the kitchen. 'Enjoy the fricassee, Kolya. There's more if you want it.'

Sheremetev stayed alone in the dining room. A couple of the security guards wandered in and took servings of cold cuts from the sideboard, and he exchanged a few words with them before going upstairs. He slept with the baby monitor on his bedside table. The vague rustlings and mumblings that were always coming out of it didn't disturb him. It was the nights when Vladimir suddenly started shouting that he dreaded.

Just after three am, the monitor squawked into life. Sheremetev woke and lay for a couple of minutes, listening groggily.

'Come here, you fucking Chechen!'

Thump.

'You stinking dead Chechen!'

Sheremetev groaned. The door to Vladimir's suite was only a few metres from his room. He got up and opened it quietly. Inside, there was a small antechamber with two doors. The one on the left led to Vladimir's sitting room, and one directly in front of him was the door to the bedroom.

Warily, Sheremetev turned the handle of the bedroom door and peeked in.

Bathed in the dim glow of the night light, Vladimir stood by his bed in his sky-blue pyjamas, his wispy grey hair awry, fists raised, legs spread in a judo pose, eyes fixed on a spot somewhere towards the window on the far side of the room.

Quickly, before Vladimir could notice him, Sheremetov closed the door. If he got to him early enough, he could sometimes calm Vladimir and get him back into bed, but by the time Vladimir had reached this point, by the time he was striking his judo poses, there was only one way to handle the situation. Vladimir might seem like any other old man, frail and hesitant, but when the delusions took hold of him, he had the strength of a man thirty years younger and a martial arts technique with which to channel it. Sheremetev went to a phone on the wall outside the suite and called the security man who was posted in the entrance hall of the dacha. The phone rang for what seemed like minutes before someone answered. Then Sheremetev went to a locked cupboard in his room and took out a vial of tranquilliser. There were fifty milligrams in the vial – he carefully drew up five milligrams into a syringe, the dose prescribed to calm Vladimir when he was acutely agitated.

In his bedroom, the ex-president took a silent, stealthy step forward, then stopped again, muscles tensed, his eyes fixed on the spot in the air where he saw the Chechen's head hovering, its sunken eyes cloudy and blind, its huge swollen tongue thrusting out from between its clenched, yellow teeth. Vladimir knew what it wanted – what it always wanted: to plant that black tongue on his face and smother him with the slime of death like a giant mollusc suffocating him in the putrid mucus of its muscular foot.

During the Chechen war, a Chechen prisoner about to be executed in front of Vladimir by a Russian firing squad – one that had got into the interesting habit of shooting their prisoners from point blank range in the face, usually after cutting off their ears – had prophesied to him that he would die a slow and excruciating death. Vladimir knew that if that tongue ever planted its poison on him, the prophecy would come true.

Suddenly the head shot off around the room, weaving, darting, bobbing. Then it swung and came straight for him. Vladimir leapt into action with a judo manoeuvre. *Tsukkake!* He struck hard and the head went spinning away, ricocheting off the window. It stopped, hanging in the air, the blind eyes watching him, the black tongue dripping its toxic slime.

Vladimir bounced softly from foot to foot, poised, ready to spring into another judo manoeuvre. 'You fucking Chechen!' he cried. 'What now, huh? Come on! Give it a try! Let's see what you've got, you boy-fucker!' That he was engaged in a mortal combat, Vladimir had no doubt, just as Russia, it was no exaggeration to say, had been caught in mortal combat with the Chechen rebels in their tiny, faraway republic. Yet at the same time, there was something exhilarating about the fight. Just him and the Chechen's head, one on one – winner take all. He had already written – or ghostwritten – three books about judo, but they were about the conventional art. No one, he thought, had laid down the principles of this type of combat before. He would write a book, he thought, about the art of judo against a head.

It flew at him again. He was ready. *Sode-tore! Ushiro-dore!* Then down on his knees – *Tsukkomi!* The head shot up and smashed into the ceiling. Ha! The Chechen wasn't expecting that.

'Now, what, you stinking head?' he shouted, as the head bobbed under the ceiling. 'Go! Crawl back into the toilet with the rest of your body! Let the maggots crawl back into your eyes and finish their feast—'

Suddenly he was flat on his face.

'Careful!' cried Sheremetev at the two security guards. 'Don't hurt him.'

One of the guards yelled as Vladimir elbowed him.

'Hold him down carefully. That's it! Careful!'

'*Ah! What the fuck!*' yelled the guard, as Vladimir elbowed him again.

Vladimir's legs thrashed. Sheremetev struggled to pull down the former president's pyjamas with one hand while holding the syringe in the other. In the end he gave up and simply rammed the needle into Vladimir's buttock through the fabric and injected the tranquilliser.

A minute or so later, the thrashing lessened.

'Let him go,' said Sheremetev.

The two guards stood up warily. One of them, Artur, a tall fair-haired man with green eyes and prominent cheekbones, was the leader of the security detail at the dacha. 'Shall we put him on the bed?' he asked.

Sheremetev nodded. 'Gently.'

They turned Vladimir over and lifted him onto the mattress. He lay motionless. Under his part-closed lids, his eyeballs had rolled back, leaving two slivers of white as if in a face out of a horror movie.

The other guard, whose nose was bleeding from the blows he had taken from Vladimir's elbow, gave a slight shiver. 'Is he dead?' he whispered.

Sheremetev shook his head.

'Shame.'

Artur looked at him sharply. 'Get the hell out of here!'

'But—'

'Out! Now! And clean your nose. You're bleeding like a stuck pig.'

The guard put his hand to his nose and looked at the blood on his fingers. He muttered something and left.

'I apologise for that, Nikolai Ilyich,' said Artur.

'He was hurt.'

'Still, it's not acceptable. I'll speak with him. He needs to improve his attitude. If he can't, I'll get rid of him. To be entrusted with the safety of Vladimir Vladimirovich is a sacred duty. I see it as a privilege, Nikolai Ilyich, not a job. A bit of borsht from the nose is nothing to complain about!' Artur paused, as if overcome with patriotic emotion. He took a deep breath. 'Will there be anything else, Nikolai Ilyich?'

'No. It's a shame. We'd had quite a good month up to now.' He paused, gazing at Vladimir, who was breathing steadily, eyes fully closed now. 'Thank you, Artur. I don't think we'll have any more trouble tonight.'

'If you do,' said Artur, 'just call. We're here to help.'

The guard left. Sheremetev straightened Vladimir's pyjamas, then covered him with the quilt.

It was a terrible thing, dementia, a disease that struck at the very core of what made a person who he was. No matter how many times Sheremetev saw it, it never became less sad. And for such a thing to have happened to Vladimir Vladimirovich, five times president of Russia...

Sometimes, when Vladimir looked at him, Sheremetev saw in the ex-president's eyes such confusion and fear, it was almost heartbreaking. He had seen that same look in so many of his dementia patients. What they needed most then was nothing that drugs or other treatments could give them, but simple human comfort. The fact that Vladimir had been five times president of Russia didn't lessen what it must feel like for him in those moments, thankfully fewer and fewer now as his condition progressed, when he was suddenly aware that he didn't know where he was or who was with him or why anything was happening around him.

The old man lay on his back, snoring peacefully.

Sheremetev leaned over him and smoothed his ruffled hair. 'I'm sorry I had to use the injection,' he murmured. 'Sleep well, Vladimir Vladimirovich.'

He left, closing the door quietly behind him.

Soon, all was quiet again in the dacha. Vladimir snored, visions of the Chechen, temporarily, dissolved by the tranquilliser in his blood. A few metres away, Sheremetev had gone back to sleep, the baby monitor rustling quietly on the bedside table beside him. Downstairs, Stepanin slumbered in the arms of the maid, Elena Dmitrovna Mirzayev, his lover. Behind the door off the main entrance hall, the guard on duty lay asleep on a comfortable bed that the security contingent had set up in a warm, cosy antechamber.

Only the new housekeeper, Galina Ivanovna Barkovskaya, was awake. She sat at the desk in her office, a table lamp glowing, poring over the dacha's accounts.

4

THE NEXT MORNING, PROFESSOR Kalin arrived at ten o'clock for his monthly visit. He brought with him another expert, Professor L P Andreevsky, who visited only every second or third time to oversee Vladimir's general physical health. Sheremetev took the two doctors upstairs to the sitting room, where Vladimir was waiting for them.

At each visit, Professor Kalin attempted to evaluate Vladimir's awareness and memory, charting its decline in the notes he dictated in his car after he left the dacha. Vladimir never made it easy for him, perhaps, at some level, sensing that the professor's questions carried an implication of illness, even if he no longer had any insight into what that illness was.

Professor Kalin crouched in front of the ex-president and started off on his usual questions to test if Vladimir had any awareness of his current time and place. Sheremetev and Andreevsky exchanged a glance. Vladimir hadn't given a correct answer to even one of those questions for the last twelve months.

The professor nodded to himself. 'Do you know this man here?' he asked, pointing at Sheremetev.

'Do *you*?' riposted Vladimir, which was one of his stock evasions when asked a question he had no idea how to answer.

'Yes.'

'Then who is he?'

'Don't you know?' asked the professor.

'Don't you?' shot back Vladimir.

'Do you know, Vladimir Vladimirovich?'

'Why should I tell you? Who are you, anyway?'

'Don't you remember?'

'I've never met you in my life.'

'I'm Professor Kalin,' said the professor for the fifth time that morning.

'What about him?' demanded Vladimir, pointing to the other doctor.

'That's Professor Andreevsky. He's another doctor, like me. He's been looking after you for years.'

Vladimir grunted dismissively.

Professor Kalin stood up. He glanced at his colleague and gestured towards Vladimir, inviting Andreevsky to take over.

Andreevsky drew out his stethoscope. 'May I, Vladimir Vladimirovich?'

Vladimir turned to Sheremetev. 'Is he a doctor?'

Sheremetev nodded.

Vladimir scrutinised Andreevsky for a moment, then slowly unbuttoned his pyjama top.

The professor laid his stethoscope on Vladimir's chest. He listened to his heart, then began to move the stethoscope from place to place. 'Breathe in... Breathe out... Very good. Continue please. In... Out... In... Out...'

'That's enough,' said Vladimir irritably, and pushed the stethoscope away.

Andreevsky stepped back. 'Blood pressure?' he said to Sheremetev.

Sheremetev pulled out the chart on which he recorded the blood pressure readings that he had been instructed to take twice a week.

The results of the urine tests that he regularly took were there as well, together with other pages detailing the medications that Vladimir had received and notes on his behaviour.

Andreevsky looked over the blood pressure chart. 'Fit as an ox,' he murmured, handing the chart to Kalin.

'Fit as a Siberian ox!' declared Vladimir, whose hearing showed no sign of accompanying his intellect into decrepitude.

Kalin turned the page and scanned the behaviour charts. He saw the note that Sheremetev had made that morning of the episode that had taken place overnight. Prior to that, there had been almost three weeks without the need for an injection to top up the tranquilliser and sedative tablets that Vladimir took each night before bed.

'What happened exactly last night?' asked Kalin.

'He thought he was fighting with someone,' said Sheremetev.

'But he'd had his tablets?'

'Of course.'

'Do you know who he was fighting with?'

Sheremetev glanced at Vladimir, who was staring straight ahead, as if oblivious to the conversation going on around him. 'The same as always.'

Vladimir's eyes narrowed and his nose wrinkled slightly.

Kalin handed the charts back to Sheremetev. 'Vladimir Vladimirovich,' he said, crouching down to his eye level again, 'did someone come here last night?'

'Last night?' said Vladimir.

Kalin nodded.

Vladimir shrugged. 'Do I know you?'

'I'm Professor Kalin. I look after you.'

'Why do you look after me? I'm as strong as . . . something or other.'

'That's good,' said Kalin. 'It's good to be strong. Does anyone come to bother you?'

'Do you know what I would do if someone came to bother me?' countered Vladimir.

'Tell me. What would you do?'

Vladimir smiled craftily. Never reveal your strategy, he knew, not even to your friends. Especially not your friends. 'If you want to find out, I'd advise you to try,' he replied, and then chuckled to himself.

Kalin watched him for a moment. 'Vladimir Vladimirovich, is there anything else you want to tell us before we go?'

'What should I tell you?'

'Whatever you like.'

'You're the doctor, aren't you? *You* should be telling me!'

'Alright,' said Kalin. 'Well, I'll tell you what – I'll see you again in a month, alright?'

'Where will you see me?' said Vladimir.

'Here. We'll come back.'

'How do you know I'll be here?'

'If you're not here, we'll find you.'

Vladimir grinned. 'No, you won't.'

Kalin stood up. 'Goodbye, Vladimir Vladimirovich. I'll see you again in a month.'

Vladimir didn't reply, as if keeping his counsel.

Sheremetev accompanied the two professors out of the room. Once the door to the suite was closed behind them, Kalin stopped.

'I could increase the tranquilliser, I suppose,' he said to Andreev-sky, in a weary, dispirited tone.

'If you're asking my opinion, Vyacha,' responded Andreevksy brightly, 'from a cardiovascular and respiratory perspective, he could take it.'

Kalin gave his colleague an irritable look. That opinion did nothing to solve his dilemma, and from the jauntiness with which Andreevsky had pronounced it, Kalin suspected the fact amused him.

The professor held out his hand to Sheremetev for the charts. He made a show of minutely examining the notes on Vladimir's behaviour. After a while he began to rub at his nose as if he had an itch, a habit he had, Sheremetev knew by now, whenever he was trying to disguise his procrastination.

The dilemma was the same dilemma that confronted Professor Kalin each month, and everyone in the corridor – not only Kalin himself, but Sheremetev and Andreevsky as well – knew it. The tranquilliser that the professor had prescribed to reduce the rages when Vladimir still had insight into his condition had numerous potential side effects, which included, paradoxically, delusions, hallucinations and agitation. Right now, that was exactly what Vladimir had. Reducing the dose of tranquilliser might therefore solve the problem. On the other hand, these delusions, hallucinations and agitation might have nothing at all to do with the medication, but be due to Vladimir's dementia, and it might be the medication that was keeping them in check – in which case, increasing the dose might solve the problem. The only way to tell for certain would be to reduce the dose and see what happened, but the one thing one could say for certain about reducing the medication after so many years of use was that there would be severe withdrawal effects, which might well include . . . delusions, hallucinations and agitation. All in all it was an unholy mess and it would take months and months to sort it out, months in which the medication would have to be reduced in gradual, tiny steps and during which Vladimir would need to be monitored closely and assessed, ideally, once a week.

It took a good half a day out of Professor Kalin's schedule to come to the dacha outside Odinstovo, half a day in which he could otherwise be attending to his eye-wateringly lucrative private practice, for which there was already a waiting list of over three months – coming even once a month was already costing him a small fortune. Coming once a week would cost him a large one. Naturally, Professor Kalin was as patriotic as the next man, and was truly grateful – as were his British-educated children – for the health system presided over by Vladimir, in which people would literally crawl out of public wards in fear for their lives – he had witnessed it with his own eyes, not once, but twice – to get themselves into private hospitals, in a number of which the professor held considerable shares. But even so, there were limits to what could be expected from him. And really, looking at this chart, it was only every few days that Vladimir had an episode of agitation, and only every second or third of those was so extreme as to require an injection, and just this month there had been almost three full weeks in which he had been injection-free . . .

'It really isn't *that* bad,' said Kalin.

'No,' said Sheremetev.

'You could almost say it's improving,' said Andreevsky, peering over Kalin's shoulder at the chart.

Kalin glanced at him suspiciously, then turned back to Sheremetev. 'It's always this Chechen, is it?'

'When he's fighting, yes, it's always him.'

'And he really fights him? I mean, he physically gets up and fights him?'

Sheremetev nodded.

'Who is he? Someone he knew? Someone he worked with?'

'I have no idea.'

'You could increase the dose if you want to,' said Andreevsky. 'His heart could take it.'

'I thought you said it was improving!' said Kalin.

Andreevsky shrugged. 'Up to you, Vyacha.'

Kalin studied the charts again and rubbed at his nose. Andreevsky stole a glance at Sheremetev and grinned. Kalin had no idea what to do but couldn't bear to show it in front of a colleague or a nurse. The nose-scratching was a sure sign. In the end, Andreevsky and Sheremetev both knew, he was going to do nothing, as he always did, and say that he would review things in a month.

'Does he wander?' asked Kalin suddenly.

'Wander?' said Sheremetev.

'Vladimir Vladimirovich! Does he wander?'

'No.'

'At night?'

Sheremetev shook his head.

'Do you keep his door locked?'

'He never wanders.'

'Never?'

'Never.'

'Still, you should lock his door, Nikolai Ilyich.'

Sheremetev had no intention of locking Vladimir's door. He hated the idea of such a thing unless there was really no alternative. It was a momentous betrayal of trust, to confine someone like an infant. And it wasn't necessary. First, Vladimir didn't wander. And second, if he did, Sheremetev would surely hear him through the monitor.

Kalin gave his nose a final scratch. 'In my opinion, it's best to leave things as they are for now,' he said sagely, handing back the charts. 'I'll review the situation next month.'

'I agree,' replied Andreevsky in his gravest, most professorial voice.

'Be sure to make a note of every episode, Nikolai Ilyich,' said

Kalin, holding up an admonitory finger. 'I'll need to make a full assessment.'

'*Every* episode,' said Andreevsky.

The two professors walked to the stairs, Sheremetev following a step behind.

'Does anyone come to see him?' asked Kalin, glancing over his shoulder.

'Not much,' said Sheremetev. 'Three days ago President Lebedev was here to take photos with him.'

'I saw in the paper. How was he?'

Sheremetev shrugged. 'He was what he was. They wanted him to give the president his blessing, but he refused to say anything.'

'Did he say why?'

'I got the feeling that he and President Lebedev didn't like each other much.'

Professor Andreevksy laughed.

'Do you think he knew what was going on?' asked Kalin.

'I think he knew more than you would think. At first he thought Lebedev had come to make a report to him, that he was still some kind of minister. Then I think he realised that something else was going on.' Sheremetev smiled. 'He liked the cameras. As soon as he walked in the room, you could see him stand taller.'

Kalin glanced at Andreevsky and chuckled. 'Vanity. It's like I always tell my students: the deepest part of a person's character is the one that goes last.'

They went down the stairs. The security guard in the entrance hall stepped forward from his post and opened the door for the two professors. Outside, their car was waiting.

'Do you still take him on his walk each day?' Kalin asked Sheremetev.

'Yes. Every morning. If not, in the afternoon. No matter how bad the weather, we try to go. Occasionally he resists, but not usually. He enjoys it.'

'How long does he walk for?'

Sheremetev shrugged. 'Half an hour. Longer if he wants. If he's had a disturbed night, if he's tired, it might be less. I have to watch that. We have problems if he gets too tired.'

'And away from the dacha? Do you ever go out anywhere else?'

'Not for a long time.'

'Maybe you should take him out, Nikolai Ilyich.'

'Do you think I should?'

'Why not?' said Kalin. 'Have an outing. Somewhere different.'

Andreevsky nodded. 'It'll be good for him.'

The two professors headed for the door. 'Shame his heart's so strong,' Sheremetev heard Andreevsky saying. 'He could go on for years.'

THE VISIT OF THE doctors left Sheremetev feeling dejected. Andreevsky was right – it was a shame that Vladimir's heart was so strong. Better to keel over with a heart attack and be gone than to linger in this twilight for so long, neglected, abandoned by family and friends, cared for only by strangers who were paid to do the job.

Over the years, Sheremetev had seen the visitors to the dacha slow from a flood to a stream to a trickle that by now had dried up almost entirely. The horde of parasites which had hummed around Vladimir when Sheremetev first arrived had flown off the moment they realised the ex-president no longer exercised any influence with his successor. At the start they had been everywhere – a year later not even their echoes were heard. Official visits from Russian politicians and foreign dignitaries who felt obliged to pay their respects lasted longer, but came to an end when Vladimir's condition had become so obvious that the visits were an embarrassment to the government and word was discreetly put out that the former president had retired from all public duties to enjoy his richly deserved retirement. As for his private visitors, the old cronies who might have felt some loyalty to Vladimir, if not affection, were mostly themselves either ill or dead, and those who weren't too frail to visit found little pleasure in coming to see a man who no longer recognised them. After a while, even a lingering sense of duty wasn't sufficient to bring them out to the dacha. That left only Vladimir's family. His first wife was dead, but the second one, the one Vladimir had married in secret, was very much alive, thirty years his junior and constantly linked with one billionaire or another. She had left him in reality, if not officially, even before he stepped down from the presidency. In earlier years, his children and grandchildren had come from abroad to visit at Christmas or Easter, but nowadays an excuse invariably arrived in their place. Thankfully, thought Sheremetev, Vladimir had no awareness of the feast days and didn't know the extent to which he was neglected.

As for Sheremetev himself, he didn't think that he was a stranger for Vladimir. He wasn't a friend, he wasn't family, but he felt sure that he was something more to the ex-president than a faceless nurse. He was certain that Vladimir knew him and was at ease with him, even if he couldn't remember his name. He was the only one who could calm him before his agitation became too great. And when the look of confusion and fear came into Vladimir's eyes, it was him that he looked for. Sheremetev, for his part, regarded the ex-president as more than a mere patient. How could he not, having looked after him so intimately for the last six years? They had been through Vladimir's rages together, the slow, stuttering extinction of his insight into his condition, the eruption out of the remains of his mind of his delusions and hallucinations. Whatever was left of Vladimir's consciousness on any given day, whatever world he lived in, he was still a person, still Vladimir Vladimirovich, still someone who could feel, shout, cry, question, laugh. You can't live so closely for so long and go through such things with someone and not develop a relationship with them, a sense of concern and even affection, that goes beyond the merely professional, even if that person has no idea who you are.

But no one else in the dacha had such a relationship with Vladimir. Even those who came to the upper floor, the maids and house attendants who saw him each day, rarely exchanged a word with him, and were generally tentative, uncertain, tongue-tied, partly because dementia often has that effect on people unaccustomed to dealing with it, partly because of the aura of who Vladimir had been. The others who lived in the dacha saw him only by chance, in passing, when he was out for his daily walk. Other than Sheremetev, the ex-president was surrounded by people he didn't know and who regarded him as unknowable, like some kind of living statue. It made the responsibility that Sheremetev felt as the only person in the dacha who knew and cared for Vladimir seem sometimes insupportable. At other times, when the second wife had waltzed in for the first time in six months and then waltzed out again twenty minutes later, as if fulfilling some kind of duty that was required to retain access to whatever funds financed her existence, it almost broke his heart.

As a nurse, Sheremetev had seen many people die over the years, some quickly, some slowly, some resigned to their fate, some raging against it, some peacefully, some in pain. But by far the worst death, in his opinion – apart from a death experienced with agony racking one's bones – was to die alone. Surely it was at the foundation of civility that a man should have some comfort from those who had loved him when his time came to depart, and surely it was at the foundation of love that they would want to give it to him. What kind of civilisation, he wondered, would allow Vladimir to live out his final days like this? And if this is all that Vladimir could expect – after his years of public life and all that he had done for the motherland – then what could anyone else hope for?

Well, Sheremetev wouldn't let the worst happen to him. He wouldn't let him die with no one to comfort him. That much, at least, he could ensure.

The doctors had said he should take him for an outing. Why not? Both he and Vladimir could do with a change of scenery.

When he returned after seeing the doctors out, Vladimir was sitting where Sheremetev had left him, deep in conversation with an armchair.

'Vladimir Vladimirovich,' he said brightly, 'let's do something you'll enjoy. Shall we go to the lake? We used to go, do you remember? It's a nice day for a walk. Maybe we'll get Stepanin to pack us a lunch.'

Vladimir looked out the window.

'See? It's sunny. I'll find something nice for you to wear.'

Sheremetev went into the dressing room. It was lined on all sides by shelves, hanging rails and drawers, and was many times larger than the little room in which Sheremetev himself slept each night. On one set of rails were at least three dozen overcoats, some fur, some leather, some wool; on others must have hung sixty or eighty suits. Elsewhere were rails of jackets, blazers and bomber jackets, shelves of sweaters, shirts and shoes, drawers of underwear, socks, belts and cufflinks. Sheremetev selected a suit, a shirt, tie, belt and shoes, then he put the clothes down on a chair and opened a freestanding cabinet that stood in the middle of the room.

The cabinet was about a metre and a half in height and half a metre in width and depth. Made bespoke for Vladimir out of a polished hardwood, it had a pair of doors that opened to reveal a column of drawers, each only five centimetres in height. Sheremetev applied a slight pressure to the front of one of the drawers, which slid smoothly out. The drawer was lined in black velvet and had three rows of five niches. In each of the niches nestled a watch.

Sheremetev perused the watches in the tray, then pushed it back in and opened another, from which he selected a silver timepiece with a blue face.

He closed the cabinet, gathered up the clothes, and took everything into the bedroom.

'Come on, Vladimir Vladimirovich, let's get dressed.'

As much as was possible, it was good for Vladimir still to do things himself. This meant that simple activities took longer than they might have done, but Sheremetev was determined to help Vladimir preserve his capacities for as long as he could. He stood with the ex-president as Vladimir fumbled with his clothes, gently prompting him when he forgot what he was doing.

'I wore this on election night,' said Vladimir, as he slipped on the suit jacket.

'This suit?'

'Look, it's got a spot.' He raised his left arm and pointed at a place near the elbow.

Sheremetev saw a very faint darkening in the material. 'Which election night?' he asked. In the early years, Vladimir had often told him stories stimulated by items of clothing that he was wearing – meeting President Bush for the first time, hunting a Siberian tiger, flying into Chechnya at the height of the war, opening the Olympics, banqueting in Beijing with President Xi. The stories were endless, as one might expect from a man who had led such a life.

Vladimir frowned.

'Well, doesn't matter which election, Vladimir Vladimirovich. It's a good suit.'

'Seventy-two percent on a turnout of slightly over seventy!' said Vladimir suddenly. 'First round! What do you think of that?'

'That's good, Vladimir Vladimirovich.'

'Good? It's perfect! At the start we were naïve – the higher the vote the better. Now, of course, we know, a vote can look too high. Seventy and seventy, that's what we want. Seventy turnout, seventy in favour, the perfect recipe – actually, just over, so you can say however many turned out, more than fifty percent in absolute terms voted in favour. Once in a while you throw in a lower result to make it look like anything can happen.' He chuckled. 'Of course, no matter how we do it, in the west they still say it's rigged. Last month, in Vienna, some reporter told me that he followed a bus from one polling station to the next and said he saw everyone voting twice. Some Italian reporter. How the hell did he get in anyway? He confronted me at the press conference after the nuclear talks. Thought he was going to catch me out. Takes more than some journalist with a smart arse question to do that, I can tell you! Do you know what I said? "Who did they vote for, these people you say you saw in the bus? Did you ask them?" He said they said they voted for me. Then I said: "So how can you believe such people? They admit to voting twice. You can't believe a word that comes out of their mouth. They're self-confessed criminals!"' Vladimir laughed. 'What do you think? That shut him up alright!'

Sheremetev handed Vladimir his shoes and went to the phone

that stood on a table in the dressing room. He called the security post in the hall and asked the guard to arrange for Eleyekov, the driver, to bring a car around. 'Put your shoes on please, Vladimir Vladimirovich,' he said as he waited for the guard to call back. When the phone rang, the guard told him that Eleyekov had said that the Mercedes in which Vladimir was supposed to travel, a bulletproof S class, had broken down and wouldn't be ready for use until late the following day. Sheremetev told him to tell Eleyekov that they were only going to the lake and they could take the other car that was kept at the dacha, an armoured, bespoke Range Rover. The guard, sounding doubtful, said he'd call again and ask.

Vladimir sat gazing vacantly at the floor, one shoe on and the other in his hand.

Sheremetev prompted him, but Vladimir looked up at him in confusion.

Sheremetev eased the other shoe onto his foot and watched as Vladimir tried to tie the laces. He completed the bows for him. Then he handed Vladimir the watch that he had selected. Vladimir stared at it, a slight frown coming over his face.

'What is it, Vladimir Vladimirovich?' said Sheremetev. 'Would you prefer another watch?'

Vladimir looked up at him. 'What?'

'Would you like me to help you with the watch?'

Vladimir looked at him as if he was an imbecile. 'I can do it!'

The phone rang. The guard told him that the Range Rover was unavailable too.

'They're *both* broken down?' said Sheremetev incredulously.

'And Vadim Sergeyevich just told me that the Mercedes – you remember I said it would be available tomorrow afternoon – he just got a call and now it won't be ready until the following morning.'

Sheremetev put the phone down in disbelief. Both cars broken down? What if they really needed them? There should be some emergency plan, he thought. Well, luckily, going to the lake wasn't a matter of life or death.

'No lake today,' he said to Vladimir Vladimirovich. 'Let's go for a walk instead.'

'Where?' said Vladimir.

'Wherever you like.'

'The seafront.'

'Well, let's see how we go,' said Sheremetev, and he took the watch, which Vladimir was still holding, and fastened it on his wrist.

5

THE NOTION OF GOING to the seafront didn't stick long in Vladimir's mind, not long enough to make it down the stairs. Sheremetev took him outside. Immediately surrounding the dacha was an area of lawn, and beyond it, in one direction, some of the birch forest that had originally covered the land. When Sheremetev had first arrived at the dacha, the rest of the estate had been a stately, landscaped expanse of meadows, rockeries and arbours, with a stream and a pond and couple of ornamental bridges, but the land had since been dug up and flattened and then covered with ugly long sausages of plastic greenhouses in which grew fruit- and flower-bearing plants alien to any Russian field. The stream had been diverted into pipes to irrigate them. Every thirty metres or so along the tunnels stood a giant steel installation with a huge pipe that fed hot air inside the plastic. The heaters weren't operating yet, but in the winter, if you walked between the tunnels, their low, vibrating thrum went straight to the stomach. Here and there amongst the tunnels stood a bench that survived from the time before the greenhouses had been erected, as if a reminder of what had been before.

Sheremetev usually left it up to Vladimir to decide which way they went. Today he marched straight up to one of the greenhouses. Inside, the air was warm and moist. Large-leafed plants were staked into the soil of raised beds on either side of the tunnel, thickly hung with dark, glossy aubergines ripening on the vine. A pair of labourers was working at each of the beds, weeding and picking off snails and slugs.

The workers stopped and stared as Vladimir approached.

Vladimir beamed at them, airily bidding them continue their work. The pickers smiled back at him uncertainly.

One of the dacha's three gardeners was there as well. Arkady Maksimovich Goroviev, a man of about fifty with thick greying hair and somewhat pockmarked skin, walked with a slight limp. Sheremetev had heard talk that Goroviev had had some kind of problems with the authorities in the past, but in Sheremetev's experience the gardener was a kind, gentle man, unfailingly restrained and polite. He was the only other person in the dacha who was uncowed by the ex-president and seemed able to see him as a fellow human being, rather than as some distant and awe-inspiring icon, and to speak to him normally. Whenever Goroviev encountered Vladimir, he always addressed him respectfully and inquired after his health in a fashion that suggested that he was genuinely interested in his condition from a human perspective, as one person ought to be interested in another. Today, after the demoralising visit from the doctors and the disappointment of his hopes of taking Vladimir on an outing from the dacha, Sheremetev was glad to have run into him.

Goroviev put down his tools. 'Good morning, Vladimir Vladimirovich. How are you today?'

Vladimir didn't answer.

'We're going for a walk,' said Sheremetev.

Goroviev smiled. 'I can see. And yourself, Nikolai Ilyich? All is well with you?'

'All well, thank you. Yourself, Arkady Maksimovich?'

'All well. We have some flowers in the next greenhouse. Roses.

They're in wonderful shape – tomorrow we'll cut them. Would Vladimir Vladimirovich care to see?'

'Vladimir Vladimirovich?' said Sheremetev.

Vladimir was frowning, as if in concentration, but he didn't reply.

'Let's go and see,' said Sheremetev.

He gave Vladimir a nudge and they walked with Goroviev out of a door beside the incoming shaft of one of the heaters. For a moment there was a shock of fresh air – not at all cool for October, but momentarily bracing after the warmth and humidity of the greenhouse – and then Goroviev opened another door and they were inside again. Warmth and humidity hit them. Sheremetev wondered if Vladimir was too hot in the suit in which he had dressed him, but the ex-president ignored the question when Sheremetev asked him.

An enveloping scent of flowers filled the greenhouse, almost too heady. Roses bloomed. Down the length of the tunnel, sections of one type of flower followed another in banks of colour.

'These are Empress Josephines, Vladimir Vladimirovich,' explained Goroviev as he led them past fragrant buds of deep pink. 'A very classical rose. They were first cultivated for the wife of the emperor Napoleon in the nineteenth century. They're much in demand again.' He stopped, pulled out a pair of small secateurs, snipped off a stem with a perfect bud and expertly removed the thorns before handing the bud to Vladimir.

'I'll give this to Marishka,' said Vladimir.

'That sounds like a good idea,' said Goroviev. 'Come, Vladimir Vladimirovich, let's look at some others.'

The gardener led them past other beds of roses, each time patiently explaining the provenance of the variety and stopping to select a prime bud for Vladimir.

'Would Vladimir Vladimirovich care to see something else?'

asked the gardener when they came to the end of the greenhouse.

Sheremetev glanced at Vladimir to see if he was getting tired. If Vladimir reached a certain point of fatigue, he might decide that he needed a nap and would simply refuse to go on. There had been times when he had simply dropped to the ground and Sheremetev had had to call a contingent of security men to carry him back – which Vladimir usually resisted. Then it would be a question of giving him an injection of tranquilliser or letting him sleep where he had dropped for an hour or two. That wasn't such a bad thing in the summer, but it was a different matter if they were out for a walk in January with the snow a metre high on either side of the path.

Vladimir didn't look tired yet, but it had been a turbulent night, and the doctors' visit had meant that they had started their walk later than normal. Sheremetev checked his watch. Lunch wasn't far away. Hunger was another thing he had to watch out for.

'I think we might go back,' said Sheremetev. 'Do you want to go back now, Vladimir Vladimirovich?'

Vladimir shrugged.

'I think we'd better go.'

'Goodbye, then, Vladimir Vladimirovich,' said Goroviev.

Suddenly Vladimir looked at him probingly. 'What do you do?'

'I'm a gardener, Vladimir Vladimirovich.'

Vladimir stared at Goroviev a moment longer. Then the energy went out of his gaze and he grunted and turned away.

Sheremetev led Vladimir back towards the dacha. As they came in sight of the house, he saw Stepanin pacing around on the grass behind the kitchen. Even from a distance, the cook looked agitated. He marched up and down like a caged animal, head bowed, one fist clenched, a cigarette clutched in the other. Suddenly he stopped and kicked out at a branch that lay on the ground, sending it flying.

The cook was given to explosions of rage, Sheremetev knew, but normally a good shout at one of the potwashers was enough to mollify him.

Suddenly Sheremetev looked around. Vladimir had kept walking. He hurried to catch up.

UPSTAIRS, THEY WENT BACK to the sitting room, where Vladimir's lunch would soon be brought.

'Shall we get changed out of your suit?' said Sheremetev.

'Why?' demanded Vladimir. 'I won an election in this suit.'

'I know, Vladimir Vladimirovich.'

'Do you think the election was rigged? Is that what you're saying?'

'No.'

'Seventy-two percent!' said Vladimir, his voice rising. 'On a turnout of seventy.'

'Yes, Vladimir Vladimirovich.'

Vladimir gazed at him suspiciously for a moment. 'Get Monarov.'

'I don't think Monarov's—'

'Get him! I'm waiting.' He tapped on his watch portentously.

'Would you like to sit at the table, Vladimir Vladimirovich?' said Sheremetev. 'It's almost time for lunch.'

'Good. Here he is.'

'There's no one else here, Vladimir Vladimirovich.'

'Monarov, have you eaten?'

'No,' said Monarov.

Vladimir laughed, rubbing his hands.

Dishes of caviar, herring, roe and pickles were laid out on the table. Monarov took a spoonful of caviar and ate it neat, chasing it with a glass of vodka, as he liked to do. Vladimir did likewise, spilling a little of the caviar on his jacket sleeve as he raised the spoon. He brushed it away. 'Shit!' he said, looking at the stain it had left.

Monarov laughed.

'Caviar never comes out,' muttered Vladimir.

'It's good luck.' Monarov filled their glasses again. 'To another election! To all those who voted again . . . and again . . . and again . . .'

Vladimir pretended to still be angry for a moment, then they both roared with laughter.

There were few people with whom Vladimir allowed himself to be at ease – actually, no one – but with Evgeny Monarov he came closest. Monarov was a true Chekist, one of the old boys from the Leningrad KGB. He had been with Vladimir ever since he came to Moscow, filling various roles, from chief of the president's staff to chairman of a state oil company to finance minister to head of homeland security. But whatever he was nominally doing, there was one role he had always had: handling the money. The arrangement was that he kept for himself twenty percent of Vladimir's share, building his own not inconsiderable fortune, and, as far as Vladimir could ascertain from the various secret investigations he had ordered into him, doing it with scrupulous honesty.

Monarov took another spoonful of caviar, then stopped with the spoon halfway to his mouth. 'You're not happy, Vova? I can see that look on your face.'

'I wouldn't say I'm unhappy. Thoughtful.'

'About?'

Vladimir sighed. 'I can't go on forever. One more election victory, yes, but when I go, who follows? Where are the great men, Evgeny? Only a strong man can rule Russia. Where's the next Czar?'

'In jail,' said Monarov, smiling. 'Or in London. Or dead. You should know that better than anyone, Vova.'

'Very funny.'

Monarov put the caviar in his mouth.

'They're in jail or in London or dead,' said Vladimir, 'precisely because they were not great. One way or another, they had a poor conception of the reality of Russia. Look at the oligarchs. For them, it was only about money.'

'Kolyakov, yes. He'd do anything you said if it would get him another contract. But the others? Trikovsky? What about him?'

'Trikovsky more than any of them! The hypocrite. A democrat, sure – a democrat once he had a television station to broadcast his propaganda and the money to buy an election. Before that, Zhenya, where was his love of democracy then? Let him rot in Switzerland, issuing his manifestoes. Water off a duck's back. Okay, then look at the liberals. They'd take us back to the days of Boris Nikolayevich. Do you remember what it was like? People forget, they have a rosy view. Chaos! Another year of it and the whole country would have been down the pan. The only smart decision the Old Man made was to get out when he did, the bloated pig.'

'And to appoint you.'

'And to appoint me. True. Alright, two smart decisions. At the end I couldn't bear to look at him. I'd think: what have you done to Russia, you fucking pig? Look at the chance you had and what you did with it! I knew then it would take me years to get us back. And it did. Years! And now what's going to happen?'

Monarov shook his head.

Vladimir noticed that others were at the table as well, Luschkin, Narzayev, Serensky, all boys from the KGB who had been with him in the Kremlin for years. Not everyone from the agencies had supported him. His old supervisor from the KGB, Grisha Rastchev, had joined the refounded communist party and had turned into a real thorn in his side, even ending up in jail on various charges over the years. That was a shame. Rastchev had helped him in his early career and Vladimir would have liked to make him rich – but you can only do so much. What can you do if the horse won't even go near the water, let alone drink it? And not only that, but keeps yelling to the other horses that you've poisoned it? But the ones who had come with him, the loyal ones, they were the rocks on which his governments were erected, from whom shot out the iron fists needed to keep the opponents at bay. They had reaped the rewards. And why not? In every country, someone has to be rich. Why should Russia be an exception?

Yet none of them had the strength and the vision that he had, none of them were capable of taking his place. And besides, the boys were old now, older than him. Only Narzayev was younger.

They all agreed that there was no one. It didn't even need to be said.

'What can we do, Vova?' said Serensky. 'No one lives for ever.'

'Who knows what our Vova can do?' said Luschkin. 'Maybe he'll never die!'

Vladimir glanced at him, wondering how someone could say something so stupid. Oleg Luschkin was a big man with strong, Slavic cheekbones of which, as a fierce Russian nationalist, he was inordinately proud. A face lift had stretched his skin tight. It was almost painful to watch him smile, so close did the skin seem to be to the point of tearing across those bones of which he was so vain. He was loyal, or always had been, and had served in a series of roles for which Vladimir required someone safe, solid and unimaginative. But when people started saying things so stupid to prove their loyalty, it was time to be careful of them.

'What about Gena Sverkov?' suggested Narzayev.

'Lightweight,' muttered Vladimir dismissively, amidst chuckles from his cronies, Narzayev included. Vladimir considered that all his prime ministers, including those with whom he had alternated the presidency, were lightweights – which was the reason he had chosen them.

'Seriously, though, Vova, Sverkov's someone we can control. That way we can preserve your legacy.'

Vladimir knew what Narzayev meant by that – their interests. And it was no small thing. If the wrong person got his hands on the Kremlin after he was gone, there was no telling what might happen. It wasn't just a matter of losing influence or money. In Russia, anyone could end up in jail, no matter how high they had flown, once the political wind changed. Vladimir knew that better than anyone. The most important thing was to make sure that whoever came after you wouldn't allow any investigations to be made, as he had guaranteed to Boris Nikolayevich and his family when he had taken the throne. The difficulty in ensuring this was one of the reasons Vladimir had never dared to retire, not after the third presidency, nor even after the fourth, when he had certainly considered it.

'Fedorov?' said Serensky.

Vladimir snorted. 'Too liberal.'

'Repov?'

'He hasn't been the same since the plane crash.'

'Well, if we can't find someone, the risk is it'll be Lebedev.'

Vladimir was silent.

'He's so corrupt himself he couldn't come after any of us,' said Serensky. 'At least that's one thing. Every pie there is, he's had his finger in it.'

'Lebedev has rotten values,' said Vladimir. 'He turns the order of things on its head. Lebedev's only after money and power, and the greatness and stability of Russia is merely a means to that end. In that situation, chaos follows. Why is there no chaos now? Because I'm dedicated to the greatness and stability of Russia, and money and power – if there is any – follow from that.'

There was quiet for a moment, then Luschkin burst out laughing. Vladimir silenced him with a glance.

Yet Vladimir had a haunting, taunting feeling that it would be Lebedev who would succeed him, this man who, alone amongst all the others, he had somehow failed to cut off at the knees, that somehow it was inevitable, just as it had been inevitable in the last days of the Soviet era that Boris Nikolayevich would somehow rise up and overthrow Mikhail Sergeyevich once Mikhail Sergeyevich had turned him out of his government. That was why Vladimir kept bringing Lebedev into the Kremlin, loathe him though he did. But that wasn't a solution. Deep in his gut, Vladimir had a horrible premonition that somehow Lebedev would find a way up after he had gone. Maybe not at once. Maybe Vladimir would be able to determine who succeeded him at first, but after that, he knew, his grip on the Kremlin would loosen. At the first election, Lebedev probably wouldn't even run. Another few years of putting more money away, buying more supporters, strutting the stage as Uncle Kostya, everyone's favourite relative . . . and then he would strike.

'I should write a testament,' said Vladimir grimly. 'Like Lenin. "Anyone but Lebedev."'

'Didn't do much to keep Stalin out,' observed Narzayev.

Vladimir looked around disconsolately. 'Lebedev will drag Russia into the mud. After me we need . . .'

The four men watched him, wondering what he was going to say. But he had no words for it. After him, he wanted to say, Russia needed another him.

'Well, you've got another six years before you need to worry about that,' said Monarov. 'Tonight, let's enjoy what you've achieved.' He raised his glass. 'Vladimir Vladimirovich, our president for the fifth time: To your health!'

They drank.

Then they put down their glasses. Suddenly they looked older, greyer, anxious. Vladimir knew there was something wrong. What was it? Why had they all come to see him?

'Vladimir Vladimirovich,' said Monarov. 'It's time to go.'

'I'm the elected president! I have another year to serve!'

'Yes. And now it's time to go.'

He looked around at the others. Luschkin, Narzayev, Serensky, they all stared back at him, faces grim.

'Vova, we came to see you together, so you wouldn't suspect that any one of us was plotting. We all agree. You can't go on. People are noticing.'

'What?' demanded Vladimir. 'What are they noticing?'

'I just told you.'

'No, you didn't.'

'I did. See, you can't remember.'

'I can! I can remember everything!'

'You're forgetting things all the time.'

Was he? There seemed to be words in his head, something that he had just been told, floating somewhere in there, but he couldn't quite grasp them. 'That's a lie!' he shouted. 'You just want to get me out!'

'Vova, we're your friends. Your most loyal friends. Resign now. Put in Sverkov—'

'Sverkov's nothing. Sverkov's a piece of stuffing you put here, you put there, wherever there's a hole you want to fill.'

'Put in Sverkov, Vova, and he'll win us the next election. That way we keep Lebedev out for at least the next six years.'

'No.'

'Every day you stay, Lebedev gets stronger.'

'I don't care. I control Russia. I control the money, I control the agencies—'

'Actually, Vova, that's not quite true. You remember the decrees you signed?'

'What decrees?'

'The decrees,' said Monarov.

Vladimir looked around. Luschkin, Narzayev and Serensky were gone. 'What decrees?' he cried.

'The decrees,' said Monarov.

'*What decrees?*' he cried in panic. 'Zhenya? What did I sign? I can't remember! What decrees?'

Monarov was gone too now. Then Vladimir remembered that Monarov was dead. Yes, he had been to his funeral. And yet there he had been sitting in the chair, eating caviar by the spoonful!

He frowned in confusion.

'What is it, Vladimir Vladimirovich?' asked Sheremetev, who had come back from the dressing room with a set of casual clothes in case he could persuade Vladimir to change.

'Who are you?'

'Sheremetev, Vladimir Vladimirovich. Are you hungry?'

Vladimir looked at him suspiciously. 'Yes, I'm hungry.'

There was a knock on the door.

'Here's lunch,' said Sheremetev.

He went to the door. One of the house attendants was standing outside with Vladimir's lunch.

'Is everything alright in the kitchen?' asked Sheremetev, taking the tray, still struck by the glimpse he had caught of Stepanin pacing around on the grass outside the dacha.

The attendant shrugged.

'With the cook? Is he alright?'

'I didn't see the cook,' muttered the attendant. 'They just gave me the food.' He stood for a moment longer. 'Can I go now?'

'Yes,' said Sheremetev. He carried the tray to the table and set it down. 'Come on, Vladimir Vladimirovich. Here's something to eat.'

'It is time already?'

'It's time. You're hungry, remember?'

'Is it breakfast?'

'Lunch.' Sheremetev smiled. 'It's easy to forget. You had your breakfast, Vladimir Vladimirovich.' Sheremetev raised him from his chair. 'Come. Let's eat.'

Sheremetev guided him to the table and put a napkin around his neck. He tied it cautiously. 'Is this okay? Not too tight?'

'It's okay,' said Vladimir.

There was a bowl of chicken soup on the tray. Sheremetev put a spoon in Vladimir's hand.

Vladimir fidgeted with it. After a couple of minutes, Sheremetev gently released it from his hand and raised a spoonful of the soup to Vladimir's lips.

'How is that? Is it good?'

Vladimir smiled. 'It's good.'

Sheremetev raised another spoonful. Vladimir sipped at it noisily.

6

STEPANIN HAD ABOUT AS much ability to hide his feelings as a Russian bear trying to hide itself in a snow field. That night he sat brooding in the staff dining room, stubbing out one cigarette and lighting another, throwing back one glass of vodka and reaching for the bottle to pour himself the next. Whatever it was that had had him fuming outside the dacha that morning was still eating at him.

'Something wrong?' asked Sheremetev eventually.

The cook grunted. He got up and opened the door to the kitchen and yelled at one of the potwashers, then came back and slumped disconsolately in his chair, fingering his vodka glass with a look of disgust.

'Vitya?'

Stepanin looked up. 'What's the boss been like today? Okay? Give you any trouble?'

'I was going to take him out, but the cars were broken down.'

'Both cars?' said Stepanin disbelievingly.

Sheremetev shrugged.

'An S-class Mercedes and a Range Rover?'

Sheremetev shrugged again.

'What fuckery! Broken down? Sure. Eleyekov! What a gangster.'

'He's a gangster?' said Sheremetev.

'No, I don't mean a gangster. Not a *gangster*.'

'Then what do you mean?'

Stepanin gave Sheremetev a look, the kind Sheremetev had been accustomed to receiving ever since he first confided to one of his fellow conscripts in the army his belief that their captain would soon be exposed and punished for hiring them out like slaves. 'Eleyekov's okay,' muttered Stepanin. Everything's okay for *him*.' The cook angrily stubbed out his cigarette, picked up the box, toyed with the idea of lighting another one, then threw it down in disgust.

Sheremetev watched him.

'It's the chickens,' growled the cook.

Sheremetev was none the wiser.

'The chickens! Barkovskaya, that slut, suddenly has a cousin who sells chickens. Where has he come from, this cousin? From under which stone has he crawled? Yesterday there was no cousin – today there is. They're probably stolen chickens, if you ask me.'

'Stolen from where?'

'Who knows?' Stepanin fixed Sheremetev with a furious glare. 'Do you have any idea how many ways there are to steal chickens? Do you even know how many places you can steal them from?' Stepanin poured himself another vodka, watching the liquid cascading into the glass. 'Not only chickens! Ducks, pheasants, geese. Anything with feathers.' The cook threw down the vodka, swallowed hard, and grimaced. 'Put a feather on it,' he rasped, momentarily hoarse, 'give it wings, put a beak on its face – and Barkovskaya's cousin, the shit, has it.'

'Aren't they fresh?' inquired Sheremetev.

'They're fresh!' retorted Stepanin. 'Why shouldn't they be fresh?'

'What about the quality?'

'The quality's fine!'

'Then . . . ?'

Stepanin sighed, and gave Sheremetev another one of those looks, but worse this time, as if he was gazing upon a fool whose imbecility was of a depth so extraordinary, whose innocence was of a simple-mindedness so complete and so utterly unsullied by knowledge or experience, that in the five billion years of its existence the world had never witnessed the like. 'Today, my chicken supplier calls me and says he's been terminated. Half an hour later, this other one turns up with chickens and grouse and God knows what. Now, Kolya, tell me, who's the chef? Stepanin or Bolkovskaya?'

'You are, of course.'

'So who decides on the suppliers? Stepanin or Bolkovskaya?'

Sheremetev, not knowing the protocol amongst chefs and housekeepers, guessed. 'Stepanin?'

'So what's Bolkovskaya doing? Hmmm?'

'It's her cousin. Perhaps she thought—'

'Exactly! Her cousin. Okay, so let's say, in this one case, I say, it's Bolkovskaya's cousin, it's fine. Let's get the chickens from her cousin. Not to mention the fact that my chicken man is a friend who goes back with me twenty years. We stood guard duty together in Crimea. Even then he was stealing chickens. He stole – I cooked. What feasts we had! Okay, but let's forget that. Let's say Bolkovskaya's cousin is more important than twenty years of friendship and guard duty on some shitty base in Crimea.' Stepanin leaned closer, his eyes narrowed. 'Do you know what else happened today?'

Apart from both cars being broken down – and Sheremetev had a hunch that wasn't what Stepanin was talking about – nothing out of the ordinary, as far as he was aware.

'A certain restaurant in the town didn't get their chickens either. Do you understand what I'm saying?'

'No,' said Sheremetev. He was utterly confused. What restaurant was Stepanin talking about? Did the friend from his days on the Crimean base supply it as well? And why should it make a difference if he did?

Stepanin stared at him, then shook his head and sat back in the chair. He pulled out another cigarette and lit it.

Sheremetev had a feeling that there was something the cook wasn't telling him. But what? There seemed to be more to this, he sensed, than mere loyalty to an old army buddy.

'What about everything else you're responsible for buying? Has Barkovskaya done anything about the rest?'

'Look, first, there's the principle!' retorted Stepanin angrily. 'It's as old as the ages. The cook chooses the suppliers. Without that principle – chaos! And second...' He hesitated, gazing shiftily at Sheremetev.

'Second...?'

'Second... Second... This is the thin end of the wedge! If I let her do this, it's exactly as you say. Next, it'll be the fishmonger. Then the butcher. Then the cheesemonger. Then the fruit and veg man. Then the dried fruit merchant. Then—'

'Dried fruit? Do we eat a lot of dried fruit?'

'A lot! You'd be surprised.'

'I never see any.'

'Well, most of it... there's a confectioner I know in town. Anyway, the point is, this is only the start.'

'Vitya, how many cousins could she have?'

'Cousins? In Barkovskaya's position, if you're looking for cousins, you'll find them everywhere!'

'But for a cousin you need an uncle and an aunt,' pointed out Sheremetev. 'You can't just—'

'If I let Bolkovskaya do this, the bitch will do it with everything, just you see. And that, Kolya, isn't right. It's not just. Things should be as they were. She's happy, I'm happy, everyone eats well, and there's peace in the world.'

'I still don't understand about the dried fruit,' said Sheremetev, deciding to forget about Stepanin's theory of endless cousins, which made no sense to him, whichever way he tried to look at it. 'Where does it go, this dried fruit? I can't remember the last time I had a piece.'

'What do you like?'

'Apricots.'

'I'll get you a packet. Look, can't you see how dangerous this is? If I let Barkovskaya win on this, it's all gone. Everything! Let someone like her take an inch, and she'll take the whole mile.'

'Maybe you should go to Barkovskaya and say...you know... let's have some kind of arrangement. Maybe one time your friend, one time her cousin. Share.'

'*Share?*' The cook's eyes almost popped out of their sockets. 'Kolya, there's the principle, and there's...there's...' Stepanin's voice trailed off. He stubbed out his cigarette, and again, and again, until it wasn't only stubbed but broken, flattened, smashed, destroyed.

'Vitya, is there something you're not telling me?'

Stepanin looked up at him sharply. 'What am I not telling you?'

'I don't know. That's what I just asked you.'

'Kolya, you know what my dream is.'

Sheremetev knew. Russian fusion! Minimalist décor! What that had to do with Barkovskaya ordering chickens from her cousin, Sheremetev had no idea.

'Is it such a terrible thing, to want to have my own restaurant? What am I asking for? To reopen the gulag? Imagine it. Russian fusion! Minimalist décor! Something totally new. The first night I'm open, you'll have a table. Is it some kind of crime, Kolya, to want this?'

'No, it's not a crime, Vitya.'

'So?' said Stepanin.

'*So?*' said Sheremetev, still at a loss to understand what the cook thought was really so terrible about what the housekeeper had done, or what it had to do with his dream of a restaurant.

Stepanin stared at him for a moment, then sat back. 'What fuckery! Fuckery with a cock on top.'

'What are you going to do?'

'I can't let this go.'

Sheremetev watched him, wondering for a moment if this was all some kind of joke.

Stepanin eyes narrowed. 'I'll do what I have to.'

'Which is what?'

'Don't worry.' He tapped the side of his nose. 'Vitya Stepanin always has a plan.'

VITYA STEPANIN DID HAVE a plan, although it wasn't of the most sophisticated subtlety. In its essence, it consisted of doing nothing – but a special kind of nothing. The next day, when Barkovskaya's cousin rang to find out what he wanted, he replied: 'Nothing.' He said the same thing the next day, and the day after that. Chickens were not required. Nor were ducks, geese, pigeons, partridges, pheasants, snipe, grouse or any of the other feathered beasts that the house-keeper's cousin purveyed. Stepanin had no idea what was going to happen next, but as far as he was concerned, Barkovskaya wasn't getting any more chicken fricassee until she backed down.

Chicken fricassee disappeared from the menu. So did chicken

soup, chicken kiev, chicken wings, chicken supreme, chicken caccia-
tore, chicken curry, chicken salad, chicken with mango and all the
other chicken dishes that Stepanin was wont to serve up. A cook
down to his fingernails, Stepanin grieved for his lost dishes, but he
hoped that in time he would send them out of his kitchen again,
and for the present there was too much at stake, he told himself, to
let sentimentality prevail.

Stepanin asked Sheremetev to apologise to Vladimir on his behalf,
knowing how partial the old man was to chicken Georgian style.
From the moment he took the job at the dacha, the cook had made
it his mission to prepare for the boss, as he called him, the foods of
which he was most fond. Not only had he questioned Sheremetev
extensively on the subject, but he had researched all he could find
about the ex-president's culinary predilections. Vladimir ate almost
all his meals at the table that had been installed for the purpose in the
sitting room of his suite, so Stepanin never saw him devouring the
results of his labours and consequently had to rely on Sheremetev's
reports of the boss's reactions. Sheremetev didn't have the heart
to tell him that Vladimir couldn't remember what he had eaten at
the start of the meal by the time he got to the end, much less an
hour or a day later, and the cook could have served up beans and
brisket, which Vladimir relished, for breakfast, lunch and dinner,
and Vladimir would have been just as happy as he was with chicken
Georgian style, boeuf à la Tversk, sole in butter sauce and all the
other immediately forgotten delicacies that arrived on trays from
the kitchen.

Accordingly, Vladimir didn't notice the disappearance of chicken
from his diet. To check, Sheremetev asked him if he had had any
recently.

'Yes,' replied Vladimir. 'At lunch.'

It was ten o'clock in the morning.

'What if I was to tell you that there'll be no more chicken?'

Vladimir laughed. 'That's preposterous. I've never heard such a stupid proposition. Get rid of the official whose idea this is.'

'There may be a problem for a time.'

'A problem?' said Vladimir. 'What sort of problem?'

'With chicken, Vladimir Vladimirovich.'

'No, there's no problem with chicken. The problem,' said Vladimir, waving a finger, 'is that Russians think chicken is the problem, when in fact, it's not chickens at all. Chickens are a distraction that our so-called friends in the west would like us to waste our time on, when it is the west itself that has caused the problem by sending us the second rate chickens they themselves won't eat. Why else would I impose sanctions on them to stop them sending us this rubbish? Yes, this is exactly what Obama, Merkel and the rest of them want to see. This whole thing is a crude attempt to retaliate for our perfectly legitimate restrictions on the distribution of gas through the Ukraine pipelines, when in reality there is no comparison between the two. Chicken is not gas! Gas is not chicken! Is that clear? Russia has no problem with chicken. Russia has no problem with anything. Every problem in Russia is the fault of the west, which can't bear to see a Russia that is strong and independent. I call on Russians to stop eating chicken and strike a blow against those in the west who would like to put us back into a cold war!'

'Yes, Vladimir Vladimirovich.'

Vladimir nodded emphatically, a fierce expression on his face.

Slowly the look changed and his face became blank again. Sheremetev tidied up around him.

'Who are you?' he said after a while.

'Sheremetev, Vladimir Vladimirovich.'

Vladimir nodded, as if he remembered now. 'Do you know my mother?'

Sheremetev shook his head.

'What about my brothers?'

'No, Vladimir Vladimirovich.'

He smiled slyly. 'How could you? They died before I was born.'

'I know,' said Sheremetev.

'How do you know?'

Sheremetev shrugged. 'Everyone knows.'

Vladimir narrowed his eyes. 'How does everyone know?'

'It's known, Vladimir Vladimirovich. It's very sad.'

Vladimir watched him suspiciously for a moment. 'Yes,' he said. 'Very sad. My mother has never recovered. She gave me this cross, you know, only last week.' He fingered a small gold crucifix that hung around his neck.

Sheremetev nodded.

'Have I had lunch?'

'No, Vladimir Vladimirovich.'

'You told me there was chicken. Is that right?'

'No.'

'I was looking forward to chicken. Have you ever had chicken Georgian style? We should go to Suliko. What a restaurant! They have a special room upstairs – they open it only for me. The boys and I went there to celebrate the war in South Ossetia.' Vladimir laughed. 'We stuck it to the Georgians, then we ate their food! Eh? Those fucking Shvillis! Get the boys together. Monarov, Luschkin, the whole gang. Let's go tonight.'

'I'll see what I can do,' said Sheremetev.

'What is this, I'll see what I can do? Do it! Go! Now!'

'Certainly, Vladimir Vladimirovich. At once.'

Sheremetev went to the dressing room and put away some clothes that had been returned from being laundered, then came back in and quietly continued tidying up. Vladimir was having a conversation with a sofa. He broke off when he noticed Sheremetev.

'Was I waiting for something?' he demanded.

'I don't think so, Vladimir Vladimirovich.'

Vladimir frowned. 'Oh,' he said. 'Then you can go.' He turned to the sofa. 'What are you talking about when you say Merkel was upset? That's nothing. If I wanted to upset her, I'd bring the dog!'

ONE DAY FOLLOWED THE next, and still there was no chicken. Stepanin lived in a state of constant anxiety, wondering what to expect. Deep in his heart, he knew that his plan was limited, if not fatally flawed. Barkovskaya could survive without fricassee, and if she could survive without it, what had he achieved but depriving everyone else of poultry dishes? With each day that passed, the cook became more tense. What if the chickens were just the start? What if Barkovskaya found another cousin who could supply meat, one to supply fish, one who was a dry goods merchant? Would he order nothing? Would the inhabitants of the dacha exist on water alone? And what if Barkovskaya had a cousin at the water board?

At night he lay in bed with his lover, staring anxiously into the darkness as she slept beside him. By day, he began to look like a hunted animal, glancing here and there as he moved, as if bracing for the fall of whatever blow Barkovskaya was preparing for him. The apprehension showed in the quality of his food. The seasoning was variable, the flavours in the sauces not quite in harmony. The curses coming out of the kitchen were louder than ever.

Then Barkovskaya made her move. One morning, up drove a

van to the dacha and out of it emerged the cousin and his helper, a two-hundred-centimetre Kazakh with a brow like a piece of granite, and proceeded to deliver four dozen chickens, ten ducks and a brace of pheasants.

'I didn't order any of this!' cried Stepanin as they pushed their way into the kitchen.

'The housekeeper did,' replied the cousin, as if she was just another customer and there was no family relationship between them. He and his helper dumped the birds on the steel work surface. 'Best quality.'

'I don't want them!' yelled Stepanin.

'Well, you've got them,' said the cousin, as the Kazakh stared stonily down at him.

Stepanin gazed angrily at the birds after the pair had left. Then he had an idea. He called Eleyekov. Naturally, the cars were unavailable, but it was possible the Range Rover would be free in the afternoon for an hour if the price was right.

That afternoon, Stepanin threw the chickens, ducks and pheasants into the back of the Range Rover and had Eleyekov's son drive him to a certain restaurant in town. When he came back, the Range Rover was empty but his pockets were full.

Two days later, Barkovskaya's cousin turned up with another delivery. This time, when Stepanin called up Eleyekov, the driver told him that both cars were off the road. Indefinitely. Having seen them head off down the drive in perfect working order at eight that morning, Stepanin knew there was a deeper message in what Eleyekov was saying, and it had nothing to do with the cars or the state of their mechanics.

'What's happening, Vadik?' he said to the driver. 'Tell me straight, what's going on?'

There was a silence on the phone.

'Vadik?' said Stepanin. 'Level with me.'

'Listen,' said Eleyekov reluctantly. 'We can't do it, alright?'

'Why not?'

Eleyekov coughed.

'*Why not?*'

'Look, Barkovskaya had a word with me.'

'What did she say?'

'She said I can't do it.'

'I'll pay you.'

'It's not that. If I want to keep my job, I can't do it. It's as simple as that. I'd like to help you, Vitya, but I'm not going to lose my job for you.'

Stepanin nodded bitterly to himself.

'I'd like to help, but I just can't. And I'd suggest…. Put it like this: anyone else who helps you out with this will discover pretty soon that they're not wanted around here.'

'What fuckery!' yelled Stepanin. 'Fuckery with a cock on top!'

'Vitya, come to an arrangement with her. She doesn't want everything, just a piece.'

'And she doesn't already have a piece? She's getting exactly as much as Pinskaya got. Why should she get more?'

'Be sensible.'

'She can't get rid of me, you know. My situation isn't like yours. I don't answer to her.'

'Vitya, all I'm saying, is you've got to be reasonable.'

'*She's* the one not being reasonable. For three years, it worked with Pinskaya. A good Russian arrangement. She had her share, I had mine, everyone was happy. Now this bitch comes along and decides it's going to be different. Did she talk to me, Vadik? Did she even ask me once?'

'Would you have said yes?' replied the driver. 'Look, if it's any consolation, Vitya, she's getting a cut from me too, more than Pinskaya got.'

'How much?'

'Thirty percent.'

'Well, she can fire you, Vadik. She can't touch me.'

'But she pays the bills, right? Whoever you buy your provisions from, if she won't pay them, they won't bring them.'

'That's why I have to fight this thing.'

Eleyekov sighed. 'Listen, I don't like her any more than you do. Thirty percent, she's costing me.'

'That's what you tell me, Vadik. Don't tell me you don't know how to water the wine.'

Eleyekov conceded the point with a shrug. 'Well, it won't be nothing. Do you think I'm happy about it? But the reality is the reality. Vitya, come on, let's have chicken on the table again. I love the way you do chicken wings with that hot sauce of yours.' The driver licked his lips. 'Come on, Vitya. Sort it out with the old bat. I'm sure you can come to an arrangement.'

Stepanin slammed down the phone and went back into the kitchen, fuming. The chicken carcases lay on the bench. For a moment he wondered how much poison you would need to put in a fricassee to kill someone.

One of the potwashers walked past.

'You!' he shouted. 'Get rid of these!'

'These, Chef? They just arrived.'

'Get rid of them.'

'Where?'

'I don't know where. Dig a fucking hole in the garden for all I care!'

So that was what the potwasher did – just what the chef said, as he was always being ordered to do. He went behind the dacha and dug a hole and threw the carcases in.

The next day more chickens arrived. And the day after that, more. Stepanin wouldn't touch them. Each morning, the potwashers went outside, enlarged the hole, and threw the chickens in. And each night, the foxes came and took them out, leaving the area behind the dacha littered with chewed chicken carcases, where they began to rot in the grass.

7

Just as the ugly plastic tunnels of the greenhouses had destroyed the beauty of the dacha's grounds, now the stench rising out of the chicken pit sullied the air around it. Inside, it was the tension between Stepanin and Barkovskaya that poisoned the atmosphere. The cook's moods were fouler, the housekeeper's words laced with threat. From the kitchen came the sounds of pots crashing as the cook marauded through his domain. Barkovskaya stalked the corridors of the house, sending maids and attendants scurrying. But through it all, Vladimir's days continued as before. Apart from the disappearance of Stepanin's chicken dishes from his menu, nothing changed. Each day, Sheremetev showered and dressed him, took him for a walk, fed him his meals, undressed him at night, gave him his tablets and put him to bed. The days were timeless, proceeding one after the other as carbon copies, enlivened only by the suspense of wondering when Vladimir's next outburst might erupt. For Sheremetev, their very unchangeability was a kind of refuge from the increasingly toxic environment around him.

But Sheremetev was not entirely cut off from the outside world. In theory, he had one day off a week, and sometimes he took it. A relief nurse called Vera would come to take his place, and he would catch the train to Moscow, usually to visit his brother, Oleg, and his wife and son, who lived near the Dmitrovskaya metro station.

And when he didn't take his day off, there was always the phone.

One afternoon, not long after the chickens began to be thrown into the pit behind the dacha, Sheremetev got a call from Oleg. His brother's voice on the phone was cryptic – something was wrong, but Oleg wouldn't say what. Try as Sheremetev might, he couldn't get Oleg to divulge any details. All Oleg would say was that the situation was serious and he needed to speak to him. Could he come to the dacha the next day? Sheremetev told him to come that night if he could, but Oleg couldn't.

Overnight, Sheremetev tortured himself, wondering what it might be. Was someone ill? Was it money trouble? Legal trouble? Why didn't Oleg want to talk about it on the phone?

Oleg worked as a mathematics teacher at a state secondary school where his wife, Nina, was a secretary. He was just two years Sheremetev's junior, and they had always been close. Like Sheremetev, he was a small man, although not quite so diminutive as his brother, and with a better head of hair, but otherwise they were like two peas from the same pod. At school they had been known as the Pinto twins, after a character in a then-popular children's comic who was knee-high in size to everyone else. Oleg would get into fights and then call on Sheremetev to rescue him. Not being a big boy, but loyal to his role as elder brother, rather than fighting hand to hand, Sheremetev developed an unusual tactic of putting his head down, letting out a bloodcurdling yell and charging at his brother's tormentors to butt them in the midriff, hopefully knocking them flat on their behinds. The sheer surprise factor made it a deceptively successful approach, at least when first used, although most of the boys who had been its target once or twice learned to sidestep and watch him go tumbling past.

Officially, neither Sheremetev nor any other members of the staff were supposed to have visitors at the dacha, but the rule was bend-able for the more senior personnel. Artur, the head of the security detail, was happy to be accommodating as long as his men were told who to expect. Sheremetev therefore left word with the secur-ity man stationed in the entrance hall of the dacha that his brother would be coming, and at three the next afternoon Sheremetev got a call to say that Oleg had arrived. He put the baby monitor in his pocket and hurried down, leaving Vladimir in front of the television in his sitting room watching the only station that he ever wanted to watch, a history channel that filled its schedule with repetitive documentaries about his glorious decades in office.

Sheremetev greeted his brother anxiously, trying to see in his face a hint of what was worrying him, then led him quickly to a small sitting room that the staff used on the ground floor.

'Something smells here,' said Oleg. 'I noticed it as I was coming up the drive outside.'

'Chickens,' said Sheremetev. 'Behind the house.'

Oleg looked at him in bemusement.

'Don't ask.' Sheremetev closed the door behind them. 'So? What is it?'

'Pavel,' replied his brother.

Sheremetev gasped. 'Pavel? What's wrong? Is he ill?'

'He's in jail.'

Sheremetev slumped in a chair. Pavel, Oleg and Nina's only child, wasn't exactly like a son to him – after all, Sheremetev had his own son, Vasily – but he sometimes wished he was. While Vasya was streetwise, cocksure and cunning, Pasha was sensitive, thoughtful and caring. Not that Sheremetev didn't love his own son as a father should, it was only that he might have found the task of loving him easier if he had turned out more like his cousin.

'What's he done?' asked Sheremetev.

Oleg drew a stapled pair of pages out of a pocket and wordlessly handed them to his brother. Sheremetev read the title.

In Honour of Konstantin Mikhailovich Lebedev on the Day he Received the Blessing of our ex-Master and Czar

'It's a blog,' said Oleg. 'Something Pasha wrote on the internet.' Oleg sighed. 'There were photos of Lebedev with the ex-president in the papers.'

'I know,' said Sheremetev. 'I was there when they were taken.'

'Obviously Pasha wasn't impressed. He doesn't like either of them, it seems. Seeing them both together was the last straw for him.'

Sheremetev looked at the page again.

In Honour of Konstantin Mikhailovich Lebedev on the Day he Received the Blessing of our ex-Master and Czar

Yesterday, our new president, Konstantin Mikhailovich Lebedev, met with our ex-Master and pres...I was about to say president, but he was really our Czar. The old Czar Vladimir gave the new one, Czar Konstantin, his blessing. And what could be more apt? One presidential term may have lapsed since Vladimir Vladimirovich went into retirement (and who can doubt, if the rumours about his mind are right, that it is only his senility that got him dislodged from the Kremlin, and if not for the merciful degeneration of his mind we would still have him with us?), and the useful fool Gena Sverkov may have been the official successor, but the truth is that it is Konstantin Mikhailovich who is his true heir.

Who in Russia is a bigger crook than our new president, a bigger taker of bribes, a bigger buyer of votes? These, ladies and gentlemen, are the skills of a president in the new Russia. And where, I ask you, did Konstantin Mikhailovich learn these necessary skills? Where, I ask, did he learn his craft? Who was his role model and his mentor, if not the old Czar himself?

So as Konstantin Mikhailovich evolves into the next despot to oppress us (and despite his warm words today, oppress us he will, mark my words, just like the bear in the story), is it really him we should blame? Or should we go back and point the finger where the blame lies? Would such a man as Konstantin Mikhailovich even be possible if not for Vladimir Vladimirovich? As clouds are the precondition for rain, so Vladimir Vladimirovich is the precondition for Konstantin Mikhailovich, the rabid pup of the mad old war dog. In other countries, he would have been strangled at birth. Only in the Russia that Vladimir Vladimirovich made could such a creature live to manhood, let alone flourish.

Officially, our old Czar has retired to enjoy the richly deserved leisure of his old age. Unofficially, we know he is senile, and had become such an embarrassment that his own henchmen had him removed. But I ask you, when did this senility begin? Was it at his last presidency, or the one before that, or the one before that? Or was it at the very first? Was he demented already, a superannuated spy who could only look back in fondness to the days of the Soviet empire and its police state, a 48-year-old with the mind, even then, of a 90-year-old?

Who could have invented such a man? Is he the spirit of

the Cheka, the personification of a hundred-year thirst for power rising out of the Lubyanka? Or is he a piece of fiction? Perhaps he's our anti-self, the projection of our basest and most debauched desires?

Imagine what he could have done. He could have been a new George Washington – and not least by exiting the stage after two terms, instead of hanging on like a frog on a windowpane. There was time, there was opportunity, there was a great will for a better society rising out of the people when Boris Nikolayevich handed Russia to him on a plate, and he could have done wonders. He could have given us the rule of law – impartially applied to everyone, no matter how great or how small. He could have given us freedom of speech, democracy, civic responsibility. He could have given us a flourishing economy, honest entrepreneurship, reward for merit. He could have given us mutually advantageous ties with our old national allies and friendship with our old foes. The moment in history was his! And instead, what did we get, what ideas came out of the paranoid little mind that returned from Germany and wheedled its way up the slippery slope to find itself sitting in the right place at the right time to lead Russia?

I ask you, what did we get?

Corruption on a scale that would have made even the Romanovs blush. Brutality that would have made even Stalin smile.

A deal with the swindlers who had stolen Russia's wealth – keep quiet and you can keep your criminal fortunes. A deal with the rest of us – keep quiet and you'll get a bit more bread. And circuses as well, ladies and gentlemen. The Winter

Olympics. The World Cup. Remember those? Events that cost five times as much to stage as they would in any other country, because in reality they weren't events at all, but schemes to transfer wealth from the state into the pockets of Czar Vladimir and his courtiers.

A yearning for an empire we should never have had and which never brought anything but death and destruction to those who were our subjects. And out of that yearning, things that were as bad as anything the empire had ever done. The killing of journalists. Genocide of the Chechens. Suppression inside the country. Provocation of everyone outside it. Proxies and invasions and death to our neighbours. And billions of dollars for the Czar himself. Dachas and palaces and yachts and jets and billions and billions and billions and billions and billions of dollars, a filthy flood of stinking money pouring over his head, rising up to his neck, a sewer of wealth so deep and so wide that no matter what he did, how he tried to hide it, all of Russia could smell the stench and hear it gushing past.

And I ask you, what did we, the people, get?

A state where you couldn't find the mafia because it had turned into the government, and you couldn't find the government because it had turned into the mafia. A hollow economy of oil and gas and arms sales and nothing else.

A society of bribe-takers, head-kickers, liars and embezzlers. A country where you keep your mouth shut and support the president or the tax police come knocking, faces masked and Kalshnikovs in hand. A place in which an honest, hard-working Russian woman can die of kidney failure while others less ill than her, less needy of treatment, the liars, bribe-takers and embezzlers, get treatment instead of her just because they can slip a few hundred dollars into the pockets of the white coat of the doctors, as much bribe-takers and embezzlers as their patients.

That, ladies and gentlemen, is the Russia that this monstrous invention of the Cheka, Vladimir Vladimirovich, built. Whatever is left of his mind, as death comes closer to him, does he ever stop to imagine what Russia might be like if he had chosen the other way? Or does he think, even now, with what is left of his mind, that he can take his blood-soaked billions with him?

Hail, Konstantin Mikhailovich, our new Czar! Worthy successor! Here is Russia for you to rape, ravage and pillage. Do with her as you will. We submit. For whatever you do, you can do no worse that Vladimir Vladimirovich, our crucifier.

Sheremetev was stunned, equally impressed and appalled by what he had read. 'I didn't know Pasha could write like that,' he murmured.

Oleg shrugged helplessly, his expression also torn between pride and horror.

Sheremetev glanced over the pages again, his gaze resting on a phrase here and there.

...the rabid pup of the mad old war dog...a 48-year-old with the mind, even then, of a 90-year-old...this monstrous invention of the Cheka...our crucifier...

'They took him two days ago,' said Oleg. 'Accused him of theft.'

Sheremetev looked up in disbelief. 'Theft? Pasha?'

'You remember that stuff he stole from the hospital for Karinka?'

'Olik, that was six years ago! He was fourteen! Can they still prosecute him for that?'

'The lawyer says they use all kinds of trumped-up charges. They could charge him with sedition or insulting the president, but if possible, they like to use other things. That way, the human rights organisations in the west don't know why he's really being prosecuted and they don't protest. Normally, they would have prosecuted him over tax evasion, but Pasha's never earned a kopeck in his life.' Oleg smiled bitterly. 'I used to tease him about that.'

Sheremetev handed the pages back. 'Do you agree with this, Olik, this stuff he wrote?'

'What difference does it make? Even if you agree with it, you don't *write* it.' Oleg sighed. 'You know what Pasha's like. He's young. He's impulsive. He hasn't learned there are things you can think but you can't say.'

Sheremetev was silent. Oleg's words reminded him of the stories his parents used to tell him about growing up in the Soviet Union of Brezhnev and his successors, when there were the things you could think, and the things you could say. Thank goodness those days are gone and you'll never have to live like that, they used to say to him.

'What are they going to do with him?' he asked quietly.

'That depends.' Oleg looked around for a moment, as if checking to see if anyone was listening, then sat forward in his chair. 'I got a lawyer who spoke to the prosecutor. Pasha's young, it's a first offence – also, right now, while he's new, the president doesn't want to seem too heavy-handed, kind of a honeymoon period, that's what the lawyer said . . . normally, he said, this would cost about ten thousand dollars to clear up.'

'That's what a lawyer costs?'

'No, that's what you give the prosecutor, Kolya. Some for him, some for the police, and they drop the charges. For a case like this, ten thousand would be about what they expect. Unless, of course, some bigwig wants to make an example out of it.'

'So you're saying someone wants to make an example of Pasha?'

'No. Apparently, there's been quite a bit of this kind of thing on the internet. Pasha's not the only one. Right now, Lebedev's approach is to laugh it off. Until he starts to gets angry, the prosecutors and police just see it as a way to make some money for themselves. They took Pasha but they don't really expect to prosecute him. It's just a way for them to have a nice a holiday this year in Mallorca.'

'So you need ten thousand dollars, is that what you're saying?'

Oleg shook his head. He was silent for a moment. 'Kolya, they found out about you.'

'What's to find out?'

'They found out you look after the president.'

'So?'

'So they think you must have a lot of money.'

Sheremetev stared at him, then burst out laughing. Even with the gravity of the situation, he couldn't help himself.

Oleg shrugged. 'Kolya, what can I tell you?'

'Do they know what I *do*?' asked Sheremetev incredulously.

'I told them.'

'And?'

Oleg shrugged again.

'Olik, I look after him. He's demented! I'm a nurse!'

'I told them! But in their heads, they don't imagine you can't have money. Everyone near him has money. Everyone knows it. You touch him and your fingers come away covered in gold.'

'Not mine.'

'Is that true?'

Sheremetev stared at him.

'Kolya?'

'Yes! It's true. How would I get money?'

'He's worth billions.'

'Where are they, these billions? Do you see them here?'

'It's a big dacha.'

'He doesn't have a ruble in his pocket! He's demented, Oleg! The bills are paid...I don't know how. The housekeeper does it. Me, I get my salary in the bank from some firm of lawyers in Petersburg. That's it. That's all I know. There's nothing else. If you wanted to steal from him, you wouldn't find a kopeck.'

'So you're saying no one here manages to take advantage of the situation?'

Sheremetev hesitated. After what Stepanin had said to him, it was obvious that something fishy was going on with Eleyekov and the cars, but that was the only thing he knew about.

'Look, Kolya,' said Oleg. 'When Karinka was sick, I gave you everything I had. To tell you the truth, Ninochka told me to stop.'

'You never told me that.'

'She said I was giving away our future, our retirement, and what-ever we had wasn't going to be enough and they'd still ask for more.'

Sheremetev stared. 'Oleg, you should have told me! I would have...'

'What?'

Sheremetev didn't know. Would he really have refused to take more from Oleg, when there was nowhere else he could turn? It was lucky, he thought guiltily, that Oleg hadn't told him.

'It doesn't matter. I didn't listen to her, Kolya. And anyway I...'

'What?'

'Nothing. We managed, that's what matters.'

Sheremetev frowned. 'Olik, I'll give you whatever I have. I've saved whatever I can since I came here. I have a couple of hundred thousand rubles in the bank. By now, it might be a bit more.'

'A couple of hundred thousand rubles? That's two thousand dollars. They want three hundred thousand dollars, Kolya. Three *hundred* thousand.'

Sheremetev stared at him.

'Kolya, tell me the truth. Do you have it? You've looked after him for years. Do you have it or not?'

'I don't have it. I don't have anything.'

'Do you know what's going to happen to Pasha if he ends up in prison? Right now, they're treating him well because they think there's a big payday coming from you. He won't survive, Kolya! They'll tear him limb from limb.'

'I have nothing. Just what I've got in the bank.'

'How can you *not?*' cried Oleg. 'You look after him. He's the richest man in Russia. In the world, probably. He's senile. How can you have *nothing?*'

Sheremetev had no answer.

Oleg threw back his head, eyes closed, teeth clenched in frustration. 'I'm sorry,' he said eventually. 'I shouldn't have said that. You have principles. You always have.' He laughed for a second, shaking his head. 'Pasha would approve.'

'I wish I had the money.'

'Well, you don't. That's clear, isn't it? You know, Nina says... Did you notice Pasha wrote about Karinka?' Oleg picked up the blog and read out the part where Pavel had mentioned the woman who died of kidney failure while richer people got treatment. He needn't have – Sheremetev had registered it. 'It affected him when she died, Kolya. It affected him deeply.'

'I know,' said Sheremetev.

'That's why he stole.'

'What was it? Nothing! A few hospital supplies. I've seen nurses walk out with whole suitcases full. And it was six years ago. He was a kid. Are they really going to prosecute him over that?'

Oleg shook his head helplessly. 'You know, he was only fourteen, but he knew what was going on. He knew why she wasn't getting treatment. It's funny. I don't know how he found out. I never told him. Maybe someone else did. He was never the same after she died, Kolya. Suddenly he was serious, concerned. If he heard about an injustice, someone taking bribes, he'd brood on it for days.' Oleg sighed. 'I'm not saying it's bad. I love that about him. I respect him for it. He's a good young man. Karinka's death changed him, that's all I'm saying. If you ask me, it's better to be like that than to be like…'

Oleg stopped himself. Sheremetev knew who he had been going to mention next.

'I can't speak for Vasya,' murmured Sheremetev.

'No,' said Oleg. 'But he managed, didn't he? Karinka's death didn't do anything to him.'

'It took its toll,' said Sheremetev quietly.

'Really?'

It was funny, as Oleg had said. Pavel, Karinka's nephew, had responded to the circumstances of her death by developing a social conscience. Vasily, on the other hand, Karinka's son, had responded in the opposite way. He was nineteen when Karinka died, away on his army service. He didn't come back to live with his father after that. With Karinka gone, Vasily floated away into whatever world of business – or worse, Sheremetev feared – had swallowed him up. Sheremetev didn't know exactly where he lived – he always seemed to be changing addresses. When Sheremetev had still had the apartment in Moscow, Vasily would occasionally come around. His fortunes seemed to go up and down. Sometimes he'd arrive driving a good car and bringing expensive foreign foodstuffs such as Sheremetev had never bought in his life – at other times he'd turn up on the metro with a bottle of Georgian wine. He would put whatever he had brought on the table, stay for an hour, and then he was gone.

Sheremetev didn't know what to say. The two brothers sat in the small room, the Pinto twins, two peas from the same pod even forty years after they had been given that nickname.

'How bad is he, anyway?' asked Oleg after a while.

'Who?' said Sheremetev.

Oleg raised his eyes towards the ceiling, as if Vladimir was in the room above their heads.

'He lives in his own world,' said Sheremetev. 'He has no idea what's going on. He still thinks he's president.'

'What does he do all day?'

'Sits and talks to his old friends. They're not here of course, but he imagines them.'

'What does he talk about what?'

'Who knows? I only hear half the conversation.'

'Do you listen?'

'Why would I listen? It's his conversation. He's entitled to his privacy.'

Oleg looked at his brother doubtfully. But Sheremetev was serious. To have listened to the conversations Vladimir had with his imaginary visitors, he felt, would have been no different to eavesdropping on a conversation Vladimir was having with a real person. As far as Vladimir was concerned, he *was* having that conversation, and for him, therefore, that conversation was real. It was a matter of his patient's dignity that Sheremetev should respect Vladimir's right to have those conversations in private, even if Sheremetev often couldn't avoid being in the room at the time.

'Aren't you interested to know what he's talking about?' asked Oleg.

'It's not my place,' replied Sheremetev. 'Besides, if I do happen to hear something, it's gobbledygook to me. Olik, what are they going to do to Pasha if you can't find the money?'

'The sentence for the crime is up to ten years.'

Sheremetev winced. 'You can have what I've got, every ruble, I promise.'

'If all you've got is a couple of hundred thousand, you may as well keep it.'

'Should I talk to the prosecutor? I could tell him I don't have anything.'

Oleg thought about it. 'I don't know if it would help. I can ask the lawyer.'

'Ask. If they'll see me, I could explain.'

'What about Vasya?' said Oleg. 'Does he have money?'

'Three hundred thousand dollars?'

'As much as he can! The lawyer says there may be a little room for negotiation.'

'I'll talk to him. I don't know what he's got.'

'Talk to him today, Kolya. Please.'

Sheremetev nodded. 'I'll call him.'

There was silence again. For a couple of minutes the two brothers sat without speaking, each caught up in his thoughts.

'Can I see him?' asked Oleg eventually, raising his eyes to the ceiling again.

'It's not really allowed, Olik.'

'Would he know? You said he's got no idea what's going on, right?'

'Yes.'

'Then . . . ?'

Sheremetev sighed. 'Alright. Just for a minute.'

They went up the stairs, encountering the maid who was Stepanin's lover on the way. Sheremetev opened the door to Vladimir's sitting room. Vladimir was in his chair, the TV on in front of him, a younger version of himself on the screen. At first they could see only the back of his head. Sheremetev gave Oleg a nudge and led him in.

Vladimir's head turned. Oleg froze.

'Who's this?' said Vladimir.

'My brother,' replied Sheremetev.

'What's his name?'

'Oleg.'

Vladimir gazed at him with his cold, blue eyes. 'Can you smell something?'

'Say no,' whispered Sheremetev, as he saw his brother hesitating. 'It's got nothing to do with the chickens.'

'No,' said Oleg.

'Sure?' said Vladimir.

Oleg glanced at Sheremetev, then nodded.

'The fucking Chechen's somewhere here, I can tell you. I can smell him, the son of a bitch.' Vladimir laughed. 'He can never take me by surprise, because I can *smell* him from fifty metres. I'm like a bear! Understand me?'

Oleg nodded.

Vladimir watched him a moment longer, then turned back to the television.

'Who's the Chechen?' whispered Oleg.

'No idea,' murmured Sheremetev.

At the door, Oleg stopped and looked back. Vladimir sat, eyes on the television, oblivious to them. Oleg tapped Sheremetev with the rolled-up pages of Pasha's blog. 'Do you agree with this, Kolya?' he said quietly. 'The stuff that Pasha wrote?'

Sheremetev glanced at his brother, then looked at the old, senile man who was facing away from them in the chair. He shrugged. 'I've never really thought about it.'

SHEREMETEV DIDN'T RING HIS son very often. Something held him back. He didn't know what Vasya did to earn money, and at a certain level he probably feared that he might find out.

But he rang Vasya that night, as he had promised Oleg that he would do.

To his surprise, Vasya already knew about Pasha's blog – and he was unsympathetic, to say the least. He didn't seem to regard it as unusual that the prosecutor wanted a bribe to let Pasha go. He laughed coldly when Sheremetev asked if he could pay it.

'How much do they want?'

'Three hundred thousand dollars,' said Sheremetev.

Vasya laughed again.

'Even if you can only spare a part—'

'Even if I could – which I can't – why would I give it to Pasha? So he can get out and do it again? Does he think such a thing is going to make a difference to anybody but himself? Let him spend some time inside and then maybe he'll learn some sense.'

'Let him spend some time inside?' Sheremetev was incredulous. 'Are you serious, Vasya? He's your cousin.'

'He's an idiot. What he did is an indulgence. Writing something like that makes no difference to anyone – those who agree with him, agree with him, and those who don't, don't – and nothing he says will change anyone's mind. What he writes makes not a speck of difference, so why does he do it? Because he thinks somehow it makes him better than everyone else. Pasha's always been like that. And what happens while the holy martyr is standing up there on his pedestal? Everyone suffers. Uncle Oleg suffers. You suffer. And if anyone knows he's my cousin, I suffer.'

'Why will you suffer?'

'Why will I suffer?' demanded Vasya angrily. 'Papa, what world do you live in? If the world knows that I have a cousin who's done what Pasha has done – and the world will know, or suspect, because his name's Sheremetev just like mine – then the size of some of the commissions I have to pay has just doubled. Do you understand me?'

'No, I don't understand you. What commissions?'

'Commissions! How do you think the world goes round? Mother of God! Get real, Papa! If I gave him the money to get out – which I don't have, as I told you – but *if* I gave him the money, do you know what would happen then? With some people, I couldn't do business at all, no matter how big the commissions I would pay. So you can say to Uncle Oleg, I'm sorry his son is such an idiot, but maybe after a couple of years inside he won't be such an idiot when he comes out.'

'I'm not going to say that to Uncle Oleg.'

'Fine. Don't. Only don't judge me. You live your way, I'll live mine. But tell me this: who's going to be paying for your retirement, Papa, when you're too old to work? Who's going to keep you alive when you suddenly discover that the money you've scraped to save from your salary isn't enough for even a year? Is it me or is it Pasha?'

'I'm not asking you to pay for my retirement. I'm asking if you have—'

'I don't have it! Okay? And I'm saying, if I did, I still wouldn't give it, and you can tell whoever you like!'

Sheremetev was silent.

'So how are you, anyway, Papa?' asked Vasily.

'I'm fine,' muttered Sheremetev.

'How's your patient? Is he still alive?'

'Of course he's still alive.'

'Are you sure? I saw him on the TV the other day with Lebedev. Was that him or have they stuffed his corpse like Lenin?'

'Don't say a thing like that!'

Vasily laughed. 'Do you need anything? Have you got enough money?'

'I don't need anything. Your cousin—'

'Don't start that again, Papa. I've told you. Pasha's old enough to know what he's doing. He's not a fool, and he's not a child. We live in Russia. If he did what he did, he knew what the consequences might be. Lucky he didn't end up dead. I'm serious, Papa, he should take this as a warning. People who get a reputation for writing such things don't live long in this country. Say that to Uncle Oleg.'

'I'm not going to say that to Uncle Oleg. He's worried enough.'

'Well, I can't tell you what to do.'

There was silence again.

'Papa? Is there anything else? I've got things to do.'

Commissions, thought Sheremetev. What did that really mean? To whom was Vasya paying these commissions, and what was he getting in return?

He remembered Vasya as a small boy, always smiling, running, cheeky, always pushing to the limit and sometimes beyond. He thought of Karinka and wondered what she would have made of their son now. It was the same Vasya, the same little boy he had carried to bed each night, and yet at the same time it wasn't and he felt that he hardly knew this child they had brought into the world.

'Vasya . . .' he said hesitantly.

'What, Papa? I have to go, really. What is it?'

Sheremetev took a deep breath, then blurted it out. 'What is it that you actually do?'

Vasya laughed.

'Really, Vasya, tell me.'

'You don't want to know.'

'I do.'

'Okay. Let's put it like this: I help people.'

'What kind of people?'

'Anyone.'

'What kind of help?'

'Whatever they want.'

'I don't understand.'

Vasya laughed again. 'Papa, I've got to go.'

'Why does that mean you have to pay commissions?'

'Forget I said that. I don't.'

'You said you did.'

'Sometimes there's no other way.'

'To help people?'

'Listen, Papa, I've got to go, really. Tell Uncle Oleg . . . Tell him whatever you want, but from me, there's not going to be anything.'

Sheremetev hesitated. Now that he had asked, he knew that he should ask more.

'Papa, I'm going. Goodbye.'

Still Sheremetev hesitated. Then he let it go. 'Goodbye,' he murmured.

*

SHEREMETEV RANG OLEG AFTER he gave Vladimir his dinner and told him that Vasya didn't have the money. Oleg said he had spoken to the lawyer and he didn't think it would help for Sheremetev to meet the prosecutor and tell him that he wasn't a wealthy man. It was a delicate thing, apparently, to get an official to back down from asking for a certain bribe once he had given a number. Negotiation within range of the price was one thing, but confronting him with someone who would tell him that he had made such a drastic mistake was something else. It might just make him more determined to get it. If Oleg didn't have the money, the lawyer said, and if he couldn't get it from anyone else, he would have to be patient and hope the prosecutor didn't feel he would lose too much face by moderating his demands.

And in the meantime, Pavel was locked in a cell with who knew what kind of criminals.

Sheremetev put the phone down, silently thinking of his nephew, hoping that he was alright.

He went to put Vladimir to bed. He helped him change into his pyjamas and gave him his pills, which Vladimir took with a glass of water.

'My daughter was here, you know,' said Vladimir, sitting on the edge of the bed and handing the glass back to Sheremetev.

'Today?' asked Sheremetev.

'She left a few minutes ago.'

'Really? That's nice.'

'She told me she's getting married,' said Vladimir.

'Your daughter? Congratulations. Who to?'

'I don't know him. He's an engineer. An aeronautical engineer. Works on planes.' Vladimir paused. 'That's a good profession. Clean and precise.'

'Does she have children, your daughter?'

Vladimir looked scandalised. 'Not yet! She's not married.'

'Of course. I forgot. Forgive me.'

'That's what she came to tell me! Don't you listen? They're going to be married in three months. I said, with my blessing.'

'But you don't know the groom,' said Sheremetev.

'I know him,' said Vladimir, smiling slyly. 'Of course I know him. Do you think my daughter would get to a position to marry someone and I wouldn't know about the groom?'

'No,' said Sheremetev. 'But knowing about someone isn't the same as knowing him.'

Vladimir grinned. 'That's true.'

'What does her mother think?'

'Her mother's happy. She had her doubts, but I told her, if that's what the child wants, that's what she wants.'

'So you think it's a good match?'

'Yes, it's a good match. He's an engineer. An aeronautical engineer.'

'I suppose that's a nice, clean job,' said Sheremetev.

Vladimir nodded. They spoke for a few more minutes, exchanging thoughts on aeronautical engineering and then the state of the defences on the border of the Baltic republics, to which the subject of aeronautical engineering somehow led in Vladimir's mind. Then Vladimir lapsed into silence.

'Vladimir Vladimirovich, are you ready to go to bed?'

Vladimir looked at him. 'Is that what I'm doing?'

'Yes.'

He looked down at his pyjamas and fingered the material of one of his trouser legs.

Gently, Sheremetev lifted Vladimir's legs and swivelled them onto the bed, then covered him over.

'Goodnight, Vladimir Vladimirovich,' said Sheremetev, turning on the night light.

'Goodnight,' said Vladimir.

Sheremetev went to the door and switched off the main light. A night light stood beside Vladimir's bed. In its dim, yellow glow, Vladimir lay alone, head on the pillows, eyes looking straight up, unaware, it seemed, that Sheremetev was still there.

Sheremetev thought of the things Pasha had written. But the man lying over there was his patient, and he was his nurse. Sheremetev shook his head and tried to put Pasha's words out of his mind.

8

IT WAS JUST AFTER five o'clock when Sheremetev heard Vladimir through the baby monitor. This time the ex-president wasn't agitated, just disorientated, thinking that it was time to get up. Sheremetev went in and told him that he should go back to sleep. It was worth a try, but it rarely worked. Quarter of an hour later, he had to go back in and settle Vladimir in the sitting room, where his favourite television channel was showing one of its most endlessly repeated documentaries, the one about Vladimir's border war with Belarus that led to the absorption of its northern half into the Russian Federation. Every time he saw it, Vladimir almost wept with emotion. Sheremetev went back and tried to sleep a little more, but he had one ear on the monitor, which crackled constantly with the noise of the tanks and artillery Vladimir had unleashed twenty years earlier and deployed with Russian troops supposedly in their private capacity as vacationers who had chosen to spend their holidays fighting with local patriots.

After breakfast, at the usual time, he took Vladimir for a walk. As soon as they got outside, there was a whiff of rotting chicken. Someone had thrown a cover over the pit to prevent the foxes getting in and leaving chicken heads and gnawed carcasses strewn over the lawn behind the dacha, but the hole still gave off the stench of a charnel house. As they got closer, Vladimir started wrinkling his nose. Sheremetev could see a familiar look in his eye. Any unpleasant smell, he knew, was always likely to put Vladimir in mind of the Chechen, and it might only be another moment before he jumped into one of his martial arts poses. 'This way, Vladimir Vladimirovich,' he said hurriedly, steering him away. Vladimir went with him, glancing suspiciously from side to side.

They went around the house towards the part of the estate that was still covered in birch wood and followed a path that led into the trees. Soon the air was fresh and the chirping of birdsong was all around them. The path crossed the paved track that ran from the main drive of the dacha to the garage, situated a hundred metres or so away in a clearing in the wood. Two black cars, the Mercedes and the Range Rover, stood in front of the building, and Eleyekov and his son were polishing them. Both men were red-haired, the younger Eleyekov a taller, slimmer version of the older.

'Shall we go and say hello?' he said to Vladimir.

Vladimir stopped.

'No?'

'I'm tired.'

'That's because you got up at five o'clock, Vladimir Vladimirovich. Come on, a little further.'

'Where's my bed?'

'It's not time for your nap yet. You haven't had lunch.'

'*Where's my bed?*'

'We're outside.'

'I think I'll lie down.'

'Vladimir Vladimirovich! Please don't!' Sheremetev reached for him before Vladimir dropped where he was. 'Come on, let's go back.'

Eleyekov heard the shout and looked up to see the nurse spinning the ex-president around and hurrying him away.

Sheremetev managed to march him back to the house, constantly nudging Vladimir forward and deflecting his desire to sleep through the sheer act of moving. He got him upstairs and into bed, still in his clothes. Vladimir lay on his back, staring up, as he always did before falling asleep. Sheremetev drew the curtains. By the time he turned around, Vladimir's eyes were closed.

Sheremetev took the baby monitor. After a few minutes he looked in and found Vladimir still sound asleep.

He quietly left the suite again. For a moment he stood in the corridor. The sight of the cars had reawakened his incredulity. Surely they couldn't have both been broken down when he wanted to take Vladimir for an outing the previous week.

He went outside and headed for the wood.

In front of the garage, Eleyekov and his son were still polishing the cars. The two black vehicles gleamed in the autumn sunlight.

Eleyekov spotted Sheremetev on the track and called out to him. His son looked up for a moment and then went back to work.

'Didn't I see you before with Vladimir Vladimirovich?' asked the driver when Sheremetev reached him. 'What happened? Didn't you want him to talk to us?'

'Not at all. We were coming to see you, but Vladimir Vladimirovich got tired, Vadim Sergeyevich. We had to go back. When he gets tired, if you don't go back in a hurry, he'll throw himself down just where he is.'

'Really?' said Eleyekov. He stepped back from the cars and stood beside Sheremetev, arms folded, as if examining a pair of fine animals. 'What do you think, Nikolai Ilyich? Magnificent beasts, aren't they?'

'So they're working, are they?'

'Working? Of course! What do you think? Cars like this? They're precision machines. They never break down.'

'Last week you said neither of them was working.'

'Last week? Are you crazy? I never said that! When?'

'When I wanted to take Vladimir Vladimirovich to the lake. Last week, I called down and the guard said he phoned you and the cars were being fixed.'

The driver stared at him for a moment. 'Ah... Well, technically, that was right.'

'Technically?'

'Yes, it's very technical. Everything about these cars is technical. They're precision machines, Nikolai Ilyich. A lot of computer programming. Very delicate. Very sensitive, right Borya?'

Eleyekov's son looked around and grunted.

'So were they broken down or not?'

'Depends what you mean by broken down,' said the driver. 'Could they move? Yes, if you're talking about simply pressing the accelerator. But with cars like this, that's only the beginning. Sometimes they need... tuning. Like a piano. If you use them when they're not tuned... well, yes, in an emergency, if you have to, you can use them, but let's just say I wouldn't like to take responsibility for the consequences. Look, the important thing, Nikolai Ilyich, is that these cars are always at the disposal of Vladimir Vladimirovich. Twenty-four seven! The only thing is that if he needs them, it's best if you can give me some warning.'

'How much warning?'

'Not much. A couple of days.'

Sheremetev frowned, trying to understand why he needed to give warning when the cars were constantly at Vladimir's disposal. 'But if—'

'Look, do you still want to take him to the lake?' said Eleyekov. 'Yes? When do you want to go?'

'How about tomorrow?'

'Tomorrow?' Eleyekov pulled a small notebook out of his pocket and consulted it briefly. 'What about the next day? Tomorrow the cars...they need tuning.'

'Again?'

'They need a lot of tuning. Tuning, tuning, tuning. That's the secret with cars like these. Let's do the next day? Is the next day alright?'

Sheremetev shrugged. For Vladimir, one day was as good as another.

'When shall we do it? What time would you like to go?'

'The morning would be good – instead of his walk. Say ten o'clock.'

Eleyekov checked his notebook again and grimaced. 'Mmmm... the morning's not so good. How about the afternoon? Three. No, make it two. Two? Would that be good?'

'Sometimes Vladimir Vladimirovich has a nap after lunch.'

'Perfect!' said Eleyekov cheerfully. 'He can nap in the car! How long will you spend there? About an hour, do you think?'

'Maybe a little more.'

'An hour and a half. Any more is too much for an old man.' Eleyekov pulled out a pencil and made a note in his notebook. 'Right! The day after tomorrow. Two o'clock. We leave at two, half an hour there, half an hour back, we're home by four-thirty. You're booked in!'

Into the driver's pocket went the notebook and pencil. Sheremetev watched in bemusement, utterly puzzled by the whole performance. 'And the cars will be tuned?' he ventured.

'Tuned, polished, revved. Nothing's too good for Vladimir Vladimirovich.' Eleyekov grinned. 'It will be good for him to get away for a bit, have a nice outing.'

It would be good for everyone to get away, thought Sheremetev, with the atmosphere as unpleasant as it was in the dacha. He glanced at Eleyekev, who was gazing lovingly at the cars again. The driver, he knew, was friendly with Stepanin, and perhaps knew better than him what was happening with the cook.

'Vadim Sergeyevich,' he said, 'what's going on with Stepanin? Why is he digging his heels in with Barkovskaya?'

'Why do you think?' said Eleyekov, raising an eyebrow.

'He said it's a matter of principle.'

Eleyekov laughed.

'The cook always chooses the supplier. He says it's the thin edge of the wedge.'

'It's the thin edge of the wedge, alright,' replied Eleyekov, winking.

'What does that mean?'

Suddenly Sheremetev was conscious of the driver giving him one of those looks that he was accustomed to receiving, a look of pity and amusement that intimated that there was a whole parallel world to the one in which he lived, of which he wasn't even aware.

'What, Vadim Sergeyevich?'

'Look, Nikolai Ilyich . . . It's really not my business, so I probably shouldn't tell you . . .'

'What?' demanded Sheremetev.

'I shouldn't say . . .'

'Vadim Sergeyevich! Please!'

Eleyekov sighed, as if the other man were really dragging it out of him. 'Okay. Stepanin had an arrangement with Pinskaya. Alright. Let's just leave it at that.'

'An arrangement with Pinskaya? About what?'

'Let me ask you this, Nikolai Ilyich. How do you think Pinskaya and her husband – a housekeeper and a truck driver – saved enough money to retire to a villa in Cyprus? Huh? Where did they get it from? And how do you think Vitya Stepanin is planning to get the money to open the restaurant he dreams of in Moscow? Nikolai Ilyich, what I'm saying is: there was an *arrangement*.'

Sheremetev frowned. 'What was it?'

'Honestly, I don't know the details. If I had to guess, I'd say there were two sets of invoices. One real one that she pays, and one for Pinskaya to show to whoever is supplying the funds. One, if you think about it, will be higher than the other. And the difference between the two will go into someone's pockets. Some to Stepanin, and some to Pinskaya. That's how things are usually done in Russia. But that's only a guess, Nikolai Ilyich. It could be something else.'

'And now Barkovskaya is trying to stop it?'

'Stop it?' Eleyekov shook his head incredulously. 'We tried perestroika once in Russia and look where that got us. No one wants to try that again.'

ELEYEKOV WAS ONLY PARTLY right. There had been an arrangement between Stepanin and Pinskaya – but it wasn't simply a matter of double invoices. Over the years that the cook and the housekeeper had worked together, it had evolved into something more elaborate and complex, hinging on the fact that one of Stepanin's old army friends – not the chicken rustler, but one who had worked with him in the kitchens – ran a restaurant in the nearby town of Odintsovo and that Stepanin, for some reason, had seen fit to add an extra loop into the process whereby he would send provisions to this old comrade. In short, Stepanin ordered provisions for the forty people he fed each day at the dacha, but the suppliers delivered enough for eighty, doubling their prices so they didn't lose out. Stepanin then sold the extra forty people's worth of food to his friend's restaurant, pocketing the money. Initially, this had involved Stepanin hiring a van to take the extra provisions to the restaurant, but by now the operation was so efficient that the suppliers delivered to the restaurant direct, bringing only the cash to Stepanin and recovering it in the bloated invoices they directed to the housekeeper every month. Pinskaya, in turn, had kept ten percent of the sum of the invoices for herself, as was normal practice. The suppliers not only knew this, but gave her the ten percent in cash, then inflating their invoices by an extra twenty percent, allowing not only for the housekeeper's ten percent but for a little additional profit on the side. Altogether it was a perfectly satisfactory, if not exemplary and truly patriotic arrangement, and everyone was content. Stepanin's suppliers had double the business they would have had and an extra ten percent on the top. Stepanin was steadily salting away the capital for his restaurant month by month. And Pinskaya, for whom the arrangement with Stepanin was only one block in a towering edifice of arrangements relating to every other product and service that was provided to the dacha, was busily paying off the loan for the villa in Cyprus to which she and her husband couldn't wait to decamp.

Inevitably, there was what some might have naively considered to be a flaw in this brilliant strategy, namely, that as a result of all these extra little percentages piled on top of more percentages, the provisions for the dacha cost two and a half times as much as they should have – and if anyone who knew about large-scale provisioning had bothered to take the ten minutes it might have taken to compute the number of people being fed and the amount of money it was costing to feed them, and took the two minutes to do the division to work out how much this amounted to per head, this little flaw would have stood out like a glaring red beacon with a screaming siren on top. But Stepanin and Pinskaya had not been stupid enough to start with the additional percentages at the level they had eventually reached. They had begun much more modestly, and the percentages had grown more audacious over time, as it became apparent that they could accumulate with impunity. Nothing is free, of course, and they were perfectly well aware that the extra money was coming from somewhere, so someone was paying for the restaurant in Moscow and the villa in Cyprus, but even if they had wanted to thank their unwitting benefactors – which would have been ill-advised, if not foolhardy – they wouldn't have known how. Was it the state paying the bills? Was the money coming from Vladimir's own fabled wealth? Or was it from some other donor? Whoever it was didn't seem to care. Each month, Pinskaya gathered up the ludicrously inflated invoices and receipts for all the goods and services provided to the dacha and sent them off to a firm of lawyers in Petersburg, and each month the bank account from which she withdrew the funds to pay the suppliers was replenished, ready to be emptied again.

Had he known the full scale of the cash generated by the arrangement between Stepanin and Pinskaya, Sheremetev would have been flabbergasted. After what Eleyekov had told him, he would have imagined it was a few hundred dollars a month – which to him would already have been a substantial sum – not a racket involving more than doubling the total value of all the food and alcohol that came into the dacha to feed the forty people who nominally lived there.

It was into the middle of this comfortable situation that Barkovskaya plummeted, like a goose crash landing on a lake, after Pinskaya ran off with her ill-gained riches to Cyprus. Unlike the lawyers in Petersburg, she did take the ten minutes required to compute one thing and another, and the two minutes – in fact, sixteen seconds, with the aid of a calculator – to do the division, and being well practised in all the arts of housekeeping, immediately put two and two together and got the eight that Stepanin was extracting. It was this about which she had spoken to Stepanin on the memorable day that he had felt moved to make chicken fricassee for her delectation. Confronted with the invoices, he made no attempt at denial. Not only was the evidence incontrovertible, but he guessed – correctly, as it turned out – that Barkovskaya's objective wasn't to cleanse the Augean stable of kickbacks and commissions that the dacha had become, but to ensure that she knew where to dip her bucket in the sludge of filthy money that seeped out of its every crevice. Stepanin explained the arrangement he had had with the suppliers, his friend's restaurant and Pinskaya, which he thought was perfectly fair to all involved. In response, Barkovskaya was non-committal about the terms of the deal, leaving him worried and disturbed – hence the chicken fricassee that evening, which he had made in an all too transparent attempt to curry favour. The housekeeper wasn't easily curried. When Barkovskaya made her move against the chicken supply a few days later, Stepanin knew that the fricassee was too little, too late.

But how far was she planning to go? By switching the poultry supply to her so-called cousin – and Stepanin had his doubts about the family relationship, because the cousin, as far as he could see, was as much a Kazakh as the monstrous thug who accompanied him each day – she was cutting him out. Certainly, it was only chickens, but if Barkovskaya could find a Kazakh to deliver chickens, surely it wouldn't be beyond her to find Kazakhs – or others, for that matter – to deliver everything else, and where would he be then? If he let her get away with this, he was finished.

Each day the chickens arrived, and each day they were thrown into the stinking hole. Stepanin hadn't even meant seriously that such a hole should be dug, but how was he to know that the idiot of a potwasher, who normally couldn't put the lid on a pot without being reminded and instructed three times over, would actually follow his orders this time? By now, taking the chickens out there each morning had become an established ritual in the kitchen, one which the pot-washers carried out with a degree of ceremony and even relish. The situation made Stepanin ill, and not only because of the choking off of his cashflow that it portended. As a chef, it offended his sensibilities to throw out two dozen perfectly good chickens every day, not to mention the other birds which Barkovskaya's cousin added to the nonexistent orders that he was fulfilling, all of which were of top quality and priced, no doubt, accordingly. Whoever he really was, Barkovskaya's cousin had access to fine fowl, Stepanin had to give him that. Barkovskaya, as the cook had realised soon after he decided to stop ordering chickens, could withstand this situation a lot longer than he could. She probably wasn't perturbed in the slightest by the latest turn of events. After all, she was now earning a cut of the chickens whether he used them or threw them into the charnel pit. He, on the other hand, had lost his portion of the revenue, and the fear that Barkovskaya would soon move onto another part of his business filled his sleep with nightmares.

At worst, Stepanin feared that she would try to oust him entirely. The housekeeper was responsible for hiring the maids, the gardeners, the house attendants and the driver. The security men came from he didn't know where. He himself had come by his job through a connection of an in-law of one his cousins, who had some kind of relationship with one of the lawyers at the firm in Petersburg which was responsible for disbursing the funds that paid for Vladimir's staff and living expenses. Stepanin had met the lawyer, a pale man with a mop of red hair called Lepev, only once, after which he had paid fifteen thousand dollars – every last cent of his savings, plus a hefty advance from a local loan shark – to a numbered bank account, and the job was his. He sent the lawyer a box of cakes as well. Barkovskaya, he assumed, had come by her job through a similar route, although who her patron was and how much she had paid him, he had no idea. Depending on the situation between Lepev and Barkovskaya's supporter, and who was stronger than whom – and which of them, if either, even cared – she might try to use her patron to push him out. Stepanin didn't know how far he could trust Lepev to back him. As a precaution, to remind him of his existence and the fact that he had paid good money for this job and the right to the plunder that came with it, he sent Lepev another box of cakes, and then, in what he thought was a masterstroke of irony, a box of chicken pies made from a delivery from Barkovskaya's cousin.

Still, his fears weren't assuaged. Chicken pies, he knew, would go only so far, and he wondered whether another helping of cash would be required. And even if Barkovskaya didn't try to oust him, would the lawyer do anything about the money Stepanin had already lost or the other revenues that the housekeeper, in her insatiable greed, probably coveted?

Each night, as Elena, who never seemed to have any trouble sleeping, lay snoring beside him, the cook's mind ran away with anxiety and frustration. Why had Barkovskaya come? Why her? Why now? The fifteen thousand that he had invested had been repaid many times over through the arrangement with the previous housekeeper, but he needed still more. Why couldn't that thought-less bitch Pinskaya have stayed for another two years, by which time he would have had enough money for his restaurant? But no, all she could think about was running off to Cyprus with that fat turd of a husband who drank so much it was a marvel he hadn't killed half of Russia from behind the wheel of his truck. Two more years, that's all he needed, and then he would be off. Two years, and the restaurant would be his.

STEPANIN, NORMALLY SUCH A talker, was in no mood for conversation when Sheremetev found him drinking in the staff dining room that night. Sheremetev was in no mood for conversation either, depressed by what he had discovered about the reason for Stepanin's fight with Barkovskaya and by the thought of Pasha being locked up while he was unable to do anything to help him. Stepanin pushed a glass towards him and silently poured him a vodka, then sipped glumly on his own.

The two men brooded in silence.

'Vladimir Vladimirovich liked the fish pie tonight,' said Sheremetev eventually.

'It wasn't my best.'

'Well, he liked it. He ate more than normal.'

Stepanin nodded. Not even that piece of information, which would normally have put a smile on his face, could cheer him up.

'Eleyekov told me about your arrangement with Pinskaya,' said Sheremetev after a while.

'My arrangement?' Stepanin turned towards him. 'Well, he's one to talk, isn't he? The gangster. Let me tell you about Eleyekov. How often are the cars needed for the boss, huh? What do you think Eleyekov does all day, Kolya? Sit there and polish them?'

'Well, actually, he *was*—'

'No,' continued Stepanin, who had apparently meant the

question rhetorically. 'Our friend Vadim Sergeyevich Eleyekov has a nice little business, him and his son, driving bigwigs around in two very fine cars that would cost two hundred thousand dollars each if he had to buy them. Cars which he could never afford to buy even if the Kazan Cathedral fell on his head. But does he have to buy them? No. Because they're sitting here in the garage all day and he can do what he likes with them. And he does! He's booked out every day two weeks in advance.'

'Not every day,' murmured Sheremetev. Suddenly the performance with the notebook made sense.

'Close enough. But can Barkovskaya get her claws on his business? No, because he takes the cash and she has no way of knowing how much it is. All she can do is demand thirty percent. He'll give her ten percent, maybe five, and tell her it's thirty, and how will she know the difference? She knows that herself. Whereas with me . . .' Stepanin stopped, gazing at Sheremetev, the vodka loosening his tongue by the minute. 'You really don't know, do you? Everyone around you is taking, Kolya. It's a fuckery, a grand fuckery with a cock on top. The maids steal whatever they want – linen, soap, towels, even furniture goes missing. Pinskaya never cared. The more they stole, the more she had to buy. The more she had to buy, the bigger a cut she took. The only things off limits are the boss's things. Fair's fair. We all agreed those were your domain.' Stepanin laughed. 'Like you'd steal, huh? And what's he got to take, anyway? A few old suits.' He laughed again. 'You really got the short end of the stick, Kolya!'

'I've never stolen a thing in my life,' muttered Sheremetev.

'I've heard people say that before,' said Stepanin, raising his glass, tossing down the vodka and then grimacing, teeth clenched, with a shake of the head. 'But you, Nikolai Ilyich Sheremetev, I believe. Look around you, Kolya! Have you seen the greenhouses outside?

Do you remember when they bulldozed the grounds and built them? What do you think they're for?'

'To supply the house?' said Sheremetev hesitantly, knowing, even as the words came out, that his answer was going to be as wrong as it was the time one of his fellow conscripts, stifling his laughter, had asked him what he thought they were actually building when they were bussed to an unfinished apartment block each day in the middle of Omsk, and he had replied that surely they were building an army barracks.

'You're too funny! Do you think for this one dacha you need greenhouses big enough to supply half of Moscow? Look at it! The whole fucking estate. It's like a farm!' Stepanin shook his head. 'Listen, this is what happened. A couple of years ago, the gardeners go to Pinskaya and say, look at all this land. It's pretty but a waste. We'll build greenhouses, we'll grow vegetables, and we'll sell them. You'll get ten percent, like everything. She says okay. They find the contractors to build the glasshouses. Naturally, the gardeners get ten percent of the contract. So does Pinskaya – even better. She gives the lawyers in Petersburg the same story you got, that we're building greenhouses to supply the house. They say okay. Listen, Kolya, the lawyers are probably taking ten percent of everything as well. The more we spend here, the more they take. So the greenhouses get built, and now the gardeners have a business.'

'Goroviev also? Is he involved?'

'Goroviev also,' affirmed Stepanin.

Sheremetev groaned. He would almost have expected it of the other gardeners, but not of Goroviev, the soft-spoken gardener who always seemed so genuine in his interest in Vladimir and appeared to be such a decent man. 'Is there *no one* who isn't taking?' he cried.

'Of course there is. You! Only you, Kolya.' The chef poured

himself another vodka and refilled Sheremetev's glass. 'Everyone was happy and now this bitch Barkovskaya has to poke her head in. What fuckery! Whatever Pinskaya took, Barkovskaya wants more.'

Sheremetev took his glass and drank the vodka, trying to drive out the feeling of disgust that was overwhelming him.

'By the way, she fired Elena.'

Sheremetev looked up at him. 'Elena?'

'She said she was stealing. That's a discovery! Why Elena? They all steal, all the maids, everyone knows that. Barkovskaya hasn't done anything to stop the others. No, it's me she wants to hurt. Get rid of Elena to make me suffer.'

Sheremetev frowned, thinking of the maid who had been Stepanin's lover. 'How did she take it?'

Stepanin shrugged. 'She came and cried in the kitchen for an hour. Then Barkovskaya marched in with a couple of the security guys and they took her away. They gave her ten minutes to get her stuff together and then threw her out. Left her standing outside the gate on the road. I don't know what she did. She had two suitcases with her.'

'Did you help?'

'How could I? I was cooking.'

Sheremetev imagined the crying maid dragging her suitcases two kilometres to the nearest bus. The sense of misery that he had been feeling totally engulfed him.

Stepanin nodded knowingly, as if he shared the feeling.

'My nephew's in jail,' blurted out Sheremetev suddenly.

Stepanin looked up at him with interest. 'Really? What did he do?'

'He wrote something about President Lebedev on the internet... and about Vladimir Vladimirovich as well.'

'What sort of thing?'

'Not very complimentary.'

'How old is he? Six?'

'Twenty.'

'So not very smart, huh?'

'They want three hundred thousand dollars to let him go.'

The cook recoiled slightly. 'Nikolai, I don't have—'

'No, I wasn't thinking... Actually, Vitya, can you help? Even something would be a start...'

Stepanin shook his head. The truth was that he had the required sum in the bank – in fact, a few dollars more – courtesy of the gargantuan appetite of his staff for overpriced provisions that never even arrived at the dacha and the unquestioning largesse of whoever was paying the bills, but he wasn't going to postpone his dream of having his own restaurant for the sake of some oppositionist who presumably must want to be in jail if he was dumb enough to have written something insulting about the president – and not only one president, but two presidents – and put it on the internet.

Sheremetev sighed. 'No. Of course not. I wasn't asking. I've got nothing. A couple of hundred thousand rubles, that's all. And my brother, Oleg, hasn't got much more.'

Stepanin gazed at Sheremetev pityingly. All these years with the old man, and he had taken no advantage. 'I suppose the boss has got nothing worth taking, has he?' said Stepanin, putting his mind to the problem. 'Just some old clothes. Nice ones, but still, second-hand clothes, how much would you get for them...?' Stepanin's voice trailed off. He frowned, and the frown got deeper, and then he broke into a grin.

'What?' said Sheremetev.

'Vitya Stepanin, you're a genius!' said the cook, gleefully congratulating himself.

Sheremetev watched him sceptically.

'There is something you can sell, Kolya, and it doesn't involve stealing.'

'What?'

'The chance to see him!' Stepanin raised an eyebrow meaningfully. 'You know, when he was president, they say, for a businessman it cost a million dollars just to have a meeting with him.'

'A million dollars?'

'That's what they say. Now, say someone wants to meet him now. Who would know if he's well enough or not?'

'He's usually well—'

'But who would *know*? Only one person.' Stepanin raised an eyebrow again. 'You,' he said, in case Sheremetev hadn't made the connection. 'You're his nurse. They would have to ask you.'

'I suppose so . . .' murmured Sheremetev guardedly.

'Charge them!' cried Sheremetev triumphantly. 'Charge his visitors.'

'He doesn't have any visitors.'

'Then charge the wife! She still comes, right? Charge the wife to see him. If she doesn't pay, say he's too unwell.'

'The wife?' demanded Sheremetev in horror.

'She's not dead, is she?'

'She hardly comes to see him.'

'Then charge the children.'

'The *children*?'

'Why not? Kolya, it's no hardship for them. Quite the opposite. Do you know how much money they must have? Can you imagine? And then they come to the dacha, and the man looking after their husband or their father or whatever – the only man who can stand in their way – asks for nothing. It's unrussian. I bet their handbags are stuffed with cash they're expecting to have to give you.'

It was true that once or twice Sheremetev had glimpsed a big wad of cash in a handbag of one of the daughters. But to ask a sick man's wife or daughter to pay to be allowed to see him . . . The idea of it made him ill.

Stepanin laughed, seeing the look on Sheremetev's face.

A grunt came out of Sheremetev's pocket. He pulled out the monitor and put it to his ear.

'Is he okay?' asked Stepanin.

Sheremetev listened a moment longer, then nodded.

'You think it will be a rough night tonight?'

'Who knows?' Sheremetev put the device back in his pocket.

'I don't know how you do it, Kolya. How many times a night does he wake you up? You know what? You should make him pay!' Stepanin laughed. 'That's it! *That's* what you should do! You should tell him, a thousand dollars a time. To him, it's nothing. I bet he used to pay a thousand dollars for a blow job and not think twice about it. Every time you have to go in, Kolya – a thousand dollars!'

'I don't think that would stop him.'

'You don't want to stop him! Kolya, that's the point. You want him to call you ten, twenty times a night.'

'Who's going to pay? He has no money himself.'

'Nothing?'

'Nothing! What would he use it for? Besides, I couldn't charge him for such a thing.'

Stepanin ignored the absurdity of Sheremetev's final statement, mulling over the conundrum of Vladimir's impecunity. He hadn't thought of that one – that the ex-president, for all his wealth, might not actually have any money. 'What fuckery, eh? The richest man in the world, they say he was, or in Russia, or something. And here he is, and he hasn't got a ruble in his pocket.' Stepanin paused, flabbergasted at the thought. 'Is that really true? Nothing?'

'Nothing.'

Stepanin shook his head incredulously, then finished off the vodka in his glass. Immediately, he poured himself another, then proffered the bottle. Sheremetev declined. 'What fuckery,' said Stepanin again. 'Sometimes everything seems like a fuckery, eh, Kolya?'

Sheremetev watched him for a moment. 'You know, I'm sorry about Elena,' he said quietly.

Stepanin sighed. 'She was a nice girl, that one. Although to be honest, I was getting a bit sick of her. The other one, Irina, what do you think about her? Sexy, huh? Shit, after this, she'll run a mile. Barkovskaya knows what she's doing. Come near me and you lose your job.' He sighed again. 'First the chickens, now the girls. What's next, Kolya? That bitch is mad. For three years Pinskaya and I live happily together – suddenly, Marshal Barkovskaya arrives and it's war. One blow after the next. I tell you, her greed is insatiable. Better that you don't have some scam going, Kolya – she'd be after you too. She wants every last ruble, every last crumb from the table. Mother of God, leave some for somebody else, you cunt! No, she has to have it all. What do you do with someone like that?'

'Have you spoken to her?'

'Of course I've spoken to her! Twice. I told her: Tell your fucking cousin to stay away. I'm the chef! I order from whoever I want!'

'Maybe if you go with a proposition . . . ?' suggested Sheremetev.

'That's what Eleyekov said, but I don't trust him. He just wants chicken wings again. You know the ones I make with the peppers and the onion and the hot sauce? He loves them.'

'They're too hot for me.'

'Really? You should have said. I'll make a milder sauce for you. Actually, that reminds me. Wait here.'

Stepanin went into the kitchen. Sheremetev heard him yelling at his potwashers for a moment, then he came back with a brown paper packet which he slapped down on the table.

'What's this?' said Sheremetev.

'Dried apricots!' said Stepanin. 'You told me you like them, remember? They're yours.'

Sheremetev opened the packet and took one for himself, then held out the packet to Stepanin, who extracted a handful.

'They're good,' said Sheremetev, chewing a piece.

'I told you, top quality,' replied the cook, his mouth full. 'I sell them on to this confectioner I know and I get a fantastic price. See, if only you could do something like that, you could get your nephew out of jail.'

Sheremetev shook his head glumly.

'Have another apricot,' said Stepanin.

Sheremetev took one and munched it disconsolately. So did Stepanin, his mind drifting back to his own troubles.

'Vitya,' said Sheremetev eventually, 'what do you think about Vladimir Vladimirovich?'

'What do you mean?'

'My nephew, in his blog, said he had the chance to save Russia, and instead turned it into a mess. And he said he took money from everyone, billions and billions and billions.'

The cook heaved a deep sigh. 'I don't know.'

'If he had done things differently, maybe Russia would be a better place.'

'And if my grandmother had balls, she'd be my grandfather. What can you say? It is what it is. Russia is Russia, Kolya. To live in Russia is to live in hell – isn't that what Pushkin said? That's our lot. If it wasn't Vladimir Vladimirovich who screwed us, it would have been someone else.' Stepanin poured himself the last shot of vodka in the bottle and threw it down his throat. He pushed himself up from the table. 'I'd better go and see what those fuckers are doing.'

Sheremetev watched him disappear unsteadily into the kitchen. The cook, he knew, could hold his drink, but by now he had had enough to knock out a horse.

Sheremetev lingered in the dining room. Now and then Stepanin's shouts came from the kitchen. Eventually he left.

He walked back towards the entrance hall, along the corridor of the original staff quarters. The housekeeper's office was here. He thought of everything Stepanin had said about Barkovskaya. Surely she couldn't be such a witch, as malicious and vindictive as he had made her out to be. Surely it was just a matter of talking to her and—

Her door opened. Sheremetev jumped. There she was.

'Good evening, Nikolai Ilyich,' she said calmly, as if she had half expected him to be standing here.

'Umm...Good evening, Galina Ivanovna,' stammered Sheremetev.

'Did you want to see me?'

'No. No, no.'

The housekeeper made no move to let him pass.

'Have you been talking with Viktor Alexandrovich?'

Sheremetev nodded.

'You often talk with him.'

'It's nice to wind down at the end of the day.'

'What do you talk about?'

'Nothing much.'

'It must be something, Nikolai Ilyich.'

'Gossip.'

'What gossip? I love gossip.'

'Not gossip! I mean, chat.'

'What chat?'

Sheremetev stared at her.

The silence went on, an uncomfortable silence that he didn't know how to break. The housekeeper let it continue.

'Well, I'm glad we bumped into each other, Nikolai Ilyich,' she said at last. 'I wanted to tell you that I had to get rid of Elena Dimitrovna today. Although I presume, if you have been talking to Viktor Alexandrovich, you are aware of that already.'

Sheremetev nodded.

'She was stealing things.'

'Really?' said Sheremetev.

The housekeeper came closer. 'Nikolai Ilyich, you should be careful who you spend your time with. Particularly now, after what's happened.'

'What's happened?'

'Everyone's heard about your nephew. The ex-president is an important man. He's a symbol. There are security issues. No one wants any oppositionists near the ex-president.'

'I'm not an oppositionist!' said Sheremetev. 'I've looked after him for six years. Would I do that if I was an oppositionist?'

Barkovskaya raised an eyebrow.

'My nephew, who should have known better, wrote a very wrong thing. I'm sure that he will soon learn to see things in the proper way.'

'I'd just watch who I spent my time with, if I were you, Nikolai Ilyich. Who I *chat* with. You know what they say: there's always us and them.' Barkovskaya gave him a thin, sour smile. 'Goodnight, Nikolai Ilyich.'

She went back into her office. Sheremetev stood for a moment, suddenly conscious that his heart was thumping, then hurried out of the corridor.

At the security post in the entrance hall of the dacha, the guard seemed to be absorbed in something on his phone. Sheremetev climbed the stairs and walked slowly along the upper floor hallway. He had denied his own nephew! He had called him wrong, he had said that he didn't see things in the proper way. And what was the *proper* way to see something? The way the police told you to see it? Sheremetev was stunned at what he had said, revolted at himself. There was nothing wrong about Pasha. He was decent, honest and good. If Russia could put someone like him in jail, there was something wrong with Russia!

He got back to his room and put the baby monitor down, then slumped on his bed, fully dressed.

Thoughts of Karinka came into his mind. He missed having her to talk to when he turned out the light. He missed drinking tea with her in the morning. Sometimes the feeling came upon him out of the blue, and the ache was as bad as it was in the months after she died. Six years, she had been gone. More – seven years in March. Seven years since those awful last months.

He sighed. The relief nurse, Vera, who came to look after Vladimir on his days off, carried a flame for him, and did nothing to hide it. In fact, she held it out like a blazing torch and sometimes almost singed his face with it. The truth was, he did sometimes think about her, and even fantasise about what might happen between them. He was a man, after all. But in the cold light of day, it always seemed like just that, a fantasy.

He looked around his solitary little room, thinking of Karinka and the apartment they had had in Moscow. Over the past few years, the dacha had become his home. But tonight, after what he had learned about the things its other inhabitants were really getting up to, in the air that was poisonous with the growing animosity between Stepanin and Barokovskaya over spoils to which neither of them had a right, it felt less like a home and more like a nest of vipers.

9

THE NEXT DAY WAS bright and blowy, a real autumn day. Sheremetev was looking forward to getting out of the dacha, if only for a few hours. For the trip to the lake that he had booked with the Eleyekov Chauffeur Company, as he thought of it now, he decided to dress Vladimir in something more appropriate for the outdoors than the suit he had chosen for the last, aborted attempt. After all, as any Russian citizen who had been alive in the past thirty years couldn't fail to know – at least, any Russian citizen who hadn't put out his own eyes to get away from the all-pervasive images of the great leader on television, in newspapers, on the internet, in paintings and in any other medium the Kremlin controlled or could influence – the Leningrad-born ex-president had supposedly revelled in the great Russian wild, whether in hunting gear, fishing gear, riding gear, camouflage gear, flying gear, or skiing gear; whether in furs, denims, khakis, snowsuits or even – quite often in the earlier years – insouciantly bare-chested for the entire world to see.

After lunch, Sheremetev laid out the clothes on a sofa in Vladimir's sitting room. A pair of jeans, a white T shirt, a black turtleneck sweater, a leather bomber jacket with a fur collar, thick woollen socks and a pair of black boots.

'Let's get changed, Vladimir Vladimirovich. Shall I help you?'

'No,' replied Vladimir. He got up, took off his trousers and pulled on the jeans. After that promising start, he sat on the sofa, still in his shirt, and stopped. Sheremetev waited for a couple of minutes, but it was obvious Vladimir had forgotten what he had been doing. Sheremetev glanced at his watch. He had a feeling that Eleyekov wouldn't wait long if they were late. He prompted Vladimir once more, then quickly helped him to finish.

'Who are you?' he asked, as Sheremetev knelt in front of him to put on his socks and shoes.

'Sheremetev. I've worked for you for six years, Vladimir Vladimirovich.'

'Do you know my mother?'

'No, Vladimir Vladimirovich. I never had the honour of meeting her.'

'Shame. I'll make sure you do.'

'Lift this foot up, please, Vladimir Vladimirovich. That's it. Let me put the boot on ... that's it ... Push Vladimir Vladimirovich ...'

'Are we going out?'

'Yes, we're going out. I told you already.'

'Where are we going?'

'To the lake. Now the other boot ... Okay, please stand up.' Sheremetev helped Vladimir into the bomber jacket, then stepped back. Before him stood the Vladimir Vladimirovich of the photographs Sheremetev had seen over the years. Older, of course, balder, thinner, but still recognisable, still upright, and altogether in excellent physical shape for a man of his advanced years, or even for one of ten or twenty years younger.

He smiled. 'You look good, Vladimir Vladimirovich. Wait. Let me put a watch on you.'

Sheremetev went into Vladimir's dressing room and opened the doors to the cabinet that contained the ex-president's watches.

He opened one of the drawers – a tray of gold watches, slim, very elegant, not exactly what he was looking for. He opened another tray, and then another, until he found one that he considered more appropriate, a thick watch in black and silver with mini-dials on the face and big silver buttons poking out of the case. A real sportsman's piece. He went back to the bedroom and put it on Vladimir's wrist.

'This one's from Trikovsky,' said Vladimir, watching him as he fastened the clasp.

'Is it?' replied Sheremetev, for whom the name meant nothing. 'Do you remember when he gave it to you?'

'Of course.' Vladimir chuckled. 'In the early days, we were almost friends. That's what Trikovsky was like. If he thought he could use you, you were his blood brother. Nothing was too much.'

'Okay,' said Sheremetev, stepping back. 'Let's go.'

'Where?'

'The lake.' Sheremetev looked at his own watch. 'Come on, Vladimir Vladimirovich. We'll be late.'

Downstairs, Artur was waiting with his deputy, Lyosha, a stocky man with a totally shaven head, and three other guards, all dressed in dark suits and dark shirts, about as inconspicuous for a trip to the outdoors as a flashing light on a police van. While Artur was tall and slim, with facial features that were even delicate, Lyosha was more what you might expect of a security man, thickset, strongly muscled and gruff in manner.

The cars drew up outside the front door.

Eleyekov was driving the Mercedes, a bulletproof beast of a vehicle much favoured by his private clients, many of whom had enemies and good reasons to fear them. His son drove the Range Rover, which was also armour-plated. Vladimir sat in the back of the

Mercedes beside Artur. Sheremetev sat in the front beside Eleyekov. Lyosha and the other guards bundled into the second car.

'All ready?' asked Eleyekov, eyeing Artur in the rearview mirror. Artur nodded.

Off they went. At the bottom of the drive, the guard in the security booth opened the gate onto the little-used road that ran to the main highway to the town, and one after the other the cars turned out.

They drove through the forest in silence. From time to time Sheremetev glanced over his shoulder at Vladimir, who sat belted up in the back, staring out the window. He wondered what was going through his mind, where he thought he was being taken. Now and again Vladimir sniffed, wrinkling his nose in distaste.

'What's happening with Stepanin?' murmured Eleyekov to Sheremetev quietly.

Sheremetev had been about to ask the driver the same thing. He shrugged, thinking of Barkovskaya's veiled threat to him the previous evening. 'Things are getting crazy.'

'He has to learn to live with her. If he wants to fight it, it's his own fault.'

Sheremetev didn't want to talk about it. The thought of all the thieving and extortion that apparently surrounded him in the dacha sickened him – and right here, in this very car, with Eleyekov sitting beside him, he was in the thick of it.

'He talks to you,' persisted the driver. 'Well? When are we going to have his spicy chicken wings again?'

'Can you smell something?' said Vladimir to Artur in the back.

'It's up to him what he does,' murmured Sheremetev.

Eleyekov shook his head in frustration.

'Can you smell something?' demanded Vladimir insistently.

'What's his problem back there?' muttered Eleyekov, still irritated by the thought of Stepanin's futile resistance that was costing him so many dishes that he relished. 'Why does he keep saying that? The car's as clean as a whistle. I made sure of it myself.'

'He thinks there's a Chechen,' said Sheremetev.

'In the car? A Chechen?' Eleyekov threw a glance at Artur. 'Are you a Chechen, Artyusha?'

Artur shook his head.

'Vladimir Vladimirovich, there's no Chechen,' said Eleyekov. Then he turned to Sheremetev, dropping his voice to a whisper again. 'You're not Chechen are you, Nikolai Ilyich?'

Sheremetev shook his head.

'See, Vladimir Vladimirovich?' Eleyekov glanced back again. 'There's no Chechen in the car.'

Vladimir smiled craftily. 'That's what you think.'

'Does he think there's someone in the boot?' whispered Eleyekov to Sheremetev.

'I checked the boot before we got in,' said Artur, as if the driver had offended his professional pride.

'Forget it,' murmured Sheremetev. 'He always thinks there's a Chechen.'

'Who is it? Someone he knew?'

'No idea. He always says he can smell him.'

'You can smell Chechens?'

'I knew some Chechens,' said Artur. 'They always smelled of . . . what's that thing you cook with?'

'Garlic?' offered Eleyekov.

'No.'

'Onions?'

'No. Fennel. That was it, fennel.'

'Fennel?' said Eleyekov. 'What's fennel?'

'It's a thing.'

'A herb,' said Sheremetev.

'Vladimir Vladimirovich, can you smell fennel?' asked Eleyekov loudly.

'Don't be an idiot,' retorted Vladimir. 'And where's Monarov? You were meant to get him. He was meant to be in the car waiting for me. Let's go back now!'

Eleyekov glanced questioningly at Sheremetev.

'Just keep going,' said Sheremetev quietly.

AT THE LAKE, ARTUR jumped out of the Mercedes to make sure the situation was safe before Sheremetev helped Vladimir out. Behind them, the other guards got out of the Range Rover.

'Where do you want to walk?' said Artur to Sheremetev.

'What difference does it make?' muttered Eleyekov, leaning against the car. He pointed at his watch. 'No more than an hour, Nikolai Ilyich. Remember what we said.'

'We'll go for as long as Vladimir Vladimirovich wants,' retorted Artur. He turned to Sheremetev. 'As long as he wants, Nikolai Ilyich. Don't rush.'

Eleyekov said nothing to that. Sheremetev smiled. At least there was someone else who wasn't here only to see how much he could extort from the ex-president. Artur was unfailingly polite, concerned only with doing his job and making sure Vladimir was safe. It was a matter of pride for him, Sheremetev knew, and he could tell that the question of money was irrelevant. Having Artur around on the outing did something, at least, to lessen the aftertaste that the previous day's revelations had left.

'Which way do you want to go?' asked Artur again.

Sheremetev looked around. The scenery on both sides of the lake was similar. Here and there a few other people were visible. Either way would do. Randomly, he pointed right.

Artur sent Lyosha off with another guard to move away a few people who were walking there, while the other two men followed a short distance behind once Sheremetev and Vladimir set off with Artur beside them.

The wind was blowing fresh across the water. On the birches, the leaves were just beginning to turn, lighting up the forest along the shore with daubs of flame.

'I was here last week, you know,' said Vladimir, after they had gone a hundred metres or so.

'It's very pleasant, isn't it?' said Sheremetev.

'Yes. Very. Am I going to swim?'

'Not today, Vladimir Vladimirovich.'

'Dive?'

'No.'

Vladimir looked around. 'No cameras today?'

'It's just a walk. Just a chance to get some fresh air.'

Vladimir took a few more steps. 'This is ridiculous! Did I ask for fresh air? I'm too busy. Where's Monarov? Did Monarov come?'

'Just enjoy the walk, Vladimir Vladimirovich,' said Sheremetev.

'Tell me, honestly, do you think he's plotting against me? I hear things about Monarov. Doesn't think I'm up to it any more. Lately, he hasn't been the same. They're all scared. That's the problem. They know there's only me between them and the abyss. As soon as they think the ship's sinking, they'll be off, like rats. I should have got rid of them when I could. I still can. It's not too late. I'll just—' He stopped himself, and glanced cunningly at Sheremetev. 'Get them all together. Monarov, Luschkin, Narzayev, Serensky. Get them in one place. Organise it today.' Suddenly he glowered at Artur, his eyes narrowed. 'Who are you? Do I know you? What's your name?'

'Artur Artyomovich Lukashvilli, Vladimir Vladimirovich.'

'Lukashvilli? Georgian?'

'My father's Georgian.'

'And the mother?'

'She's from Chelyabinsk.'

Vladimir grunted. He watched him suspiciously for a moment longer, then turned his head and gazed along the forested shore of the lake. He took a deep breath, exhaled, and struck a proprietorial pose with his hands on his hips. Thirty metres away in each direction, the two pairs of security guards stood at the ready. Further along the shore, the people who had been shepherded off by the agents were gazing in his direction, perhaps recognising their ex-president, perhaps wondering who it was who was being protected by all these men.

'When we gave you Georgians a spanking,' he said suddenly to Artur, 'President Bush was like a hurt little child. That man, he was an idiot. The minute I met him, I knew I could twist him round my finger. He said he could see into my soul. What a magician! A man who can see what isn't there. The Americans give themselves a man like that for president – and then they have the gall to blame me when things don't go the way they want! Well, let's not forget the promises they made to Mikhail Sergeyevich, and to Boris Nikolayevich, and to me, to my face – and they broke them, one after the other. Didn't they? Everyone knows it!' He smiled slyly. 'If you want to play that game, lads, if you want to play it with Vladimir Vladimirovich, then watch out for what you'll get back! Isn't that right? That's what that idiot Bush should have seen if he had such great eyesight.' He looked around at the trees fringing the lake. 'Are there bears in this forest?'

'I doubt it, Vladimir Vladimirovich,' said Sheremetev.

'Am I hunting today? Where's the gun?'

'Not today.'

'Am I fishing?'

'No.'

'Riding?'

'No, Vladimir Vladimirovich.'

'Then what am I doing here? Where are the cameras? Are they hidden? Why hide them? Shall I take my shirt off?'

'No.'

'People love that stuff!' Vladimir began to pull at his jacket.

'Vladimir Vladimirovich—'

He threw the jacket at Sheremetev. The zipper whipped his cheek viciously, drawing blood.

Now the black turtleneck was coming off.

'Vladimir Vladimirovich!' said Sheremetev, reaching for him. 'You don't need—'

Vladimir threw his elbow as he struggled with the sweater, catching Sheremetev in the face and tearing open the wound from the zipper. Sheremetev stumbled over a stone and ended up flat on his back. Vladimir pulled the sweater over his head and dropped it beside him.

Artur glanced from one man to the other.

'It's alright,' said Sheremetev, clambering to his feet.

'Here,' said Artur, taking a handkerchief from his pocket. 'That cut looks bad.'

Sheremetev pressed the handkerchief to his cheek and it came away red with blood. The two pairs of guards standing on either side along the shore had come closer at the sight of the disturbance. Artur held up his hand to them.

Vladimir pulled off his T shirt. He puffed himself up, the once powerful chest and arms that he had showed off so vainly to the world now scrawny and diminished, the gold cross that his mother had given him hanging in the cleavage of wrinkled skin between his pectorals.

'Where are the cameras?' He smiled knowingly. 'I know! In the trees. Telephoto lens. Ah, yes, now, I can see them.' He stood proud and turned slowly from one side to the other, giving his phantom photographers time for a shot of him against the background of the lake. Then he walked towards the trees.

Lyosha and the other guards came running from either side.

Artur glanced at Sheremetev. 'Do you want us to get him?'

Sheremetev didn't reply, pressing with the handkerchief on his lacerated cheek. They all stood, watching. Vladimir was bending down, trying to lift a fallen trunk. It was too heavy. He tried another and managed to drag it a couple of metres. He stopped and posed with it, one end of the tree raised in his arms, elbows flexed to show his biceps, chin raised.

'What the fuck is he doing?' whispered one of the guards.

'Posing for the camera,' replied Sheremetev.

'Where? Which camera?' said the guard, smoothing down his hair.

'Bring an axe!' shouted Vladimir. 'I'll show my woodsman's skills. It'll make a good picture. Come on! An axe!'

'I think they forgot to bring it,' called out Sheremetev, taking a few steps towards him.

'Idiots! Well they can put it in later. They can say I cut down the tree. I don't want anyone saying they planted the log here like it was some kind of pot.' Vladimir dropped the trunk and posed with arms up and hands clenched around an imaginary axe. He struck another couple of manful poses, swinging, chopping, then tossed the invisible implement aside and strode purposefully out of the forest. 'Okay. Enough! Show me the shots and I'll choose the ones to use.'

Vladimir stopped at the pile of clothes he had dropped on the shore. He put on his T shirt, but left the sweater and jacket on the ground. When Sheremetev tried to put them on him, he brushed him off. 'Let's go,' he said. He marched back to the Mercedes in his T shirt and settled impatiently into his seat. Everyone else scrambled into the two cars.

'To the airport,' commanded Vladimir. 'These fucking Siberian woods. Honestly, why can't we do this somewhere closer? It's not as if we don't have trees outside Moscow!'

Eleyekov glanced at Sheremetev. 'Are we going to the airport now?' he whispered. 'You said we'd be finished by four-thirty!'

Sheremetev shook his head. 'Back to the dacha,' he murmured.

'Come on!' shouted Vladimir. 'And call ahead. Make sure the plane's ready to go. I don't want to wait for some idiot of a pilot who hasn't had the plane refuelled.'

For the first half of the drive back to the dacha, Vladimir kept shouting about getting to the airport and getting out of Siberia and making sure they scheduled these photoshoots so it didn't take three days of his time to do them. He was getting more and more agitated. Every time Sheremetev looked back, Artur gave him a questioning glance. Sheremetev sat with the handkerchief pressed to the cut on his cheek, wondering how much more excited Vladimir was going to get and wishing he had brought an injection of tranquilliser with him in case things got out of hand. But then, for no apparent reason, Vladimir began to calm down. By the time they got back to the dacha he was sitting happily, confidentially telling Artur about various dealings he had had with foreign leaders and affectionately calling him Fedya. 'They thought they could push me,' he was telling him as they headed up the drive to the dacha, 'but we knew better, didn't we, Fedya? I was the one who pushed them! Just press the right button – a little bit of pressure in Ukraine, heat up the romance with China – and watch the westerners snarl and snap at each other as they try to organise a response.' He chuckled. 'Like dogs! First and foremost, Fedya, I'm a specialist in human relations. That's what you have to be, not only if you're a Chekist, but if you're a politician too.' Vladimir chuckled again. 'Not that there's much difference now that the undercover boys who were sent to work in the federal government have completed their mission!'

Eleyekov pulled up.

'We're here, Vladimir Vladimirovich,' said Sheremetev.

'About time!'

Sheremetev took Vladimir inside. Eleyekov and his son immediately drove off in their two armour-plated cars towards an appointment with a visiting Azeri mining billionaire who didn't dare step into the street without a dozen uzi-wielding henchmen to protect him.

'Do you want a hand getting Vladimir Vladimirovich upstairs?' asked Artur.

'Thank you, Artyusha,' said Sheremetev. 'He's fine. It was just the change of scenery. It excited him a little, I think. I can manage.'

Lyosha and the other security men dispersed. Artur stayed, feeling, it seemed, that his mission wasn't complete until he had personally seen Vladimir back to his suite. 'You don't want me to come with you?'

'Thank you, Artyusha. We're fine.'

'It's no trouble, Nikolai Ilyich. Being responsible for the safety of Vladimir Vladimirovich isn't a job, it's a privilege.'

Sheremetev smiled. 'He's safe, Artyusha.'

'Well, that cut on your face, Nikolai Ilyich, make sure you get it seen to.'

'I've got your handkerchief, I know. I'll return it to you as soon as I've had it washed.'

'Don't worry about that. Just get your face seen to. It doesn't look good.'

Sheremetev turned to Vladimir. 'Come on, Vladimir Vladimirovich. Let's go up.'

Vladimir started up the stairs but stopped after a couple of steps.

'Are you tired?'

Vladimir nodded.

'Come. I'll help you.' Sheremetev took Vladimir's arm and gently pulled him up.

Vladimir took a weary step.

'Come on, Vladimir Vladimirovich. One step at a time.'

'Are you sure you don't want some help?' called up Artur.

Sheremetev glanced down at him. 'No. We're fine. Vladimir Vladimirovich is strong, but he's not a young man, after all.'

'Maybe we should have an elevator installed.'

'Maybe,' said Sheremetev. There would be no shortage of people in the dacha who would be in favour of the idea, he thought, each hoping to take a cut of the cost. He turned back to Vladimir. 'We're okay, aren't we, Vladimir Vladimirovich? One step at a time...That's it. Another step...After such an outing, it's natural to be tired. We'll have a rest when we get to your room...That's it...Another one...'

The security man watched them ascend the staircase. The old man who had stood bare-chested in the forest with his arms raised in the mime of holding an axe, giving orders, telling everyone what to do, just like the head of state he had once been – suddenly he was reduced to this. A step, then a rest . . . A step, then a rest . . .

Sheremetev and the ex-president got to the top and slowly disappeared from view.

Artur felt a tug on his arm. He looked around to find Stepanin standing beside him.

The cook glanced right and left, then leaned closer. 'A word in your ear, Artyusha.'

THE CUT ON SHEREMETEV's face continued to bleed. When he finally got a chance to take a look in a mirror, he saw a gash about five centimetres long running over his cheekbone. He washed it clean. The edges of the skin were ragged and gaping. Every time he managed to staunch the bleeding, a facial movement would open the wound and restart it. When Vladimir's dinner arrived, he sat feeding him with one hand while pressing a piece of gauze on the cut with the other.

He needed stitches. Sheremetev phoned Dr Rospov, the local doctor who was contracted to provide day-to-day care to Vladimir between the visits of the grand professors from Moscow, and told him that there had been a minor accident and some stitches were required. When he arrived, the doctor wasn't too pleased to discover that it was Sheremetev who needed attention. Sheremetev took him to a suite on the upper floor, adjacent to his bedroom, explaining that he had had an accident.

'You should have gone to the hospital,' said the doctor brusquely, rubbing at Sheremetev's cheek with an iodine-soaked swab.

'I can't leave Vladimir Vladimirovich,' replied Sheremetev through teeth gritted against the pain of the doctor's cleansing.

Rospov grunted. He finished cleaning the wound and then drew out from his bag the implements he would need to suture it. He pulled on a pair of gloves. 'This'll hurt,' he announced, and injected the skin around the cut with local anaesthetic.

Sheremetev winced at the sting.

'Hold still! There. I'll give it a minute to let it work.'

The doctor looked around the room as he waited for the anaesthetic to take effect. Rospov was a plump, generally amenable type. He wasn't often needed at the dacha, but Sheremetev had got to know him over the years. Already, Sheremetev could see, his irritation at being called out was dissipating. Besides, he would probably be charging a hefty fee.

'How's that?' said the doctor, touching Sheremetev's cheek with the tip of a pair of scissors. 'Feel anything? Numb?'

Sheremetev nodded.

'Okay. I'll tidy it up first.'

He trimmed the ragged flaps of the wound with a pair of scissors, leaving the edges straight and clean. Then he sat back, examining his handiwork, made another couple of snips, and put the scissor down.

'You'll need six or seven stitches,' he said. 'It's not just a nick.'

Sheremetev nodded.

The doctor set to work. 'So how'd this accident happen?' he asked, as he drove the suture needle in for the first stitch.

'A zipper.'

The doctor looked up for a moment with an inquisitive glance, then began to tie the suture in a series of quick hand movements.

'Vladimir Vladimirovich threw a jacket at me,' said Sheremetev, as Rospov paused before inserting the second stitch. 'I took him out for a walk and he got agitated.'

The doctor nodded. 'How's that going now, the agitation?'

'He has his moments.'

'It's worse?'

'About the same.'

'The drugs are helping?'

'I don't know. Maybe.'

'And Professor Kalin, is he still coming to see him?'

'Every month. He brings another professor with him. Andreevsky. Do you know him?'

The doctor shook his head. He put in the second stitch, tied it and snipped the suture thread. 'I think we'll need seven here, Nikolai Ilyich. Is that okay?'

'Whatever you think.'

He put the next stitch in. 'Who was it you told me that he always talks about when he gets agitated? Who was it again? A Georgian? A Ukrainian? A Syrian?'

'A Chechen.'

'That's right! A Chechen. I knew it was someone he'd got us into a war against. What do you think it's about? Do you think he feels guilty?'

'I don't know.' Sheremetev couldn't recall anything to suggest that Vladimir felt any guilt towards the Chechens. His tone of voice and the way he struck at whatever he thought he was seeing weren't exactly suggestive of contrition. But then why did he constantly sense the Chechen's presence around him, and why did he feel so threatened by it?

'So that was it today? That Chechen again?'

'No, today we were at the lake.'

Sheremetev gave a brief account of the outing and the ten minutes of mayhem that ensued beside the lake. The doctor chuckled at the story of Vladimir stripping off for his imaginary photoshoot.

'When I was a kid,' he said, 'that's all you used to see. On horses, on boats, killing tigers, I don't know what. Every month, it seemed, there was a new picture of our macho president taking on the world.'

Sheremetev didn't reply. The doctor worked quietly for a couple of minutes, completing the sutures. Then he sat back and examined the wound. He prodded at it, then took another iodine-soaked swab and gave it a last rub.

'Okay, I'm finished. Once the anaesthetic wears off, if it's causing you pain, take an aspirin.' He pulled off his gloves, separated the needles and bundled everything else up.

'Leave it,' said Sheremetev. 'I'll get rid of it.'

'Will you need me to come back to take out the stitches or can you do it yourself?'

'I can do it myself.'

'Leave it for a week, then see. If you think it's closed, take them out. If not, leave them a couple of days longer. If you're not sure, I can come back.'

Sheremetev nodded.

'You'll have a scar, Nikolai Ilyich. I've done my best to close it neatly. As long as the laceration stays closed and has a chance to heal, it shouldn't be a bad one.' The doctor picked up his bag. 'Maybe I'll say hello to Vladimir Vladimirovich.'

They went along the corridor. Vladimir was sitting in front of the television. The doctor greeted him. Vladimir appraised him without a flicker of recognition in his eyes.

'I'm Dr Rospov,' said the doctor.

'Is someone sick?' replied Vladimir.

The doctor smiled. 'No, I was just passing, so I thought I'd say hello. Are you well, Vladimir Vladimirovich?'

Vladimir looked at him suspiciously.

'I'm just asking.'

'I'm well. Who are you?'

'Do you know?'

'Do you?'

'I'm Dr Rospov.'

'I know a Rospov. In the duma.'

'That was my father,' said the doctor. 'He died eight years ago.'

'Very reliable man. Always sold his vote to the highest bidder.'

The doctor coughed nervously.

'Absolutely no honour,' continued Vladimir, perhaps taking the doctor's cough as a sign of interest. 'Absolutely no principle except one – whoever pays the most gets the vote. But I'm not opposed to that. Let me tell you, a man like that, at least you know where you stand. You know exactly what you're getting. You pay more than anyone else, you get him – you pay less, you lose him. Simple. And the ones with principles, you know where you are with those ones, too, although they're not too thick on the ground. No, the tricky ones are the ones with principles *and* with a price. Sometimes one, sometimes the other. They're like a woman – one day yes means no, the next day no means yes... how the hell do you know? Just get into bed and spread your legs already, like Rospov! I'll take a man like him any day.'

'Well,' said the doctor. 'I was just—'

'I liked him. A real Russian! No airs. No shame. Always holding his hand out. Give me the money, and I'll do what you say. He's dead, you say?'

'Eight years ago,' murmured the doctor.

'Tragedy. Did I go to the funeral?'

'No, Vladimir Vladimirovich.'

Vladimir laughed. 'Well, he got enough out of me over the years. How do you know him?'

'He was my father.'

'Are you in the duma too?'

'No. I'm a doctor.'

'Why are you here? Is someone sick?'

'Do you feel sick?'

'No.'

'Let me have a look at you, now that I'm here.' The doctor reached for Vladimir's pulse. As he counted the beats, his eye wandered. 'That's a beautiful watch, Vladimir Vladimirovich.' The doctor's fingers were still on Vladimir's pulse, but he was no longer counting. 'A Hublot. Very nice.'

The doctor took a stethoscope out of his bag and listened to Vladimir's chest. He couldn't keep his eyes off the watch that Sheremetev had fastened on Vladimir's wrist before the outing to the lake.

'That's enough!' snapped Vladimir.

'Alright. You look fine, Vladimir Vladirovich.'

'Are you Rospov's son?'

'Yes.'

'Tell the old bastard that if he doesn't vote the right way next week, he'll never get another ruble. Nothing, understand? Make sure you tell him.'

'Yes.'

'Good. Go.'

'Goodbye, Vladimir Vladimirovich,' said the doctor, stealing a last, lingering look at the watch on the old man's wrist.

Vladimir waved him away without a word.

Outside the suite, Sheremetev didn't know what to say after hearing those things about the doctor's father. As they descended the stairs, the doctor shook his head. 'What a crook that man was.'

Sheremetev wasn't sure if the doctor was talking about Vladimir or his father.

'Did you see the watch he was wearing? Do you have any idea what it's worth?'

'A lot?' guessed Sheremetev.

The doctor laughed. He pulled back his sleeve and showed Sheremetev the watch he was wearing, a chunky, silver timepiece with a dark blue face and a silver band. 'I like watches, alright? It's my weakness. My wife tells me it's childish but I don't care. This is a Breitling Chronospace, so it's not nothing. Do you know what you'd pay for this one? Seven thousand. Dollars, Nikolai Ilyich, not rubles.'

Sheremetev stared at the watch on the doctor's hairy wrist.

'That's right. Seven thousand dollars, and believe me, it wasn't easy for me to find that money. But a watch like *that* one...that's out of my league. Way out of my league.'

'More than seven thousand dollars?'

The doctor laughed again. 'I bet he didn't even pay for it. Someone would have given it to him, for sure. A little sweetener to help him make a decision, a little thank you for giving someone what he wanted. A lifetime's wages for a working man, right there on his wrist, for doing someone a favour. It's absurd, Nikolai Ilyich. With all the wealth that he had, he probably never had to pay for a thing. You've got to take your hat off to him. What a crook – a world champion.' The doctor mused on it for a moment, then his expression changed. 'Did I hear from someone that you have a new housekeeper here?'

Sheremetev nodded.

'You should introduce me.'

'Certainly. I'll just have to see if she's—' The sound of Vladimir yelling came out of the monitor in Sheremetev's pocket. He looked at the doctor apologetically. 'I'd better go back to him. I don't want him to get worked up.'

'Okay. I'll meet her another time. Take care of that cut, Nikolai Ilyich. It'll be a bad scar if it opens. Don't disturb the sutures.'

Vladimir needed to go to the bathroom, and Sheremetev was soon able to settle him in front of the television again.

Later that evening, Oleg rang. He said that he had been to see Pasha, and the boy had a black eye. Apparently the kid gloves were off now, perhaps in an attempt to make the family pay up. Conversing under the watchful eye of a prison guard, Pasha had refused to say how it had happened.

'He was trying to be brave, but . . . I can't bear it, Kolya! We have to get him out.'

'Does he actually want you to do that?' asked Sheremetev.

'What are you talking about?' demanded Oleg.

Sheremetev was thinking of what Vladimir had said – some people stand by their principles, no matter what. 'Have you asked him? He might not want you to pay a bribe.'

'That might have been how he felt the day he went in, but not now. Not with a black eye. Kolya, I don't know what they'll do to him in there . . . I don't know if he'll survive it.'

His brother sounded on the verge of breaking down.

'Oleg, it's okay. We'll get him out.'

'*How?*'

'Have you seen if anyone else has any money? I've got two thousand dollars. Perhaps, little by little, we can get it.'

'Kolya, no one will give me a kopeck once they hear what he's in for. I'm a leper. "Oh, he insulted the president? And the *ex-president*? Goodbye, Oleg Ilyich." Pasha's right, Kolya – this is the Russia your Vladimir Vladimirovich made. He's almost dead, but we have to go on living in it. And now, Pasha – just because he has the courage to stand up and tell the truth – he's the one who has to pay. Is that right, Kolya? Who should pay? He should, the old man, the one who made this mess! He should be the one in prison, he should be the one who's treated like a leper! Oh, he's old, and forgetful. Oh, let's leave him alone. Well, what about it? Pasha's young and has everything in front of him, and he says one thing, he tells the truth, and look what happens! That's our Russia, Kolya. And who's to blame?'

Sheremetev was silent.

Oleg sighed. 'What about Vasya?' he said eventually. 'What does he say?'

'He can't do anything.'

'Not even for his cousin? Come on, Vasya knows all kinds of people. He's like a cat, always falling on his feet. Don't tell me there's nothing he can do. What did he say?'

'He said he doesn't have money.'

'That's all?'

'That's all.'

'He doesn't have the money?'

'Not on the scale we're talking about. I think ... I don't know about his business. Maybe it's not going so well.'

'Kolya, I swear to you, I feel people watching me. At the school. I look around and I see them. They know. They're thinking: he's the one whose son insulted the president. He's the one with the boy in jail.'

'Olik, don't be paranoid.'

'I'm not paranoid. Nina's noticed also.'

Us and them, thought Sheremetev. That was what Barkovskaya had said. Us and them. Was that how people thought, just as in the old Soviet days?

'Come on, Olik,' he said eventually. 'We'll get him out.'

'How?' cried Oleg again.

Sheremetev closed his eyes. He wished he knew.

Images came to his mind. Pasha as a little boy, a thoughtful child, always quiet when you first started talking to him, but then warming up, bright and clever and confiding ... A photograph that he had from Karinka's funeral, when Pasha was fourteen years old, standing next to Vasya, a full head shorter than his cousin ... The serious, selfless young man into which he had developed, so quick to take up a cause.

One heard of things happening in Russia, so-called injustices, but one never thought of them happening to a person one knew. Beside, you never knew what the truth was – there are always two sides to a story. But now it wasn't just a name, a face on a television screen. It was Pashik, whom he had held in his arms the day he was born. And there weren't two sides to the story – there was only one.

'It'll be alright, Olik, we'll find a way.'

'How?' said Oleg again.

Sheremetev didn't have an answer. 'I'll come and see you on Saturday,' he said instead. 'I've got the day off.'

He put his phone back in his pocket, and went upstairs to give Vladimir his medications and get him ready for the night. As he walked in and saw the ex-president, the thought of the distress he had heard in Oleg's voice and his brother's bitterness towards Vladimir hit him like a slap and made him stop in his tracks. But he endeavoured to put it out of his mind, reminding himself that he was a nurse and the old man sitting in the armchair, looking at him with a benign blankness, was his patient.

Vladimir was still wearing the T shirt and jeans from the excursion to the lake. Sheremetev could see him peering at the cut on his face as he helped him undress.

'What happened to you?'

'Nothing, Vladimir Vladimirovich.'

Vladimir put out a finger and poked at the cut.

Sheremetev jumped back. 'Don't!' he shouted angrily.

Vladimir smiled, seeming to enjoy the response.

'It hurts,' murmured Sheremetev. 'Don't touch, please.' He turned away, confused by the mist of rage that had engulfed him. His heart was thumping. Never before, in the six years he had cared for Vladimir, could he remember being angry with him. Impatient, frustrated, fed up ... yes, all of these, of course, as one was occasionally with any patient. But never anger. He took a deep breath. As a nurse, anger towards a patient wasn't an emotion he could allow himself to feel.

He waited a few moments, until he sensed the mist subsiding. Then he came closer again and cautiously helped Vladimir into his pyjamas, warily watching out for any more sudden jabs. He unfastened the watch that the doctor had envied so much and took it back, together with the clothes, to the dressing room. He opened the drawer from which the watch had come and laid it in its niche, then put his finger to the front of the tray to push it in, but hesitated. The watch he had just put back was out of his league, the doctor said, and his league obviously went up to seven thousand dollars. A lifetime's wages for a working man, he had said. And here, on this tray, was not one such watch – but fifteen.

Sheremetev opened another tray at random. Watches in gold and silver, some with white faces, some with faces in blue or green, some with what appeared to be tiny jewels set into faces or hands, some with metal wristbands, some with leather. He examined a couple of the leather straps. They were utterly smooth, never worn. He opened another tray. In this one, a niche was empty, like a missing tooth in an otherwise full jaw. Another tray. This one was full.

Sheremetev stepped back. How many trays in the cupboard? He counted them. Twenty-five. And on each tray, fifteen velvet niches, and only a few of them here and there that didn't contain a watch. Watches that were hardly ever even taken out of their hiding places. And was it true that Vladimir had never had to pay, that people had given them as gifts, watches, it seemed, that were so expensive that even a doctor couldn't afford to buy them?

As Vladimir waited in the next room to be put to bed, Sheremetev gazed at the closed trays in the beautifully made cabinet, sitting one above the other in perfect precision. Tray above tray, watch beside watch.

And Pasha lay in jail for want of a bribe, while these watches, apparently so expensive, lay all but forgotten in their niches...

Suddenly he came to his senses. Nikolai, he said to himself: what on earth are you thinking?

10

THE CUT ON HIS face, together with Dr Rospov's ministrations, had bruised Sheremetev's cheek more than he had realised. The next morning, when he looked in the mirror, he saw the narrow black line of the laceration, festooned with suture knots like tiny blood-caked cactuses, across a swelling the colour of an aubergine.

Everyone who saw him seemed to take Sheremetev's lacerated cheek as an invitation to pass comment, as if by his mere presence he was advertising a newfound desire to hear what they considered either their wisdom or their wit. 'You need to take care of yourself, Nikolai Ilyich,' said the maid in the corridor, using a tone one would normally reserve for a decrepit octogenarian. 'Been on the booze again?' offered the house attendant who brought up the breakfast tray for Vladimir, grinning from ear to ear. And Vladimir, the cause of the injury in the first place, took one look at him and said: 'Learn to use your razor, whoever you are!'

'Yes, Vladimir Vladimirovich,' muttered Sheremetev, staying out of range of his finger.

After he had helped Vladimir with breakfast, Sheremetev left him in the sitting room while he went downstairs. He found half a dozen of the security guards in the staff dining room breakfasting noisily, including Lyosha and two of the others who had been at the lake the previous day. A chorus of chortles and jokes greeted him, many of them about the danger posed by that most deadly of weapons, the zipper.

'Very funny!' declared Sheremetev irritably, and he helped himself to bread and honey.

The jokes carried on for a few more minutes, then petered out.

Eventually the guards drifted away. Sheremetev sat alone, sipping coffee, thinking about Pasha and his black eye, now and then prodding tentatively at the tender swelling around the cut on his cheek. The fear and desperation he had heard in Oleg's voice the previous night tormented him. He tried to imagine how he would feel if Vasya was in Pasha's situation – except somehow it was impossible to imagine Vasya being in such a situation, and not only for the obvious reason that Vasya would never have written the kind of thing that Pasha had produced. If Vasya was in jail, he'd probably end up running the place. But Pasha... Oleg was right – who knew what would happen to him or if he would even survive it?

And Oleg was right about another thing – it was because of Karinka. The outrage that had built up in Pasha over the years, and which had exploded out of him in that blog, had started with Karinka's death. Somehow, as Oleg said, he had found out what was going on, and he had never been the same.

Sheremetev feel a deep sense of responsibility, as if somehow he had had a part in putting Pasha in jail.

Stepanin poked his head out of the kitchen. He came out and got himself a bowl of *kasha* and a coffee.

'That looks bad,' he said, gesturing at Sheremetev's face. 'If you're going to go out brawling, Kolya, take a gun.'

'Very funny.'

Stepanin chuckled. 'On the other hand, it can be hard to defend against a zipper.'

'*And* an elbow,' muttered Sheremetev.

'The boss hit you with his elbow?' Stepanin made a show of looking impressed. 'Whatever you did, you must have really upset him.'

Sheremetev didn't rise to the bait.

The cook grinned. He seemed more like his old self. The frown of anxiety that seemed to have become a constant feature of his expression since Barkovskaya commenced her assault on his chicken supply was absent. He drizzled honey on his *kasha*, took a spoonful, and ate it with a smug expression.

Sheremetev wondered what was going on.

Stepanin ate quickly, then slurped his coffee. He put the mug down with a thump and grinned again. 'Do you think Vladimir Vladimirovich would fancy chicken Georgian style one of these days?'

Sheremetev looked at him in surprise. 'Have you sorted things out with Barkovskaya?'

Stepanin got up, an enigmatic smile on his face.

'So everything's okay?' asked Sheremetev, with a sudden sense of relief.

'It will be.'

'It *will* be?' That didn't sound good, nor the portentous tone in which the cook had said it. 'What do you mean it will be?'

'Who started this, Kolya? Was it me or was it Barkovskaya? Well? If you start a war, someone's going to get hurt.'

'Vitya, what are you talking—'

'Just tell Vladimir Vladimirovich he'll soon have Georgian chicken for lunch again.'

Sheremetev didn't know how Stepanin was planning to get Barkovskaya to back down, but the cook's dark intimations sucked away the relief he had felt and replaced it with a looming sense of foreboding. On top of his guilt and worry over Pasha, and the throbbing tenderness in his lacerated cheek, it made Sheremetev feel even more miserable. The situation with Pasha reminded him of the worst days with Karinka, when he could see her going downhill in front of his eyes, and for want of money, there was nothing he could do. He had said to Oleg that they would find a way to get Pasha out of jail, adopting the tone of an older, protective brother, but this wasn't a schoolyard in which he could put his head down and charge to Oleg's aid, and this wasn't a fight with people he could beat – not that the Pinto twins had emerged victorious from that many scuffles, anyway, not with the boys who learned to sidestep him. He had uttered the words out of an instinctive desire to comfort his brother, but the words were hollow, and if they had given Oleg any hope, then it was false. He had nowhere near enough money to get Pasha out and no idea who else might provide it.

He remembered the thoughts he had had in front of Vladimir's watch cabinet the previous night. But that was a fantasy, like a child dreaming of walking up to a hated teacher in front of the whole class and giving him a poke in the eye. Sheremetev knew himself too well. It wasn't possible that he would actually do it.

THAT MORNING, WHEN HE took Vladimir for his walk, Sheremetev kept him away from the charnel pit. It was an unusually mild day for October and the smell was high. If Stepanin did find a way to finish the stand-off with Barkovskaya, at least they could fill in the hole and that would be the end of the stench. Sheremetev didn't want to go towards Eleyekov's garage either. He steered Vladimir in another direction.

Between the long plastic tunnels that covered this part of the estate, out of the breeze, the day felt almost warm. Vladimir was muttering something to someone with whom he was apparently holding a conversation. Sheremetev brooded as he walked alongside him, caught up in his sense of impotence about Pasha. Tomorrow was his day off and he had told Oleg that he would come to visit, although Sheremetev knew that he would have nothing new to say. He wanted to see his brother, of course, but going empty handed in Oleg's hour of need made him dread it as well.

Vladimir had spotted one of the benches that still stood amongst the greenhouses – or the commercial farm, as Sheremetev now understood them to be. Normally, he kept Vladimir walking on their morning outings, since the ex-president spent enough time sitting the rest of the day. But today he felt so demoralised that he didn't care. It was a dereliction of his professional duty, but when they reached the bench, and Vladimir said that he wanted to stop, he let him sit.

Sheremetev stood beside him. Still muttering to himself, Vladimir hardly seemed aware of him. Sheremetev hesitated a moment longer, then sat.

Inside the greenhouse in front of them, silhouettes of labourers worked at the plants. Sheremetev glanced at Vladimir. The ex-president sat, arms folded, his gaze somewhere in the middle distance.

Sheremetev wondered if Vladimir's hallucinations and imaginings were getting worse. Living with him day to day, it was hard to tell, as it is hard to tell if someone's skin colour or weight is changing because of an illness when you're constantly with them – much easier to tell if you see them six months apart, and then the change hits you like a bolt. He could remember once, as Karinka became

160

really ill, coming across a picture of her that had been taken a year earlier, and suddenly realising how much she had deteriorated. It was a shock. *Only a year?*

He glanced at Vladimir again. The old man lived decades in the past. Sheremetev doubted that he recognised anyone at all in the dacha now, while only six months ago he had still been able to come up with a name from time to time. He tried to imagine what it must be like, to live surrounded entirely by people you took to be strangers. The idea was terrifying. But Vladimir at least felt a familiarity with him, Sheremetev was certain, and often mistook the other people who served him in the dacha for long-past friends – and enemies – so perhaps the world in which he was living, even if utterly distorted, was not as cold and alien as he imagined. True, it was fantasy, a memory confection that existed only in Vladimir's head, but Vladimir no longer had any insight into that fact, so as far as he was concerned, it was real. In a sense, thought Sheremetev, it was as real as the world in which he or anyone else lived.

Goroviev appeared out of the greenhouse, pushing a long, flat barrow laden with seedlings. The gardener stopped when he saw them. He left the barrow and came over.

'Good morning, Vladimir Vladimirovich,' he said politely, as he always did.

Vladimir glanced at him and then looked away again.

'Vladimir Vladimirovich is somewhat preoccupied this morning,' explained Sheremetev.

Goroviev smiled. 'Indeed? Affairs of state, no doubt. You have quite an injury to your face, Nikolai Ilyich.'

'Just an accident,' said Sheremetev. 'It's not as bad as it looks.'

'I hope it heals quickly.'

'Thank you.'

Sheremetev didn't know what to make of Goroviev now. He had formed an impression of him as a good, gentle soul, and yet it turned out that he was taking his cut, just like everyone else.

The gardener continued to stand there.

'I'm afraid Vladimir Vladimirovich isn't in a great mood for conversation this morning,' said Sheremetev eventually.

'Nikolai Ilyich ... may I sit?'

'Here?'

'Yes.'

Sheremetev hesitated for a moment, then moved up along the bench, managing to preserve a sliver of space between himself and Vladimir. The gardener sat beside him.

'I wanted ...' began Goroviev in a low voice, and then he paused, glancing at Vladimir, who was mumbling again. 'I wanted to say how sorry I was to hear about your nephew.'

Sheremetev looked at him in surprise.

'Everyone knows what's happened. I read the blog, Nikolai Ilyich. It had been taken down, of course, by the time I found out about it, but there are ways to find things. Nothing ever really disappears from the internet, does it? It was a bold thing to write, I'll say that much.'

'And now they're punishing him.'

'Yes.' The gardener sat silently for a moment. 'Nikolai Ilyich ... I suppose people have told you about me?'

'Told me?'

'About my past.'

'No.'

The gardener looked at him knowingly.

'Well, people say there was something,' confessed Sheremetev, 'but I don't know more than that, and why should I want to? What may have happened isn't any of my business, Arkady Maksimovich.'

162

Goroviev smiled. 'I'm sure whatever you're imagining I did is worse than the reality.'

'I don't know.'

'Shall I tell you?'

'You don't have to.'

'When I was young, after I left university, I was a journalist. Things were different back then, of course. Your patient over there and his cronies hadn't yet taken control of all the newspapers and television stations. Foolish as we were, we thought Russia had changed, become like every other civilised nation, and that this was the way it would be forever. We were wrong, of course. Some of us stuck our necks out too far. Some stuck them out so far they lost their heads.'

'You?' said Sheremetev. 'Is that what happened?'

'No. I mean, really – lost their heads, Nikolai Ilyich. Me, I lost my job and a few years of my life in prison. What does that amount to, by comparison? Some of us *died.* There was Anna Stepanovna, of course. Everyone remembers her, but there were others, plenty of others. In those days, to kill a journalist was like a sport. When I look back on it now, I realise that I was lucky to have got out alive.'

'So you became a gardener?'

'Not immediately. Things happened, but one way or another . . . the ins and outs don't matter. The thing is, there's something very peaceful and true about gardening, Nikolai Ilyich. Things live, things grow, things die. If you give them the right conditions, they thrive, if you give them the wrong ones, they wither. If you allow the weeds to grow, they'll choke off everything, if you cut them back, there's room for others. Isn't that the truth of life? What other truths are there, after all?'

Vladimir murmured something. Goroviev listened. Then the ex-president was silent again.

'I'd love to know what he's thinking,' said the gardener quietly. 'I've always wondered what went on in his head. He was such a liar, to Russia, to the world. You wonder, a man who tells such lies, for so long, to so many people, in the end, does he even know the truth himself?'

Sheremetev glanced at Goroviev in astonishment, amazed to hear such things coming out of his mouth. And with Vladimir sitting only a metre away! The gardener was gazing across him at the old man, but instead of condemnation in Goroviev's face, Sheremetev saw only curiosity, as if he really was pondering the question.

'What did you write about when you were a journalist?' asked Sheremetev, trying to change the subject.

Goroviev looked back at him. 'All sorts of things. But the really big thing, the thing that did for me, was when he went after Trikovsky.'

'Trikovsky!' muttered Vladimir.

'He was one of the oligarchs,' explained the gardener to Sheremetev. 'Look, Trikovsky wasn't perfect, I'll be the first to admit it. To become one of the oligarchs meant by definition that you had committed economic crimes. And personally, he was somewhat of an egomaniac. But I do think, by the time your patient here went after him, he had developed a kind of democratic vision, maybe some kind of personal conversion, and... who knows? Maybe, he could have made a difference. In any case, they had no right to do what they did to him. He wasn't a saint, but he wasn't the devil, either.'

'You think you're a saint,' said Vladimir.

Sheremetev went to say something, but the gardener quickly held a finger to his lips.

Vladimir snorted. 'You've turned all holier than thou all of a sudden.'

'We shouldn't listen—'

'*Shhhhh!*' Goroviev leaned forward slightly, one hand holding Sheremetev back, frowning as he tried to catch every word.

'You think, all you have to do is say the word "democracy",' said Vladimir, 'and suddenly you're the nation's saviour.'

Trikovsky shook his head. 'That's not true.'

'A real convert, aren't you?' said Vladimir sarcastically.

'I'm not saying I haven't done certain things that I regret, Vladimir Vladimirovich,' replied Trikovsky.

Vladimir laughed. 'Certain things!'

'A man can change course. What I may have done in the past as I constructed my business were things that the conditions of the time made—'

'Sure,' said Vladimir, cutting the oligarch off. He enjoyed doing it. Who else told an oligarch to shut up? Outside these walls, in their mansions and the boardrooms of their corporations, they were king. But not here. Not in the Kremlin. Behind the red brick walls, there was only one boss. '*There were conditions at the time . . .*' he parodied. 'Listen to me, Leva. You can be a businessman or a politician, but not both. We have to make a choice in life. One or the other. Riches or public service.' Vladimir shrugged, not betraying by even the faintest hint of a smile the patent falsity – proven above all by himself – of what he was saying. 'You've made your choice, I think.'

'All I'm saying, Vladimir Vladimirovich, is in a democracy, any person can speak. Anyone can run for office, businessman or not.'

'We saw that with Boris Nikolayevich. Anyone can do anything, say anything. What a fucking disaster! He turned Russia into a living corpse, every day being eaten away a little more by mad dogs like you. Which is why you put him there the second time, you and your friends, so you could keep on eating.'

'We put you there, too.'

'Ha!'

'Yes. What do you think Boris Nikolayevich would have done if we'd told him to choose someone else?'

Vladimir smiled. 'The old man didn't know what day it was.'

'He knew enough to listen to us,' replied the oligarch.

'Then you should have told him to get rid of me while you still had the chance, because I'm telling you this now, and for the last time, Leva.' Vladimir wagged a finger. 'Stay out of politics. It may be true the old man would never have chosen me as his successor if it wasn't for you and the others. Fine. I couldn't care less. That's between you and him. As far as I'm concerned, you were the means, not the reason. The reason I was put in this place was to bring order and stability to Russia, to stop it becoming a place where every mad bird could peck out its eyes. And that's what I'm doing!' He slapped a fist into the other palm. 'I'm putting an end to it. You'll thank me one day. Even you, Lev Fyodorovich.'

'I think there's a way we can do this,' said Trikovsky. 'You're—'

'No. There's no way. I'm not bargaining. I'm not negotiating. You see – you're thinking like a businessman. That's why you shouldn't be in politics.'

'You don't bargain in politics?'

'You do what I say in politics. And do you know what you're going to do? You're going to go to your television station and your newspaper and fire the nest of oppositionists who work there. Then you're going to make sure the rest say what I want them to say. Monarov will talk to you from time to time so there's no misunderstanding. And as far as politics is concerned, that's it. That's as much as you're going to do. Apart from that, you're going to look after your bank and your oil company and your nickel mine and you're going to make a lot of money, because while you're taking care of business,

I'll be taking care of politics, and Russia will have order, and when Russia has order, businessmen can make money, those who allow them to do so are rewarded, and everyone will be happy, including you. That's what you're going to do, and that's what all your friends are going to do.'

'And if I don't?' said Trikovsky quietly.

Vladimir sighed. 'Have your companies been audited by a tax prosecutor? Show me a company in Russia that comes out of that clean and I'll show you a cow that shits gold.'

Trikovsky shook his head. 'My companies don't owe any tax.'

'No?' Vladimir laughed. 'My guess is that if the tax prosecutor comes visiting he'll find that you owe plenty of tax, taxes you haven't even heard of yet.' He laughed again. 'You'll owe so much tax that it will bankrupt your whole company if you have to pay it. Of course he's totally independent, Leva, so I can't be sure. Call it a hunch.'

'That's an outrage!'

'The state might be prepared to take the business off your hands in lieu of the taxes, but as for you, Lev Fyodorovich, we don't tolerate tax cheats in Russia. This isn't London. Here, we make examples of them! But all of this is so unnecessary. Why are we even talking about it? You'll stay out of politics, you'll support me whenever I tell you to, and I'll support you in your business. You'll do what I tell you, you'll make a lot of money, and you'll be happy.'

'No one would tolerate what you're talking about!' retorted Trikovsky. 'Confiscating an entire corporation of this scale on the basis of falsified investigations? You can't do it. I have support in the duma.'

'Oh, you have support in the duma?'

'If you do this to me, every other businessman in Russia will be threatened. Do you know what that will do for investment?'

Vladimir smiled. 'And where will they take their money, Leva? Where else can they do what they're allowed to do in Russia? Where else can they make such profits? With order and stability in Russia, they can do even more of it. Do you think they'll throw themselves after you? No, they'll watch you go down. And as for your support in the duma...you know, I'm a specialist in human relations. In this job, you have to be. One thing I've noticed about people with a lot of money, is that they think people are personally attached to them. After a while, after you've had enough yes-men around for long enough, it's easy to mistake subservience for loyalty. Me, when I find myself starting to think that someone is loyal to me, I immediately remind myself that his loyalty only goes as far as the next commission that's going to land in his Swiss bank account. So let's remember what you are. You're a crook. You're an embezzler. When the Russian state was drowning in debt, when the Afghan veterans and their war widows were starving in the winter, you and your friends, in the goodness of your hearts, paid Boris Nikolayevich ten kopecks on the ruble for your mines and your oil wells and your banks. *That's* what people are going to remember when the tax prosecutor comes calling, Lev Fyodorovich. Now, how many of your friends in the duma are going to want to associate themselves with that? And by the way, how many of them would welcome their own visit from the tax prosecutor?'

Trikovsky gazed at him incredulously. 'Do you really think this is the way to save Russia? To have you and your KGB henchmen deciding everything?'

'Do you think it's to have you and your fellow crooks doing it?'

'I'll take my chances with the people.'

'Of course you will. With your newspaper and your television station to tell them what to think, just like any other citizen, huh?

You gave an election to Boris Nikolayevich—'

'And to you.'

'Exactly.' Vladimir sat forward. 'Do you think – do you *really* think – I'll ever take the risk that one day you'll take one away from me? Use your brains, Leva. By the time he was finished, Boris Nikolayevich was nothing but an alcohol-soaked sponge. Do I look like an alcohol-soaked sponge? What you could do to him, you can't do to me. That's why you chose me, remember?'

The oligarch didn't reply. Vladimir watched him, letting the silence stretch out, relishing the encounter more and more.

'He seems to be talking to Trikovsky,' murmured Goroviev to Sheremetev, finally letting go of his wrist. 'Is that possible? That he thinks he's talking to him?'

Sheremetev didn't reply.

Vladimir was silent, as if aware that he was being overheard.

'You know,' mused Goroviev quietly, watching the ex-president, 'I wonder about him. How did he become what he was? Sure, a Soviet KGB officer, he was never exactly going to be a natural democrat. But to turn out to be so brutal when he got power, and so corrupt...Did the KGB make him like that, or was it natural to him from the start?'

'We should go,' said Sheremetev nervously. 'If he gets upset—'

The gardener leaned across him, putting his face closer to the ex-president's. 'You were corrupt, weren't you, Vladimir Vladimiro-vich? Corrupt on a scale no one could have imagined.'

'Me?' said Vladimir.

'Yes, you.'

Vladimir laughed.

Goroviev sat back. 'See, Nikolai Ilyich? He's not upset. He's laughing.'

'Still, we should—'

'Your nephew is right, Nikolai Ilyich. He crucified us, and the Russia we live in is his. The question is, was it only because of him, or was it inevitable in some way that this would happen to us? Can one man alone do what he did to us? If he had tried to do the opposite, would the KGB boys have brought him down and put someone else in his place?'

'I really don't know, Arkady Maksimovich,' replied Sheremetev, wanting only for this conversation to end. He made to stand, but Goroviev pulled him back.

'I've asked myself, a thousand times,' he said earnestly. 'And the truth is, I don't know. It would be easier if the answer was yes, that everything is his fault. It would be easier if he was the only one we had to hate. But one man can't do everything, he can't be responsible for every ill. And yet . . . he could have made a start. If he was different, more of a democrat – or not even that, but if he was honest, at least, and not so greedy for wealth, if he had the minimum of human decency – he could have nudged us away from authoritarianism and corruption. A nudge from him, then a nudge from someone else, then more of a nudge, and by now, we would be a free country with a true leader at its head instead of a vaudeville thief like Lebedev. But instead of holding us back, nudging us away a little, he opened the floodgates and we were swept away. So for that, he's guilty. Yes. Guilty as charged.'

For a moment, Sheremetev's curiosity overcame his discomfort. He gazed at Goroviev, thinking of what the gardener had told of him of his life. 'Do you hate him, Arkady Maksimovich?'

Goroviev smiled slightly. 'There was a time, Nikolai Ilyich, if had been sitting this close to him, I would have strangled him with my bare hands. And if I'd had to have strangled you to get to him, I would have done that too. But now . . .' Goroviev shrugged. 'Yes.

I hate him. I hate him for what he was, what he wasn't, what he did, what he didn't do but should have done. I don't forgive him. He's beneath forgiveness. But the thing is, Nikolai Ilyich, for how long did he rule us? How many decades? The thing your nephew is really saying...' The gardener stopped himself. 'How old is he, by the way, your nephew?'

'Twenty.'

Goroviev nodded. 'Of course. You told me. That's young. Very young. Well, what he's really asking is the question every one of the young generation should be asking of us: how did we let this man do this to us? This small fearful personality who aspired to be a Chekist even when he was a boy. How did we put such a man, a man of so few attainments, such limited vision, at the top? Why did we tolerate him? How did we give him the time and opportunity to put Russia against a cross and put the nails through her hands, like your nephew said? It didn't happen in one night – it took years. Where were we?'

A smile crept across Vladimir's lips.

Goroviev leaned forward. 'Isn't that right, Vova? All those things you did, bit by bit, one after the other, and we were like blind men, sleepwalking, watching you do it but not seeing. How could we let you?'

Vladimir sneered at Trikovsky, who for some reason was wearing a pair of overalls now. 'You didn't *let* me do anything, Leva. I saw what had to be done and I did it in the only way it could be done.'

'And that's it, is it? For how long? Where does it end, Vova?'

Vladimir narrowed his eyes.

'Control us, control the duma, control the press. And then?'

'What *then?*'

'Does it go on forever? Is this Russia? Is this all there is?'

'*All* there is? First, I'll put order and stability into the country. Then we'll see. That's the only way.'

'The only way? To take twenty percent off every contract in the country? To have men who spent twenty years sitting behind a desk in the KGB supposedly running the nation's biggest companies, when all they're really doing is siphoning off the profits into bank accounts in Switzerland? To send the tax prosecutors after honest Russians while telling them to ignore the biggest crooks in the land? To whisper into the ear of a judge what the verdict and sentence on a young journalist will be before the trial has even begun? What kind of a Russia is that, Vladimir Vladimirovich?'

Vladimir didn't reply. One of the benefits of power, he had discovered, was the prerogative of silence, and the implicit threat it carried.

'I hope one day you'll know, Vladimir Vladimirovich, one day before you die, what you've done—'

Vladimir laughed. 'That's what they all say when they know I've won. "Just you wait, Vladimir Vladimirovich. Your turn will come." But it hasn't, has it? *Your* turn has come.'

'No, *your* turn has come. You know, inside, don't you? You must know...'

Vladimir kept laughing. He couldn't hear, wouldn't hear. The sound of his laughter drowned out the other man's words.

Then he was silent.

Vladimir could see a strange sadness in Trikovsky's eyes, as if the oligarch could see his own future now, the life that he had envisaged for himself that he was about to lose and the life that would replace it: the arrest, the trial, the cage in the courtroom, the confiscation of his businesses, the years in a Siberian jail, the release, many years later, only through Vladimir's clemency, a final act of humiliation tainting the sweetness of liberation with an indelible bitterness.

In his triumph, Vladimir felt an unexpected, unattributable unease, an unaccountable and troubling sense of doubt.

'Get out,' he murmured, suddenly sickened. 'Get out!'

Goroviev stood. 'I should go,' he said to Sheremetev. 'You were right. I've upset him. Forgive me, Nikolai Ilyich, it wasn't my intention. I only wanted to say, as I said at the start, that I'm sorry for your nephew. I hope he gets out soon.'

Sheremetev stood as well. 'I don't understand. How did you get this job here if you have this record of being such an oppositionist?'

'I had a job here long before Vladimir Vladimirovich arrived. That's already eight years ago. To be honest, back then, I don't think anyone bothered to check. I'm just a gardener, right? And how many mansions did Vladimir Vladimirovich own? This was just one of many. Back then, he never came here. It was only Mitya Zaminsky and me, looking after the estate. Then when they brought Vladimir Vladimirovich here to stay, we added a third gardener, and then, of course, everything else...'

'Is it true what I heard, that all these greenhouses grow produce that you sell for your own profit?'

'And the profit of a few other people,' said Goroviev. 'Yes, it's true.'

'But it's not legal?'

Goroviev shrugged. 'Legal? Illegal? Is there a difference in Russia, Nikolai Ilyich? All that matters is whether something is possible or impossible. That's the correct question.'

'I don't understand, Arkady Maksimovich. From what you tell me, this corruption, this thievery... this was exactly what you fought against.'

'But Nikolai Ilyich...I lost' Goroviev shrugged, a helpless smile on his face. 'I couldn't change the world. I tried, in my way, but by the time I was twenty-six, I had failed. And I discovered then that I wasn't very brave, and that was actually a surprise to me. I thought I had enough courage to face up to anything. But when people were being murdered around me, when the man who had been my editor one day was shot to death in front of our office the next, I found out that I didn't, not enough to go on trying. I didn't want to die as well.'

'Is that really how it was?' whispered Sheremetev.

Goroviev nodded. 'Your nephew, Nikolai Ilyich, get him out of jail and send him far away, out of this country. If he has a voice, it will only be silenced here, one way or another.' The gardener gestured towards Vladimir. 'In the Russia that this man made, you can't exist in opposition. In the end, either you give in, or they put an end to you.'

'Do you think he made it? I thought you said no man can do everything alone?'

'No, but he used the others to do what he wanted. This is *his* country, Nikolai Ilyich. Everything about it is his. Nothing is an accident – whatever you see, he wanted.'

Sheremetev gazed at the gardener, frowning, shaking his head slightly.

'Look, Russia is what it is, and he did what he did. What really matters to me now is what he thinks. Does he believe this is his creation? Is there anything he would have changed? If not, whether he could have done it alone or not, it's the same as if everything is his responsibility.'

Sheremetev turned to look at the ex-president. So did Goroviev. They both stared down at the old man on the bench, who gazed blankly at the plastic sheeting of the greenhouse in front of him.

'Listen, Nikolai Ilyich,' said Goroviev. 'You ask me how I can do what I do. At my second trial, when I was found guilty – actually, I had been found guilty the day they decided to try me, so I should say, the day I was pronounced guilty – the judge, who was not such a bad man, really, and in sending me to jail for five years was only doing what he had been told to do by this man here, which was his job, after all . . . He said to me, Arkady Maksimovich, you're obviously a man of talent. You must learn to adapt your talent to reality. As our president, Vladimir Vladimirovich has often said, we must all do what we can to build the new Russia.' Goroviev glanced at Vladimir, who was still sitting on the bench, gazing at nothing obvious. 'What did *he* do to build the new Russia? I'll tell you. He gouged us every way he could. He took our money by the truckload and sent it to his banks all over the world, and he let his friends do the same. That was the way he showed us. Now, obviously, I'm not in his league. I'm nothing but a gardener. But I have to do my bit, as we all must, like the judge said. It's our patriotic duty. So I do. Every time I send a tray of vegetables from here to the market, grown on his land, in greenhouses that he paid for, by labourers that he pays but for money that I keep, I like to think that Vladimir Vladimirovich would be proud of me, even in a small way, for gouging him back.'

II

JUST AS STEPANIN HAD promised, chicken Georgian style arrived on Vladimir's lunch tray the next day. Sheremetev wasn't there to witness this miracle of modern peacemaking. It was his day off, and he had gone to visit Oleg. Vladimir was being looked after by the relief nurse, Vera. Vladimir had no recognition of her, although she had been coming for almost two years now. He usually thought she was his mother.

Vera worked occasional shifts in a hospital in Odintsovo, as well as doing private work, such as the weekly shift covering for Sheremetev. She was a single mother of two, abandoned by a husband who, from her account, was a drunken womaniser with bad breath and strong body odour. From the stories Vera told, Sheremetev had built a picture in his mind almost of a beggar lying in a gutter with a bottle of rotgut and his hand out trying to cadge a kopeck or two from the people stepping over him. It had been a genuine surprise when Vera let slip one day that he was a pharmacist with a shop in Odintsovo. It also eventuated that his abandonment involved an orderly divorce, support payments for the children and regular contact with the kids, aged eleven and eight.

Still, Sheremetev was quite fond of Vera – who was more than fond of him. She was loud, over-made up, and opinionated, but funny, warm and generous, and the hair-raising stories about her ex-husband were always told with a certain knowing, tongue-in-cheek humour. Early on, she had coyly admitted to Sheremetev that she found small men attractive, even batting her eyelids as she spoke, and each week, when she took over from him, she always insinuated that he must be off to visit a lady love, while at the same time managing to convey that she knew perfectly well that he wasn't, but that if he was interested in such a thing...

Sheremetev was supposed to have a full twenty-four hours off, with Vera staying to cover for him overnight, but he always came back after dinner, or even before, and let her leave. Vladimir's disorientation was greater at night, and if he was to awake and find an unfamiliar face trying to calm him, it was likely to send him off into a full blown episode that only the security men and an injection of tranquilliser would be able to quell.

Vera had arrived at ten. 'Where are you off to today, Kolya?' she asked. 'Just once, I'd love to come with you. But I suppose,' she said, her eyes twinkling with innuendo, 'that would be inconvenient.'

'Particularly because if you did come with me, there'd be no one to look after Vladimir Vladimirovich,' replied Sheremetev drily.

Vera laughed.

'I won't be late, Verochka.'

'With you, it would never be too late,' she said suggestively. She paused, letting the *double entendre* sink in, then laughed.

There was no bus on the road that led to the dacha. Sometimes Eleyekov or his son, if they were heading to town, gave Sheremetev a lift. Otherwise it was possible to call for a taxi. On pleasant days, he sometimes walked the two kilometres to the main road and waited there for the bus that ran to Odintsovo.

This time, Artur took him. He was driving a dark blue BMW with darkened windows and a smell of fresh leather. Artur took a look at Sheremetev's face as he got in and said: 'That was really a nasty cut. Is it healing alright?'

'I think so.'

'Does it hurt?'

'Not hurt, really. It's tight, for instance, if I smile.'

'Then you mustn't smile, Nikolai Ilyich,' said Artur.

Sheremetev did just that.

'How is Vladimir Vladimirovich?'

'He's well, thank you.'

Artur nodded. He started the car and they set off down the drive to the dacha gate. As they turned onto the road, Artur said that he had heard about Sheremetev's nephew and hoped the situation would soon be resolved. Sheremetev thanked him. He glanced at Artur as the younger man drove. It was odd, he thought, to find someone so well mannered in security.

'If you don't mind me asking,' he said, 'how did you end up working in the job you're doing?'

'It was never my intention, Nikolai Ilyich,' replied Artur. 'I was studying electrical engineering at a technical college in Moscow and to earn some money I used to do shifts down here for a security firm my cousin owned. It was very simple – Saturday, Sunday, I would do a shift, then back to the institute for the week.'

'What about your studies?' asked Sheremetev. 'Did you finish them?'

Artur shook his head. 'Unfortunately, my cousin had an accident.'

'A car accident?'

'Something like that.'

'I'm sorry to hear it.'

'What can you do? Suddenly, there was no one to lead the firm. I already knew something about the business so I had to take over. Then we got the contract to provide security for Vladimir Vladimirovich, and of course I couldn't say no. It's not about the contract, Nikolia Ilyich – it's a privilege to do this work. One couldn't refuse.'

'Yes, I felt the same when I was asked to take responsibility for his care.'

'Exactly. I do regret having to give up my studies. I hope one day I can go back and finish my degree.'

'My nephew Pasha is at university as well.'

'Well, let's hope he can get back to his studies soon.'

Artur dropped him at the station. From there, Sheremetev caught the commuter train to Belorusskaya station in Moscow and then went down to the connected metro station, with its coffered plaster ceiling and black and grey marble floor. He got off the metro at Dmitrovksaya, near where his brother lived in a Soviet era apartment block. The walk to the apartment took him fifteen minutes. On the way, Sheremetev stopped and bought a box of chocolates.

When he arrived, Oleg and Nina stared at his lacerated cheek. Sheremetev told them it was nothing, just an accident, and came inside. Over a glass of tea and a dish of vatrushkas, they reported that Pasha was okay, but they looked worried and unsure. Nina had been to see him once since the time Oleg had seen Pasha's black eye – each visit in addition to the one officially allowed per month cost a hundred dollars in bribes – and said that Pasha was still in good spirits. She wiped away a tear. 'They say they treat them alright as long as they think the family might pay up – after that, they treat them worse than everyone.'

Sheremetev was silent. The guilt that he felt over Pasha was doubled in Nina's presence. He saw her glancing at Oleg, who sipped at his tea.

'I don't have the money,' said Sheremetev. 'Nina, I'll tell you what I've got. Two hundred and twenty-three thousand rubles. You can have every kopeck.'

'And Vasya?' said Nina. 'He's the businessman. I don't believe he has nothing.'

'I've asked him.'

She shook her head, her nose wrinkling in distaste.

'Nina, I called him the day Oleg came—'

'It's him who should be in there, Kolya! Not Pasha. It's because of Karinka that Pasha's like this. And who's Karinka's son? *Who?* Not Pasha!'

Sheremetev bowed his head. After what Oleg had said when they met, he had expected something like this. It wasn't quite fair. After all, he couldn't be responsible for the way a person reacted to a tragedy, and he could hardly be blamed if Pasha had gone one way and Vasya another. Still, as a nurse he knew that allowances must be made for someone who is naturally worried sick about a person they love. Nina must have been beside herself. In the current circumstances, she was entitled to say a few things she might regret later.

'Kolya,' said Oleg quietly, 'do you really not know anybody? A word from the right person – and Pasha's out.'

'You mean from Vladimir Vladimirovich?'

Oleg shrugged.

'Olik, you've see him. Nina, did Olik tell you what he's like? He doesn't remember anything you tell him. He lives in the past.'

'Still,' said Oleg, 'if Vladimir Vladimirovich said the right word...'

'Olik, for a start...' Sheremetev stopped, trying not to get impatient. 'Listen, I want to help. I'll do anything for Pasha, but believe me, I could tell Vladimir Vladimirovich this minute to say that Pavel Olegovich Sheremetev should be released, and in thirty seconds from now he would have no recollection, not of the name nor or what he was meant to do about it. Nothing. That's how senility works – he remember things from the past, things you wouldn't imagine anyone could remember, but he retains nothing of the present. I've looked after him for six years, and he no longer knows who I am. Can you imagine? I shower him, I dress him, I feed him, I put him to bed and every day – five times a day, ten times a day – he asks me who I am.'

'Get him to write something,' said Oleg. 'Write something for him saying Pasha should be released and he can sign it.'

Sheremetev considered the idea for a moment. 'I could write something for him and possibly get him to sign it – you can never be sure what he'll do – but then who would I give it to? No one listens to him. No one's coming to him for his advice. Anyone who knows him would know that such a thing means nothing.'

'The president was there only a fortnight ago,' said Nina.

'Did you hear what he said?'

'I saw pictures.'

'I was there, Ninochka. Let me tell you what was going on. Vladimir Vladimirovich thought Lebedev was his minister of finance, and you know what he was doing? He was firing him! Banging his fist on the chair, saying, you're no good, the Ministry of Finance is a disgrace, out you go!'

'I didn't see him banging his fist.'

'Well, I suppose they didn't show it. Lebedev, let me tell you, used a few choice words in return. All the time he was smiling, but you should have heard what he was saying, real bar room stuff. Let's just say I wouldn't repeat it in front of present company.'

'What about someone else?' said Oleg. 'One of the people who comes to visit him. Maybe they'd do you a favour.'

'No one comes.'

Nina looked at him sceptically.

'Ninochka, I'm telling you, none of his friends come.'

'What about his family?'

'The second wife... The last time I saw her I think was six months ago. She stayed for twenty minutes. And the daughters... Two or three times in the last couple of years. And even if one of them came tomorrow, and even if they agreed to help, if they pick up the phone and said to someone, I want you to release Pavel Sheremetev, is it going to make a difference? After what I saw the day Lebedev came to visit, it might be even worse for Pasha if someone close to Vladimir Vladimirovich makes an appeal on his behalf.' Sheremetev paused. 'Ninochka, how can I help? Tell me! I'll do anything. Maybe you don't believe what I'm telling you, but truly, Vladimir Vladimirovich is alone. There's no family, no friends. No one.'

'What about his money?'

'I don't know about that. I get my salary, that's all I know. Turns out, people are embezzling hand over fist, the housekeeper—'

'You didn't tell me about that,' said Oleg.

'I only found out. It's shocking. The cook, the driver, the maids, even the gardeners, everyone who can get anything. Only the security men haven't got some kind of racket. The rest of them, they're like rats in a corn barrel, trying to get as much as they can for themselves. Now there's a terrible fight between—'

'But not you,' broke in Nina. 'Oh, no. Not Nikolai Ilyich Sheremetev.'

'What?'

'You're not trying to get anything, right? Of course not. Not brother Kolya.'

'Nina...' said Oleg, and he put a hand on her wrist, but she pushed it angrily away.

Sheremetev shrugged. 'Maybe that's my failing.'

'Oh, so righteous!'

'Nina!'

'What, Oleg? The only man in Russia who's never taken a commission, and he happens to be your brother. Tell me, is that something to be proud of?'

'I don't mean to say I'm proud of it,' said Sheremetev. 'I'm not a businessman. I wouldn't even know how to start.'

'How hard is it to know how to steal?'

Sheremetev bit his tongue, telling himself again that he had to make allowances for Nina's distress.

'No, not you. Not brother Kolya. Such a man of principle. A man who'd prefer to let his brother do the dirty work for him.'

'Nina!'

'A man who'd let his wife die before—'

'*Nina!*'

Nina stopped.

'Before what?' said Sheremetev. 'What are you talking about? Let my wife die before what?'

Nina and Oleg exchanged a glance. 'Nothing,' muttered Nina.

There was silence. It persisted, heavy, tense.

'Come on,' said Oleg. 'Let's have lunch.'

Nina produced cold cuts, cheese and bread. Oleg opened a bottle of wine.

No one had anything to say.

'Do you see Vasya much?' asked Oleg eventually.

'Not much,' said Sheremetev.

There was silence again. Only the sound of sipping and chewing, but little enough of that. No one seemed to have much of an appetite.

'How can you bear to look after him?' demanded Nina suddenly.

Sheremetev frowned at the question. 'Vladimir Vladimirovich? He's an old man, Nina.'

'Don't you ever stop to think about what he did to this country?'

'I've looked after him for six years. You've never said anything before.'

'I'm saying it now! Pasha did – why shouldn't I? Look at what he did to us! Look at what we are!'

The truth was, Sheremetev had begun to think about that since Pasha was thrown into jail, and the conversation with Goroviev the previous day had made the questions in his mind even more acute. But he knew that was a dangerous path to go down for someone in his profession, and he tried to stop himself. 'I'm a nurse, Nina, and he's an old, demented man who needs care. That's all I've ever thought about. All my life I've looked after people who need help, and I've never asked what they've done or haven't done in their lives. Vladimir Vladimirovich is no different.'

'If it wasn't for him, Pasha wouldn't be in jail.'

'He wasn't the one who had Pasha arrested.'

'Are you defending him?'

'I'm sure Kolya's not defending him,' said Oleg.

'Then let him say what he thinks! Well, Kolya? Are you defending him?'

Sheremetev thought of Goroviev. The gardener's attitude puzzled him. It seemed that he still blamed the ex-president, still hated him, and yet his hatred was directed to someone – or something – that no longer existed, and the physical shell of the man who had been Vladimir Vladimirovich, president of Russia, that part of him that still did exist, was no longer worth hating.

'I'm not defending or accusing him,' said Sheremetev eventually. 'I'm a nurse, Nina, not a politician.'

'And you're a man! You're an uncle!'

'Look, Nina, whatever you think of what he did to Russia, he's not the same man.'

'He's *always* the same man, Kolya. Anything else is an excuse!'

Sheremetev shook his head. 'No. He's old and sick and confused. Doesn't he deserve the care that anyone else would have?'

'I don't know what he deserves! It's a judge who should decide that, and I'm not a judge. But even if he does deserve the same care as anyone else, *you* don't have to be the one giving it to him.'

'I don't discriminate between those who deserve more or less. I give as one needs. That's my duty.'

'So righteous!' sneered Nina. 'What was your duty to your wife, Kolya? Can you tell me that? Did you give as one needed when it came to Karinka? Did you do everything you—'

'Nina, *please!*' cried Oleg despairingly. 'Please stop! How does this help? It has nothing to do with Karinka.'

'No? Kolya should think about what he's doing when he looks after that monster!'

Oleg took a deep breath. 'Nina, will it help Pasha if Kolya stops looking after Vladimir Vladimirovich?'

'He should at least think about it!'

'It's not up to us to tell Kolya what to think.'

'Maybe I should go,' said Sheremetev.

Oleg shook his head.

Nina folded her arms and remained pointedly silent, not asking him to stay.

Sheremetev left soon after. Oleg walked with him to the metro. They stopped at the entrance. For a moment they just looked at each other.

'I'm sorry I haven't got any money,' said Sheremetev. 'All around me, all my life, people have been taking.' He shrugged despondently. 'I never did.'

'Nina had no right to say the things she said, especially about Karinka. We both know the kind of man you are. We know you have your principles.'

'Are you any different? I didn't take from people who wanted to bribe me to favour their relatives. I tried to give care to everyone according to their need. What's so special about that? What kind of a country do we live in if that's so remarkable? Come on, Olik! Would you take from people who want to cheat to get a better grade for their child? If a pupil came to you with a bribe and asked you to bump up his score, would you do it? I mean even a big bribe, a lot of money? Of course not!'

Oleg looked at his feet.

'Olik?'

Oleg was silent a moment longer. Suddenly he looked up at his brother. 'Would I do it if my sister-in-law was dying and that was the only way I could get the money for her? Would I do it when she was gone and I was in debt because of everything I had given for her?'

Sheremetev stared at him. 'Olik . . .' he murmured in disbelief.

'What?'

'You took money . . .'

'Yes! Yes, I took money! I took money!' He shook his head miserably. 'Do you think I'm proud of it? What a mess! What a fucking mess this whole country is in.' Oleg paused again and took a deep breath, unable to look his brother in the eye. 'Look, I'm sorry Nina said those things, anyway.'

'I won't hold it against her,' murmured Sheremetev, still stunned at what he had just learned.

People came and went around the two brothers standing at the entrance to the metro station.

'So what's going to happen?' asked Sheremetev eventually.

'I don't know. I don't see a way out of this.' Suddenly Oleg put his face in his hands. 'They might put him away for years.'

Sheremetev didn't know what to say. He put his arms around his brother. Oleg buried his face against his shoulder.

For a moment they stood together like a rock balanced precariously against the tide, against the shameless, grasping bureaucracy of Russia, in danger of being knocked over and submerged.

Sheremetev straightened up. 'We'll solve this, Oleg.'

Oleg nodded, but not with any show of belief. He took a deep breath and stepped back, wiping at the tears on his cheeks. Then he turned and walked way.

Sheremetev watched his brother leave, his head bowed, his pace barely more than a shuffle.

BY THE TIME HE got back, Vera, the stand-in nurse, had heard about Pasha from someone in the house. Sheremetev shrugged helplessly when she asked if they would be able to get him out.

'You look upset about it, Kolya,' she said.

'Well, it's upsetting.'

She gave him a meaningful look. 'Can I do anything to help?'

Sheremetev shook his head.

'Really?'

'Vera...'

'If only you'd let me in, Kolya!' She gazed at him imploringly. 'I really wish you would. You're such a good man. You need someone. How long is it since your wife died? Six years?'

He didn't reply.

Vera smiled wistfully, then sighed. 'I'll see you next week, but if you need anything, Kolya, call me, huh?'

'Thank you.'

'I mean it. Please.'

He watched her go down the stairs. At the bottom, she turned and waved to him. The guard in the lobby saw the gesture, looked up at Sheremetev, and winked lewdly.

Sheremetev helped Vladimir with his dinner and later put him to bed. For his own dinner, Stepanin proudly presented him with a dish of chicken fricassee, made from chickens that his own supplier had delivered. Barkovskaya had refused to eat it, he announced, grinning broadly.

'She knows when she's beaten!' he crowed.

'What did you do?'

'I made her see sense, that's all.'

'How?'

Stepanin grinned again and tapped the side of his nose. 'Don't worry about that, Nikolai Ilyich.'

Sheremetev didn't. He had too many other things on his mind. He went to bed. From Vladimir's room, through the baby monitor, came the stirrings and snorings and murmurings that went on all night. Sheremetev thought about the things Nina had said to him that day. He knew that Oleg didn't blame him for what had happened to Pasha. He might have wished that things were otherwise – that Pasha had grown up differently, or that Sheremetev had the money or knew someone who could get him out – but he didn't blame him for any of this. Nina, on the other hand... when the initial pain and shock, and the desire to find someone to blame, blew over, he couldn't tell how much of her anger would be left.

Karinka had always believed that Nina was jealous of them. She said that Oleg idolised him, and Nina saw that and was resentful. Sheremetev, for his part, had never considered that Oleg idolised him, or anything like it, knowing there was so little to idolise. Karinka used to laugh at him. You can't see what's in front of your nose, Kolya, she would say.

Karinka...

Nina's words had sliced through him like a knife. Had he let her die? His own wife?

Karinka had developed kidney disease when she was only forty-four. After a couple of years, her kidneys had stopped working and she needed dialysis. That was when the doctors really started asking for bribes. A thousand dollars to go on the clinic list, for a start. A hundred dollars for each treatment. Not for them, of course – oh, no, of course not – but to help pay for the equipment and consumables, which anyway were supposed to be free for the patient. First, Sheremetev used his and Karinka's savings. Then he sold all but the most necessary of their household possessions and furniture. Then he was forced to ask Oleg for help. Getting Karinka on the list for a kidney transplant was out of the question, that would have cost thousands. Oleg's money ran out. The dialysis wasn't stopped completely, but it was fitful. Instead of three or four times a week, it was once or twice. Karinka would become bloated by the time each treatment came around, her blood pressure soaring. Then Oleg would somehow produce more money and for a few weeks the treatments would be more frequent.

This went on for another couple of years. And then Karinka died, suddenly, one day, from a heart attack.

And had he really never asked himself where Oleg's windfalls were coming from? Was it only today that he had found out? *Really?*

And why had he never said, okay, if this is how it is, I'll take bribes too? Take from others, as he was being forced to give? How was it possible, he thought, that he hadn't done that? Even *thought* about it?

Perhaps he hadn't thought that Karinka would die. But eventually, what is going to happen to a person who needs dialysis three times a week and gets it once?

Nina's words lacerated him again. *'What was your duty to your wife, Kolya? Can you tell me that?'* The question left him flailing and bereft. There was no way to address it and reconcile the answer with what he had done – or failed to do.

Eventually Sheremetev fell into a fitful sleep. A couple of hours later he awoke and immediately felt that something was wrong. He lay for a couple of minutes, trying to put his finger on it. Then he knew. The baby monitor was silent. None of the usual rustlings and rumblings.

He checked it. The volume was turned up to its usual level. He put the speaker to his ear. Only the faintest, staticky hiss of the machine itself. Otherwise – nothing.

For another couple of minutes he lay in bed, the monitor pressed to an ear. A thought struck him: what if Vladimir had died?

He considered that for a moment. Would it be so terrible? What kind of a life did he have? And whatever he had now, it was only going to get worse. It would be a blessing if he had slipped away peacefully in his sleep.

He got up and went to Vladimir's suite.

The door to the bedroom was ajar and the light was on. Sheremetev peeked in. The bed was empty. Sheremetev shivered. Vladimir was probably engaged in a battle with the Chechen, hiding somewhere, keeping still, waiting to pounce.

'Vladimir Vladimirovich?' he called quietly.

No response.

Cautiously, Sheremetev went into the bedroom, bracing himself for Vladimir to spring up from somewhere and come hurtling towards him.

Nothing.

Crossing to the bathroom, Sheremetev turned on the light and quickly drew back. Then he peered around the doorway. Nobody there. He turned and went to the dressing room.

'Vladimir Vladimirovich?' he called, loudly this time.

He went to the sitting room. Empty as well. 'No...' he said to himself. He should have locked the door as Professor Kalin had said.

He ran to the closest phone and called down to the security guard in the lobby. The phone rang and rang. Eventually a sleepy voice said: 'Yes?'

'Have you seen Vladimir Vladimirovich?' demanded Sheremetev.

'Vladimir Vladimirovich?'

'Have you seen him?'

'No. Isn't he—'

'He's gone. Stay at your post in case he's on the way out. Get people to look outside. Quick! I'll check upstairs.'

Still in his pyjamas, Sheremetev ran along the corridor, throwing open door after door onto cold, dark, empty rooms, turning on lights and calling Vladimir's name into suites that had not been used in years. Where had he gone? He must be fighting the Chechen, but where had the fight taken him?

Sheremetev ran down the stairs and found the security guard in the lobby.

'Did you see Vladimir Vladimirovich come through?'

'No.'

'What about before I called you?'

The guard shook his head.

'Were you asleep?'

The guard quickly shook his head again.

Sheremetev didn't believe him. 'Have you told people to look outside?'

'Yes.'

'Who?'

'The whole security detail.'

'How many is that?'

'Everybody, Nikolai Ilyich.'

'*How many?*'

'Two,' murmured the guard sheepishly, gazing at his feet.

'Is that including you?'

The guard bit his lip. 'Me and Gorya.'

'Where's everybody else?' demanded Sheremetev indignantly.

The guard shrugged.

'What about Artur? Is Artur here?'

'Artur's . . . I don't know where exactly.'

'And Lyosha?'

'Lyosha . . . also . . .'

Barkovskaya came out of the corridor that led to the staff quarters, wearing a dressing gown and slippers. 'What's going on?' she demanded.

'Vladimir Vladimirovich has disappeared,' said Sheremetev.

She put her hand to her mouth. 'Mother of God! Has someone taken him?'

It hadn't occurred to Sheremetev that Vladimir might have been kidnapped.

'Shall we call the police?'

Sheremetev reacted strongly against the idea. 'He's probably wandered, Galina Ivanovna. Let's see if we find him. I've been through the upper floor. We've got the security detail – I mean, what there is of it – looking outside. Can you check down here? And get some of the others to go outside. Eleyekov, Stepanin . . .' Sheremetev paused at the look of distaste that crossed the housekeeper's face. 'Anyone you can rouse.'

'What about you?' said the housekeeper.

'I'm going out as well!'

Sheremetev ran back upstairs, threw on a coat, slipped his feet into a pair of boots, and ran down again.

'Here, Nikolai Ilyich!' called the guard at the door, holding out a torch to him.

Sheremetev grabbed it. 'Get one for yourself and follow me!' He ran out, the security guard close behind. In the direction of the main drive, he saw the light of a torch poking into the darkness.

'That'll be Gorya,' said the guard behind him.

'Then let's go that way.' Sheremetev ran around to the other side of the house. Immediately he sniffed the charnel pit. He had a horrible thought. 'Check in there,' he called out to the guard.

'In *there?*'

'In case he's fallen in. I'll go that way.'

The gigantic grotesque sausages of the greenhouses loomed at him out of the darkness. Sheremetev ran into the nearest one. Warm, humid air hit him. The beam of his torch pried into lines of plants stretching off into the shadows, ripe aubergines hanging plump and black in the darkness.

'Vladimir Vladimirovich?' He ran along the lines of plants, leaves brushing at his arms, calling out his name. At the end of the greenhouse he ran out the door and headed for the next one.

Sheremetev stopped. There was a glow in the darkness, some distance away on his right. A lantern was on the ground, and two figures sat on a bench, lit from below, as in a picture out of a children's storybook.

Sheremetev went closer, still breathing heavily from his run.

Goroviev, the gardener, was on the bench. And beside him sat Vladimir in his pyjamas, a coat thrown over his shoulders.

'Nikolai Ilyich!' called out the gardener.

'Vladimir Vladimirovich,' said Sheremetev when he reached them. 'Are you alright?'

'He's fine,' said Goroviev.

Sheremetev peered at the gardener suspiciously. 'What are you doing here with him?'

'I found him sitting on this bench.'

'When?'

'Just now. I was trying to get him to come back, wasn't I, Vladimir Vladimirovich? Come on, Vladimir Vladimirovich. It's too cold for you to be out like this.'

'What were you doing here?' asked Sheremetev.

'I couldn't sleep. I thought I'd go and do a bit of work with the tomatoes.'

Sheremetev gazed at him disbelievingly.

Goroviev smiled. 'I'm often up at night. Ask the security guys. They've seen me many times.'

'Is that your coat he's wearing?'

Goroviev nodded.

Sheremetev made to take his own coat off with the intention of replacing the gardener's.

'It's okay,' said Goroviev. 'Leave it with the guard in the hall. I'll pick it up in the morning.'

'But you'll be cold.'

'No. I think I'll go back to the lodge now. The tomatoes can wait until morning.' The gardener got up. 'Goodnight, Vladimir Vladimirovich.'

Vladimir looked at him. 'Goodnight.'

The gardener picked up his lantern. 'Goodnight, Nikolai Ilyich,' he said, and walked away.

Sheremetev watched him go, dumbfounded. Was it really possible that the gardener had just happened to find Vladimir sitting here, in this place, on the exact same bench where they had all sat the previous day? That the two of them should by chance converge here at three in the morning? But otherwise, what? How else had it happened?

The gardener, who had confessed that there was a time when he would have strangled the ex-president, could have done anything he wanted to him in the time that they were sitting there. Vladimir was entirely at his mercy.

'Are you alright, Vladimir Vladimirovich?'

Vladimir nodded.

'Do you know where you are?'

'Praskoveevka.'

'And what are you doing, Vladimir Vladimirovich?'

'What am I doing?'

Sheremetev nodded.

'What are *you* doing?'

'Did that man who was here . . . did he do anything?'

'Who was here?'

'A gardener. Goroviev.'

Vladimir frowned. 'You mean Boroviev, that bastard?'

'No, Goroviev. Arkady Maksimovich.'

'He changed his name?'

'No.'

'He ran away to London, the coward. If we could have got him back here, the place I would have put him would have made the gulag look like a holiday camp!'

'Let's go back, Vladimir Vladimirovich. It's too cold to be sitting here.'

'Do you think so? Who are you, anyway?'

'Sheremetev.'

'Oh. I thought you were talking about Boroviev. Do you know Boroviev?'

'No.'

'Boy-fucking bastard. Traitor! Pig!'

Sheremetev sighed. 'Come, Vladimir Vladimirovich.'

'Still, he didn't last long, did he? People have a habit of dying in London if they're not careful.' Vladimir laughed. 'It's that English tea they're always drinking. There's more than one way to make it hot!'

'Please, Vladimir Vladimirovich,' said Sheremetev, who had no idea what Vladimir found so funny in what he had just said. He pulled gently at his arm. 'It's cold. You'll get ill. Please stand up.'

Vladimir stood. Sheremetev took one last look around the bench, shining his torch on it, then they started walking back.

Barkovskaya was waiting in the hall. 'Thank God,' she whispered, fingering a crucifix at her neck, as the ex-president appeared.

'It's okay,' said Sheremetev. 'Everything's okay.'

'Are you sure?' Barkovskaya peered anxiously at Vladimir.

'I'm taking him upstairs. Please let the others know that he's safe, Galina Ivanovna.'

He guided Vladimir up the stairs and into the bedroom. Now Sheremetev took a good look at the ex-president. His pyjamas were wet and muddy, but otherwise he looked unharmed. Sheremetev took a new pair of pyjamas from the dressing room and helped Vladimir into them. Vladimir cooperated, as docile as a lamb. Sheremetev took him to the toilet, then brought him back to the bed.

The old man looked at him and smiled.

'Are you tired, Vladimir Vladimirovich?'

Vladimir nodded.

Sheremetev went to the bathroom, unlocked the cabinet in which he kept Vladimir's tablets, and came back with a sedative. After what had happened, he thought, it wouldn't hurt for Vladimir to have an extra one. He took a glass of water off the bedside table and gave it to him. 'Here,' he said, turning over Vladimir's other hand and pressing the pill into his palm. 'Take this.'

Vladimir put it in his mouth and swallowed a couple of mouthfuls of water. His Adam's apple worked up and down noisily in his throat.

Sheremetev took back the glass and set it down. He helped Vladimir into bed and turned off the light, leaving only the night light glowing.

'Goodnight, Vladimir Vladimirovich.'

There was no response.

At the door, Sheremetev stopped and looked back at the old man lying in the bed. Vladimir's eyes were already closed. In another moment, a light, rasping snoring began.

Sheremetev rested his head against the door jamb. What was it that Nina had said? How hard was it to know how to steal?

He knew how to steal, thought Sheremetev, watching Vladimir sleeping peacefully. If even half the things people said were true – or a quarter, or a tenth – he had been the biggest crook in Russia, the king of bribe-takers and embezzlers. What would he do if *his* nephew was in prison? He wouldn't hesitate.

Only he, Sheremetev, would. Only Saint Nikolai, as his colleagues had derisively called him.

Sheremetev closed his eyes. He remembered Stepanin laughing, saying that Sheremetev had drawn the short straw because the old man had nothing that was worth taking, nothing but old clothes. But Stepanin didn't know what else was up here.

There were a couple of empty niches in the watch cabinet that stood in Vladimir's dressing room. Occasionally Sheremetev had come across a watch somewhere – down the back of a sofa, in a sock drawer – which Vladimir must have taken at some point and forgot where he left it. Was that why the niches were empty? Or had they never been filled? Or were they the evidence of earlier thefts? In six years, Sheremetev had never seen anyone check the contents of the cabinet. But surely there must be an inventory of these watches? But if there was, surely he would have seen someone check from time to time – or at least once in his time with the ex-president – to see that everything was still there.

Yet he was afraid that there was, and that if he did what he was thinking of doing, someone would find out.

So was that all that had ever stopped him? Fear? The fear that someone would catch him if he did something wrong as a conscript, the fear that someone would discipline him if he took a bribe as a nurse – even though all the time he knew that everyone else was doing it? Not only fear, but cowardice. Extreme, snivelling cowardice. Everyone always thought it was principle, and in the very sharpness of their mockery of him, he knew, there was a certain grudging acknowledgement of his supposed integrity. Funnily enough, the mockery had sometimes made his resolve to stick to his principles even stronger. But how much principle had he really ever had?

There was some, surely. He hadn't been able to let the poor patients languish just because the rich ones had money, and that wasn't only because of fear. But was that principle or softness? Well, there was no room for softness in Russia, and if it was principle, there was even less room for that. Wasn't that what all of this was showing him?

He was a fraud. Cowardice dressed up as virtue – making his brother commit the offence for him. He wondered if Oleg still did such things today. And why not? Why shouldn't Oleg do it when the whole of Russia was doing it as well? Why be like his idiot older brother?

And he – Sheremetev – what if he had never been afraid? What would he have done then? Would he still have stuck to his so-called principles?

Was he going to continue to be afraid? Now? Always?

Quietly, Sheremetev went to the dressing room. A soft glow came in from the night light next door. Sheremetev peeked back into the bedroom for a moment to check that Vladimir still slept.

He turned. In front of him stood the cabinet. He opened its doors.

Sheremetev counted the trays. Twenty-five, each one resting neatly in its slot.

Twenty-five!

What about his duty to his wife? Nina had flung that at him, and it had cut him to the bone. Had he been too proud, too self-righteous to sacrifice his so-called principles? Even for Karinka?

But Karinka was gone now, and nothing could bring her back, and what he had done he had done – and what he hadn't done he hadn't done – and somehow he would have to live with that. But Pasha could still be saved.

In front of the cabinet, with its tray above tray of watch beside watch, Nikolai Sheremetev asked himself: what about his principles now, and what about his duty to his nephew?

12

Sheremetev didn't get much sleep that night. It was almost a relief when he heard Vladimir stirring and had a reason to get out of bed and stop thinking about the questions that had kept him awake. He knew what he was going to do. It wasn't exactly a decision to do it, more a resignation to the fact that it had to be done. He didn't know whether it was wrong or right – both, probably – and he didn't know how to balance one side against the other, and so he gave up trying. Pasha was in jail. That was enough.

After getting Vladimir showered and dressed, Sheremetev went outside and called his brother.

'Oleg,' he said, 'I've had an idea.' Sheremetev looked around to make sure there was no one nearby who could hear him. Even so, he lowered his voice. 'I have something. Something that . . . maybe I could sell.'

'What?' said Oleg.

'Like I told you, I've never got any money out of caring for Vladimir Vladimirovich, just my salary. I know Nina thinks I'm a fool—'

'Kolya, listen, she shouldn't have said those things. I want to apologise—'

'Wait. Let me finish. In the early days, when he still had most of his faculties, there were times when Vladimir Vladimirovich did want to show his appreciation. I told him it wasn't necessary, and I didn't feel comfortable, but he insisted, and he was a hard man to refuse.'

'Naturally. He was the president.'

'I wouldn't accept such a thing now, of course, because he really doesn't know what he's doing. But back then, you know, the forgetfulness was much less, and when he said he wanted to do something, he really did know what he wanted. I mean, I think it was ethical to accept, you understand.'

'Anything you did, Kolya, I'm sure it was ethical.'

Sheremetev hesitated. He had worried that he wouldn't be able to lie, that Oleg would discern something in his voice, but actually, the story he had made up was sounding remarkably believable, even to his own ears, and surprisingly, almost disturbingly, easy to tell.

'When you came to me, and yesterday, again, when you asked if there was any way I could help, any way at all ... well, naturally, I thought of what I had in the bank. But last night, I realised, maybe there's something that has some value, maybe I could sell it. So anyway, the thing is ...' Sheremetev paused again, knowing that if he kept going he was about to cross a dividing line, and even if he did nothing further, even if Oleg turned down his offer, he would never be able to go back, at least in his mind.

'What is it, Kolya?'

Sheremetev took a deep breath, then blurted it out. 'He gave me a watch.'

'A watch?' said Oleg. 'What kind of watch?'

'Some ... watch. I don't know exactly. But it's a nice looking watch and Vladimir Vladimirovich's doctor happened to be here the other day and he had a watch on his wrist and he said this watch cost him seven thousand dollars – the watch he was wearing, I mean, not the one I have – and there are others that are even more expensive.

For example, he said that the one that Vladimir Vladimirovich was wearing at the time was worth much more. A lifetime's wages for a working man, Olik! And knowing Vladimir Vladimirovich, when he gave me the watch that I have, it was a year after I started working for him – it was to mark the year, I think – and he was genuinely showing gratitude, so I don't think he would have given me something that isn't worth anything. Who knows how much it's worth? Maybe he gave me one that's really worth a lot.'

There was silence.

'Oleg?' said Sheremetev.

'You'd sell it for Pasha?'

'Of course I'd sell it for Pasha! It's a watch, Oleg. Who cares? I don't even wear it. The old watch I bought when I got my first job is good enough for me. This one just sits in my cupboard. The thing is, it's not going to be three hundred thousand dollars, right? But it might be something. It might be a start. And if the prosecutor realises that we don't have the kind of money he wants, maybe in the end this will be enough. I mean, you said normally ten thousand is enough. Who knows? Before I spoke to the doctor, I had never imagined it, but this watch could be worth that much.'

Again, there was silence on the phone.

'Well, watches can be expensive,' said Oleg. 'But so much?'

'I don't know. I'm saying it's possible.'

'And you're prepared to sell it?'

'Why not?'

'It might mean a lot to you.'

'More than Pasha? Oleg, for God's sake! It's a watch. A watch is a watch. I couldn't care less about it. I care about my nephew. I care about my brother.'

'I'm sorry about the things Nina said yesterday.'

'Well, I even care about her as well.'

Oleg laughed for a moment. 'She said some terrible things. She shouldn't have asked you to compromise your principles.'

Sheremetev sighed. 'I don't know if those principles are right any more. I don't even know if they are principles, if they ever were. Anyway, in Russia, I don't know if one can live by them. Maybe I should have taken the money, all those years when I was working in hospitals. People came in with bundles of notes, Oleg. I said no and off they went to someone else. I didn't even save them anything – they still paid. I could have done it. Maybe I should have.'

Sheremetev listened to himself. The idea of what he was saying revolted him. Thank God, he thought, that he hadn't had to make this choice back then. But he had, hadn't he? He did make a choice, not even thinking as he did it, when Karinka was dying. He had been paying the bribe-takers, but hadn't considered becoming one himself when the money ran out. Not even for Karinka's sake. What had been *wrong* with him?

'Kolya? Kolya! Are you still there?'

'Sorry. Yes, I'm here.'

'What do you want to do?'

'This watch, Olik, where would I go to sell it? Who would give me a good price?'

'You don't know anyone?'

'Do I go around selling watches all day?'

'You want me to help you? You definitely want to sell this thing?'

'Yes! I dont know how much we'll get, but whatever it is, it's yours.'

Oleg laughed. 'Kolya, I don't know what to say!'

'Don't say anything. We're brothers. Can you find me someone to buy the watch?'

'Why don't you to talk to Vasya? I would have thought this would be his kind of thing.'

'I don't want to get Vasya involved.'

'But Kolya—'

'No, not Vasya!' Sheremetev found himself reacting viscerally against the suggestion. 'Can you find me someone?'

'I'll try. If you're prepared to sell, it's the least I can do.'

'Good. Give me a call when you know.'

Sheremetev put his phone away. Suddenly he found that he was shaking. He had done it – and you don't give up fifty years of honesty just like that. But that wasn't the thing that had sent a chill through him. It was his immediate, instinctive reaction to Oleg's suggestion to call Vasya. No, not Vasya! What did it mean, that he felt like that? Sheremetev realised that he didn't trust his own son.

SHEREMETEV STAYED OUTSIDE FOR a few minutes more, delaying the moment of going back inside. Two of Stepanin's potwashers come out, carrying a big black tub between them. They stopped beside the chicken pit, put the tub on the ground, and then raised the wooden lid that covered the hole. Even from a distance, Sheremetev could smell the fetid air that immediately wafted out of it. As he watched, the two potwashers upended the tub and a spillage of fresh pink carcases tumbled in.

He went a little closer. 'What's going on?'

The potwashers were putting the lid back on the pit, each holding it with one hand and their nose with the other. One of them glanced at him and shrugged.

In the kitchen, Stepanin sat glumly at one of his steel benches, a glass of vodka in his hand and the bottle in front of him.

'What happened?' asked Sheremetev. 'You're throwing chickens out again.'

The cook swallowed the vodka and poured another glass without saying a word.

'Vitya?'

'They firebombed my supplier,' muttered Stepanin.

'They *firebombed*...?' Sheremetev was aghast. 'Who firebombed?'

'Barkovskaya.'

'*Barkovskaya* firebombed your supplier? When? Last night? But I saw her here—'

Stepanin turned to him. 'Not Barkovskaya herself! Someone did it for her, obviously.'

'And they told you they were doing it for her?'

'They didn't need to.' Stepanin threw back the vodka and winced at the liquor's ferocity. 'There are some things you don't need to say.' He shook his head. 'What fuckery!'

'Vitya,' said Sheremetev slowly, 'what did you do to make Barkovskaya's cousin stop delivering chickens?'

The cook shrugged.

'Vitya?'

'Let's just say someone taught him a lesson.'

'What kind of lesson?'

'The kind of lesson where you break a leg or two.'

'You broke his legs?' demanded Sheremetev in disbelief.

'Not me personally!'

'You got someone to do it? Are you insane? What were you thinking?'

'What do you mean, what was I thinking? This is my future, Kolya! My dream! Everything depends on it. You understand? And that bitch Barkovskaya isn't going to stop me!' Stepanin picked up the vodka bottle and angrily poured again, sloshing some of the liquor on the steel bench. 'You want some?'

'No.'

Stepanin drank. 'It's simpler to be like you,' he said bitterly. 'Take your salary and that's it. No complications. Of course, you live a miserable life and die in poverty, but that's not so bad, I suppose.'

'Thank you,' said Sheremetev, feeling like bashing the cook over the head with the bottle.

Stepanin raised his glass in a mock tribute to Sheremetev.

Sheremetev snatched the bottle away from him. 'It's nine o'clock and you're already drunk. You're not going to be able to cook.'

Stepanin waved a hand. 'Who gives a fuck?' He glared at the potwashers. 'Clean that fucking stove down, I told you! What are you waiting for? I'm going to start in a minute. And you,' he yelled, turning his ire on one of his assistants, 'where's the stock, you fucking idiot?'

'We used it yesterday, Chef!'

'And you didn't make more? I have to tell you every time? You moron!' Stepanin looked back at Sheremetev. 'See? Look what I have to work with here. A cook of my talents! Classically trained!'

'Who did you get to teach Barkovskaya's cousin a lesson?' asked Sheremetev.

'What?'

'Who did you get to break Barkovskaya's cousin's legs?'

'I don't know if he broke his legs. It might have been his arms.'

'*Who?*'

'Who do you think? Artyusha.'

'*Artyusha?* Our Artyusha? The security guy?'

'Who else?'

'But...but...' Sheremetev stared, utterly lost for words.

Stepanin laughed. 'You really don't know anything, do you, Kolya? Have you seen the BMWs he drives? Every six months he changes it – the latest model! Even if you knew nothing, if you saw that, you'd realise something was going on. The Lukashvillis run the biggest protection racket in Odintsovo. It started with Artur's cousin, who was shot dead in his car a few years ago by another group of gangsters. After that, Artyusha took over. When he was finished with the other gang, no one but the Lukashvillis was left in the town.'

'But he told me he was studying to be an electrical engineer!'

'Maybe he was. Who cares? You want to run a business in Odintsovo, you want to have a restaurant – shit, you want to take your kid for a walk – you pay Lukashvilli. In return, he keeps the cops off your backs.'

'How does he—'

'What do you think all these security guards are doing here, Kolya? Last night, when you needed them to find Vladimir Vladimirovich, how many of them were actually here? And they're only some of his foot soldiers. He has plenty more. Artyusha's got them hired out as bouncers, bodyguards, anything you like. You want security in Odintsovo, you come to Lukashvilli. You should talk to your son – he knows all about it.'

'My son?'

'Yes. What's his name again?'

'Vasya,' whispered Sheremetev.

'Vasya! That's it. Vasya.'

'He works with Artur?' asked Sheremetev in horror.

'No. Artur told me he talked to him one time. Sheremetev's son, he said. Apparently he had to organise some protection for someone, down here in Odintsovo. If you do that, you have to talk to Artur.'

Sheremetev shook his head, fighting a losing battle to comprehend what he was hearing.

Stepanin laughed. 'The ex-presidential dacha! Who would imagine that you would run a protection operation from here? But think about it. Lukashvilli's smart. Blanket surveillance, electrified fences, a legitimate security business in case anyone ever asks why you've got so many thugs on your payroll . . . not that they would. You couldn't ask for more.'

'What else does he do, my son?' whispered Sheremetev.

'How should I know? Ask him yourself, Kolya.' The cook paused – the look on Sheremetev's face was almost pleading. 'Look, from what Artur said, he sounds like he's just one of these guys who helps people.'

'What does that mean?' implored Sheremetev. 'I don't understand.'

Stepanin sighed. 'Say you've got a restaurant. Say you've got a really important person who's coming to dine. This person is obviously going to have enemies. He'll turn up with his bodyguards, of course. Fine. But you don't want trouble. You don't want the bodyguards to actually have to do anything. It won't help your restaurant if something happens, and if the police somehow end up getting involved, you'll never stop having to pay them. So you might decide you want to get some people yourself for the night just to keep away anyone who might have ideas. For that, you might turn to someone who can help you.'

'Help you what? Find some people?'

'Exactly. The sort of people to keep things quiet.'

'And that's what Vasya would do?'

'I'm guessing, Kolya. From what Artyusha said, it sounded like it. They're everywhere, these guys. You want one – you'll find a dozen of them buzzing around, all stabbing each other in the back to get your business, all telling you they can find better people than the others.' The cook grinned. 'Your boy wasn't involved in any of this business with Barkovskaya's cousin, anyway, so don't worry. He's not in that league. That was strictly Artyusha and his boys. Of course, I had to pay, but I got a big discount, on account of the fact that I cook for him. Anything he wants, I'll make him. He told me he had his guys smash up Barkovskaya's cousin's delivery van as well. An extra. I didn't ask him to do it. He said it was on the house. That's very decent, don't you think?'

'Does Barkovskaya know?'

'Do I care? What's she going to do about it? Fight the Lukashvillis?'

'Well, someone firebombed your supplier.'

'Yeah, well, I think ... he owed Artur a bit of money.'

'So *Artur* firebombed him?'

'No, the situation wasn't that bad. I just don't think Artur was protecting him. If he was protecting him, no one would have touched him. Still, Artyusha won't be happy. If anyone gets punished in Odintsovo, it's the Lukashvillis who do it. It's their patch.'

Sheremetev put his head in his hands. 'Vitya, this is out of control! You have to talk to Barkovskaya.'

'And say what? Thank you for taking away my chickens – please tell me what else you would like? In Russia, Kolya, if you show weakness in one thing, you show weakness in all.'

'What's your supplier going to do? Has he gone to the police?'

'Over a firebombing? Are you crazy? Do you know how much he'd have to give them to get them on his side? Once they know there's a feud on, for the cops, it's like Easter and Christmas have come at once. A Dutch auction. Whoever has more money wins. They're experts at driving up the price.'

'I think you drive the price down in a Dutch auction.'

'Well, then, it's the opposite. What is that? A French auction? Hey, you fucker!' he yelled, suddenly noticing one of the potwashers taking apart the gas burners on the stove. 'Only I do that! I've told you before!'

'So what are you going to do, Vitya?'

'Last time, they fucked the burner up so bad I couldn't cook on it for a week.'

'Viktor! What are you going to do?'

Stepanin was silent, then he shrugged. 'I don't know. I can't let this go. In two years, if I can keep going, I'll have enough to open a restaurant in Moscow. Do you know how much that costs? I mean a restaurant like the one I'm thinking of. We're talking half a million dollars, Kolya. I get that, and I'm out of here. I'm over halfway. Tell me, honestly, do you think Vladimir Vladimirovich is going to live another two years? Can you make sure of that for me?'

Sheremetev wondered if he had heard right. Stepanin needed half a million dollars – and he was over halfway! That was enough to get Pasha out. 'You know, my nephew is still in jail.'

'Well, if you do something so stupid, what do you think is going to happen?' remarked Stepanin, apparently too drunk now to get the hint or to feel any embarrassment if he did.

Sheremetev watched the cook, who sat fingering his empty vodka glass in frustration. Suddenly, Stepanin reached for the bottle that Sheremetev had taken from him. Sheremetev let him have it. Drink, he said to himself. Drink yourself to death, you pig.

Everyone in Russia was selfish, thought Sheremetev. Selfish for themselves and, at best, for their family.

He felt weary and demoralised. He had always liked Stepanin, but suddenly he couldn't care less about them. Let the cook and the housekeeper fight themselves to the death in their envy and greed.

It would serve them both right.

Sheremetev stood up.

'Tell Vladimir Vladimirovich there might not be any chicken for a while,' muttered Stepanin. 'I'll try to make it up to him.'

Sheremetev had no interest in maintaining the pretence any longer for the cook's sake. 'Who cares? He doesn't know what you cook him. Between mouthfuls, he forgets.'

Stepanin gazed at Sheremetev with real in pain in his expression. Good, thought Sheremetev.

That afternoon, Stepanin received a note from Barkovskaya telling him that from tomorrow he would be receiving meat from a new supplier, and if his old supplier made a delivery, he would not be paid for it. Stepanin, mincing pork and liver at the moment one of the house attendants delivered the note, tore it up in a rage and threw it in, feeding it back to Barkovskaya that evening in a terrine he made just for her.

For the rest of the household, he prepared a beef stroganoff with rice, letting everyone know it might be the last time they had meat for a while. The attendant carried a tray upstairs for Vladimir and set it out on the table in his sitting room.

Sheremetev was there when the tray arrived. He asked Vladimir if he was ready for dinner. Vladimir shrugged him off. He was too busy to be disturbed. He had just been listening to Dima Kolyakov, the billionaire, who had a plan to build a ring road for Moscow, which, frankly, the city needed like a hole in the head, as everyone knew, but which had certain benefits to recommend it, to himself at least. At a commission of twenty percent out of a cost of billions, it would be hard to say no. And then Kolyakov had to go, because Vladimir's secretly married wife wanted to talk with the businessman about some kind of charity gala for which he and she were joint patrons, and suddenly, Grigory Rastchev was there, the KGB colonel who had commanded Vladimir when he was stationed as an agent in East Germany. After the end of the Soviet Union, Rastchev had become a member of the Russian duma for the born-again communist party and had turned into that rarest of creatures, an ex-KGB officer who wouldn't keep his mouth shut but seemed to want no place at the Kremlin trough. One or the other, alright, but not both. In particular, he had a habit of making unwelcome remarks – many of them in print – about Vladimir's time in the agency, some of which could be indisputably verified. Consequently – and not with any sense of pleasure – Vladimir had had to have him jailed a number of times on various charges, some of which were arguably justified. In the last instance he had been behind bars for three years.

Now Rastchev had asked to see him. Vladimir agreed. He didn't regard himself as a sentimental man, but he thought that after all Rastchev had been through at his hands, as a fellow KGB officer he deserved at least the chance to talk to him.

And why not? Rastchev was broken. Tall, always on the lean side, he was now bald, thin and pale, like a stick of white asparagus. His nose took a leftward angle about halfway down the bridge, which hadn't been a feature of his proboscis the last time Vladimir had seen him, and he doubted it had been put there by a plastic surgeon. Rastchev had obviously served real jail time.

'So?' said Vladimir. 'What can I do for you, Grigory Markovich?'

'I'm finished, Vladimir Vladimirovich,' replied Rastchev. 'I can't take any more. From now on, you don't have to worry about Rastchev.'

Tactfully, Vladimir didn't point out that he had never really worried about Rastchev, only found him an irritant, the more so because Rastchev had never seemed to take a hint and had forced

Vladimir to have him incarcerated, which was the last thing he wanted to do to a man who had mentored him through his early days as a foreign agent.

'Why do you say you're finished?'

'I'm weak...this last spell inside...I couldn't take that again.'

'Did they treat you badly?'

'Don't you know, Vladimir Vladimirovich?' asked Rastchev insinuatingly.

'I only know what I'm told. If anyone mistreated you, give me their names and I'll personally see to it that they answer for any irregularities according to the strictest dictates of the law. You have my word as the president of Russia.'

Rastchev gazed at him, one old Chekist to another, knowing exactly what that pledge was worth.

Vladimir smiled. 'Grisha, what can I tell you? You're on the wrong side of history. You chose to look backwards – I choose to look forward.'

'Is it wrong to want the best for the people?' demanded Rastchev, with a little of the old fire showing in his eyes. 'Is that what you call looking backwards? Is it wrong to renounce corruption, graft, embezzlement, propaganda, lies, deception and outright intimidation?'

'Renounce? Of course – privately renounce what you want. But denounce? No. Besides, what kind of a communist do you call yourself if you renounce those things?'

'A communist like Lenin! Everything that came after him was gimmickry and distortion.'

'That's a lot of distortion,' mused Vladimir. 'Seventy years. And I'm not sure if I'd call the gulags gimmickry.'

Rastchev shrugged dismissively.

'You're an idealist, Grisha. Very unusual in a KGB man. How did that happen?'

'Vova, the breakup of the union was the greatest disaster of the twentieth century.'

'I agree. I've said so many times, and in public, as well. That's why I did what I did in Chechnya. No more separatism! It was the very first thing I did when becoming president. People didn't want another war. A bomb or two in an apartment building – then they did. Magic! After that, I could do what I wanted. They smell, by the way. The Chechens, I mean. Let me warn you. If the head's been lying on the ground for more than a day or two, they stink. Can you smell it now? Try... See? He's always here, the Chechen. Thinks he'll kill me if he can get me with the tongue, but I'm too quick for him. I'm writing a book on judo for heads. What do you think? Good idea?' Vladimir nodded smugly. 'Huh?'

'That was the only good thing you did, Chechnya.'

'The only good thing? What about Georgia?'

'You didn't go far enough. Should have taken them out when you had the chance.'

'What about Crimea? I got that back, didn't I? And eastern Ukraine. And Belarus.'

'Alright, Crimea. Yes. I'll give you that. How that cretin Khrushchev gave it to the Ukrainians I'll never understand. What a pygmy of a man. Lenin would never have done that. And Belarus. Okay. I'll give you that as well. But what about the rest of Ukraine, Vova? All you have to do is turn off the gas and they'll freeze to death.'

'It's complicated.'

'Complicated – bullshit! Is that what Lenin said when he got off the train at the Finland Station? Comrades, we'll try to storm the Winter Palace – but it will be complicated!'

'Fuck Lenin!' said Vladimir irritably. 'Stop talking about him.'

'Fuck Lenin? You don't stand comparison, Vova. He was a giant and you're a cockroach sitting on his throne.'

'Right. Thank you. I'll remember that one. If you repeat it in public, Grisha, you'll be back in the same cell and this time they'll break your nose in the other direction. Now, what do you want from me?'

Rastchev sat forward.

'Vladimir, you and I both saw what happens when the mob is allowed to rule. You remember those days in Germany? We went from everything to nothing...' he clicked his fingers, 'like that. There was no need for it. A few tanks, a few shots, and that would have put an end to it.'

'The will wasn't there.'

'Exactly,' said Rastchev. 'A few tanks—'

'Not tanks. You don't need tanks. There are better ways. Look, the will wasn't there, Grisha, but now it is. You're looking at it. The vertical of power starts with one man. In Russia, it always has. Strength. Stability. Unity. One man, one party, one country.'

'I thought you said I was on the wrong side of history.'

'You are. Strength, stability, unity – but not communism. That was a blind alley. There are better ways. Managed democracy, that's the way you do it. A handpicked opposition, elections, the results are never in doubt. It works beautifully.'

'The rule of thieves.'

Vladimir smiled and wagged a finger. 'You know, if you hadn't kept saying things like that, Grisha, you wouldn't have ended up in prison so much.'

'Did you give the orders? Did you tell them to arrest me?'

Vladimir noticed a piece of fluff on his jacket. He picked it off and dropped it on the floor. 'At a certain point, one doesn't have to give the order, Grisha. People know what you want and they just do it. You see, people think power is when you can tell someone that you want something, and they'll do it for you. No, that's only the first level. *Real* power, Grisha, the top level, is when you don't even have to tell them. They just do it. When that happens, you know that you not only can control what they do, you control their minds.'

Rastchev snorted. 'It's still the rule of thieves.'

'Government of thieves, country of thieves...' Vladimir shrugged. 'Call it what you will. I've never worried about words. The country's stable. People know what to expect. There's order, there's bread. If you don't like it, you can leave – the borders are open. Compare that with the last years of Boris Nikolayevich and don't tell me the people wouldn't prefer it.'

'Like saying you prefer the slower poison to the quicker. Vova, no one had a chance like you. You could have made us pure.'

Vladimir laughed. 'Pure? Is that what you call purity? Listen, your communists, in their seventy years of gimmickry and distortion, as you call it, wasn't it the rule of thieves? The nomenklatura, the apparatchiks, all getting their better clothes and their better food. Wasn't that theft from the people, who got the worst of everything – when they were lucky enough to get anything? But these thieves, not only were they thieves, they were stupid thieves. Idiots! They had this system and it gave them nothing. What was there to steal in this godforsaken economy they created? Tell me. A better coat? A better sausage? Even the best thing we had was worth nothing compared to what an ordinary citizen in West Germany could buy in a supermarket every day of the week. And for that you needed to fill a gulag with ten million slaves? For God's sake, such morons! Sure, rule the country, steal from the people – nothing wrong with that. In every country, those who rule, steal, one way or another. Fine. But first make sure there's something to take!' Vladimir paused for a moment. 'That's what the boys from the agencies, the ones who came with me, understood. They saw what the real thieves, the oligarchs, had got, and they wanted their share. But not by destroying the golden goose, like those idiots Lenin and Stalin and the fools who came after them, but by looking after it. Making it bigger. Using those oligarchs to produce even more golden eggs, and then taking them away. Not all of them, not every one. The trick is to leave the goose with just enough to keep it wanting to make more. That's what we've done, Grisha. That's what you've never understood.'

'You not only let the others take, you took yourself.'

Vladimir shrugged, as if the point was barely worthy of mention.

'You had the chance to be a great leader, to take us back to what could have been when Lenin died, before Stalin came.'

'Grisha, you're giving me a headache. History says: fuck the martyrs! They sacrifice themselves and the world goes on. Those who take, take, and those who don't, don't.'

'And what did you do, Vladimir Vladimirovich?' asked Sheremetev, who had been standing beside him, listening, as he had never listened before.

'I took. Why not? With one hand, I gave Russia order, and with the other I took for myself. It's a fair trade.'

'What did you take?'

Vladimir smiled to himself. 'Everything.'

'And others? Should they take as well?'

'Let them. Let he who can, take.' Vladimir laughed. 'We have all of Russia, Grisha. There's plenty to go round. Support me – and you can have what you want. Why? Because I've given order. When my time as president comes to an end, that will be my legacy. Order, strength, stability, unity. Not the Russia of Boris Nikolayevich, falling apart like a senile old man, but a strong Russia, a Russia that can be proud, a Russia that the United States and the rest of them will fear, not laugh at.'

'This is it, is it?' said Sheremetev.

'This is it. Look around, Grigory Markovich. This is Russia.'

'Your Russia? Your creation?'

'Yes,' said Vladimir smugly. 'My Russia. The Russia I made. No one else could have done it.'

'And you wouldn't change anything?'

'Nothing.'

Sheremetev picked up the knife and fork from Vladimir's dinner tray and slammed them down on the table.

Vladimir jumped.

'Eat!' Sheremetev stepped back. 'There's your food, Vladimir Vladimirovich! Go on! Eat!'

Vladimir looked up at him. His eyes filled with confusion.

Sheremetev turned away and took a deep breath. When he turned back, Vladimir was still gazing at him with the same heart-rending look.

'Okay,' whispered Sheremetev, more to himself than to Vladimir. He sat down and began to fasten a napkin around Vladimir's neck. 'Let's eat.'

'Who are you?' asked Vladimir.

'Sheremetev. I look after you. Pick up your fork, Vladimir Vladimirovich.'

Vladimir made no move, perhaps sensing the uncharacteristic lack of warmth in Sheremetev's voice. Sheremetev took another deep breath, trying to find the strength in himself to want to care for this man.

'Are you hungry, Vladimir Vladimirovich?' he asked.

Vladimir nodded.

'Let's eat, then, shall we? We've got beef stroganoff. You like beef stroganoff, don't you?'

Vladimir nodded again.

Sheremetev closed his eyes for a moment, then opened them again and forced himself to smile. Vladimir smiled back.

'I'm having beef stroganoff!' he said.

'I know,' replied Sheremetev. 'Your fork, Vladimir Vladimirovich. Would you like to pick it up?'

Sheremetev waited a moment, but Vladimir made no move, so he picked it up for him.

Later that night, Sheremetev got a call from Oleg. His brother had the name of someone who bought watches.

13

THE ADDRESS THAT OLEG gave him turned out to be a shop in the centre of Moscow, in an alley near the Arbat. In the window was a dusty display of watches and pieces of jewellery that looked as if they had been there for centuries. Across the glass, in ornate gold letters, was written the name Rostkhenkovsky, and beside the door, which was locked, was a bell.

Sheremetev rang it. He heard a click. Tentatively, he pushed on the door and it swung open. The shop was long and narrow, with jewellery cabinets along either side. As he stepped inside, an inner door opened at the other end of the shop.

He was momentarily taken aback. In such a place, he had expected to find some wrinkled old shopkeeper with bushy nasal hair and sagging trousers. Instead, he found himself confronted by a smart, petite young woman in a cream and grey pinafore dress, with short brown hair cut stylishly to fall across one side of her pixieish face, almost covering an eye.

'Yes?' she said.

Sheremetev coughed nervously. 'I've been told that you buy watches.'

The woman nodded.

Sheremetev waited, expecting her to say that she was going to go and find the resident horologist, but instead she continued to stand facing him on the other side of the counter.

'*You* buy them?'

The woman nodded again.

'So should I...?'

The woman cocked her head. 'If you have a watch you'd like to sell, if I can't see it, I can't tell you if I want to buy it, can I?'

'It's just – you'll excuse me – you look very young.'

'Twenty-eight,' said the woman combatively.

'You look younger.'

'That's meant to be a compliment?'

'No,' said Sheremetev. 'It's just...the truth.'

'Listen, my father died four weeks ago. Now the shop's mine. I worked with him from the day I left school. That's ten years. Even before that, I practically lived in this shop. If you think you know something about watches that I don't, I'd like to know what it is.'

'I'm sorry about your father,' said Sheremetev.

'Thank you. He built this business. Did someone send you here?'

'In a way.'

'In a way? What does that mean? Who sent you?'

'I heard about you.'

'You've got quite a nasty cut there.'

'Where?'

'There, on your face.'

'Oh.' Sheremetev's hand went to his cheek. The bruising had started to come down, but the sutures were still embedded along the line of the laceration.

'If you'll excuse me, you don't look like the kind to get into fights.'

'It was an accident.'

The woman scrutinised him for a moment, as if wondering whether to throw him out. If she was, she decided against it. 'Okay.

Let me explain how it is. Everything we do is legal, in case you're wondering.'

'I didn't mean—'

'Well, it is. So, we buy watches. If it's just an ordinary watch – two, three thousand dollars – we sell it here ourselves. If it's something special, there are other places we take it to. Some are shops, some are dealers who work privately with certain clients. Not every watch should be displayed in a shop window, if you understand what I mean. So anything you've got, believe me, one way or another, we can handle it for you.'

Sheremetev frowned. A watch that cost two or three thousand dollars was just an ordinary watch?

'What's your name?'

Sheremetev hesitated. 'Nikolai Ilyich.'

'Nikolai Ilyich . . . ?' She waited.

'Just Nikolai Ilyich.'

'Okay. Suit yourself. I'm Anna Mikhailovna Rostkhenkovskaya. So, are you going to show me something, Nikolai Ilyich, or have you just come for a chat?'

Sheremetev reached into the inside pocket of his coat and fished out a small bundle wrapped in a handkerchief, trying to keep his hands from trembling. Under the young woman's eyes, he put it down on the down on the counter and drew back the wrapping.

Anna Rostkhenkovskaya had a healthy scepticism when people came in off the street and announced that they wanted to sell her a watch. Half the time, they pulled out a treasured Swatch. But as soon as she saw this one emerging from its wadding, she knew she was dealing with something serious.

'May I?' she asked.

'Please,' said Sheremetev.

She pushed back her hair with a quick flick of her fingers and picked up the watch. Nothing in her expression gave any indication of what she was thinking as she examined the timepiece.

What had come out of the handkerchief, to Rostkhenkovskaya's surprise, was a Rolex Oyster Perpetual Daytona in gold and platinum with a gold strap. What was even more surprising, as she studied it, was what appeared to be a series of sparkling, baguette-cut diamonds in place of the hour markers around the watch face and embedded in each of the watch hands.

Rostkhenkovskaya had seen plenty of Rolex Daytonas, but never one bejewelled like this. She wasn't aware of Rolex ever having produced such a series, which meant that this was a bespoke piece, either produced to order by Rolex itself – presumably at significant expense – or tailored after purchase by an expert watchmaker.

'Just a moment,' she said.

Rostkhenkovskaya opened a drawer and took out a jeweller's loupe. She examined each of the diamonds through the lens. They appeared to be flawless and of exceptional clarity and colour. She took another careful look at the watch itself, which seemed to be in mint condition. She doubted that it had ever been worn.

As she studied the piece, Rostkhenkovskaya ran through the numbers in her head. A standard gold and platinum Daytona that looked as if it had just come out of its box – thirty thousand dollars. With the diamonds: double that for the value of the jewels alone, and possibly double it again for the uniqueness of the piece. With an interesting provenance, you could double it once more.

'This is yours?' she asked, putting the watch down at last.

Sheremetev nodded.

'You bought it?'

'It was a gift.'

'Who from?'

'An uncle.'

'Does he have a receipt, your uncle?'

'He's no longer– he's senile.'

'I'm sorry. And this is a gift, you say?'

Sheremetev nodded.

'A very generous man, your uncle.'

Sheremetev didn't reply.

The young woman was silent for a moment. 'The diamonds are interesting. There wouldn't be many Daytonas like this.' She paused. 'Rolex probably knows exactly who bought each one.'

'Are they diamonds?' asked Sheremetev, missing the young woman's insinuation.

'What did you think they were?'

Sheremetev shrugged.

Rostkhenkovskaya folded her arms. 'Okay, so what are we saying, Nikolai Ilyich? You want to sell this watch, yes?'

'That's why I'm here.'

'Despite the fact that your doting uncle gave it to you?'

'I need the money. If my uncle still had his senses, he'd be the first to tell me to sell it.'

'So not a very sentimental man?'

'Not really.'

'Would I know him?'

'No.'

'You know, it doesn't look like the watch was ever used.'

'He has a lot of watches. People used to give them to him.'

'*Give* them to him? Watches like this one?'

Instinctively, Sheremetev's hand went to his mouth. He had said too much. He had worked out the uncle story on the train in to the city, but who had an uncle who was *given* watches like this?

Rostkhenkovskaya noticed the reaction. She wondered how much of the story she could believe. Maybe the watch was stolen, but the man in front of her was an unlikely thief. Could be a fence, though. But what kind of a fence would turn up like this, with a face that looked as if he had just danced a tango with a chainsaw? Who would ever forget it?

'Okay,' she said eventually. 'The problem, Nikolai Ilyich, is that with a watch like this – such a unique watch – someone might recognise it. To be honest, I've seen plenty of Daytonas, but never one with diamond insets. It's one of a kind.'

'Would that make a difference to what it's worth?' asked Sheremetev.

'At this level, the watch world is quite a small world. Such a unique watch...If someone recognises it, and the way you got it isn't one hundred percent above board...' She shrugged. 'Do you understand?'

Sheremetev frowned.

'So let me ask you again – forgive me – but you have no documentation for this piece, is that correct?'

'My uncle gave it to me.'

'And do you have a certificate of gift?'

'What's that?'

'It's a certificate that says he gave it to you as a gift.'

Sheremetev shook his head.

Rostkhenkovskaya had a dealer in mind who would jump at this watch. But was it stolen? The small man who had walked into the shop with it didn't have the manner of a criminal. It didn't look as if he had done any research on the piece before trying to offload it. If she had to guess, he had no idea what it was worth.

The dealer she was thinking of would sell this on, she estimated, at a minimum of one hundred thousand dollars. If that was what he thought he could get for it, he would pay her around seventy-five thousand for the piece. Her father's rule of thumb was to offer the seller two-thirds of the price he would receive, which in this case would amount to fifty thousand dollars. But if there was a question of the piece being stolen, the calculation changed. If a theft came to light, the insurance company would normally pay something to get it back – twenty percent of the value was the norm. That would make the insurance payment for this watch twenty thousand, perhaps more. Her father's rule had been to offer half the likely insurance payment, which still left a healthy profit if it turned out that the piece was identified as having been stolen, and an even healthier one if no one ever found out. For this watch: ten thousand.

But all of that depended on how much you thought the seller knew.

'Five thousand dollars,' she announced.

'Five thousand?' murmured Sheremetev.

'You have a second-hand, platinum and gold Daytona with some very small baguette-cut diamonds of average quality, Nikolai Ilyich. On the market, at the very best, unless you can prove to me that, I don't know, President Lebedev wore it when he was sworn in, that's worth ten thousand dollars. I give you half of that, so that's five thousand.'

Rostkhenkovskaya waited to see how Sheremetev would react. He gazed glumly at the watch.

'What, Nikolai Ilyich?'

In his dreams, Sheremetev had fantasised that the watch might bring him many multiples of that sum, as Dr Rospov had intimated that the one he had seen on Vladimir's wrist might have done. In his more realistic moments, he had told himself that maybe he would get ten thousand, the price of Pasha's freedom if the prosecutor saw sense. But five thousand... What good was that going to do? Was it worth selling?

'Look,' said Rostkhenkovskaya, 'I'm giving you a fair offer. If we're lucky someone will end up buying this for ten thousand, as I said. But they might not – the price might be lower. I give you five, but I don't keep the other five. I take it to someone else who's going to sell it. I keep maybe a few hundred for myself.'

'I understand.' Sheremetev sighed. 'My nephew's in jail. I'm trying to get him out. If only I could have ten...'

'Nikolai Ilyich, really, what would that leave for me?'

'I understand.' Sheremetev hesitated, then began to wrap the watch in the handkerchief.

'Nikolai Ilyich, stop. Listen. I want to help, okay? Let's see what we can do. Your nephew's in jail. It's a terrible thing, and everyone in Russia is corrupt.' Rostkhenkovskaya paused and shook her head as if in disbelief at her own weakness, as she had watched her father do since she was old enough to remember. 'Seven and a half. Would it help if I made it seven and half thousand?'

Sheremetev frowned, then gave a shrug and nodded. Rostkhenkovskaya smiled.

'Thank you,' he said.

'You're a hard negotiator, Nikolai Ilyich. Seven and a half thousand! I'm not going to make a ruble... but, who cares, if it helps your nephew get out of jail? Not everything's about money, is it?'

'It's a start,' said Sheremetev.

'Good. A start. So do we have deal?'

'I feel bad, if you're not going to make a ruble.'

'It's okay, please! Do we have a deal?'

Sheremetev thought for a moment. 'Okay.'

'I'll go and get the money.'

'Now?'

Rostkhenkovskaya turned on her heel. 'Yes. Now.'

She vanished into the back of the shop. An older woman appeared in the doorway while she was gone and stood, watching. Sheremetev smiled at her. She gazed blankly back at him.

Rostkhenkovskaya came back and the other woman disappeared.

The young woman examined the watch again to make sure, unlikely as it seemed, that this apparently guileless customer hadn't pulled a switch under the eyes of her mother. Then she counted out seven hundred thousand rubles in five thousand ruble notes.

'It's actually seven thousand five hundred and forty dollars,' she said as she handed them over. 'I rounded up.'

'I'll give you change!'

'No, Nikolai Ilyich. Let's not quibble.'

Sheremetev thanked her again. 'It's quite a lot, isn't it?' he said anxiously, gripping the wad.

'Put it in a couple of pockets,' advised Rostkhenkovskaya.

As she watched, Sheremetev proceeded to do so, just like a schoolboy following the advice of his teacher, dividing the money between the two inside pockets of his jacket.

'Do you want a receipt?'

He shook his head.

'Listen ... I'm sorry I couldn't give you all the money you need. If you need more ... Nikolai Ilyich, you said your uncle had a lot of watches. He didn't ... you know, give you any more, did he?'

Sheremetev coughed. 'There might be a couple more.'

'Really? I don't suppose you know what names they might have.

This one's a Rolex. Do you know what the others are called? Are they all Rolex?'

Sheremetev tried to recall the name of the watch the doctor had seen on Vladimir's wrist. 'There's Hablet or Hoblet...'

'Hublot?'

'That's it.' Sheremetev had seen other names on Vladimir's watches over the years. 'Patek something.'

'Patek Philippe?'

'That's right. And Vach... Vach...'

'Vacheron?' said Rostkhenkovskaya, digging deep into her resources of self control to conceal her excitement.

'Vacheron, that's it. Are they worth anything, those things?'

Rostkhenkovskaya took a deep breath, recovering her composure. She shrugged nonchalantly. 'Well, it depends. Maybe it would be worth me taking a look. Shall I come to your house?'

'No,' said Sheremetev quickly.

'But you know it's quite risky carrying watches like that – I mean, not that they're worth *that* much – but still, it is taking a chance. I could come and—

'No.'

'Okay. Look, Nikolai Ilyich, if you need more money to get your nephew out of jail, why don't you bring me a couple more and I could see if they're worth anything? The others, though. Not more Rolexes.'

'Aren't the Rolexes good?'

'Of course. They're fine. But let's look at some of the others next time. A Vacheron, a Patek Philippe, a Hublot. Others as well, if you have any. Bring as many as you like. What do you think? Shall we do that?'

Sheremetev frowned. 'I'll think about it.'

'Do you want to give me your phone number?'

He shook his head.

Rostkhenkovskaya held out a card. 'Here's mine.'

Sheremetev slipped the card in a pocket. 'Goodbye, Anna Mikhailovna.'

'Goodbye, Nikolai Ilyich. Come back with the other watches.' She gave him a coquettish smile. 'I'll be waiting.'

Rostkhenkovskaya pressed a button to unlock the door and watched the unlikely little man step outside.

Sheremetev walked quickly back to the Arbatskaya metro, conscious of the bundles of notes in his pockets as if they were a pair of dead weights pulling him down.

WHEN HE GOT BACK to the dacha, Sheremetev crept guiltily into the house, feeling that the security guard in the entrance hall, the house attendant he passed on the stairs, must surely be able to sense that he was up to something. Vera, who had come to cover for him at short notice, was upstairs with Vladimir. He got rid of her as quickly as he could, then retrieved the cash from his jacket pockets and hid it under his mattress.

Sheremetev wasn't much of a drinker, but right now he craved the fire of a vodka in his throat. Vladimir was in his sitting room. He had had his dinner and was waiting to be put to bed. He could wait a few minutes more.

Sheremetev headed downstairs. Seven or eight of the security guards were in there, slouching around with the remains of their dinner in front of them. After what Stepanin had told him about Artur, he looked at them differently now. They were probably getting ready to go out for their night's thuggery. He went to the sideboard, poured himself a vodka and threw it down in one gulp. The security boys at the table watched him, grinning.

'How's the face, Nikolai Ilyich?' one of them called out. 'Been in any more fights?'

Sheremetev scowled, and they laughed.

When he went back upstairs, Vladimir was sniffing the air and muttering darkly about the Chechen. Sometimes Sheremetev thought that if he could understand who the Chechen was, he would understand Vladimir Vladimirovich, unlock the secret of the man. But Vladimir never said anything about him, just called whoever he thought he was seeing the Chechen and hurled abuse at him.

Sheremetev helped Vladimir change into his pyjamas, prompting him each time he forgot what he was doing, nodding each time the old man looked at him for confirmation. Sheremetev felt Vladimir's vulnerability and need for him as acutely as ever. But yesterday he had listened to him for the first time – really listened to him – and had heard, out of Vladimir's own mouth, a confession of unmitigated abuse and corruption, without even the faintest hint of contrition to relieve it. He had asked the questions Goroviev had wanted to ask and received the answers he least wanted to hear.

How could he continue to stay at the dacha to look after this man? But with Vladimir looking at him like that, how could he leave?

Vladimir climbed into bed. Sheremetev gave him his medications.

'Goodnight, Vladimir Vladimirovich,' he said.

Vladimir said nothing, as always, but lay on his back, staring up at the ceiling.

Sheremetev turned off his light. He withstood the temptation to go to the cabinet in Vladimir's dressing room where so many more watches lay waiting. He needed to think. He retreated to his own room and lay down, conscious of the wads of money under his mattress, imagining that he could feel them through the springs.

His phone rang. It was Oleg. He wanted to know if Sheremetev had been to the watch shop.

Sheremetev hesitated. 'Not yet,' he said. 'How's Pasha?'

'Okay. When are you going to the shop?'

'I couldn't get away today. Tomorrow, I hope.'

'Do you really think you'll get something for the watch?'

'I don't know, Oleg. I'll have to see. Listen, I have to go.'

'Kolya, what's going on?'

'Nothing. I'll try to go there tomorrow.' Sheremetev put the phone down before Oleg could ask any more questions.

He rested back on his pillow and closed his eyes. Already he had under the mattress more money than he would ever have imagined one could get for a watch before Dr Rospov had enlightened him. He felt bad when he thought about the young lady in the watch shop, and how he had made her pay him so much that she wouldn't make any money for herself. But still it wasn't enough. Certainly, if he took the money he had got for the watch, and added to it what he had in the bank, and perhaps a little more from Oleg, they would have ten thousand for the prosecutor – but would the prosecutor really suddenly agree to drop his price? Might not the unexpected offer of ten thousand merely encourage him to hold out for more, and to make Pasha's life even harder until it was delivered? And in the meantime, how many more watches were there in Vladimir's cabinet? Hundreds! Enough to fully quench the greed of the prosecutor.

Sheremetev felt the fear he had always felt when faced with the prospect of wrongdoing, fear that everyone else around him seemed to be able to ignore. Somewhere, he thought, there must exist an inventory of Vladimir's watches and one day, someone would check it. And if things were missing, who would they blame?

But other people had access to the dressing room. The maids, for instance, who were always taking things. After all, just a few days ago one of them had been dismissed for theft even though her real crime was sleeping with Stepanin. Surely it would be assumed that the maids had done it.

But would he then allow the maids to be sent to jail for a crime that he had committed? On the other hand, they had committed plenty of crimes, according to Stepanin, so what difference would it make if they were punished for something they hadn't done rather than something they had?

No, he couldn't imagine himself standing by and allowing that to happen. But then he could never have imagined himself stealing and selling a watch – and he had done it!

Maybe there wasn't an inventory. No, there must be one, he thought.

Even if there was an inventory, would anyone worry about one missing watch when the other three hundred were in place? For all anyone knew, Vladimir himself might have taken it and before long it would turn up behind a cushion or in a sock drawer. It was natural that at any given moment one might be missing. More than one, however, and people might start to wonder.

But what if it was only a few more, say three or four? Would anyone really care? But he needed three hundred thousand dollars for Pasha, and three or four watches wouldn't be enough. Besides, what would he say to Oleg? That he had sold *one* watch for so many hundreds of thousands of dollars?

He stopped. 'Kolya,' he said to himself, 'what are you *talking* about? Stealing watches, one after the other? Is that what you've become? A common thief?'

But it was in a just cause. What right did the prosecutor have to demand three hundred thousand dollars to free Pasha from a charge that should never have been brought? What was that but common thievery, even if it was perpetrated by a man in a suit?

Sheremetev felt ill with fear and uncertainty and self-loathing. He touched gingerly at the laceration on his face. Even now, four days after Vladimir had injured him, it was still tender.

He wondered what Karinka would say. She had never, not once, in all the months she had been dying, ever asked him to take bribes. He wished she had. He wished she had made him confront himself as Nina had done.

But watches, more watches...Stealing them...

It was hunger that finally interrupted his thoughts. He looked in on Vladimir, who was sleeping peacefully, took the monitor and went downstairs. He was later than usual. He knocked on the kitchen door and one of the potwashers opened it.

'Can I have something to eat?' he asked.

The potwasher yelled over his shoulder: 'Nikolai Ilyich wants something to eat.'

Sheremetev sat at the dining table. Stepanin came out with a couple of dishes and put them in front of him. Then he sat as well. Sheremetev felt like telling him to go away – the last thing he wanted now was to have to listen to Stepanin whining about his endless feud with Barkovskaya.

In front of him was a dish of fried potatoes with egg and a kind of stew that appeared to contain aubergines and salami in sour cream.

Sheremetev looked questioningly at the cook.

'I'm not using that bitch's meat. Into the pit it goes with the chickens.'

Sheremetev didn't think that was going to work for very long. The security boys might have tolerated the disappearance of poultry from their diet, but meat was another matter. 'What are you going to cook with, Vitya? Air?'

'I can't let her do this.'

'Vitya,' said Sheremetev wearily, 'she's going to win. She's the one who pays the bills. You can't beat that. How many arms and legs do you want to break? How many of your suppliers do you want to have firebombed? Talk to her and see if she'll come to an arrangement.'

'It's too late for that.'

'What does that mean?'

Stepanin didn't reply.

Sheremetev shook his head in exasperation and began to eat.

'How is it?' asked Stepanin after a while.

Sheremetev shrugged. 'Better than it looks.'

Stepanin couldn't hold back a grin. He explained enthusiastically how he had created the potato dish, a new twist on a classic. Sheremetev's irritation with him evaporated. The truth was, he was a good cook, and he wanted people to enjoy his food, and what else can one ask of a cook? Even these two dishes, that he had concocted, it seemed, out of spite for Barkovskaya, were tasty. And in the end, was he really such a bad man? Was it so terrible, what he wanted, to set up his own restaurant in Moscow? Russian fusion, minimalist décor – was it such an abominable dream? And everything had been going so well for him. True, he had been skimming a little off the top – or a lot off the top, if what he had told Sheremetev about his astronomical savings was true – but who didn't? Only him, Sheremetev.

And what right did he have to sit in judgement, after what he had just done and with two thick wads of cash hidden under his mattress? And whose money was the cook taking, after all? If it was Vladimir's, it had been obtained through theft, and the cook, like Goroviev, was simply taking it from him in turn. Siphoning it off seemed far less of a crime than the stealing of a watch out of a defenceless man's cabinet – and not just any man, but a patient who was in his care – in which he, Sheremetev, had just indulged, and which he was thinking of repeating.

'Vitya,' he said, suddenly feeling sympathetic towards the cook. 'Don't be rash. Talk to Barkovskaya. See what she'll do. She's probably more reasonable than you think.'

Stepanin shook his head grimly. 'There's only one language that woman understands.'

THAT NIGHT, THE PREMISES of Bolkovskaya's meat supplier were firebombed. Sheremetev guessed something like that must have happened when veal cutlets, lamb *plov*, boeuf à la Tversk, pork chops, stewed liver, fried brains, braised tongue and ham terrine all turned up on the sideboard at lunch, an extravaganza of meat that seemed to have exploded out of Stepanin like the triumphant crowing of a cock over its dead foe.

Even the vegetable dishes had meat. Barkovskaya took one look and walked out of the dining room.

Meanwhile, Sheremetev ruminated about what he should do, conscious that every day that passed was another day for Pasha in jail. The money he had under his bed was a bigger sum than he had ever physically held before, but it wasn't enough. A drop in the ocean.

Heavy rain had fallen through the morning. In the afternoon, the clouds cleared and Sheremetev took Vladimir out for his walk.

The plastic of the greenhouses, normally so drab and ugly, sparkled with sunlight refracting through the raindrops. Vladimir headed for them enthusiastically.

Sheremetev followed. He had no desire to run into Goroviev again. Sheremetev still couldn't work out what had happened the night Vladimir disappeared from his room. How was it that he had ended up sitting with Goroviev on the exact same bench where they had sat before? He had begun to wonder whether the gardener had taken Vladimir from his suite, although how he would have got up there and then smuggled Vladimir out past the guard in the lobby, Sheremetev didn't know. Unless the guard was asleep. That wasn't unlikely, to judge from the length of time it took him to answer the phone, but would the gardener still have been able to get the ex-president up and out without being detected, not least by Sheremetev himself, who would surely have been woken by noise from the baby monitor? And why would he take him? To talk? Something worse? Had Sheremetev, by finding them, interrupted some long-planned act of revenge? Or had the gardener really just happened to find him, calm him, warm him with his coat, wait with him until he was found? This same gardener who had confessed that there was a time when, if he could have got his hands on Vladimir, he would have strangled him.

They went into a greenhouse full of tomatoes and strawberries. There was no sign of Goroviev, but half a dozen labourers were at work. Vladimir smiled at them approvingly and encouraged them to keep at it. They stared back at him solemnly.

The next greenhouse, full of cucumbers just beginning to swell below yellow flowers, was deserted. Vladimir moved slowly along the beds, occasionally putting out a hand to brush at the blooms.

Sheremetev's mind went back to his dilemma. Was there an inventory of the watches? If he took more, would he be caught?

There was no one else here, just him, the flowers and Vladimir, and Vladimir was no more likely than the flowers to remember anything he said.

They walked on, past plant after plant.

'Vladimir Vladimirovich,' Sheremetev blurted out, 'who knows about your watches?'

Vladimir said nothing.

'Your watches!'

'My mother gave me a watch when I was ten,' murmured Vladimir. 'Not a bad watch. Sometimes I still wear it when I see her. Mother likes to see it on me. Do you know my mother?'

'No, Vladimir Vladimirovich.'

'That's a shame. Next time she comes, I'll make sure you meet her.'

'What about your other watches? The ones you have in the cabinet?'

'A man only needs one watch, you know. One watch is enough for a man for his whole life, if it's a good one, and if he looks after it.'

Sheremetev raised an eyebrow. Could there be a more incongruous philosophy, coming from a man who had a cabinet such as the one in Vladimir's dressing room. 'I mean the other watches, Vladimir Vladimirovich. The Rolexes, the Hublots...'

Vladimir laughed. 'Just by looking at a watch, I can have it. Have I ever told you about the time Dima Kolyakov came to get my permission for the new ring road? That was the best one! In he comes and he's sitting there with a Vacheron Tour de l'Ile, and he's playing with it smugly – it's obvious he just got it – and I just look at it, and a minute later, he's trying to get it off his wrist!' Vladimir chortled.

'He's shitting himself to get it off his wrist, so I say, don't worry, Dima, I've got two already. You should have seen his face! Anyway, the next day, he sends it to me, with a note that says: Why have two when you can have three? Huh? What do you think of that?'

'What is that worth, such a watch?'

'Which watch?'

'The one you just talked about.'

Vladimir looked at him blankly.

'Vladimir Vladimirovich, you mentioned a Vacheron something.'

'A Vacheron something? What Vacheron something?'

'You gave it a name.'

'Did I?' Vladimir peered at him suspiciously. 'A name? What name are you talking about?'

Sheremetev wondered if this was mischief or dementia. Sometimes it was hard to tell. 'A Vacheron watch, Vladimir Vladimirovich.'

'What about it?'

'Dima Kolyakov gave it to you.'

'How do you know? Were you there? That's a slander, do you understand me! No one ever gave me anything!'

Sheremetev clenched his fists in exasperation. 'Vladimir Vladimirovich, who knows about the watches?'

'Now, it's true my mother gave me a watch. Did I ever tell you about that? I was ten, and I came home and—'

'*The watches!*' yelled Sheremetev, his frustration bursting out of him. He grabbed the old man by the shoulders. 'Who knows about the watches? Is there a register? Is there an inventory? Does anyone have it? Barkovskaya?'

Vladimir looked at him in confusion.

'Does she? Does Barkovskaya have it?'

Vladimir kept staring at him with the same fearful look.

Sheremetev let his hands drop. He gazed down at them for a moment, appalled at what he was doing. 'Come on,' he said quietly. 'Let's go back, Vladimir Vladimirovich.'

THAT NIGHT, AFTER VLADIMIR was asleep, Sheremetev stood in front of the open doors of the watch cabinet. He felt clammy and nauseated, unable to move, as if in the presence of some sacred altar or relic imbued with a majestic, ineffable power. Eventually he reached forward and pulled out one of the trays. Three rows of faces stared back at him, mostly white or silver. Amongst them was one green one. Sheremetev stared at it, mesmerised.

He had no idea of the value of any of these watches. The only one about which he had even the slightest sense was the one Dr Rospov had seen on Vladimir's wrist, but Sheremetev didn't dare take that one to the shop off the Arbat, for fear that, if anyone suspected that he had stolen the watches, Rospov would be able to testify that that one, at least, had still been in Vladimir's possession as recently as this last week. Sheremetev certainly had no awareness of the true difference in the price of the watches in the cabinet, the fact that some, from the early days of Vladimir's rule, were worth mere tens of thousands of dollars, and others a million. In his mind they all fell into the same category, objects that had fallen into his path out of an alien realm of barely imaginable wealth.

He heard a noise from Vladimir's bedroom. Sheremetev switched off the light in the dressing room and listened. Vladimir was murmuring, but not aggressively. Sheremetev poked his head around the doorway. Vladimir was sitting up in the bed, gazing ahead. The glow from the night light was yellowish and low.

'Yes, Mama.'

As Sherememtev watched, Vladimir frowned slightly.

'Of course, Mama.'

His mother looked at him seriously. 'Vova, Papa and I have decided that you're old enough. But a watch isn't a toy, do you understand?'

'I understand, Mama.'

'You have to look after it. You have to take care of it. If you break it, there won't be another one. It's very expensive, Vova. Papa and I have saved and saved to get it for you, because you make us very proud, and we love you. But you have to take care of it, Vova. Will you do that?'

'Yes, Mama. Can I put it on now?'

His mother smiled. 'Of course. Let me help you.'

She unclipped the clasp of the linked metal band and slid it over his wrist, then clipped it fast.

'Papa shortened it for you. See? It fits just right. When you get bigger, he'll make it bigger again. Now, you have to learn how to open and close it.'

She showed him how to use the clasp, and he practised it a couple of times. He looked up at her with a smile.

She ruffled his hair. 'Do you like it?'

'I love it, Mamochka! A Poljot! They're the best!'

He gazed at the watch in delight, taking in every detail. It had a white face and slender gold hour and minute hands. Twelve and six were marked in gold numbers, and the other hours by narrow gold rhomboids. The second hand was an almost impossibly thin reed, and around the outside of the dial the seconds were marked and divided into fifths, and every fifth second was marked with its number. Two other timer dials were set into the face. Just under the number twelve, in slender black letters, was the word Poljot.

'This is the best watch in the world, Mama! I won't break it ever!

241

And I won't lose it, I promise. I'll always have it.'

Vladimir's mother smiled. 'That's good, Vova. My father, your grandfather, only ever had one watch. His papa gave it to him when he was a boy, and he kept it all those years. He still had it the last time I saw him. That was before the siege. He used to say, a man only needs one watch for his life, if it's a good one, and if he looks after it.'

'Yes, Mama.'

'And your papa's father, did you know he cooked for Lenin? And not only Lenin, Stalin. You know that, don't you?'

'Yes, Mama.'

'That's something to be proud of. To be able to serve a great man, that's something, Vova. Don't forget.'

'I won't forget, Mama.'

'Maybe you'll be able to serve a great man one day, too, Vova.'

Vladimir nodded, his eyes stealing back to the wonderful watch on his wrist. 'This is a good one, Mama! A Poljot! They're better even than the western watches.'

'So you'll look after it? Do you promise?'

'Yes, Mama. This is the only watch I'll ever have. I'll look after it every day.'

Vladimir's mother leaned forward and kissed him on the forehead. 'Keep it safe, Vova. May you have it for as long as you live.'

As Sheremetev watched, Vladimir continued to sit for a minute or so, looking up slightly, then lay down again and pulled up the covers.

Sheremetev turned and went back into the dressing room, where the cabinet still stood open.

14

THE NEXT MORNING, SOON after he got up, Sheremetev called Vera. She was on a hospital shift but agreed to come to the dacha when she was finished. By three o'clock he had handed Vladimir over to her and was downstairs, with three small bundles hidden in his jacket, waiting for Eleyekov, who was off to pick up a client in Vladimir's Mercedes and had offered to drop Sheremetev at the station.

Eleyekov drove silently down the drive. 'Have you heard about Artur?' he asked as they turned out of the dacha gate and onto the road.

Sheremetev nodded glumly. 'He's a gangster. Like everyone else here, it seems.'

'No, I mean about what happened last night.' Eleyekov glanced at him questioningly. 'You don't know, do you? Someone shot him.'

'Artur?'

'He wasn't killed, but it's not good. He's in hospital. According to what I heard, they took three bullets out of him.'

Sheremetev was dumbstruck. This was madness. It was as if the dacha and all who lived in it were dragging themselves deeper and deeper into some kind of living hell.

'Yeah. It's gone too far,' said Eleyekov. 'Shooting Artyusha Lukash-villi! I don't know who would have had the balls. Must be some gang from Moscow. Khazakhs...Chechens...Maybe another bunch of

Georgians. Who would have thought Barkovskaya would even know such people? And what's going to happen now?' Eleyekov shook his head. 'I suppose if you're in a business like Artyusha's, you can almost expect that something like this will happen sooner or later. But it's only the start, Kolya. It's going to be war. The security boys, they all work for Lukashvilli. They're already planning something, I'm sure. If I was Barkovskaya, I'd sleep with a gun tonight.'

'Are you sure she had something to do with it?'

'Well, we had meat for dinner yesterday, and it came from Stepanin's man. Someone firebombed her cousin, or whoever her supplier was. I don't know, maybe you're right. Maybe this is all just an excuse. Who would go to war with the Lukashvillis for some housekeeper? Maybe some other gang has been waiting for an excuse to muscle in on Artyusha's territory.' Eleyekov shrugged to himself, eyes on the road. 'Well, whether Barkovskaya's involved in it or not, there's going to be a war. And we're going to be in the middle of it.'

Sheremetev sat dejectedly beside Eleyekov. There seemed to be nothing solid or wholesome left in his life at the dacha, and what he was doing – his little mission to the shop off the Arbat with more watches in his pockets – only added to his sense of misery. He wished he had never come to this dacha. He wished he never had to go back.

He thought about it. Seriously. Get on the train to Moscow and not come back. Stay with Oleg, perhaps, while he found a new job and got on his feet again.

But then he imagined the reality of it. He had told Vera he would be back by nine. Say he didn't come back. She would have to go home to look after her children. Who would put Vladimir to bed? Barkovskaya? One of the maids? One of the security guards? Who would be there if he woke in the night? Who would know what to do with him or how to calm him? He imagined the confusion and fear in Vladimir's eyes, no one able to take it away.

'Nikolai Ilyich,' said Eleyekov. 'Did you say we're going to the station?'

Sheremetev looked around. 'What?'

'The station? Is that where you said we're going? The station?'

'Yes,' said Sheremetev. 'To the station.'

THE TRAIN RIDE INTO Belorusskaya took forty minutes. It was a heavy day, the sky grey and low. The birch forests blazed with autumn fire. Normally, the sight would have lifted Sheremetev's spirits, but not today.

From Belorusskaya, he took the metro to Arbatskaya station and came up into the Moscow evening as dusk fell. He walked quickly down the Arbat towards the alley where Rostkhenkovskaya had her shop.

He rang the bell. The door clicked and he pushed it open. Rostkhenkovskaya greeted him with a smile. Sheremetev was struck, again, by her youth, so unexpected in this mausoleum of trinkets and watches.

'Good evening, Nikolai Ilyich. I wondered if I would see you again.'

'Good evening, Anna Mikhailovna,' he murmured.

'So what have you brought me? Something interesting?'

Sheremetev reached into one of his jacket pockets and extracted two hankerchief-wrapped watches, which he laid down on the counter. He took a third out of another pocket.

Rostkhenkovskaya tried to still the slight, expectant tremble that suddenly shook her hands. 'May I?'

Sheremetev nodded.

It wasn't logical for Sheremetev to have brought only three watches from Vladimir's cabinet, because he knew that three would not be enough to get Pasha out of jail, but if someone did have an inventory, perhaps they wouldn't look too hard if only a few watches were missing. He lacked the courage to take more, and despised himself for it.

Rostkhenkovskaya unwrapped the first watch and set it on the glass of the counter. She unwrapped the second. As the third came out of its handkerchief, her heart gave a thump.

The first one that she had unwrapped was a Hublot, although not the one that Dr Rospov had seen. As Rostkhenkovskaya looked at it lying on the glass of the counter in front of her, she estimated that it was worth around seventy thousand dollars. Another, the one with the emerald face that had so mesmerised Sheremetev, was the least valuable of the three, a Bruguet worth around forty thousand. But he had hit the jackpot with the third one, a Patek Philippe by Tiffany in mint condition. It was one of the more valuable in Vladimir's collection, given to him during his later years in office when those who could still get access to him knew – and if they didn't, Zhenya Monarov soon made sure they did – that if they were going to give him a watch, it had to be something truly extraordinary. Rostkhenkovskaya knew of Patek Philippes by Tiffany, but had never actually held one. She couldn't price it at a glance, but it would be no less than half a million dollars, and possibly more.

'These were given to you by your uncle?' she asked.

'Yes,' said Sheremetev, or thought he did – somehow the word didn't come out. He cleared his throat. 'Yes.'

'Do you have more?'

'Possibly.'

Rostkhenkovskaya didn't point out the absurdity of such an answer. Either he had more or he didn't, and surely he would have known what his uncle had given him – assuming there was such an uncle, or that an act of giving had actually taken place, both of which, by now, Rostkhenkovskaya doubted.

'And if there were any more,' asked Rostkhenkovskaya, 'would you want to sell them too?'

'That depends,' said Sheremetev.

'On what?'

'On how much I get for these.'

'Okay.' Rostkhenkovskaya drew a deep breath. 'These two,' she said, pointing to the Hublot and the Bruguet, 'ten thousand dollars for the pair.' She paused for a moment. 'This one...'

Rostkhenkovskaya picked up the Patek Philippe again, as if examining it once more and trying to determine a price for it. She stole a surreptitious glance at Sheremetev. Could this funny little man – could anyone – really come into possession of a Patek Philippe by Tiffany – by whatever means – and have *no* idea of its worth? If so, she could offer him a few thousand, as for the others, and end up with a profit in her pocket in the many hundreds of thousands. If not, and she made such an offer, he might walk away and it would be out of her hands forever – this watch and the others that he might 'possibly' have.

From the minute he had appeared in her shop two days earlier, Rostkhenkovskaya had believed that he knew nothing about watches. Now she doubted herself. What if he really had a collection that he – or his uncle – wanted to get rid of, very quietly, for reasons of his own, and without public notice? What if he – or the uncle – was testing her? Perhaps he could afford to give away the Rolex at the ridiculous price she had paid him. Bring her a couple more – nice watches, but not extraordinary watches – and then throw in a real prize, to see what she would do.

She picked up a loupe and examined the watch through the lens, trying to decide. No, she thought. He couldn't be so naïve, not if he had a watch like this.

In her mind she heard what he had said when she asked if he would want to sell any more watches: it would depend on the price for these ones.

She took the loupe away from her eye.

'You say there could be more, Nikolai Ilyich?'

He shrugged, almost casually, thought Rostkhenkovskaya. His apparent naivete now seemed subtly calculated.

She heard the words in her mind again. *It would depend on the price.* Suddenly, their meaning for her changed.

'Quarter of a million,' she said.

Sheremetev stared.

'Alright, three hundred thousand.'

'How much did you say?'

'Three hundred thousand.'

'Dollars?'

She laughed. 'What do you think? Rubles? But I need to do some checking on this one first, to verify. And obviously, I don't have that kind of money in the back of the shop. Leave it with me and come back tomorrow.'

'I can't leave it with you,' said Sheremetev.

'Then I'll take a picture.'

'No pictures.'

'Okay. Let me look at it again carefully.' Rostkhenkovskaya took out a notebook. She examined the Patek Philippe with the eyeglass, front and back, making notes. Then she wrapped the watch up carefully in the handkerchief in which it had arrived and handed it back to Sheremetev. 'Do you want the money for the other two now?'

'No, I'll—'

'Yes, I know. The price was low. I was just…Forget what I said. Twenty thousand.'

Sheremetev's eyebrows rose.

'Twenty-five thousand?' Rostkhenkovskaya was prepared to go to thirty, forty, even fifty, if that was what it took to get him to come back with the rest of his watches.

He nodded.

'Twenty-five? Okay. I'll get it for you now.'

Rostkhenkovskaya left the shop, and the old woman who had been there on the previous occasion came out to watch him. Sheremetev smiled at her and she stared stonily back.

'Are you the widow of the late Rostkhenkovsky?' he asked.

The woman nodded.

'My condolences.'

The woman nodded again.

Her daughter reappeared with a thick wad of notes and the old woman retreated. Rostkhenkovskaya counted the money in front of Sheremetev. He distributed it in his pockets, as he had done the last time, on this occasion without having to be told. The Patek Philippe went in as well.

He felt as if the money was bursting out of his jacket all over. He put on his coat and zipped it up, hoping it was bulky enough to cover the bulges.

'Your uncle must have been quite a collector,' said the young woman, thinking of the other watches that would hopefully follow these ones.

'Uncle?' For an instant, the story about the supposed uncle

having given him the watches had gone out of Sheremetev's mind. 'Oh, yes, of course! Yes, a very big collector.'

Anna Rostkhenkovskaya smiled her most winning smile. 'I don't suppose you want to give me his name?'

Sheremetev shook his head.

'Not even for me?' Rostkhenkovskaya smiled sweetly a moment longer. 'Okay. So, I need to do some checking, but if this Patek Philippe is what I think it is, three hundred thousand is the price. Agreed? If it's all okay, I'll get the money tomorrow. And you know, I meant to tell you, I've done a bit of research, and the price I paid you for the Rolex the other day was somewhat low. I'll add another fifty thousand for that one when you come back. And let's add another twenty-five for the ones you've sold me tonight. I assume you'll want it all in cash?'

Sheremetev nodded, flabbergasted by the sums of money the young woman seemed to be throwing him. 'But are you sure...' he began, thinking of how Rostkhenkovskaya had said she wouldn't make any money on the Rolex even at the price she had paid him, and wondering if she had been so moved by his story of having a nephew in jail that she was bankrupting herself to help him.

'I'm sure!'

'But—'

You know, with an amount like this, we'd be happy to bring it to you...'

'No,' said Sheremetev. 'I'll come here.'

'Are you certain?'

'Yes.'

'Fine.' Rostkhenkovskaya smiled. 'Don't forget the watch!'

Outside, hunching his shoulders to reduce the bulges in his jacket, Sheremetev walked back along the Arbat. He wasn't aware of it, but a smile was plastered across his face, and as he walked, the smile got bigger. Passersby wondered if the little man with the grin had some kind of mental defect. Three hundred thousand! Not to mention the extra seventy-five that Rostkhenkovskaya wanted to give him. Enough to get Pasha out, and all from one watch. He couldn't wait to tell Oleg.

He felt guilty for taking the money for the other two watches. Twenty-five thousand dollars! And the same again when he came back. His smile went as he thought about it. He didn't need that for Pasha, and he felt that he was taking advantage of Rostkhenkovskaya's sympathetic nature. Somehow, getting the money required to get Pasha out of jail was justifiable – but taking money for the other watches, that was theft, pure and simple.

Only four watches though, he said to himself – no one would notice that. Four amongst all the watches in that cabinet . . . But the one he still had, the one worth three hundred thousand dollars that was nestled in his pocket – maybe if anyone ever checked, they would want to know where that one was.

He felt a sense of panic. For a moment he doubted that he could go through with it. Calm down, he told himself. One watch, however valuable it was, was more likely to go missing than ten or twenty, which was what he might have to sell in order to get Pasha out if he didn't sell that one. And he was going to get Pasha out. That much, he had decided.

Three hundred thousand. From one watch. And what if there were more such watches in the cabinet? He had selected four and had found one like that. Maybe that was lucky. But what if every fifth, or tenth, or even twentieth was worth such a sum? As he waited for the train at Arbatskaya station, the sheer scale of the wealth locked up in that cabinet suddenly hit him. He did some simple multiplication

– and the result staggered him. Had he overestimated by a zero or two? He did the sum again. If there was so much wealth locked away in one cabinet of watches that everyone seemed to have forgotten about, how much else must Vladimir have had? And how had he got it? Was a president of Russia paid in watches? Was that how he got his salary?

Pasha had written that the biggest crook in Russia was Vladimir Vladimirovich. To a man like Sheremetev, who had lived all his life on a nurse's salary, the true scale of the sums involved in Vladimir's embezzlement as president of Russia, if he had known them, would have been inconceivable. Perhaps they would be inconceivable to any man, including the one who had stolen them. But the number Sheremetev produced in his head from the contents of that cabinet was not inconceivable. It was big enough to boggle his mind, but not too big for his mind to contain. For the first time, what Pasha had written about the scale of Vladimir's theft was real to him.

The train pulled into the station. Sheremetev stepped on, jacket buttoned and coat zipped, laden down with more wealth than any of the people in that carriage would see in a lifetime.

At that moment, in a room behind the shop in the alley off the Arbat, Anna Rostkhenkovskaya sat at her desk, while her mother reclined in an armchair nearby. The Patek Philippe she had seen was a tantalising prize. A watch like that didn't come along every day. Even if she paid three hundred thousand dollars for it, she would probably make a hundred thousand in profit, and possibly more, when she sold it on. But the story of the watches she hadn't seen tantalised her more. How many were there? Ten? Twenty? Could there be even more? And what other prizes would she find amongst them? The strange little man had mentioned Vacherons last time he came. What if there was a Tour l'Ile amongst the collection? Why not? After seeing that Patek Philippe emerge from its handkerchief, anything was possible. She imagined a kind of Aladdin's cave, and if only she could get into it, then in one fell swoop she might make more than her father had made in thirty years.

But what if the little man decided, after all, that he didn't want to sell her any more pieces? What if the prices she had offered weren't high enough? What if he came back with the Patek Philippe – and that was it?

What if he didn't even come back with the Patek Philippe? But she had offered to give him another seventy-five thousand for the other ones she had taken. She was glad that she had had the impulse to do it. That would bring him back even if he didn't want to sell her the Patek Philippe. She would have one more chance, at least.

Rostkhenkovskaya glanced at her mother. The older woman had never been very strong, often depressed, and her husband's death a month earlier at the age of fifty-nine had totally floored her. Anna didn't know how much she even registered now of what was happening around her. She had her mother mind the shop when there was a customer and she had to do something in the back, but that was more of a bluff than anything else. If the customer actually reached under the counter and grabbed something and ran off, she doubted her mother would even cry out.

Of her two parents, it was her father Anna took after. As the Soviet empire tottered and fell, the young Mikhail Rostkhenkovsky had been a junior manager, an apparatchik in the making, in charge of one of the forty sections of one of the four vast warehouses through which the centralised planners of the Soviet economy routed Moscow's food supply. Such was life in the communist paradise that the job was greatly coveted for the opportunity to put a handful of pilfered sausages on the table at home or to earn a ruble or two by selling a bunch of stolen tomatoes and Rostkhenkovsky had been widely and enviously congratulated when he was awarded the position. But now, for a short moment in time, it offered riches beyond imagining. As starvation threatened the city, as officials abandoned the pretence of fulfilling their responsibilities and scrambled to seize what they could of the disintegrating infrastructure of the Soviet economy, Rostkhenkovsky, like so many of the younger generation who would soon style themselves Russia's new entrepreneurs, took his chance. He walked into the warehouse and filled lorries with food and drove them into Moscow, not worrying about such niceties as his legal right to purloin entire container loads of cheese, sausage or flour, and proceeded to sell the contents as if they were his own – not for rubles, that were devaluing by the day, but for dollars, and if people didn't have dollars, for anything small, moveable and valuable. And what is small, moveable and valuable? Jewellery! Rings, watches, necklaces, brooches, bracelets. A pair of earrings, Madamoiselle, for a kilo of bread. Your wedding band, Madam, for a stick of salami. Soon he had whole cupboards stashed with trinkets. By the time the crisis was over and some kind of order was restored, Mikhail Rostkhenkovsky was out of the warehouse and into the jewellery business.

Anna Rostkhenkovskaya had grown up on that story. 'It was the chance of a lifetime,' Mikhail Rostkhenkovsky would tell her in later years, reminiscing about the wild days when he would load a lorry and hawk it around Moscow. 'It was madness, the things that were happening. Those of us who jumped in were set up for life. Those who didn't are starving to death on their pensions. Such a chance, if it comes at all, will only come once in a lifetime, Anushka. If it does, seize it, my daughter. Seize it! Do whatever you have to – don't think twice!'

If the father was an opportunist, the daughter was something altogether more determined. Mikhail Rostkhenkovsky had been satisfied with the shop that became dustier and less fashionable by the year, but for Anna, that would never be enough. Her pixieish looks and the smile she could put on belied the depth of her resolve. She had greater ambitions – and no illusions. In Russia, you fought your way up to the top, or you stayed with everyone else at the bottom.

Her father had had his once in a lifetime chance, and had taken it. She had often wondered in what shape hers would present itself. And now she knew – in the shape of a little man who had stepped in off the street like a Rumpelstiltskin in a fairy tale. Whatever else this man who called himself Nikolai Ilyich had – and there was more, she knew it – she was going to get it. The Patek Philippe wasn't enough.

Anna picked up her phone. A conversation of about twenty minutes ensued, beginning on the subject of the Patek Philippe but moving quickly on to the question of the other watches hanging in the Aladdin's cave of Rostkhenkovskaya's imagination and how she could be sure of getting them.

Anna's mother stared across the room, her eyes empty. Nothing suggested that she had registered a thing her daughter was saying.

'We'll need some muscle in case things turn nasty,' said the man on the phone. 'There's someone I use whenever I need some help.'

'I know,' said Rostkhenkovskaya. 'I've used him too.'

'Do you want me to ring him?'

'I'll do it.'

Anna ended the call. She glanced at her mother, who was still gazing listlessly into space.

She rang a second number.

'Vasya?' she said. 'It's Anna Rostkhenkovskaya.'

*

WHEN HE GOT BACK to the dacha, Sheremetev paused outside and called Oleg to tell him the good news.

'You're going to get three hundred thousand dollars for one watch?' his brother said in disbelief.

'For one watch!' replied Sheremetev.

'You know, I looked online to see what some watches might be worth, but I didn't see anything like that!'

'I'm going back tomorrow to get the money.'

'I'm amazed!'

'So am I,' said Sheremetev, laughing.

'Kolya,' said Oleg, his voice suddenly changing. 'I spoke to Pasha yesterday. He said, if he gets out, he's going to leave Russia.'

'Leave? Why does he want to leave?'

'He says he can't be silent, and if he can't be silent, he'll never be safe here.'

Sheremetev dropped his head and heaved a sigh. Then he looked around the moonlit grounds. The dacha stood in the middle, all but one of the windows in its upper storey darkened.

'Where will he go?' asked Sheremetev eventually.

'I don't know.'

'What will he do?'

'Who knows?'

'What does Nina say?'

'What can she say? He's not a child. If he wants to go, he'll go. And who's to say he's wrong? What if they pick him up again, Kolya? Could you get him out again next time? Do you have another watch you can sell?'

Sheremetev didn't reply.

'Anyway, this is great news, Kolya! One watch! Who could believe it? I don't know how I can thank you.'

'You don't need to thank me. If I had a hundred watches, I'd sell them all.'

'I can't tell you what this means.'

'Olik...please...'

'You know, the things Ninochka said...'

'Forget it. I understand. When all of this is done, none of that will matter.'

Sheremetev went inside. Upstairs, he dropped his jacket, still containing the money and the watch, on the bed in his room. Then he went to tell Vera that she could go home. Vladimir had eaten his dinner indifferently, she reported, alternating between talking to her as if she was his mother and asking her who she was. Sheremetev told her that he needed her again tomorrow.

Vera looked at him doubtfully. 'He's not an easy man to look after, Kolya.'

'I know.'

'He misses you when you're away.'

'He doesn't show it.'

'He does. When he sees that you're back, he's different. When you're gone, he's never fully at ease. I can see it. He knows something's wrong.'

Sheremetev said nothing to that.

'I can tell, Kolya.'

'Listen, Verochka, please, can you come again tomorrow?'

She looked at him for a moment, then smiled. 'Kolya, how can I resist when I see that look on your face? But tell me, where are you going? All these trysts... Who is she?'

'No one,' said Sheremetev.

'So there *is* a she!'

'No, there isn't. Please. It's family business.'

'Oh! *Family business!*'

'Will you come tomorrow?'

'Do you really need me?'

Sheremetev nodded.

'Life and death?'

'Just about.'

'So you're saying you can't live without me, Kolya?'

They gazed at each other. Sheremetev shook his head. 'Vera . . .'

She laughed, but with a hint of longing in her eyes. 'Okay. I'll come.'

'Thank you, Verochka. It's important. Thank you.'

When Vera had left, Sheremetev looked in on Vladimir. He was in front of the television in his sitting room, murmuring to himself.

'Vladimir Vladimirovich?' Sheremetev waited. 'Vladimir Vladimirovich!'

The old man's head turned.

'Have you eaten enough? Are you hungry?'

'Is it lunch time?'

'No, you've just had dinner. Do you want something more?'

'Do you?'

'How about a sandwich? Or *pirozhki*, if the cook has any?'

Vladimir shook his head.

'I'll get you a sandwich,' said Sheremetev, knowing that if Vladimir woke up hungry in the night he'd think it was time for breakfast, and there would be no getting him back to sleep.

Sheremetev called down to the kitchen and spoke to one of Stepanin's assistants, who said he would have something brought up. In the meantime, he went back to his room. He took the money out of the jacket and hid it under his mattress, alongside the wads he had brought back two days previously. He put the Patek Philippe in the drawer of the little table that stood beside his bed, not having any safer place to hide it. After a few minutes he thought better of that and went to Vladimir's dressing room, where he opened the cabinet and slipped the watch back into its niche. He was struck again by the astonishing, almost unimaginable wealth in that cabinet alone. How did Vladimir get the watches? he wondered. If he bought them, that showed how much money he must have stolen from the people. And if he had been given them, well, why would anyone give such things if not in return for illicit favours that he had granted?

He went back to the sitting room. Vladimir ignored him. Sheremetev gazed at the old man. In the last few days, Sheremetev had found his feelings for the ex-president veering from compassion to revulsion, often in seconds.

'How did you get the watches, Vladimir Vladimirovich?' he demanded suddenly.

Vladimir's head turned towards him.

'Who are you?'

'Sheremetev. I've been looking after you for six years.'

Vladimir snorted. 'That's ridiculous.'

'How did you get the watches?'

Vladimir smiled. 'My mother gave me a watch when I was only ten, but I kept it and I looked after it, just like I promised her.'

'What about the others?'

'What others?'

'The other watches.'

'You only need one watch in life, if it's a good one and if you look after it. That's what my grandfather said.'

There was a knock on the door. The house attendant stood outside carrying a tray with two sandwiches and a plate of fruit salad, together with a bottle of water. Sheremetev took the tray from him and closed the door.

He looked at the sandwiches. One was smoked salmon and dill, the other ham and mustard.

'Are you hungry, Vladimir Vladimirovich?'

Vladimir shook his head.

Sheremetev tucked a napkin under Vladimir's chin, put the plate of sandwiches on a table next to his armchair, and brought over a chair to sit beside him. He picked up half of the ham sandwich and put it to Vladimir's lips.

'Come on, Vladimir Vladimirovich. This is good. Eat.'

Vladimir's lips parted and mechanically he took a bite.

Sheremetev waited until Vladimir swallowed, then put the sandwich to Vladimir's mouth again. He was conscious of feeling a kind of unreal detachment as he watched Vladimir eat – not empathy, but not antagonism, either. Almost a kind of numbness.

Again, he wondered, how could he stay in this place – but how could he leave? He had begun to think that he hated this man, and yet he couldn't bear the thought of the confused, fearful look that Vladimir got in his eyes and the trauma he would inflict on him by leaving.

Vladimir ate only half a sandwich. Eventually, Sheremetev took the food to his room and finished the other pieces himself. Then he took the tray downstairs. The atmosphere in the house was tense. The guard in the hall watched him come down without a word. Three more security guards sat in the staff dining room having a conversation in low voices. They stopped as soon as Sheremetev came in.

'How's Artyusha?' he asked.

The guards glanced at each other.

'Alive,' growled Lyosha, Artur's shaven-headed deputy.

'Is he going to be alright?'

Lyosha looked at Sheremetev suspiciously and then shrugged.

Sheremetev found Stepanin brooding in the staff sitting room, smoking and nervously tapping the ash of his cigarette into a saucer.

'What's going on, Vitya?' asked Sheremetev.

'You heard about Artyusha?'

Sheremetev nodded.

'What fuckery!' Stepanin drew deeply on his cigarette and the smoke billowed from his nose. 'I got a note today from Barkovskaya saying she has suppliers for everything, and I should tell my guys to stay away. All of them! She's gone mad, Kolya. Shooting Artyusha? What the fuck is that about?'

Sheremetev refrained from pointing out that it was Stepanin himself who had described this as a war and had remarked sanguinely that in a war, people get hurt.

'Does she know who he is? Does she know what's going to happen now? What a piece of fucking fucked-up fuckery! Fuckery with a cock on top! This is going to be bad, Kolya. I'm telling you, this is going to be bad.'

Stepanin took a final drag on his cigarette, then ground out the butt on the saucer, pushing down hard with a snarl on his face.

'Vitya,' said Sheremetev, 'it's enough, don't you think?'

'What's enough?' retorted the cook.

'With Barkovskaya.'

'Enough? It's enough, alright! This is it, Kolya. She wants everything. The whole lot! What am I going to do? Walk away?'

'Maybe you should.' It occurred to Sheremetev that there was no alternative for Stepanin now, and at least if he walked away, no one would get killed.

'Sure, and let her win, huh? Is that what you want? I've only got half of what I need, Kolya. What am I going to do? Open half a restaurant? Serve my diners half a dish?'

Sheremetev thought of the watches. In that one cabinet upstairs was enough to satisfy everyone. Enough to get Pasha out, enough for Stepanin to have his restaurant, and enough, surely, even for Barkovskaya.

'What is it?' growled Stepanin. 'I'm not walking away, so don't say that again. Have you got any other ideas?'

Sheremetev shook his head.

The cook poured himself a vodka and threw it down.

'Vitya, what are you going to do?'

'It's me or her, Kolya. Isn't that clear? It's not my fault. I didn't start this thing. Everything was fine until she arrived. This is it, Kolya! The finish, the finale, the end game.'

'Vitya, don't do anything rash.'

Stepanin laughed, almost choking on his hatred.

It seemed to Sheremetev that the cook was like a hog on a spit, roasting and blackening in his own caustic juices. Sadly, he remembered the jovial, garrulous cook of days gone by. He stayed for another couple of minutes, then got up, leaving Stepanin throwing down another drink.

Upstairs, Vladimir was sniffing suspiciously and muttering dark imprecations about the Chechen.

'There's no Chechen,' said Sheremetev, trying to get him into his pyjamas. 'There's only me, Sheremetev.'

Vladimir looked probingly at the short, balding man who was standing in front of him with a pyjama top in his hands. Suddenly the Chechen's head poked out from behind him – then it was gone.

'Vladimir Vladimirovich, let's get your shirt off.'

There! He saw it again for an instant before it disappeared, the huge slimy black slug of a tongue lolling from the mouth, the lips stretched in a teeth-baring grin.

Vladimir let Sheremetev unbutton his shirt, glancing surreptitiously around the room, trying to spot the Chechen while he was off his guard. He put one arm after the other through the sleeves.

'Now the trousers.'

Again! There it was! Vladimir snapped into a judo pose and launched his attack. *Tai Otoshi!*

The blow swept Sheremetev off his feet and sent him sprawling on his back. 'Vladimir Vladimirovich!' he cried.

Vladimir looked down at him in confusion. What was that man doing on the floor? But he couldn't afford to be distracted. He peered carefully around the room. The Chechen was so cunning and so quick. He'd do anything to get his death tongue onto his face.

Sheremetev hauled himself up and hurried off to get Vladimir's tablets. If he got them into him quickly enough, he thought, he might be able to avoid using an injection. He caught sight of himself in a mirror – the laceration on his cheek, which had been healing well, was bleeding. He took a closer look. The scar had opened between a couple of the sutures when Vladimir had thrown him. Sheremetev pressed on the cut to staunch the blood, remembering what Dr Rospov had said about making sure the wound stayed closed to prevent it scarring. Eventually he went back and warily handed Vladimir a glass of water, then his pills, standing as far back from him as he could.

'Take them please, Vladimir Vladimirovich. They're good for you.'

Vladimir swallowed a couple.

'Also the others ... Good.' After what he had just seen, Sheremetev had added an extra sedative.

He took Vladimir to the bathroom. Vladimir looked suspiciously around the room as he led him back to bed and helped him in. He left Vladimir staring up, as he always did, and prayed that the sedatives would soon kick in and do their job.

Sheremetev didn't go back downstairs that night. The atmosphere in the dacha was poisonous. He had a pain at the base of his spine, where he had landed after Vladimir's judo attack, and his cheek was throbbing where the scar had been opened.

How much longer could he bear to stay here? In the last couple of weeks, the dacha, where he had thought he would stay until Vladimir died, had become like some kind of hell on earth. So why not leave? Perhaps not tonight, or tomorrow, but in a few days, so they had time to find a nurse to replace him. That wouldn't be abandoning his patient. That's all that Vladimir was to him. A patient, and he was just a nurse. Another nurse would be as good.

But Vladimir would never find the same familiarity with another nurse as he found with him. He had reached a stage in his disease when traces of recognition could never again be created – only forgotten. And even though he asked ten times a day who Sheremetev was, underneath it, that familiarity, that ease, was still there, as Vera had discerned. That was why he could resolve the look of fear and confusion in Vladimir's eyes with a word, a touch, when no one else could. If he left, that look would never be dispelled.

What if Vladimir died? The thought came into his head. Families of some other patients who had reached this stage had even said that they thought it would be for the best, occasionally going so far as to ask for his help. What kind of life did Vladimir have? There was no dignity or quality in it. And if Vladimir died, he could leave.

It had to happen sooner or later. Maybe it would be best for everybody if it was sooner.

He drove the thought out of his head.

His mind drifted. He thought of the money under the mattress on which he was lying. Thirty-two and a half thousand dollars, including what he had got for the first watch and what he had got for the second two. He was glad now that he had sold them, even if the other watch by itself was enough. There would be something for Pasha when he got out, something he could take with him from Russia to start a new life.

What if he sold more watches? What if he swallowed his distaste for Vladimir and stayed on at the dacha for a while, after all, and built himself up a nice nest egg? Sell a watch each week, for example, on his day off. Not always to Rostkhenkovskaya. There must be others who would buy. Mix it up a bit so no one would be suspicious. After a few months, he would have a fortune.

Be like Goroviev. Gouge Vladimir back for all the gouging he had done.

He grimaced, disgusted at himself.

And yet the thought persisted. Why not? Maybe give some of the proceeds to Stepanin, so he could leave his hopeless feud with Barkovskaya before it killed him. Who would know? Who would ever miss those watches? Why leave them for others to have after Vladimir was dead, people who almost certainly already had so much wealth that the whole cabinet of watches would add barely a speck to the mountain of their riches?

The *whole* cabinet of watches...

Again, Sheremetev tried to put the idea forcibly out of his mind, dismayed at the way it kept coming back. First things first. Tomorrow, he had to get the three hundred thousand for Pasha. Right now, that was all he should be thinking about: how he would safely carry the watch, how he would get to the shop, how he would transport the money to Oleg.

He lay in bed, resting on the mattress with the money hidden underneath it, his back aching, his cheek throbbing, torn between disgust for himself and hope for Pasha, thinking about tomorrow.

15

THE NEXT MORNING DAWNED grey and drizzly. The atmosphere in the dacha was oppressive. In the staff dining room, the security guards ate their breakfast gloomily. Stepanin's assistants came out of the kitchen to refill the *kasha* pot and went back in without uttering a word.

Just before ten o'clock, the drizzle petered out and the clouds parted for a time, allowing through rays of weak, watery sunshine. Sheremetev took Vladimir out for his walk. Goroviev passed by with a hoe in his hand. He stopped and asked how Vladimir was. Vladimir ignored him. The gardener walked with them for a few minutes, but Sheremetev had nothing to say to him, and eventually Goroviev went away.

At around the same time, in the staff wing of the dacha, Stepanin knocked on the door of Barkovskaya's office. 'Come in,' called out Barkovskaya's voice. The cook entered and closed the door behind him.

VLADIMIR'S LUNCH CAME UP at one o'clock: vegetarian stew with polenta cakes. Sheremetev fed Vladimir in his sitting room, then took the tray away and finished the leftovers himself, not wanting to go downstairs. Vera was due at three o'clock. A few minutes before she arrived, Sheremetev left Vladimir watching footage of himself on the television and went into the dressing room. He retrieved the Patek Philippe from the cabinet and slipped it into his pocket.

Eleyekov drove him into town, where a client had scheduled a pickup for three-thirty. Sheremetev had toyed with the idea of paying Eleyekov to drive him all the way to Moscow and wait for him while he settled his business at Rostkhenkovskaya's shop, then take him to Oleg's, thus avoiding the risk of carrying the watch and later the money on the metro. But it occurred to him that if an inventory of Vladimir's watches actually existed, and if the ones he had taken were ever missed, the last thing he needed was for Vladimir's driver to recall that he had taken Sheremetev to a watch shop in Moscow. Even getting him to wait out of sight, so he didn't know exactly where Sheremetev was going, would have been a risk.

Once he had the money, Sheremetev thought, he would get a taxi. There were always taxis around Arbatskaya station.

'Guess what's for dinner tonight,'said Eleyekov, glancing at Sheremetev with a knowing smile on his face as they cruised down the drive of the dacha.

'Fried air?' suggested Sheremetev. Air was all Stepanin had left now if he persisted in refusing to cook anything that Barkovskaya's suppliers were bringing.

Eleyekov laughed, pulling up in front of the security barrier at the gate. 'Fried air! That's good. No. Guess.' The barrier rose as Eleyekov waited for Sheremetev to reply. 'Chicken fricassee!' he announced, glancing at Sheremetev to see what he would make of such momentous news.

'Chicken fricassee?'

Eleyekov grinned and drove out of the gate. 'Stepanin's made it up with Barkovskaya.'

'No!'

'Yes! This morning. He finally bit the bullet and went and talked to her. It's all okay, apparently. He'll get something. Not as much as before – in fact, between you and me, reading between the lines, I think it's quite a lot less – but still, something is better than nothing, right? If you can't have the whole loaf, at least make sure you get a few crumbs from the table.'

'Are you sure?'

'Barkovskaya's won. That's clear to him now. The fricassee is his surrender. She loves it, you know. Well, she'll eat this one with double pleasure! She's a tough one, Barkovskaya, there's no doubt about that. But that's what it takes to get ahead, right, Nikolai Ilyich?'

Sheremetev was amazed at what the driver had just told him. After what Stepanin had said yesterday, he would never have imagined that the cook would capitulate. But in reality, what else could he do? One person beaten up, two places firebombed, another person shot . . . What next? Burn down the dacha? It couldn't go on. Barkovskaya held the trump card, that was what all of this had proved, and finally Stepanin himself had had to accept it.

'If he had done it earlier,' said Eleyekov, 'he would have got more. I told him. Vitya, I said, talk to her.'

'So did I.'

'You know, at the start, it might really have only been her cousin with the chickens that she was trying to help. If he'd accepted that, she might not have gone any further. Still . . . Who knows? Maybe he was right to fight it. She's so tough, maybe she would have given him even less if he had simply given up.' The driver frowned, considering the conundrum. 'Hard to say.'

'And what about this business with Artur?'

'Ah, that's something else. If I was Barkovskaya . . . I told you yesterday, I'd be shitting in my pants. But maybe she knows some-thing we don't know. Maybe she has protection. You know, Stepanin's lucky it's Artyusha in the hospital and not him.'

'How is he?'

'Artyusha?' Eleyekov let out a long breath, shaking his head. He took his eyes off the road for a moment and glanced at Sheremetev. 'Not good. They're not sure if he'll walk again. From what I under-stand, one of the bullets hit his spine. That's not good, is it?'

'They're saying he might end up in a wheelchair?'

'I think so.'

Sheremetev still didn't know quite how to think about Artur. On the one hand, personally, he had always found him polite and thoughtful, by far the most amenable of the security contingent, and he couldn't deny that he had taken a liking to him. On the other hand, he ran a protection racket that apparently had all of Odintsovo quaking in its boots, and although Sheremetev was no expert in the arts of intimidation and punishment, he knew enough to imagine that this must involve a fair helping of violence, as the breaking of the arms of Barkovskaya's cousin demonstrated. Still, somehow, the idea of Artur being in a wheelchair for the rest of his life was appalling.

'What are things coming to?' murmured Sheremetev.

Eleyekov laughed. 'That's what each generation says as it gets older. Do you think things were better when we were young? They've always been shit. Shit piled on shit piled on shit. That's Russia, Nikolai Ilyich. It was the same in the days of Ivan the Terrible and it was the same in the days of Stalin and it's the same now. What do you expect? Every so often you get your head above the surface for a second and that's when you realise it, there's nothing around you but shit. After that – you're in again.'

Sheremetev didn't reply, wondering glumly if the times they were living in were really no better than those of the two terrible autocrats Eleyekov had mentioned.

The driver stole a glance at him. 'Tell me something, Nikolai Ilyich. Seriously...Vladimir Vladimirovich...How long do you think he'll live?'

Sheremetev closed his eyes, revolted by the question. They were all the same, every single person in the dacha. The only thing they cared about was how long the feast would go on, like fish gorging themselves on a whale's flesh even while the whale was still alive.

Then Sheremetev thought of why he was in this car and what he carried in his pocket and of his thoughts last night: week by week, sell a watch, build up a nest egg...How much better was he?

'You're a nurse, Nikolai Ilyich. You've seen this before. How much longer? What do you think? Six months? A year?'

'You never know,' murmured Sheremetev. 'He could go on for a long time.'

'Really?' said Eleyekov, a note of relief in his voice. 'Because I had a friend who told me, once they lose their marbles, it's quick after that.'

'No. It's all about how strong the heart is.'

'And how strong is his heart?'

Sheremetev shrugged. 'Any one of us could go at any time, Vadim Sergeyevich. You or me included. That's all I know.'

Eleyekov glanced at him for a moment, then laughed.

Sheremetev gazed out the window. Already they were at the out-skirts of the town. He watched the first apartment blocks pass by on either side.

He really was amazed that Stepanin had given in. But in the end, what else could he do?

Well, the feud between the cook and the housekeeper was over, and in another couple of hours, he would have the money to set Pasha free.

THE RITUAL OF PRESSING the bell, hearing the click of the lock and then pushing open the door was becoming familiar now. From the back of the shop emerged Rostkhenkovskaya, this time wearing a black pinafore dress and a silver brooch in the shape of a bird of some sort.

'Good evening, Nikolai Ilyich,' she said. 'I'm glad to see you.'

Sheremetev reached into his pocket, produced the usual handkerchief-wrapped bundle, and laid it on the counter.

Rostkhenkovskaya unwrapped it. A smile played on her lips as she examined the Patek Philippe. 'Just wait a moment please.'

She left the watch on the counter and disappeared into the back of the shop. When she returned she was accompanied by a large man with brown eyes and wavy dark hair in a well-cut, pinstriped suit.

'Nikolai Ilyich, this is Aleksandr Semyonovich Belkin. He's an expert in Patek Philippes. Given the sum of money we're talking about, I felt I needed a second opinion. I hope that's alright.'

'Yes,' replied Sheremetev. 'It's alright.'

'Good evening, Nikolai Ilyich.' Belkin extended a fleshy hand, but his eye was already on the watch. 'Is this it?' Without waiting for an answer, Belkin dropped Sheremetev's hand and picked up the watch. He adroitly slotted a loupe in his right eye socket and proceeded to examine the Patek Philippe minutely, handling it as gently as if it was a newborn child. 'Hmmm...' he said. Then another 'Hmmm...' in a slightly higher register.

The expert put the watch down. He disposed of the eyepiece by releasing the contraction of his facial muscles and letting it drop, neatly catching it in the palm of his hand and secreting it in a pocket. Then he glanced at Rostkhenkovskaya and gave her a nod. He turned to Sheremetev. 'A beautiful watch, Nikolai Ilyich. You know, there are very few of this particular watch known to be made. We're talking about fewer than forty. Of those, I know who owns probably fifty percent – in Russia, probably all of them. If any of the owners wanted to sell, I'd be the first person they'd consult. But you, Nikolai Ilyich, I don't know.'

'It was my uncle's,' said Sheremetev.

'So I must know your uncle.'

Sheremetev didn't reply.

The expert watched him closely, a half smile on his face. 'Anna says you sold her three more watches. Not quite in this class, but not bad ones. That's quite a collection, Nikolai Ilyich.'

'My uncle was very generous.'

'And still is, it seems.'

Sheremetev didn't say anything to that.

'Listen, Nikolai Ilyich, what else do you have ... or should I say, what else might he be inclined to give you?'

'Nothing.'

'That's it?'

'Yes.'

'Ah. I thought you were going to bring more.'

'No.'

'Your uncle has no more?'

'He has more but they're—'

'But he has more?'

Sheremetev didn't like the look in the expert's eyes. 'I don't know.

This is what I've got. This is what I'd like to sell. That's it.' He glanced at Rostkhenkovskaya.

She smiled slightly.

'The thing is,' said Belkin, 'what you bring is of such high quality, and of such demand amongst our customers, that we'd like a little more.'

We, thought Sheremetev, increasingly uneasy. Who was *we*?

'I only have what I have,' he said.

'We could give you a commission,' continued Belkin, as if he hadn't heard him. 'Say, ten percent.'

'They're not my watches to sell.'

'And this is?' Belkin looked at him pointedly.

Sheremetev reached for the Patek Philippe, but the other man's hand was quicker. He snatched the watch up and held it away from Sheremetev.

Sheremetev looked at Rostkhenkovskaya again. 'Anna Mikhailovna, you told me you would pay three hundred thousand dollars for this watch. We had an agreement. All I'm asking for is what you promised.'

'That was yesterday,' replied Belkin.

'Anna Mikhailovna!'

She shrugged. 'Aleksandr Semyonovich is right. That was yesterday.'

Sheremetev stared at her in disbelief.

'Things change, Nikolai Ilyich.'

Sheremetev hesitated, but nothing in Rostkhenkovskaya's expression changed, and he finally understood that no help was going to come to him from her. Suddenly he lunged across the counter for the watch. Belkin batted him away with ease.

'Well, Nikolai Ilyich, what do you say?'

Sheremetev was red-faced with anger. 'Give me the watch back and I'll think about it.'

Belkin laughed. 'Give you the watch back, and we'll never see you again. You need to decide now, Nikolai Ilyich. You need to decide now, and then we need to go.'

'Go where?'

'To the watches.'

Sheremetev stared for a moment, then shook his head.

'Yes, Nikolai Ilyich. We need to go there now.'

Sheremetev glanced around the room, hurriedly considering his options. Taking these horological gangsters to the watches meant taking them to the dacha – which was impossible. Getting the watch out of Belkin's grasp also seemed impossible, or at least unlikely. All he could do, it seemed to Sheremetev, was walk out, leave the watch and let Belkin and Rostkhenkovskaya do what they wanted with it. The idea was offensive – but in the end, what difference would it make to him? True, that would leave Rostkhenkovskaya and this reptile holding a watch they had stolen and would presumably sell for many hundreds of thousands of dollars, but so what? Personally, he would have lost nothing, since he had never had that money to start with, and more importantly, there were another three hundred watches in Vladimir's cabinet, and surely in amongst all those others must be one or two more as valuable as this. Next time he might even look on the internet to see how much they were worth, as he should have done, he realised, from the start. And there must be other watch buyers in Moscow, and he wouldn't make the mistake again of letting anyone think he had more than he proposed to sell them. Or perhaps he would go to St Petersburg. He was supposed to be able to take four weeks holiday each year but he hadn't taken a single day since moving to the dacha three years previously. He could leave Vera in charge and head off for a week with a bag full of watches.

Rostkhenkovskaya had seemed such a sweet, sympathetic girl. Well, she had taken him in completely.

Sheremetev looked at her. 'Keep it,' he said, and went to the door. It was locked.

'It wasn't a question, Nikolai Ilyich,' said Belkin. 'We need to go to the watches tonight.'

'I can't take you.'

'I think you can.'

'Keep that one. Isn't it enough for you?'

'No. Nowhere near enough.'

Sheremetev tried the door again. Behind him, Belkin was laughing. Sheremetev looked desperately around. A wooden mantle clock stood at the end of the counter. He grabbed it and hurled it through the glass door, shattering the pane and leaving razor-sharp shards hanging from the frame. He began to kick at them.

Suddenly he felt hands on his shoulders dragging him away from the door. They dumped him on the ground.

Sheremetev looked up. Above him stood five thugs in leather jackets who had materialised from the back of the shop, and behind them were Belkin and Rostkhenkovskaya. He got to his feet, angrily straightening his clothes.

'Vasya!' called Rostkhenkovskaya. 'What are you doing? Come out!'

From the back of the shop, sheepishly, came a sixth man.

Sheremetev's mouth dropped.

Vasily looked down in embarrassment. 'What the fuck are you doing, Papa? Why don't you just do what they tell you?'

'*Papa?*' said Rostkhenkovskaya.

'You didn't tell me his name!' snapped Vasya. 'You think if I knew who he is I'd be here?'

'I didn't know his name!' replied Rostkhenkovskaya. 'All he told me was that he's called Nikolai Ilyich.'

'You could have told me that!'

'Would that have helped? How many Nikolai Ilyich's do you think there are in Moscow?'

Vasya shook his head angrily. 'Papa, what have you done to your face?'

'It's a cut,' said Sheremetev.

'How did you get it?'

'What difference does it make? What are you *doing*, Vasya?'

'Who gives a fuck?' shouted Belkin. 'I don't care if he's your father or your brother or your fucking mother. Nothing's changed. We're going! You,' he said, pointing at Sheremetev, 'are going to take us to the watches, or the consequences are going to be very painful.'

'Papa,' said Vasya, 'whose watches are they?'

Sheremetev glared at him angrily. 'Whose do you think?'

Vasya frowned for a moment, then his eyes widened. 'Jesus Christ!'

Belkin turned to Vasya. 'Do you know whose they are?'

Vasya didn't reply. He raised an eyebrow at his father.

'The ex-president's,' muttered Sheremetev guiltily.

There was a stunned silence. For several seconds, nobody did anything. Then Belkin began to laugh. 'Vladimir Vladimirovich?'

Sheremetev nodded miserably. At least that would be an end of it now. They weren't going to go and steal the watches from the ex-president of Russia.

But Belkin showed no sign of discouragement. He glanced excitedly at Rostkhenkovskaya. 'I should have known. What quality! They say not a contract was signed in Russia without our President Vova getting a little watch as a gift. Tell me,' he said to Sheremetev, 'is he as senile as they all say?'

Sheremetev nodded again.

'And how do you happen to—'

'I'm his nurse,' blurted out Sheremetev, overcome with shame.

'His nurse! How long have you looked after him?'

'Six years.'

Belkin tutted. 'Nikolai Ilyich! What a betrayal – six years, and all this time you've been stealing from your patient!'

'I have not!' he replied indignantly. 'I've never taken a thing before this. Now I . . . I have a reason. Vasya knows.'

'Yes, there's always a reason,' remarked Belkin airily. 'Well, if he's as senile as you say, he won't notice if his watches are gone, will he?'

'You still want to go?' demanded Sheremetev in disbelief. 'He's surrounded by guards. You're crazy!'

'Nikolai Ilyich,' said Rostkhenkovskaya, 'how many watches are there? Tell us the truth.'

'I haven't counted them.'

'Roughly.'

'Another half dozen, perhaps.'

Belkin threw a glance at one of the thugs. He moved closer to Sheremetev, menacingly cupping the fist of one hand in the palm of the other.

Sheremetev glanced at Vasya, but his son had averted his eyes.

'How many, Nikolai Ilyich?' repeated Rostkhenkovskaya.

'I don't know,' he muttered. 'A couple of hundred, maybe.'

Belkin grinned. 'That sounds more like it. A couple of hundred, probably the best couple of hundred in Russia. And no record of ownership, because every one of them was a bribe. What could be better? Be honest. How long have you been selling them?'

'I've only sold the ones I brought here.'

'Come on, Nikolai Ilyich. Really?'

'My father's very honest,' said Vasya.

'Obviously,' observed Belkin.

'I've never stolen a thing in my life! I need the money for my nephew.'

'Pasha's an idiot, Papa. I told you—'

'How much do you need?' said Rostkhenkovskaya to Sheremetev.

'Three hund— Five hundred thousand.'

'Five hundred thousand? Dollars?'

Sheremetev nodded.

'Yesterday you seemed to be happy with three hundred thousand.'

'You said you were going to give me another fifty thousand for the first one and twenty-five for the others. And I was going to sell more elsewhere. I didn't want everything in one place.'

'Tell us the truth. Can you take us to the watches?'

'No. It's impossible.'

Rostkhenkovskaya glanced at Belkin.

The expert sighed, as if what he was about to say troubled him deeply. 'Well, in that case, Nikolai Ilyich, here's how things are going to work. Anna is going to take the three watches you sold her to the police and tell them that you brought them and how much she paid for them, and then the police are going to come and arrest you. We, in the meantime, will keep this lovely little Patek Philippe, which Anna of course won't mention. So the upshot is, Anna will have paid you what has she given you so far, which is how much?'

'Thirty-two and a half thousand dollars,' said Rostkhenkovskaya coolly.

'Thirty-two and a half thousand dollars. The police will take that from you when they arrest you, and we'll get some of it back after they deduct their commission. Not much, it's true, but on the other hand, we'll have a watch we got for free and that we'll sell for a million dollars, which is a pretty good profit. Oh, and I forgot. You're going to spend ten years in jail. Or ...' Belkin paused. 'It could work out differently. You could find a way to take us to the watches and we could give you five hundred thousand dollars and you could do whatever you want with it, including getting this idiot Pasha out of whatever trouble he's in, if that's what you want.'

'He's my nephew,' said Sheremetev, his voice barely more than a whisper. 'And he's not an idiot.'

'Idiot...not an idiot...Who cares? What do you think of my proposal, Nikolai Ilyich? It's your choice. Let me ask you once more: Can you take us to the watches or can't you?'

Sheremetev tried to catch Vasya's eye again, but his son seemed remarkably interested in scrutinising the old rings and necklaces in the nearest display case.

'What are you going to do with the watches if I take you to them?' asked Sheremetev at last, delaying the inevitable rather than really expecting an answer that would help him decide.

'Really, Nikolai Ilyich,' said Belkin knowingly. 'What do you think we're going to do?'

There was silence in the shop. Belkin, Rostkhenkovskaya, the five thugs and even Vasya – surreptitiously sneaking a glance at his father – watched Sheremetev as he thought over the choice. As if he really had one.

'When can I have the money?' he asked quietly.

'As soon as we've got the watches,' replied Belkin.

'Tonight?'

'We've got two briefcases full of cash in the back of the shop.'

'Five hundred thousand? I thought you were going to give me three hundred for the Patek Philippe.'

'We thought you might bring some more,' said Rostkhenkovskaya.

'So now you can get us to the watches, can you?' said Belkin. 'Well, let me warn you. If you've got some plan in your head that you're going to take us there and somehow turn us over to these guards you told us about, the story will be the same. You sold us three watches, which we'll hand over, and you asked us to come out to value the others. Us? We bought the watches in good faith. We drove with you to wherever you were taking us without knowing where we were going. We've done nothing wrong. So don't play games with us, Nikolai Ilyich, or it will end badly for you, I promise.'

Sheremetev closed his eyes. He didn't want to play games. He just wanted this to be over. He wanted to get the money for Pasha and then...then get away from the dacha and the filth and corruption that seemed to ooze out of its very pores to infect everything around them and which now seemed to be oozing out of his.

He opened his eyes. Again, everyone in the room was watching him. His gaze rested on Vasya. This time Vasya met his eyes. He gave a slight, almost imperceptible shrug.

Sheremetev turned back to Belkin. 'Okay.'

'So there's a way to do it, is there?'

Despising himself, Sheremetev nodded.

'Good!' Belkin went to the back of the shop and returned a moment later with two briefcases. 'Let's go.'

A PAIR OF VEHICLES was waiting around the corner. Sheremetev was put into the back seat of a Mercedes between Vasya and Rostkhenkovskaya. Belkin put the briefcases in the boot and then climbed into the front passenger seat. One of the thugs sat behind the wheel – the others piled into the second car.

Sheremetev told them to head for the Odintsovo. Soon they were in the Moscow traffic

After a few minutes Sheremetev's phone rang.

'It's my brother,' he said.

'Answer it,' replied Belkin.

Oleg had expected to hear from Sheremetev by now and had rung to check that everything was alright.

'There's been a hiccup,' said Sheremetev guardedly.

'What kind of hiccup?' asked Oleg .

'Umm . . . Listen, Oleg, I couldn't get away today.'

'What do you mean, you couldn't get away?'

'The relief nurse didn't turn up.'

'So what's going to happen?'

'I'll go tomorrow.'

'But you told me the watch buyer's expecting you today!'

'I phoned her. It's okay. I'll bring you the money tomorrow. Oleg, I promise, alright?'

'Do you want me to come with you tomorrow?'

'Oleg, I told you—'

'I told Pasha I was getting the money tonight and I'd have him out tomorrow.'

'Well, it might have to be the next day.'

There was silence.

'Okay,' said Oleg eventually. 'I guess another day's not going to kill him.'

'I'll see you tomorrow, Oleg.'

Sheremetev put the phone away.

'Nice lying, Dad,' said Vasya.

Sheremetev glared at his son. 'What are you doing, Vasya? This is a kidnap. Is this what you do? Go around hijacking people? I should go to the police!'

Vasya laughed, pointing a thumb at the thug driving the car. 'That guy *is* the police. There are four more in the car behind us. Moscow's finest.'

Sheremetev frowned. 'What is this? Some kind of investigation?'

Belkin chuckled.

'Jesus Christ, Papa!' hissed Vasya. 'How naïve can you be? You're embarrassing me! How do you think a policeman like that earns enough to feed his family?'

'It's better than taking bribes on the street, Sheremetev!' growled the driver.

'Sure,' retorted Vasya. 'And you don't do that as well?'

The driver grinned.

'So you bribe policemen?' said Sheremetev.

'No, I don't bribe policemen,' retorted Vasya. 'Not if I don't have to. Look – right now he's working for me. Why shouldn't I pay him?' Vasya sighed impatiently. 'Papa, I get things done, alright? Someone wants something, I fix it for them. Someone needs help, I get it for them. Anushka rings me up and says she needs some guys with a bit of muscle. Nothing nasty, just a bit of persuasion. So I get them for her.'

'So this isn't the first time? You help her steal things all the time, do you?'

'Every situation's different. Sometimes, someone needs protection. People know I always deliver. Word of mouth. I have a lot of customers in the jewellery business.'

'And what about me? Shouldn't I have had protection?'

'Did you call me?'

Sheremetev fumed. 'And you need five guys?' he demanded. 'Five guys for me?'

'First of all, I didn't know who you were, okay? What do you think I am? I wouldn't have got involved in this if I knew. She didn't tell me your name.'

'He didn't *tell* me, Vasya!' said Rostkhenkovskaya.

'Alright, fine. Whatever. Secondly, who knows if you're going to come with anybody else or what weapons you might have? Or what might happen when we get to wherever we're going to? It's not for me to question. I get the guys for her – that's it. It was going to be six, but one pulled out at the last minute, which is why I came myself. Incidentally, Seva, what the fuck happened to Gleb?'

'Don't know,' grunted the driver.

'If you see him, tell him, he can forget about me. That's it for him. Zero tolerance! No one fucks with Vasya Sheremetev. If Gleb thinks I can't get more where he came from, tell him to have a look around next time he goes to work.'

The driver nodded.

Vasya looked back at his father. 'See, you want some guys, I get them. It's only a question of money. It's not only policemen. If Anna had asked for ballerinas, I could get her half the chorus line for the Bolshoi. Trust me, I've done it before. You can have whatever you want. Not that any—' His phone rang. 'Excuse me.'

Vasya answered the phone. For the next minute or so he gave a series of monosyllabic answers, then put it away.

He turned again to Sheremetev. 'What was I saying?'

'Nothing,' muttered Sheremetev. As if Stepanin hadn't told him enough, he was sick at what he now understood of his son's profession, if that was the right word for it. He would never be able to pretend again that he didn't know.

They were driving stop-start on an eight-lane road with thousands of other vehicles all trying to get out of central Moscow. Sheremetev had lost track of where they were – he only knew that every minute they were in the car brought them closer to the dacha.

Suddenly he looked back at Vasya. 'Do you think it's because of Mama?'

'What?'

'This stuff that you do. Do you think it's because of the way Mama died?'

'Papa...' growled Vasya.

'I remember the way you cried—'

'Papa! Please!'

Sheremetev was quiet for a moment. Then he turned to Rostkhenkovskaya. 'His mother died when he was nineteen.'

'Papa!'

'What?' demanded Sheremetev. 'Are you ashamed of it?'

'Why should I be ashamed of it?'

'Then be quiet! You were nineteen. A boy's mother dies. He shouldn't cry?'

'Of course he should cry,' said Rostkhenkovskaya.

'My mother only died last year,' chipped in the driver, 'and I cried like a baby.'

'Seva, you shut the fuck up!'

'How did she die?' asked Rostkhenkovskaya.

'Oh, for God's sake!'

'Kidney failure,' said Sheremetev. 'We didn't have the money for the bribes. Others did.'

Rostkhenkovskaya leaned forward and looked past Sheremetev at Vasya. 'Vasya, is that true?'

Vasya shrugged.

'Is it?'

Vasya grunted.

'And did you know it was because your dad didn't have the money?'

Vasya shrugged again.

'So is this . . . what you do, is that to get back at him?'

Vasya didn't reply.

There was silence in the car – a silence that prickled with the tension of people straining to hear more. Belkin had turned to look at Vasya. Seva, the driver, was frowning, hunched slightly, waiting for the response.

'Vasily,' said Sheremetev. 'Is that why you do this? This life that you live, this work that you do – is to punish me?'

Vasya wiped at his eyes. 'No, it's not to punish you! It's so, if I ever have a wife and I ever have a son, he won't have to watch her die because I'm so damn honest and so damn noble and so damn upright that I don't have the pathetic few thousand dollars it will take to save her!'

Sheremetev recoiled.

'How much was that watch you brought in today, Papa? Ask yourself that. Three hundred thousand dollars. That's what Anushka offered you, right? And for the sake of how much did Mama die? Was it even three thousand? The watch alone could have saved a hundred of her. And that crook, that man you call your patient, was probably taking that watch from some filthy oligarch the very same day she died. That's what it is to live in Russia, Papa. That's something you've never understood. You have to be like him – or you end up emptying his bedpan.'

Vasya's phone went off. 'Yes?' he barked.

'Vasya's not so bad,' whispered Rostkhenkovskaya to Sheremetev, as Vasya snapped answers into his phone.

Sheremetev glanced at her in disbelief. How, he wondered, had he come to be sitting in this car beside his son, the gangster, taking comfort from an extortionist in a black pinafore dress?

The car drove on, a capsule full of greed and recrimination and misery travelling through the Moscow night.

IT TOOK ALMOST THREE hours to get to the dacha in the traffic crawling out of the city. When they finally arrived, they stopped out of sight of the gate. Sheremetev had told them that if he tried to get the five policemen into the house, suspicions would be raised – especially now that the whole dacha was on edge and everyone was waiting for some kind of war to break out between the Lukashvillis and whoever had shot Artur, although he didn't tell them about that. The driver, Seva, got out of the car and went to join his fellow moonlighting cops in the second car, which parked on a verge at the side of the road. Vasya took his place at the steering wheel.

They drove up to the gate. A security guard came out of the booth to see who was there. Sheremetev lowered his window.

'I've got a couple of contractors here who have come to see about installing some equipment for Vladimir Vladimirovich,' he said.

'What kind of equipment?' asked the guard suspiciously.

'A lift for the stairs. It's getting harder and harder for Vladimir Vladimirovich to walk up and down.'

The guard looked at his watch. 'So late?'

'They had to come from Moscow.'

The guard consulted his clipboard. 'Did you clear them?'

'They're doing me a favour. They agreed to come at short notice.'

The guard peered into the car. 'Turn off the engine,' he said to Vasya.

'You want me to turn it off?'

'Yes! Turn it off!'

Vasya turned it off. 'Touchy,' he said.

The guard gave him a hostile glance and then looked carefully at the other occupants. Rostkhenkovskaya gave him a winning smile. He didn't react.

'Do you know these people personally, Nikolai Ilyich?' he asked.

'Of course,' said Sheremetev. 'I can vouch for them.'

The guard looked them over again. Sheremetev waited. Normally, the guard would have waved them through by now, but everyone in the dacha was jittery.

The guard walked around the car. 'Open the boot,' he called out. Vasya released the boot lock and the guard looked inside, then slammed the door closed.

He came back to the window. 'You know you're meant to get people cleared in advance, Nikolai Ilyich.'

Sheremetev nodded. 'It was short notice.'

'I need to see identification.'

Belkin and Rostkhenkovskaya pulled out their driving licences. Vasya did the same.

The guard took the licences and noted down the names and date of birth of each person. H returned them without a word and then went back to the booth.

They could see the guard making a call.

'Remember what I told you,' said Belkin to Sheremetev as they waited. 'If you try anything, we show the watches and say you sold them to us.' He clicked his fingers. 'Like that! Ten years in jail for you, minimum.'

Still the gate didn't open.

'What's the holdup?' muttered Vasya.

'Things are a bit . . . It's just takes a little while,' said Sheremetev. He frowned. 'Funny he didn't notice you've got the same name as me.'

Vasya rolled his eyes, as if his father's naivete knew no bounds. 'That's not the name on the licence, Dad.'

By the time Sheremetev understood what his son meant, the guard inside the booth had put down the phone. The security gate opened a few seconds later.

Vasya restarted the engine and they headed up the drive.

16

WITHOUT UTTERING A WORD, the security guard in the hall ran a metal detector over them and checked the briefcases that Belkin and Rostkhenkovskaya carried. Lyosha stood beside him, watchful and silent. When the guard was finished, Lyosha gestured for them to come through.

Upstairs, Sheremetev left Vasya, Belkin and Rostkhenkovskaya in an empty room while he went to get rid of Vera. Vladimir was in his sitting room, mumbling aggressively.

'How has he been?' asked Sheremetev.

Vera rolled her eyes.

'I'm sorry,' said Sheremetev. He would need Vera again the next day so that he could take Oleg the money that he was going to get from Belkin. 'Listen, Verochka, can you come again tomorrow?'

'Kolya, I don't think so.'

'Please. One more day. He's getting used to you.'

She looked unconvinced.

'Come on, Verochka. It's important.'

'What are you doing every day, anyway?'

'I just need to get away a little. I told myself, this week, I'll take a few afternoons off.'

She looked at him knowingly. 'Have you met someone?'

'No.'

'You have!'

'I haven't,' he said impatiently. Vasya and the two extortionists were sitting in a room not ten metres away, and although he had told them explicitly to stay there until he came for them, he knew that if he left it too long they might decide he was trying to pull some kind of trick – and there was no knowing what they would do then.

'Kolya, it's six years since your wife died. It's time you met someone. Give yourself some credit. You're very attractive to a woman if she likes small men.'

'Thank you, Verochka, but now's not the time.'

'Now *is* the time!'

'Believe me,' said Sheremetev, 'it isn't.'

'Kolya, it's too easy to keep saying that. How much longer will you wait?' Vera shook her head, eyes filled with emotion. 'Kolya, if you're not careful, you'll be an old man before you know it and your whole life will have passed. You deserve more than that.'

'We'll discuss it,' he said, trying to push her out the door.

She held firm. 'When?'

'Not now.'

'Kolya, don't pretend.'

'Pretend what?'

Vera batted her eyelids coyly. 'You know what.'

Sheremetev felt like tearing his hair out.

She came closer.

'Vera,' he said, trying again to usher her out of Vladimir's suite, 'let's talk about this tomorrow.'

'Tomorrow? Really?'

'When you come to look after Vladimir Vladimirovich.'

Vera sighed. 'Oh, I'm really not sure I can come tomorrow.'

'Vera, please! I need you tomorrow. We can talk then.'

'But you won't be here.'

'When I come back. I'll only be gone for a few hours. I'll put Vladimir to bed, then we'll have plenty of time.'

'All night?'

'If we need it.'

'What do you have in mind?'

'Wait and see,' he said, finally shoving her out the door and into the corridor.

She stopped. 'Kolya, you devil! You've been playing hard to get. The things you made me say! Shall I bring something special tomorrow for when you get back?'

'Whatever you like,' he replied hurriedly, pulling on her arm to get her moving again.

She raised an eyebrow. 'Lingerie?'

'Whatever!'

'Yes?'

'Yes! Yes!' He stopped at the top of the stairs.

Vera ran a finger under Sheremetev's chin. 'Until tomorrow, Nikolasha.' She gazed at him, and then sashayed down the stairs.

He stayed, stifling his urge to run back, knowing that she would turn at the bottom and look at him again. She did. He smiled, seeming to remember that he had heard Vera mention lingerie and only now thinking about what he had said and wondering how he would get out of it tomorrow. She walked past Lyosha, who was still there with the other security guard, and disappeared

Sheremetev turned to go back but caught a glimpse of Stepanin crossing the lobby below him. As Sheremetev watched, the chef leaned close to Lyosha and whispered something in his ear. Lyosha nodded and they walked away together.

What was Stepanin, who hardly ever emerged from the kitchen, doing in the entrance hall? And where was Lyosha going with him?

Suddenly he remembered the three interlopers. He ran back to the room where he had deposited them. 'Wait!' he said breathlessly. 'Five more minutes. Stay until I come to get you!' Then he ran back to Vladimir's sitting room.

Vladimir was still mumbling to himself.

'How are you this evening, Vladimir Vladimirovich?' asked Sheremetev, trying to slow himself down and keep his anxiety out of his voice.

Vladimir looked around at him. 'Who are you?'

'Sheremetev, Vladimir Vladimirovich.'

'What are you doing here?'

'I'm looking after you.'

Vladimir sniffed. 'Can you smell him?'

'No,' said Sheremetev. 'I think he's gone.'

'He's never gone,' growled Vladimir.

'Vladimir Vladimirovich, I have a couple of visitors.'

'Who is it?' demanded Vladimir. 'Is it Monarov? I told him to have the latest on Trikovsky on my desk this morning. Where is he? Has he got it?'

'I don't know, Vladimir Vladimirovich.'

'He's been twelve years in prison. I don't understand why no one's arranged an accident!'

'It's just three workers who need to check something in your dressing room.'

'Who?'

'The people who are here. They'll only take a few minutes. Just stay here, Vladimir Vladimirovich, and they won't disturb you.'

'Go on, then! Why are you taking my time up with such a thing? What do I care? I've got more important things to attend to.' He paused. 'That fucking Chechen is here somewhere, I'm telling you. If you find him in the dressing room, let me know.'

'I think he's gone.'

'He's here!'

Sheremetev left. A minute later he returned with Vasya, Belkin and Rostkhenkovskaya and led them past the closed door of the sitting room into Vladimir's bedroom.

'Where is he?' whispered Belkin.

'In another room. Come through. The watches are here.'

Sheremetev took them into the dressing room. He turned on the light and gestured to the wooden cabinet.

Belkin opened the doors. He hesitated, as if heightening the moment of climax, and then slid out the top tray.

At the sight of the fifteen watches nestled in their velvet-lined clefts, he and Rostkhenkovskaya exchanged an awed glance.

'A Vacheron Tour de l'Ile,' whispered Belkin, pointing.

Rostkhenkovskaya nodded. 'And another one! There. Look.'

For an instant longer, they stared as if the objects of their lust had momentarily paralysed them. Then Belkin opened his briefcase and his thick, sausage-like fingers reached for the watches. In four quick handfuls, he had cleared the tray.

He opened the second tray and grabbed another clutch of watches as Rostkhenkovskaya did the same. They emptied the third tray, and the fourth. They weren't even looking at the pieces now, just scooping the watches up and dropping them in by the handful. Their greed oozed out of them like an oily sheen.

Sheremetev tried to get a peek into Belkin's case. As far as he could tell, it was empty but for the watches that had just gone into it. But then . . . where was the money they had said they were bringing for him?

Sheremetev took a step closer, trying to get a look into the brief-case Rostkhenkovskaya was filling.

'Where's Monarov?'

Sheremetev jumped. Belkin and Rostkhenkovskaya froze, watches in hand, then turned to see an old man in a blue sweater and grey trousers standing behind them.

'Where's Monarov?' demanded Vladimir, peering at each of them to see if anyone was his dead crony. His eyes lingered on Vasya, who stared back at him, mouth agape.

'I told you, Vladimir Vladimirovich,' said Sheremetev, 'he's coming later.' Sheremetev took Vladimir by the arm. 'Come on, let's go back. It's just workmen here. They need to finish what they're doing.'

'Monarov's coming, is he?'

'Yes, he's coming. Soon.'

Vladimir looked at Sheremetev suspiciously. 'You're sure?'

'I'm sure. I'll let you know as soon as he's here.'

'With his report!'

'Yes, Vladimir Vladimirovich, with his report.'

Sheremetev nudged Vladimir again, and the old man shuffled away with him back to the sitting room.

A couple of minutes later, Sheremetev returned. Belkin and Rostkhenkovskaya had finished ransacking the cabinet. When they had run out of space in their cases, they had filled their pockets.

'Well?' said Sheremetev.

Belkin grinned. 'He really knows nothing, does he?'

The tone of Belkin's question and the repulsive grin on his face brought out a protective instinct in Sheremetev. 'He's got dementia. That's how it is. It can happen to any of us.'

'He's worse than he looks on the TV.'

'Watch out it doesn't happen to you,' retorted Sheremetev. 'All the watches you can steal will mean nothing then.'

Belkin laughed. 'They'll mean a lot until it happens, though. Right! We're ready. Thank you, Nikolai Ilyich. You've been very helpful. We'll be going now.'

'And the money, Aleksandr Semyonovich? The half million?'

'Yes, the half million. Listen, Nikolai Ilyich, we've been thinking...' Belkin grimaced, as if it was a difficult decision that he had to announce. 'We can't give it to you.'

'You mean you don't have it with you? Do I have to come and get it tomorrow?'

'No, I mean, we're not going to give it to you. At all.'

Sheremetev stared at him.

'See, the way I look at it – excuse me for putting it bluntly, Nikolai Ilyich – half a million dollars isn't a puff of air, and even if one can afford to give it, if one doesn't have to, why should one? What are you going to do? Are you going to go to someone and say, I did a deal with these people to let them steal all of Vladimir Vladimirovich's watches, but then they didn't give me my cut? I don't think you're going to do that. Believe me, if you do, you'll be in prison longer than me. I'll buy my way out of the charges. What will you do?'

Sheremetev's mind reeled. He turned to Rostkhenkovskaya. 'You never even brought it, did you?'

She didn't reply.

Sheremetev searched for something to say. All he could think of was what Stepanin had done. 'I'll get someone to firebomb you,' he muttered.

Rostkhenkovskaya smiled.

'Come on, Nikolai Ilyich,' said Belkin, 'you're not that kind of guy. You know, I really do believe you're an honest fellow. A rarity – and a conundrum! An honest man stealing watches. What has Russia come to when we see such a thing?' He laughed. 'You should be thankful to us for relieving you of the temptation. Don't eat yourself up about it. What have you lost? How many years did you say you worked here? Six? For six years, you didn't touch these watches. You were never going to. Here they stayed – now I've got them. They weren't yours before, they're not yours now. You've lost nothing.'

'But Pasha...'

'Ah, yes, the nephew. That really is what this is all about, isn't it? Tell me, how much do you really need for him?'

'Three hundred thousand dollars.'

Belkin tutted. 'So you lied as well. Shame on you, Nikolai Ilyich.'

'He needs some money to leave the country.'

'Two hundred thousand?'

'Forget that. Give me three hundred thousand. Just let me get him out of jail.'

Belkin laughed.

'Please,' he begged. 'Three hundred, that's all.'

'Or what?'

Sheremetev had no reply to that. He turned his gaze on Vasya. 'Are you going to let them do this?'

'Papa...'

'Are you?'

'It's business, Papa. What do you want me to do? They're the client, not you.'

'But they lied to me!'

'You lied to them too.'

'It's not the same.'

Vasya shrugged.

'And your cousin?'

'He's an idiot. How many times do I have to tell you that? I'm not responsible. Let him write what he wants and let him take the consequences.'

'But this is wrong!' cried Sheremetev. 'Vasya! These two people promised me half a million in return for the millions and millions they've got in those bags. You heard them! And now, nothing? Is that right? Is that just? Go! Go outside and get your thugs. They'll do anything you say.'

'Papa...listen...I can't do that. I'm a businessman. It's a cut-throat world, you have no idea. I have nothing but my reputation. I told you, I have a good business with the jewellery people. One talks to the other. Do you know what would happen if I did what you say? No one would trust me. I'd never get another client.'

Belkin nodded gravely. 'The relationship with the client is sacred, Nikolai Ilyich. You should understand, you're a nurse. It's like you and your patients.'

Sheremetev shook his head, stunned and horrified by the analogy.

'That's how it is, Papa. You can ask them yourself for the money. I can't do anything. If they say no, it's no.'

Swallowing his loathing for the other man, Sheremetev turned again to Belkin. 'Please,' he said. 'Please give me the money to get my nephew Pasha out of jail.'

Belkin glanced at Rostkhenkovskaya, then gestured towards her, as if leaving the decision in her hands.

A flame of hope came alight in Sheremetev's heart.

'No,' she said.

'But Anna Mikhailovna—'

'No.'

'Aleksandr Semyonovich?' cried Sheremetev in desperation.

'You heard her.'

The two watch thieves headed out of the dressing room.

'Wait!' said Sheremetev, running after them.

'What now?' demanded Belkin irritably.

'You've taken everything!'

'So?'

'You have to leave something. People are used to seeing a watch on his wrist. One day one watch, one day another. If they don't, they'll start to wonder what's happened. Someone will investigate. And people saw you come in today, even if you gave a false identity. There are cameras here also.'

'He's got a point, Sasha,' said Rostkhenkovskaya.

'You think so?' said Belkin. 'I think it's a trick to make us leave him something. If anyone does investigate, how much will it take to buy them off?'

'In the case of the ex-president's watches,' said Rostkhen-kovskaya, 'who knows?'

She gazed at him pointedly. Eventually Belkin sighed and shook his head. He put his briefcase down on Vladimir's bed and opened it, looked over the tangled mass of watches, selected half a dozen and put them on Vladimir's bedside table. As he went to close the case, he stopped and fished another one out.

'You can have this one for yourself,' he said derisively, and he tossed it to Sheremetev. 'In the whole collection, this was the only piece of shit.'

He snapped the briefcase closed.

Rostkhenkovskaya was already heading for the door. Belkin went with her.

Vasya gazed at his father, who stood helplessly, arms by his sides, his face with its lacerated cheek torn between confusion and despair. For a moment, their eyes met.

Vasya shrugged and followed his clients out.

Sheremetev slumped to the floor. He looked at the watch that Belkin had thrown him. You didn't have to be an expert to recognise this one. Even he knew what it was – a plain old Poljot from Soviet times, battered, scratched and worn.

DISBELIEF. HUMILIATION. HOPELESSNESS. SHEREMETEV felt like an old rag that someone had picked up and wiped themselves with and thrown away. He was nothing: Nikolai Ilyich Sheremetev, a worm, a slug, a mushroom, a little man who knew nothing about how anything worked, a fool who had been taken advantage of all his life in this Russia which was a paradise, above all, for those who took advantage of fools. Well, here he was, unable to find a way to get even a few hundred thousand dollars to save his nephew when for six years he had had a cabinet of watches worth – How much? Ten million dollars? Twenty million? – at his sole disposal.

He keeled over and lay flat on the floor in self-hatred and misery.

Eventually the sound of Vladimir's mumblings and grumblings, growing in volume, penetrated his consciousness. He lay listening for a while. He had to get Vladimir up, get him into his pyjamas, get him into bed . . . And for what? So he could do the same thing tomorrow, and the day after, and the day after, as he had done for the last six years . . . And in the meantime, his son had turned into a gangster, and not just any kind of gangster. A gangster who would stand by and watch as his own father was cheated and abused.

He got wearily to his feet and put the Poljot watch with the others that Belkin had left on Vladimir's bedside table. The laceration in his cheek, which had been partially reopened the previous day, throbbed a little, just enough for him to be conscious of it.

He went to the sitting room.

'Come on, Vladimir Vladimirovich,' said Sheremetev quietly, feeling that he didn't have the energy even to hate this man any more, as he had started to do. 'It's time for bed.'

Vladimir scrutinised the face that had suddenly loomed up in front of him. He could smell the Chechen. He was definitely somewhere here. Vladimir tried to peer around the small man in front of him to see if the Chechen was behind him.

'Vladimir Vladimirovich,' said Sheremetev, almost in tears, 'please.'

He pulled gently on Vladimir's arm. After a moment, the old man got up and Sheremetev led him to the bedroom.

As Sheremetev got him changed, Vladimir kept scanning the room. Sheremetev slipped him an extra sedative tablet with his pills. Vladimir lay in bed staring straight up, as always, in that pose of his that made him seem so alone as he went to sleep.

'Goodnight, Vladimir Vladimirovich,' murmured Sheremetev, and left.

He felt numb, not knowing how even to start to understand what had happened to him that evening. He had had no food since he ate Vladimir's leftovers from lunch. Maybe, he thought, having something to eat would make him feel better – it certainly couldn't make him feel worse. He remembered Eleyekov saying that Stepanin had made it up with Barkovskaya. The thought didn't do much to lift his spirits, but it was something. At least he could go down without having to hear about another firebombing or arm-breaking or shooting.

In the dining room, Sheremetev found Lyosha and half a dozen of the security men gathered around the table with bottles of vodka, looking as if those weren't the first ones they had opened.

The conversation stopped.

'Good evening,' said Sheremetev.

A couple of them grunted in reply.

Sheremetev glanced at his watch. Normally, at this time, the dining room was empty.

He spotted a big dish of chicken fricassee on the sideboard, still warm. Sheremetev took a helping and sat down.

No one said a word.

He took a mouthful of the fricassee. Over the past couple of weeks, he had come to realise that you could tell Stepanin's mood from the quality of his cooking. The cook had obviously cheered up.

He ate more. The guards around him drank.

'How's Artur?' he said.

Lyosha shrugged. 'Not too bad. Not too good,' he muttered. His shaven scalp gleamed with a slick of alcohol-induced sweat. He had obviously put a lot away since Sheremetev had glimpsed Stepanin with him earlier in the evening.

'Any news on whether he'll walk again?'

There was no reply.

'Shouldn't you boys be out terrorising someone?' Sheremetev asked, only half jokingly.

'How do you know we aren't?' retorted one of them, slurring his words.

Sheremetev ignored that, thinking it was just a smart-aleck remark, as he took another forkful of the fricassee.

'So Stepanin has made it up with Barkovskaya, huh?' he said, chewing on the chicken.

The guards exchanged glances. There were a couple of smirks.

'He made it up with her, didn't he? Eleyekov told me today.'

'Oh, yes, he made up with her alright,' said one of the guards. 'She had a big dish of fricassee to celebrate.'

The sniggers were turning to laughter.

'What is it?' said Sheremetev. 'What's so funny?'

One of the guards, drunker than the rest, giggled. 'Stepanin's—'

'Shhhhh!' hissed Lyosha, but he had drunk as much as the others and was struggling to keep a straight face.

'What?' said Sheremetev, taking a mouthful of fricassee.

The giggling guard threw back his head, laughing. 'The chickens will have company.'

'What chickens?'

'The chickens outside.'

Sheremetev didn't understand. The guards were laughing so much now they were almost crying. Lyosha made a last, vain attempt to stop them, and then, throwing a vodka down his throat, joined in.

'The chickens outside?' repeated Sheremetev uncomprehendingly.

'In the pit,' squeaked one of the guards.

'The pit? What do you mean? The pit outside where—'

'You've got to watch what you eat with a cook like Stepanin,' blurted out another, before collapsing in amusement.

'What's he done?' demanded Sheremetev.

The guards around the table, doubled up, didn't even hear him.

Sheremetev jumped up and pushed open the doors to the kitchen. Stepanin stood by a stock pot, spoon to his lips. 'Vitya,' demanded Sheremetev, 'what's going on?'

The cook looked around. 'Have you tried the fricassee, Kolya?'

Suddenly Sheremetev's blood ran cold. He clutched at his throat.

Stepanin laughed. 'It's okay. You didn't get the special batch. Only Barkovskaya got that.'

'What have you done?'

'Not so loud.' He glanced around at the potwashers.

'*What?*'

'The only thing I could do.'

'Vitya, you can't kill her!'

'Not so loud!' hissed the cook. 'Whatever happens to her, it's her own fault. She left me no choice. She knew that herself.' Stepanin turned calmly back to the pot and tasted with his spoon again. 'Needs seasoning,' he murmured to himself, and he threw in a big pinch of salt.

Sheremetev watched him for a moment. The cook had been drinking, that was obvious, but there was something eerie about the way he was behaving. He seemed to be both completely insane and perfectly rational at the same time.

'Where is she?' demanded Sheremetev.

'In her room.'

'Is she still alive?'

Stepanin shrugged.

'I'm calling an ambulance.'

'No.'

Sheremetev reached for his phone.

Stepanin grabbed his arm. 'I can't let you do that, Kolya.'

'You can't stop me.'

'Can't I?' He hurled Sheremetev across the room.

Sheremetev crashed under a bench, smashing the back of his head against a steel leg and knocking over a large bin of refuse that covered him in chicken carcases and offal and a stinking brown sludge that oozed over his shirt.

Stepanin rushed to him. 'Are you okay? I told those fucking pot-washers to empty that stuff—'

Sheremetev kicked at the cook, striking him hard on the knee, and got to his feet while Stepanin jumped in pain, slipping on chicken guts. He ran. The cook ran after him. He got to the kitchen door and . . . a wall of surly, drunken guards confronted him, not showing any signs of amusement now.

One of them pushed him down on a chair.

'He stinks,' said another, holding his nose.

Stepanin had followed him out. 'Have some fricassee,' he said, dishing up a fresh helping of the chicken.

'I don't want it,' said Sheremetev.

'It's fine!' said the cook, and he angrily shoved a forkful into his own mouth to demonstrate its safety.

'You expect me to eat while you've poisoned a woman and she's dying? I'm not hungry.' Sheremetev rubbed at the back of his head where he had hit the bench. His fingers came away smeared with blood.

'Eat!'

'Vitya, you can't kill her!' cried Sheremetev.

'Of course I can.'

'What do you want?'

'I want her to go away.'

'Very good way of making her,' slurred a guard, wagging a finger. 'Excellent plan.'

'Not like this!'

'Yes like this!' snapped the cook. 'Exactly like this!'

'No!'

'Yes!'

'Well what if . . .' Sheremetev's mind raced. An idea sprang to his mind. 'What if she agrees to go? What if she signs something saying she resigns?'

'That's fucking ridiculous!' retorted Stepanin. 'Why would she do that?'

'Because . . . otherwise she's going to die. What if she signs it and then we send her to the hospital and we say you realised you made a mistake with her food and accidentally poisoned her? Then she's gone, just like you want. We have the paper. She's resigned.'

Stepanin's eyes narrowed. Sheremetev watched him anxiously. It occurred to him that he had got the idea from Oleg's suggestion that he get Vladimir to sign a request to have Pasha released. He didn't think it had been a very smart suggestion when Oleg suggested it, and in this situation, the version of the idea he had come up with was even more absurd, worse than something in a movie. On the other hand, the cook's behaviour was so erratic that he might just be persuaded by it.

Stepanin shook his head. 'No. She'd come back.'

'She had Artyusha shot,' said one of the guards. 'She's got to die!'

The other guards nodded.

'Did Artyusha say that?' said Sheremetev.

There was silence for a moment. 'He'd want us to do it,' said the guard, but something in his tone was less than certain.

Sheremetev knew nothing about gangsters apart from what he had seen in movies, and he had totally misjudged Artur Lukashvilli, but he had a feeling that a gang boss didn't keep a bunch of men like this under control by letting them kill whoever they felt like killing. 'What happened the last time you killed someone Artur didn't tell you to kill?'

The question hung in the air.

'Remember Tolya?' murmured someone.

The guards glanced nervously at each other. A couple of them grimaced. 'We should take her to hospital,' one of them said.

Stepanin looked at them in dismay.

306

'Come on, lads,' said Lyosha. 'Let's go and get her! We'll say it was all the cook's idea.'

'No!' cried Stepanin. 'No one gets her!' He turned on Sheremetev. 'She's not going to hospital! Understand? I've told you before! I've got three hundred thousand dollars. To open my restaurant, I need five! Five! And I've only got three!'

The guards glanced at each other.

'She is not ... going ... to *hospital*!' shouted Stepanin, shaking Sheremetev by the shoulders.

Another guard appeared in the doorway. He went quickly to Lyosha and whispered into his ear.

Lyosha nodded. 'Well,' he said to Stepanin, 'looks like it's not a question any more.'

'Has someone taken her already?' asked one of the guards.

'Idiot!' said Lyosha, giving him a slap on the head. 'She's dead.'

There was silence.

'Fuck!' muttered one of the guards.

Sheremetev looked up at Stepanin, who was still standing over him. In his moment of triumph, the cook seemed to be frozen, bewildered.

'Looks like you've got what you wanted,' said Lyosha.

Still Stepanin didn't speak.

'Vitya,' said Lyosha to the cook, 'what was that you said before?'

'What?'

'You said something about three hundred thousand dollars.'

The cook's face reddened. 'No.'

Lyosha came closer.

'No, that was just talk ... just ...' Stepanin looked around. The other guards were coming nearer as well.

'Don't lie to me, Vitya,' said Lyosha. 'If you lie to me, you're lying to Artyusha. And do you know what Artyusha does to people who lie to him?'

The other guards surrounded him now.

'Silence costs,' said Lyosha. 'For poisoning someone, it can cost a lot. Hundreds of thousands, Vitya.'

'That wasn't what we agreed!' cried Stepanin. 'We both wanted to get rid of her!'

'But you did it, Vitya. We . . . who's to say we even knew?'

Stepanin looked frantically around. 'What about him?' he shouted suddenly, pointing at Sheremetev.

'Him?' Lyosha laughed. 'What does he have? Three hundred thousand kopecks? Besides, he didn't poison anybody.'

Stepanin stared at him, ashen-faced.

'You,' said Lyosha to Sheremetev, 'I don't have to warn you what will happen if you say anything to anyone.'

Sheremetev shook his head. 'No,' he murmured. 'You don't.'

'Go.'

Sheremetev stood. He threw a last glance at Stepanin, whom he had once thought of as a friend. The cook, surrounded by Artur's drunken men, looked back at him, eyes full of a desperate regret, but for what – for killing Barkovskaya, or letting slip in front of Artur's men the amount of money that he had – Sheremetev didn't know.

He left the dining room, stinking from putrefying kitchen juices. The guard in the entrance hall silently watched him. The journey up the stairs was unreal. Barkovskaya was dead. Dead! It was inconceivable. He stopped. Maybe she wasn't. Maybe it was some kind of an act that they had put on as a joke and soon Stepanin was going to come up and boom at him with a big grin: 'What fuckery!'

No, that wasn't going to happen. She was dead, really dead, and they were going to throw her in with the chickens. He was scared to look out a window in case he saw them carrying her to the pit.

What more could happen? The day had started full of hope. Today, he had thought, he would get the money to get Pasha out of jail. And it had ended with nothing. No money, no hope – nothing. He had been abused, degraded, pummelled, discarded. First by thieves, then by murderers. Sheremetev was filled with a fierce, impotent rage. He felt like flinging out his arms and crying to the heavens: *What else can you do to me? What? Do it now, while you have the chance, because soon there'll be nothing left of me!*

He leaned his head against the wood panelling of the upstairs corridor, feeling as if he couldn't take another step, sobbing silent tears.

A noise came out of the monitor in his pocket. Vladimir was awake, shouting about something.

Even after all this, after everything that had happened, the nurse's instinct in Sheremetev stirred. He took a deep breath. He waited a moment longer, then went to Vladimir's room and cautiously opened the door.

Inside, Vladimir sniffed. What a stench! The Chechen was coming. He must be close now, very close.

Vladimir knelt on the bed, turning his head watchfully from one side of the room to the other.

'Vladimir Vladimirovich,' said Sheremetev, hoping that it wasn't too late to settle him without an injection. 'Please, lie down.'

Vladimir's gaze focused on him.

'Vladimir Vladimirovich,' urged Sheremetev, coming closer, 'lie down again now. Please. Everything's okay.'

The smell grew stronger. Stronger than ever. This was it! The Chechen was here to finish it once and for all, a fight to the death.

'Vladimir Vladimirovich . . .'

There it was! The head!

Vladimir leapt. *Ouchi Gari!* Then quick as a flash – *Tsukkomi Jime!*

Sheremetev's skull thudded against the floor and Vladimir crashed down on top of him. 'Stop!' cried Sheremetev hoarsely. Vladimir's strength was like that of a man thirty years younger. 'You're choking . . .'

'Ah, you fucking Chechen! See!' Vladimir let go of his neck and leapt up, then pranced around triumphantly in his pyjamas.

'Vladimir Vladimiro—'

Two quick blows to Sheremetev's face silenced him. Vladimir went off dancing around the room, singing an obscene army song about Chechen women.

Sheremetev climbed warily to his feet. Vladimir stopped, eyeing his adversary once more. He started slowly to approach him, arms tensed, knees flexed, preparing to unleash another assault.

Sheremetev threw a quick glance at the phone on the other side of the room, considering his chances of being able to get there to call the security guards – provided any of them weren't too drunk to respond. But even if he got there, he couldn't imagine he would have the time to make the call before Vladimir was on top of him.

Vladimir had taken another couple of steps closer. 'You fucking Chechen. That was just the appetiser. Now, I'm going to kill you. Once and for all. This is it. Come on. Scared, you boy-fucker?' He narrowed his eyes. 'You're dead.'

Sheremetev breathed heavily. Pasha had said that Vladimir had carried out a genocide of the Chechens. Now, even in his senility, he still wanted to kill them.

He watched Vladimir stepping softly towards him. Why was he looking after this man? Why had he ever looked after him? Twice tonight the back of his head had been smashed. The laceration in his cheek, he realised, was bleeding again. His windpipe was bruised and tender. He was covered in stinking kitchen juice. And why? For what?

Every man, no matter how gentle or humane, has his breaking point. After all that he had been through that day, as Vladimir padded intently towards him, Nikolai Ilyich Sheremetev reached his. The anger that had been building up in him that night – that had been building up in him since the news of Pasha's arrest – finally erupted. Everything was the fault of this man who was creeping inexorably closer to him. His nephew was in prison and his son was a gangster and jewellers were thieves and policemen were kidnappers and security men were extortionists and drivers and housekeepers and gardeners and cooks were embezzlers and fraudsters and cheats and murderers and it was all because of *this* man, because this was *his* country, because this was what *he* had made of it for everybody else, as he had himself proclaimed, this place where nothing counted but money and if you had it you could have everything and if you didn't they left your wife to die.

'Come on, you fucking Chechen!' Vladimir started running at him. 'Come on! Scared? You're—'

Sheremetev let out a yell and for the first time in forty years, put his head down and charged. Two seconds later he connected with Vladimir's belly and sent him flying. The back of Vladimir's head hit the floor with a crack and Sheremetev tumbled down on top of him.

Vladimir saw the Chechen's face leering over him, the black tongue coming at him to cover him with the slime of death. He punched at it.

Sheremetev punched back, all restraint gone. 'You destroyed everything! You killed my wife! You corrupted my son! You turned me into a thief and an accomplice to murder!'

'You're all thieves and murderers, you fucking Chechens!' cried

Vladimir gleefully, punching harder.

The old man's punches were well aimed. Sheremetev tried to shield himself from the blows. Another one came, and another, tearing out the sutures and opening the cut in his cheek and smashing across his nose. He pulled back and struggled to get up, pushing down with his hand on Vladimir's face and slamming the old man's head back onto the floor as he rose – and again, and again – as he got to his feet.

'You're not getting away, you fucking Chechen!' yelled Vladimir, rising behind him.

Sheremetev ran. Vladimir chased him. The old man threw himself at Sheremetev's legs and dragged him back. Sheremetev kicked like a mule and stumbled free. He ran to his room and slammed the door. Feverishly, he scrabbled for his keys and unlocked the cupboard containing the tranquilliser.

There was a thumping on the door. 'I'm coming for you, you Checken prick!'

He leaned back against it, not trusting that the lock would hold, juggling needle and syringe in trembling fingers. He could feel Vladimir's thumping coming through the wood. He had the vial of tranquilliser and plunged the needle through the rubber stopper. What was the dose? How much? *Thump!* He sucked the whole lot into the syringe.

He opened the door.

Vladimir punched him in the face.

He fell back, needle in hand, Vladimir on top of him and still swinging his fists. He turned his head this way and that, trying to evade the blows as he felt for Vladimir's buttock with one hand and readied the syringe with the other. He stabbed. '*Ahhh!*' A searing pain shot through his other hand. He pulled the needle out of it. Vladimir hit him across the nose. He stabbed with the needle again. This time it went into the old man's buttock, all the way to the hilt. He pressed down hard on the plunger and drove the drug in.

Vladimir was still punching. Sheremetev dropped the syringe and put his hands up to protect himself.

Vladimir landed a good blow on the rotting, grinning face. Then another. 'You fucking Chechen!' he cried triumphantly. 'I've got you now. Die! Die!' But suddenly he felt dizzy, and his arms were like lead, and he felt his head falling, and the Chechen's empty sockets and black tongue were coming closer and a terrible fear took hold of Vladimir as he knew that suddenly he couldn't lift himself away and in another instant the slime of death would be smeared across him. 'No!' he screamed. 'You fucking . . .'

In the split second that remained to him before he lost consciousness, Vladimir felt the slime of death wiping itself across his cheek and he knew that now – just as that earless Chechen prisoner had prophesied to him decades earlier in the moments before a squad of Russian soldiers riddled his face with bullets – he was lost.

His head dropped.

Sheremetev lay with Vladimir on top of him, the old man's leg twitching occasionally, one side of Vladimir's face buried in the putrefying liquid that soaked Sheremetev's shirt.

After a moment he pushed Vladimir off. The ex-president lay on his back, breathing slowly and deeply in loud, ragged snores. Sheremetev dragged him by the shoulders back to his suite and left him on the floor of his bedroom while he went to get a moistened towel. He wiped the brown kitchen juice off Vladimir's face. There were some grazes from the punches Sheremetev had thrown, and he cleaned and dried them. Some of Vladimir's knuckles were grazed, and he cleaned them as well.

He dragged Vladimir onto the bed and laid him down, placing his head on the pillow and then straightening his pyjamas. Finally he covered him up.

Sheremetev stood back, gazing down at the old man. He was unutterably ashamed of himself. He had acted in self defence – but he had gone much further than that. He had attacked him as well. Whatever Vladimir had once been, he was an old, senile man. The person who was responsible for the things he had done had already departed. Sheremetev had vented his rage on an empty shell.

'Goodnight, Vladimir Vladimirovich,' he murmured in despair. 'Let's hope things seem better in the morning.'

Sheremetev locked the door, as he had taken to doing after the night Vladimir went wandering, and went back to his room. He took a look at himself in a mirror. His cheek was gaping and ragged and elsewhere on his face were grazes and bruises left by Vladimir's punches. His throat, where Vladimir had gouged him with his thumbs, was streaked with a pair of red weals. He felt at the back of his head and his fingers came away sticky with blood.

He took off his filthy clothes. The stench of the kitchen juice was on his skin. Exhausted and demoralised as he was, he had a shower, to wash off the juice, the day, everything.

He lay in bed and thought about nothing, because there was too much to think about, all of it inconceivable. He slept, but fitfully, waking frequently to some recollection of the day which seemed to be more of a nightmare than any dream he had ever had, feeling lost and confused and miserable. Finally, in the early hours, he fell into a deep sleep and didn't wake until after eight.

There was no sound from the baby monitor other than its usual low static. Normally, Vladimir would have been awake by now, yelling for attention, but after such a disturbed night, and with the extra tranquilliser Sheremetev had given him, he must have still been deeply asleep. Sheremetev lay in bed, not wanting to get up, not wanting to reenter the world of madness that awaited him in the dacha. Was it even real? Could it be? Where was Barkovskaya's body? Had they really thrown it into the pit with the chickens? Were they all going to walk around pretending that nothing had happened and no one knew anything as it lay rotting in the pit?

He thought of what had happened with the watches. And of Vasya. He had lost his son, he knew that now. There was no hiding from it any longer. In a different way perhaps, he was also going to lose a nephew. What was he going to say to Oleg? There would be no three hundred thousand dollars. He had thirty-two and a half thousand from the thief in the pinafore dress, and that would have to be enough.

But what about the watches Belkin had left behind? Suddenly he remembered them. How many were there? Five or six, excluding the old Poljot he had added as a joke. Put them together, they might be worth something, maybe even enough to persuade the prosecutor to let Pasha out. He sat up to check that the thirty-two and a half thousand from the other watches was still under the mattress. Pain shot through his head. He got out of bed tentatively, testing the extent of his injuries.

He'd take the watches, he thought. Leave the old Poljot for Vladimir. What did he care? After the crimes that had been committed in this place, that would be nothing.

And then he would leave. Take the watches and go. The dacha and everyone in it revolted him.

Only don't look at me with that look, Vladimir Vladimirovich, he thought. Don't let me see the confusion and fear in your eyes.

Sheremetev glanced at his watch. Eight-thirty. Still no sound from

315

Vladimir's room. Gingerly, he dressed and went to look in on him.

The ex-president was lying in the bed just as he had left him, face up, eyes open – stone cold.

17

SHEREMETEV MET DR ROSPOV at the door of the dacha. The doctor took one look at the gaping wound on his cheek and grimaced.

'What happened to you?'

'Come upstairs,' said Sheremetev, conscious of the security guard watching them. 'I'll tell you when we get up there.'

They climbed the stairs and walked along the corridor to Vladimir's suite. 'You're sure he's dead?' said the doctor in a low voice.

Sheremetev nodded. 'Vladimir Vladimirovich was very agitated last night. He attacked me...' Sheremetev gestured towards his face.

'Did you sedate him?'

'Eventually. But he managed to do this first. It wasn't an easy situation, I can tell you.'

'I'll fix you up,' said Rospov. 'Let's go and see him first.'

Sheremetev unlocked the door. Vladimir was lying where Sheremetev had found him, flat on his back in the bed. Rospov went to the bed and opened his bag.

Sheremetev watched as the doctor began to examine the body, trying to hide his anxiety.

He had had no choice but to call the doctor – you couldn't just throw the ex-president of Russia into a pit full of chickens, as you could apparently dispose of a housekeeper. What would Rospov do?

If he had any suspicion over the cause of death, he would be required by law to order an autopsy. After the struggle of the previous night, there was no telling what the findings of an autopsy would be and how they might implicate Sheremetev in Vladimir's death.

But Rospov didn't have to order an autopsy. He could decide that the ex-president's demise was a death from natural causes, and there was no need to investigate further. And Sheremetev had seen enough of doctors to know that the other two physicians involved in Vladimir's care, Kalin and Andreevsky, would be grateful to let it go at that. Why would either of them want an autopsy when there was always the possibility that it would reveal a shortcoming in their treatment?

Rospov felt at Vladimir's neck for a pulse. Then he touched his eye with a tissue and laid a stethoscope on his chest. He listened for a full minute. Finally he put the stethoscope away and closed his bag.

'Well, there's no doubt about it. He's dead. When did you last see him?'

'I came up at about eleven o'clock. He was awake. He was talking – quite aggressively. Nothing unusual, but I sensed there might be trouble. I put my head in to try to calm him. He thought I was the Chechen.'

'Do you know why?' asked the doctor.

Sheremetev shook his head. If he had to describe the reason he was covered in the stink of kitchen juices, a whole new snake's nest in the dacha would be revealed, which would hardly make the doctor feel more confident that there had been no suspicious circumstances surrounding the ex-president's death. 'He was disorientated, I suppose – he always was when he woke up at night. You know, Doctor, he was a martial arts champion. If he hadn't lost some of his strength because of his age, he would have killed me last night.'

'Did you fear for your life?'

'Certainly. At one point he had me down on the ground and he was choking me.' Sheremetev touched his throat, where the thumb-prints left by Vladimir were visible as a pair of red, tender weals. 'I tell you, Dr Rospov, if he hadn't let go of me, I think he might have strangled me.'

Rospov shook his head. 'So what did you do? Did you hit back at him?'

'I defended myself. I had no choice.'

'Do you hit him hard enough to hurt him?'

'No! Just self defence. I didn't hit him – I was just keeping his punches off me while I tried to get away. I ran to where I keep the tranquilliser. He was coming after me, but I managed to draw it up and then I got the injection into him. After that he was quiet. I got him back into bed, cleaned him up. By then he was asleep. Everything was normal. He was breathing easily. I went to bed. The next thing I knew, it was morning, and this is what I found.'

The doctor gazed at the grazes on Vladimir's face. 'These,' he said, pointing. 'Are these from blows you struck?'

'I don't know, Dr Rospov. I really don't know.'

The doctor scrutinised the grazes. 'With respect, Nikolai Ilyich, I think I'd better have a proper look at the body.'

Sheremetev nodded, feeling sick with foreboding. Why had he even talked about a fight? Why hadn't he said that he had fallen – or something – and torn open the laceration on his cheek? Nothing to do with Vladimir. The doctor might not have even noticed the grazes that he now found so interesting.

Rospov unbuttoned Vladimir's pyjama top and examined his chest and abdomen. There was a faint bruise on the left side below the ribs. Sheremetev stole a surreptitious glance at Rospov and saw that the doctor had noticed it. 'Let's lift him up,' said Rospov. They sat the corpse up and Vladimir's chin flopped onto his chest, exposing the back of his head. Another bruise discoloured the skin, detectable through the wisps of Vladimir's hair. Rospov looked questioningly at Sheremetev, who couldn't bear to meet his gaze. They laid him down and then removed the pyjama trousers and Rospov examined the legs.

'Alright,' said the doctor.

'I only did what I had to do to defend myself,' said Sheremetev.

'Of course, Nikolai Ilyich.' Rospov took a step back and folded his arms. 'Please.'

Sheremetev rearranged the pyjamas and then pulled the sheet up over Vladimir's face.

'And the tranquilliser, Nikolai Ilyich ... You said you injected him. How much did you actually give?'

'The usual dose.'

'How much was that?'

'Five milligrams,' muttered Sheremetev.

'Five?'

'Yes. Five. That's the usual dose.'

'You didn't give him a little more, perhaps, considering how agitated he was?'

'Maybe I gave him ten.'

'Was it ten or was it five?'

Sheremetev's mind raced. *Why* had he said that? Why had he said ten?

'Professor Kalin said he could have up to ten if necessary,' he murmured at last.

'So you gave him ten?'

'Ten, yes. I think it was ten.'

'Perhaps you got confused. From the way you described the situation, it sounds as if it might have been difficult to be precise when you drew it up. Perhaps you gave him more than ten.'

'No, ten. Definitely no more. The door was locked.'

'The door?' said the doctor.

'I keep the tranquilliser in a cupboard in my room. I got back to my room and locked the door behind me. That way I was safe – then I could draw it up. I gave him ten, Doctor. Ten milligrams. No more.'

Rospov peered at him, eyes slightly narrowed. 'Do you think, when you fought him, something could have happened?'

'Like what, Dr Rospov?'

'Oh, I don't know, like a blow to the upper part of the abdomen perhaps, on the left, where it might have ruptured his spleen.'

'Ruptured his spleen?' Sheremetev remembered the sensation of the top of his head connecting with Vladimir's belly. 'No, Doctor. Definitely not!'

'Or a blow to the back of the head, perhaps?'

Sheremetev shook his head, hearing in his mind the crack of Vladimir's skull hitting the floor, and again, as he struggled up with his hand on Vladimir's face.

'In an older person, Nikolai Ilyich, even a relatively mild blow to the head can cause bleeding around the brain.'

'I only held him off, Doctor, like I said. I was only trying to keep his blows off.'

'Hmmm,' mused the doctor. He gazed at the body, which was now covered. Vladimir's nose made a point in the sheet. 'Well, under normal circumstances, I would just write a death certificate: he was old, he had dementia – something in him gave up. But there has been some kind of a fight, drugs have been used, and he was our

321

president, after all, so we can't take shortcuts. No disrespect to you, Nikolai Ilyich, but in view of these facts, I have to conclude that an autopsy is in order.'

Sheremetev stared at him. He felt clammy with fear.

'Nikolai Ilyich, are you alright?'

Sheremetev hesitated. 'I have ... some money,' he murmured in barely more than a whisper.

The doctor laughed. Sheremetev's reputation for probity was known even to him.

'Thirty two and a half thousand—'

'What? Rubles?'

'Dollars!'

'Of course you do. And where is it, under your mattress? I'm a professional man, Nikolai Ilyich. You're insulting me.'

'I have it! I swear I have it.'

'Thirty-two and a half thousand dollars? Really? How?'

'It doesn't matter how.'

The doctor eyed Sheremetev for a moment, then turned back to the corpse, as if weighing up the offer. After a minute, he was still staring.

Sheremetev peered around to see that he was looking at. It wasn't the corpse – it was the bedside table, where the watches left by Belkin still lay in a jumble.

Suddenly Rospov turned back to him.

'Nothing serious happened in the fight?' said Rospov.

'No.'

'You just fended off his blows? You didn't strike him yourself?'

'No.'

'And you gave him only ten milligrams of the tranquilliser? No more?'

'No more.'

Rospov stepped forward to the bedside table. Six watches. Each, he knew, would put his Breitling Chronospace in the shade, each worth five or six times as much.

Rospov ran his fingers over them as one might over the delicate skin of a newborn child, gently turning them this way and that.

'Vladimir Vladimirovich was strongly opposed to the idea of an autopsy being carried out on him, wasn't he?' murmured Rospov, still caressing the watches. 'I remember once, when I first met him, he told me explicitly.'

Sheremetev could remember no such thing.

'One shouldn't go against a person's wishes in such a thing, not unless there's an overwhelming need.'

'No,' said Sheremetev.

'And there's no such need, is there?'

'No,' said Sheremetev.

The doctor looked around at Sheremetev. Their eyes met. Both men knew exactly the bargain they were about to strike. Rospov knew what Sheremetev's offer of a bribe signified – and Sheremetev knew what Rospov's greed for the watches portended. Nothing even needed to be said.

As Sheremetev looked on, the doctor opened his bag and put the watches in, one after the other. He stopped only when it came to the seventh watch on the table, lying a little apart from the others, the old Poljot that Belkin had thrown away. 'Rubbish,' he muttered, and he left it where it was. Then he closed the latch over the other watches in his bag with a snap.

The doctor turned back to him. 'I don't think we need an autopsy. The case is clear.'

'I agree,' said Sheremetev.

'You held him off in self defence. He had the same dose of drugs he'd had a hundred times.'

'Yes,' said Sheremetev.

Rospov smiled. 'Good. I'll write the death certificate. A man of his age with dementia – sooner or later his heart's going to give up.'

The doctor picked up his bag and headed for the door. 'Take me to the housekeeper, please. You were going to introduce me last time, remember? I should inform her that Vladimir Vladimirovich has passed on and that I will be letting the appropriate authorities know.'

'Ah, the housekeeper, Dr Rospov...' Sheremetev tried to think of a plausible excuse for her absence. But after all the lies he had told, it seemed that this was one lie too far. His mind went blank.

'What, Nikolai Ilyich?' demanded the doctor, turning the door handle.

'Well, she...'

He stopped as Rospov pulled back the door. The corridor outside the suite was full of people. Word had spread in the dacha that the doctor had arrived for the boss, and somehow everyone sensed the worst. For the last fifteen minutes, they had been coming up the stairs and waiting for that door to open

But the doctor wasn't taken aback. 'I have bad news!' announced Rospov, who relished the opportunity to be the centre of attention provided by births, deaths and major injury. 'I have just been to see Vladimir Vladimirovich. The great man, Russia's great leader, is dead.'

The inhabitants of the dacha stared back at him, stunned. They couldn't care less how great a leader – or how terrible – Vladimir had been. Their concerns were entirely more selfish.

'He died of natural causes. No foul play is suspected! I am going to inform the authorities. In the meantime, Nikolai Ilyich will stay with the deceased to ensure that nothing is disturbed.'

Sheremetev gazed at his fellow denizens of the dacha. Maids, gardeners, security guards, all had come to find out if they would continue to feast on the living corpse of the ex-president or if the party had come to an end – and now they knew.

He recognised four or five of the guards who had been in the dining room last night when Barkovskaya was dying. Near them stood Eleyekov with a frown on his face, wondering, no doubt, what would happen to his highly tuned vehicles. Stepanin was there along with his potwashers, unshaven, heavy bags under his eyes, misery etched into his features. He didn't look as if he had had much sleep the previous night. Their eyes met for an instant before the cook looked away. What fuckery, thought Sheremetev. Eh, Vitya? You beat Barkovskaya, and now Artyusha's boys will clean you out of every kopeck you've saved.

And there was Goroviev, gazing at him knowingly, with even a faint hint of a smile. It occurred to Sheremetev that the gardener wouldn't grieve for the loss of his illicit income, no matter how large it had been. Things live, things grow, things die. That was what Goroviev had said to him. That was the truth of life. He was the only one, thought Sheremetev, who knew how to live in the Russia that Vladimir had created. To hate quietly, and to take. He was the only one who had got it right.

'Now, I must ask you all to disperse,' said Rospov solemnly. He had forgotten about being introduced to the housekeeper. Besides, there was hardly any need to tell her personally what had happened, now that everyone knew, and in any case, this would probably be his last visit here. 'I'm sure you'll have the opportunity to pay your respects at a later time. Please. Clear the way.'

Slowly at first, then more quickly, people began to move along the corridor and down the stairs.

'Nikolai Ilyich,' said the doctor, ushering Sheremetev back into Vladimir's suite. 'Please.'

HE DIDN'T KNOW HOW long he had been sitting there. Could have been two minutes. Could have been two hours.

He had locked the door behind him and then he had sat, in a chair that stood a few metres from the bed, lost in his thoughts. Eventually he got up. He raised the sheet that covered Vladimir's corpse. The face on the pillow was familiar and yet strange, as a face always is in death, features one knows but that are somehow different, lax, lacking something that had been there in life, as if a facsimile of the real thing.

He let the sheet drop. Now there was no dilemma for him. He could leave the dacha. He wouldn't have to imagine Vladimir with that look of confusion and fear in his eyes, unable to be comforted.

Sheremetev felt at his cheek. The wound was open. He shook his head, smiling helplessly at the predictability of it. Rospov had left without tending to him. Once he got the watches in his bag, all he wanted to do was get out of there.

The watches, Pasha's last hope. How much would they have been worth? It didn't matter, he thought hopelessly. That wasn't a question any more. He felt as if he had been thinking about stealing watches forever – now he would never have to wonder about the worth of a watch again.

But Pasha? What was going to happen? Unless the prosecutor was prepared to drop his price by ninety percent and release him in exchange for the money Sheremetev had under his bed, there was no way out for him.

He had traded his freedom for Pasha's, the autopsy for the watches. Or had he? Even in the depths of his self-revulsion, Sheremetev knew that once the doctor had noticed those watches, he would never have been able to keep them. Even if he had said to the doctor, yes, do an autopsy, Rospov's greed for them was so transparent, that he would have found a way to get hold of them.

An autopsy would have revealed a huge dose of tranquilliser in Vladimir's blood, enough to fell an elephant, and perhaps a haemorrhage around the brain or the spleen. The tranquilliser by itself would have been enough to convict him, if not of murder, surely of manslaughter or some other charge.

Maybe Vladimir would have approved, to trade justice for a few trinkets. He had often done the equivalent, Sheremetev suspected, although on an incomparably larger scale. What a liar he had been, what a criminal. Now, Sheremetev could at least say that openly to himself. He was no longer Vladimir's nurse, and the ex-president was no longer his patient. There was no need for him to hold his thoughts in check. It served him right, Sheremetev thought, for justice to be cheated for the sake of a handful of watches. Die as you lived, Vladimir Vladimirovich. At least have the decency to do that.

Did he mean to kill him? What was it really, murder or manslaughter? Sheremetev tried to remember what was going through his mind in those last terrifying moments, tried to relive the chaotic stream of events. As he got up, with his hand on Vladimir's face, did he really need to thump his head against the floor? As he ran to his room, as he locked himself in, panicked, hands trembling, heart thumping, feeling the vibrations of Vladimir pounding on the door behind him, could he really not calculate the dose of the tranquilliser that he had administered so many times before, could he really not steady himself sufficiently to draw up less than the whole vial – the *whole* vial – into the syringe?

But he had been scared, genuinely scared, thinking that any second Vladimir might come smashing through the door. Maybe that was the explanation. Or maybe he wanted Vladimir to die. Or maybe he didn't care, which was almost as bad.

But if he had wanted to kill him – why? What difference would it make? Vladimir had had his time and had done what he had done – his death neither ameliorated nor undid it. And if it was revenge on behalf of Karinka and Pasha and...on behalf of Vasya, yes, even Vasya, and Barkovskaya, who was dead, and Stepanin, who had murdered his dream along with her, and the whole of Russia that seemed somehow to have become a reflection of the small, corrupt and brutal mind of the man who had been Vladimir Vladimirovich...then what kind of revenge was it when the victim had no knowledge that it was being exacted? A wasted revenge. A pointless one.

Who was the Chechen? All these years that he had looked after Vladimir, he had never managed to find out. He remembered the bloodcurdling scream Vladimir had emitted in the last seconds as the tranquilliser took effect and his head fell forward. Thinking of it sent a shiver down his spine. Whatever hallucination the ex-president was seeing at that moment, whoever he deludedly thought he was fighting, Sheremetev hoped that as part of that delusion he believed he was being punished for one of his many crimes, that he felt the terror and doom and desolation of being beyond all rescue, even if only for a split second in his life.

Sheremetev shook his head, disgusted at the way he was thinking, that he had become so corrupted, so degraded, that he wanted some kind of revenge to have been enacted on a senile old man.

And yet at the same time he knew that it was only because of the things that had been done by Vladimir himself that his thoughts had been debased.

He sighed, gazing at the outline of the corpse under the sheet. Yes, there was a sense of relief in him that the old man was dead, that his dilemma about leaving the dacha was gone. Maybe he had killed him because that was the only way he could free himself from him. Maybe it was as simple as that.

Or maybe it was that, and everything else. As simple, and as complicated.

Sheremetev looked at the watch the doctor had left behind on the bedside table. The old Soviet Poljot, like so many Sheremetev had seen before. When he was a boy, that was all anyone had, and you could wait for months to get one. Now, it was worth nothing.

He should call Vera and tell her that she wouldn't need to come back today, or any other day. Soon he and everyone else would leave the dacha. With Vladimir dead, the reason for this miserable little band of fraudsters and cheats to be gathered here was gone. For a moment, Sheremetev toyed with the idea of keeping the Poljot as a memento, but that seemed incongruous. It was of purely sentimental value. Wasn't that the opposite of what Vladimir had yearned for? The Russia of his desire was a place where the only worth of anything was its worth in money, and those who spoke the truth of it were silenced.

It was Vladimir who had won. He had built the Russia he wanted and crushed out everything else. Sentiment had no place here.

Sheremetev raised the Poljot. 'To you, Vladimir Vladimirovich,' he said solemnly, holding it out towards the corpse. 'Look what you did to us.'

He dropped the watch on the floor and crunched it underfoot.